Way
Beyond the
Spanking Stick

BY THE SAME AUTHOR

Beyond The Spanking Stick

Way Beyond the Spanking Stick

(Brothers Six)

ANTHONY J. MAJOR

iUniverse

WAY BEYOND THE SPANKING STICK
(BROTHERS SIX)

iUniverse books may be ordered through booksellers or by contacting:

iUniverse
1663 Liberty Drive
Bloomington, IN 47403
www.iuniverse.com
844-349-9409

ISBN: 978-1-6632-5667-6 (sc)
ISBN: 978-1-6632-5668-3 (e)

Library of Congress Control Number: 2023921385

Print information available on the last page.

iUniverse rev. date: 12/08/2023

For my brothers, Peter, Christopher, Philip, Stephen, and Timothy. The six of us together are not a melting pot within the Major family. Instead, we are a tossed salad where every individual brother adds to the wonderful flavor.

"A brother is like a strong tree to lean against in a storm."

(Derived from the poem *Like a Strong Tree* by Claude McKay.)

Contents

Chapter 1   Sixth Grade 1

Chapter 2   The Fight 32

Chapter 3   Rose Lake 45

Chapter 4   The Kellogg Police 70

Chapter 5   Kit 85

Chapter 6   The North Country 105

Chapter 7   The Frozen Hell 116

Chapter 8   Phil, Craig, and the Cliff 134

Chapter 9   Stephen Attacks 143

Chapter 10 The Dummy 150

Chapter 11 Uncle Bill 156

Chapter 12 Burn Bean 165

Chapter 13 Joe Mandoli versus the Cops 171

Chapter 14 Peter Takes Charge 185

Chapter 15 School Election Upset 225

Chapter 16 Tim and the Cliff Inferno 243

Chapter 17 Two-Time Champions 250

Epilogue (Two Years Later) 269

Contents

Chapter 1

Sixth Grade

The school year had ended so abruptly—almost violently. Everything that had transpired over the past nine months was nothing but a blur to me now. Something had gone terribly wrong, and I had to figure out what it was. For several days in a row, I hiked up the hillside, sat in the grass, and in the warm June sunshine, looked down at my beloved elementary school. Apparently, there had been a wrinkle in time, and I had taken a personal descent into madness. Now that it is all over, I have come to one unalterable conclusion: I am certifiably insane.

On the first day of school, when I entered the sixth grade, I knew that day would forever be fateful for two people on this planet: me and my new teacher. The moment that Mr. Razor walked into my classroom to begin the first year of his teaching career, I could tell by the look on his face that he had no idea what was in store for him. I took one look at him and realized that this young man was fresh meat, and I was going to make his life a living hell without even trying to do so. Seriously, I didn't mean to do it on purpose; it's just that the setting was nothing less than a perfect storm. Here I was, the most obstreperous student in the world, and he was the most naïve grade school teacher alive, not a good combination. Secondly, his entrance into the classroom surprised me because I had never had a male teacher before. The dynamics would be so different this school year, and no one could predict what would happen.

With the initial shock of seeing this young teacher stroll into my minefield wearing off, I began to reflect on my life and what the present moment might mean for me. I found myself in the sixth grade, the top class in the entire school. I was King Shit. This meant that I was now in the Sunnyside School elite. We sixth graders were the cocks of the walk. We ruled the school. Deep inside, I knew I had to make every moment count in these final days of being a grade schooler because, in just one short year, I would find myself in a totally different dimension when we reached junior high school.

After Mr. Razor made his grand entrance, I looked around the room and noticed that I was not the only tyrant in the crowd. The notorious Lonnie Sissons and the rough-cut Tim Peterson had also joined me. Luckily for Mr. Razor, the world's greatest troublemaker, my old nemesis, Bert Hoover, had been assigned to another class just across the hall from us. Thank God, there is no such thing as a quadruple failure.

Immediately, I started to analyze Mr. Razor. He was young and thin and had straight brown hair that he neatly combed over to one side of his head. Just above his thick broom-like mustache, his dark, beaming eyes held a mix of intense focus and some deep internal apprehension that he had probably carried around with him since childhood. Mr. Razor wore a neatly starched short-sleeved shirt, buttoned to the top, and sported a thin, professional black tie. Evidently, he was anxious, inexperienced, and naïve with his notion that he could somehow change the world from inside a grade school classroom. From the first moment of meeting him, I could tell that he was an idealist, out to contribute to the youth of our town. But somehow, I was out just the same to make my mark on him. Despite the frailties I detected in the man, I admired him. I liked him very much without knowing anything about him yet. However, boys will be boys, and there was nothing to stop me from testing him in every possible way.

Mr. Rasor

After taking attendance, Mr. Razor called each of us to come to the front of the room and introduce ourselves to the class. We had to say something about ourselves, like what our hobbies were, what our favorite TV shows were, etc. I absolutely hated that type of bullshit, glad-handing, and back-slapping. I had a belly full of all this pussy shit, like holding hands at summer camp and singing Koom-By-Yah around the campfire. I had better things to do. Even though I silently rejected the status quo, I looked around the room and noticed something different this year: some of the girls were growing lovely sets of tits (unfortunately, the big fat girl didn't count--her tits were just blubber). Not only were there mammary glands jumping out at me, but there were also a few particular girls that caught my attention. I think I was actually attracted to them. One of them was Wendy Wieselheimer. She was thin, sexy, bright-eyed, and had a nice set of ruby-red kissing lips. Unfortunately, she was a little bitchy.

I did my best that first day by playing along with Mr. Razor's shit well enough, and by doing so, the day seemed to fly by. However, there were times that I looked around the room to see what Tim Peterson and Lonnie Sissons were up to. You know, I did have to size up my competition. Forget Ron Hartley, though; he seemed to be no threat. He spent most of the day eating single, chocolate and peanut butter Reese's candy bars. He kept pulling them out of his desk one by one as if he had an endless supply. He, ever so gently and without interrupting the class, kept gently unwrapping each of them. He forced the entire cups into his mouth without bothering to break them into bites. With his mouth gorged with these Reese's, the pimples on his face seemed to swell to the point of bursting, threatening an eruption, before he had a chance to take a lavatory break where he could pop them at his leisure in the mirror.

By the end of the day, I felt so proud of Mr. Razor. He had indeed put his best foot forward by introducing one subject after another with the utmost enthusiasm and vigor. He kept us so busy with fractions and decimals, dangling modifiers, and split participles that no one in the class felt the need to act up. Part of the reason is that we were still sizing him up.

After the 3:00 bell rang, I ran down the stairs to meet up with Bert Hoover, who stood near the flagpole and scanned the crowd, looking anxiously for me. We found each other and then walked the two blocks back to my house. We shared our experiences of our first day back in the classroom. Even though Bert was not in my class, he seemed overly excited about all the possible terror he could bring to his own class. We discussed such things as pea shooters, rubber band fights, and even sneaking live dog shit into the class and putting it in the teacher's desk drawer. The possibilities were endless.

On the second day of school, the morning flew by just as it had the day before. When we returned from lunch, Mr. Razor brought the class to order and announced that he would institute a twenty-minute story time session every day immediately after lunch. He said that we could lay our heads on our desks and doze off if we wanted to, or we could look out the window and daydream, or listen to the story being read, just as long as we remained quiet. After his proclamation, he leaned back in his swivel chair. He propped his feet up on the desk, not crossed together as people typically do, but separated as if he were waiting for a gynecology exam. He read slowly for about five minutes until he accidentally farted. It wasn't terribly loud, but the entire class heard it. Within a millisecond of the embarrassing act, he said, "Ooo, ya got me," and kept reading as if nothing happened. His little mishap gave me one helluva idea! I couldn't wait to meet Bert Hoover after school and tell him what happened.

"Bert! This guy was reading us a story and then farted. Right in class!"

"Shit, you should have farted right back!"

I considered it.

On the third day, I felt comfortable enough in my surroundings to begin testing the waters with Mr. Razor. After lunch, we took our seats and prepared for story time. I looked around, surveyed the entire class from front to rear, and waited for things to settle down. As the story was being read, I waited until some of my fellow students were dozing off or staring blankly out the window before I slowly and inconspicuously as possible, slipped my right hand into my shirt. I cupped my hand in my armpit with an airtight grip. I gently raised my left arm and violently squeezed the air out with a short drop. RIP! I sent the most beautiful sound of someone flatulating, echoing disrespectfully around the room. The frog-like sound surprised Mr. Razor. He stopped reading for a second as several heads turned around to see who had shit their pants.

My brave move seemed to bolster a couple of my unruly colleagues. Tim Peterson looked over at me from two aisles away. He smiled because he knew that it was I who had made the noise. Tim and I weren't really friends; we were more like rivals. It could have been a bit of jealousy mixed in with a slight annoyance because he wanted to be the head troublemaker in the class and deny me the crown. At this moment, he could not let me steal the show. Whatever I had done in the past, he just had to one-up me. Taking over my lead, Tim carefully reached his hand into his shirt, cupped it in his armpit, and made the same frog-like farting sound I had. This time, Mr. Razor stopped reading and looked around the room, more intently than ever, to find the culprit. He knew that twice in a row was no accident.

With no perpetrator identified, Mr. Razor returned to reading, and I once again scanned the room, looking for another opportunity. But to my surprise, before I could stage another disturbance, I noticed Lonnie Sissons was itching to get in on the action. He reached his hand into his shirt and prepared to cup it in his armpit. At first, I thought he was crazy because he sat in the far row, near the front of the class. He was way too close to Mr. Razor. He'd surely be caught, but I would let him fill his boots. Just then, a brilliant idea flashed through my mind. I was going to beat Lonnie to it. In a split second, I reached into my shirt, cupped my armpit, and dropped my left arm. The fart sound shot across the room before Lonnie could complete his task. Mr. Razor looked up and immediately noticed Lonnie in his seat with his hand buried in his shirt. Lonnie was busted. Mr. Razor slammed the book shut and said, "Lonnie, out to the hallway now!"

Lonnie sat there in defiance.

"Out into the hallway now, Lonnie!"

When Lonnie refused once again, Mr. Razor got out of his swivel chair and marched towards Lonnie. He grabbed him by the arm and yanked him out of his seat. Lonnie resisted as Mr. Razor dragged him across the room and to the classroom door. Lonnie resisted going out to the hallway so violently that Mr. Razor picked him up off the ground by at least a foot and slammed him against the door. After the loud thud of his back hitting the wood, Lonnie screamed into Mr. Razor's face, "Leave me alone, you punk!"

Hearing this enraged Mr. Razor all the more. He immediately dropped Lonnie onto his feet, and using his left hand, he wrestled with the doorknob. Mr. Razor finally opened the door, and he and Lonnie disappeared outside the room. The sound of their feet shuffled down the stairwell quickly faded away. The rest of the class was horrified by what they had just witnessed.

A short while later, after all the ooos and awes quieted down, Mr. Razor returned to the classroom—minus one Lonnie. With that rebellion quelled, no one dared to act up for the rest of the day. As the time slowly passed until the 3:00 bell, I almost couldn't contain myself. Boy, did I have a story to tell Bert Hoover!

A day later, Lonnie rejoined the class, and with that incident now behind us, the rest of the week went by without anything else substantial taking place. Regardless, I could tell that a few of us in the room were growing increasingly restless as time passed. Day after day, Tim Peterson kept eyeballing me, wondering what I would instigate next because whatever I did, he planned to outdo me, but my attention was elsewhere. I kept glancing over at Wendy Wieselheimer, thinking she was quite attractive, but for some reason, she always knew I was looking at her and would give me an evil stare. Without any form of reciprocity from her, my admiration quickly turned into disdain. She wouldn't ever smile back. Instead, she gave me a look of total disgust as if I were a bug crawling around her cereal bowl. Soon enough, all my hopes were dashed, and I knew, with certitude, that I couldn't stand the bitch. I was confident that, in time, I would think of a way to get back at her for treating me with such contempt.

Without any new pranks coming from my section of the classroom for a while, Tim Peterson finally took the initiative. He didn't seem to care much for the farting routine any longer. Mr. Razor was onto that one. So, Tim went straight for the rubber band shooting. He randomly launched them at any class member he chose: the big-titted fat girl, the prudish Wendy Wieselheimer, the weird Julie Essman, and, in the end, even me.

After morning recess that day, Tim resumed his onslaught against the entire class and all of civilized society. Unfortunately, Mr. Razor saw Tim fire a rubber band across the room that barely missed the head of an inconspicuous student whose nose was buried deep in his math book.

The look on Mr. Razor's face grew so frazzled that he went directly into deliberations on what he should do. At first, he hesitated, especially with the scuffle with Lonnie Sissons still fresh on his mind. However, his deliberation didn't last long because when Tim fired a salvo at the teacher's pet, the one and only Wendy Wieselheimer, Mr. Razor had had enough. And just like with Lonnie, Mr. Razor ordered Tim to go out into the hallway and sit outside the class for a while until he felt like calling him back in. Tim reluctantly left the classroom and disappeared—only for a moment. When Mr. Razor re-opened the textbook and began to read our assignment, two hands appeared in the doorway. Tim hid just outside, but with his hands completely visible to the entire class (all except for Mr. Razor). He balled up his fists, then fully raised his two middle fingers and flipped off Mr. Razor, all from behind his back. Several of us giggled, and Mr. Razor was none the wiser about Tim's disrespectful salute to him. Virtually everyone in the class thoroughly enjoyed it—all except Wendy.

With Tim one-upping me that day, I remembered how much I liked flipping the 'bird' at people. In fact, I excelled at it. The last time I did it in style was a mere month ago during a Little League all-star game.

Looking back at what happened just a month earlier, with it so clear in my mind, I mentally replayed the scene of the last inning of the final game of my Little League baseball season. We were playing the Mullan team on their home turf. We were getting our asses kicked really bad. We were worse than the Bad News Bears. We all screwed up. No one could get a hit. No one could put someone out, etc. Everyone fucked up, everyone except my cousin Marian Russell. She outshone all of us on the team. She was a superstar. But her help wasn't enough to change the outcome of this game. Our collective performance was pathetic. We simply needed to be put out of our misery. Just when we thought it might happen, the game being over with just one more strike-out, this huge player steps up to the plate. He was spitting, scratching his cleats into the dirt, and breathing fire while taking a few practice swings with his size 1000 bat. It was the bottom of the ninth. Everyone just wanted it to be over: the crowd, our coach, and everyone on the team.

Suddenly, the batter hit a fly ball right to center field, exactly where I played—a perfect hit to catch. Stupid me, I wasn't paying attention because I had been watching some random jet fly bay and leaving its vapor trail across the sky when the ball came my way. I took notice alright but ended up not positioning myself at all. I didn't even move an inch. I just lethargically reached up with my glove and stood there like a sinner, waiting to be blessed by a priest. The ball flew right over my head. Dammit! I missed what would have been the final and perfect out of the season.

Half the crowd booed as the ball hit the ground and bounced in the grass behind me. Hearing that, I stopped dead in my tracks. I wasn't going to stand for that kind of shit. And so, I didn't even go after the ball. Instead, I just stood there, tore off my glove, and with both middle fingers, flipped off the whole fucking crowd. "Take that all, you assholes!" It was a great move for an eleven-year-old kid, I have to admit. It was something right out of the Tony Major playbook. Surprisingly, I didn't even get in trouble for it. Instead, after the game, I got a juicy hamburger, hot French fries, and a delicious milkshake. I was on top of my game. It couldn't have gotten any better than that!

My sixth-grade class photo.

As the school days passed, we immersed ourselves deeply into our studies. Mr. Razor and I got to know each other a little bit better. In time, I began to realize the magnitude of what our beloved educator was facing as a first-year teacher. In addition to all the duties thrust upon him, he had me, Tim Peterson, and Lonnie Sissons to contend with. Just one of us was enough for any teacher; he had the three of us instead. While my heart went out to him personally, it did not go out to another person in the class. A great nemesis of mine was also developing a strong bond with our beloved Mr. Razor at the same time. Wendy Wieselheimer swooped right in and cut me off to the chase. She had Mr. Razor eating right out of her hand. The stronger their bond grew, the more arrogant she became—and the more I hated her. The tension between her and me rose so high that I was scrambling to do anything to topple her off her high horse. It didn't take me long to figure something out because after I tried one last time to win her over, I declared an all-out war against this heartless wench.

One morning after recess, as we were all climbing the stairs and heading to our classroom, I noticed that Wendy was directly in front of me. She had her hair neatly braided into two ponytails. I couldn't help myself. I reached up and gently tugged on one of them in an innocent, grade-school, flirtatious gesture. This would be my last chance. At that moment, deep inside, I still felt there was a remote possibility (a million to one) that we could end all hostilities and begin to like each other. I could never have been more wrong. After I gave one of her ponytails a gentle tug, I expected a smile from her, but instead of turning around and smiling, she glared at me with the red glowing eyes of Lucifer. She slugged me in the stomach and almost knocked the wind right out of me. Right then, I knew that according to my rules of the game, she was toast. She was going down, and I was the one who was going to do it!

For the rest of the afternoon, I fussed and fumed about how I could get back at her for such a rejection. Right before the 3:00 bell, I came up with the most brilliant idea. I took a piece of paper and quickly drew up a 'wanted' poster for her. I described her as a notorious outlaw and put a $10,000 price tag on her head. I stated that she needed to be brought immediately to justice. Although I am not much of an artist, I did my best to draw an image of her with two ponytails, dark, evil eyes, multiple facial scars, and a pig snout. But I didn't stop at that; I decided to make an enterprise out of it. After a minute of precise fiscal calculations, I arrived at the appropriate price of five cents for my one-of-a-kind promotional poster. I envisioned running through the hallways, selling them like snake oil in the Old West.

We all rushed out of class when the day's final bell rang. However, I decided not to meet up with Bert Hoover this time. Instead, I ran down all the flights of stairs to the lowest level—down into the bowels of the school. I approached the door to the technical equipment room. There I found my mother. She no longer taught in a formal classroom like in the past. She now served as a special education teacher in a program known as

Title One. She had a group of special needs students to tend to (the ones with IQs that didn't even reach the double digits). My mother took her job very seriously. So seriously that she spent hours every week making up educational tools and props with the available school equipment and supplies. I didn't give a rat's ass about all that shit; I just wanted her to print me up a hundred copies of my wanted poster. And so, I politely asked her to make up the batch of my artwork on the mimeograph machine before the end of the day. In an attempt to cover my ass, I made sure to downplay the actual content of my media production. It was probably the worst performance of my life, but my mother didn't doubt me for a second. Luckily, she was so entranced in her latest project for her students (like how to pronounce the word 'the') that she wanted to terminate my interruption as quickly as possible and return to her work.

She placed my original hand drawing onto the machine without reading it and ran off a hundred fresh copies just as I had asked. She quickly handed me a stack of warm, freshly printed-off flyers, then returned to her work. I thanked her with a semi-sincere tone, mostly sincere because I realized that I had inadvertently made my mother a co-conspirator in my plot to destroy the dreaded Wendy Wieselheimer. I sincerely didn't want my mother to get into any trouble at my trial.

The following morning, I arrived at the school fifteen minutes early, on purpose. I would sell and distribute as many copies of my work as possible before class started. In no time, I could not believe the fanatical response I received from all the students on the playground. They seemed so eager to spend a nickel on my scandalous piece of paper. Every student who handed me their five cents tore the sheet of mimeographed paper out of my hand and shrieked with joy. Apparently, many of them hated her as severely as I did. My pocket began bulging with all the nickels I had gathered. I was going to be rich, rich, rich!

I meandered up the stairs and into my class only seconds before the opening bell rang. I sat down, and Mr. Razor started the class. Within minutes of being seated, I realized that the news of my widespread propaganda campaign had not yet been noticed. Breathing a sigh of relief, I slipped the rest of the unsold posters into my desk and concocted plans of how to finish distributing them.

When the recess bell rang, everyone ran out onto the playground, everyone except me. I crept down the stairs to the basement floor of the building and snuck into the same supply room where my mother had printed the flyers. I secured a roll of cellophane tape from one of the shelves and quickly bolted out of the room. I then started roaming the hallway in the east wing of the school. I worked fast. I taped the posters on every wall and even to the doors of several classrooms. When I finally ran out of posters, I returned to the third floor and entered my classroom. Just then, the bell rang. Crap, I was safe! I felt an elevated state of euphoria. I stared out the window and didn't pay attention to anything. It was as if I got sucked into some time warp because the time passed so quickly. The next thing I knew, the lunch bell rang. Everything that I had planned had gone off so perfectly! Filled with joy, I ran down the stairs to the first floor, out the school's front door, and ran the two blocks home. I decided to make the most delectable tuna fish sandwich to celebrate.

In the comfort of my own home, instead of being in a stinky cafeteria, I enjoyed my sandwich, pretending that it was caviar, and enjoyed watching the TV. But then, I looked at the clock. Fuck, time had evaded me. I panicked. I had stayed too long. I ran out the back door and sprinted back to the school. I rushed up the stairs and then calmly walked into class. Yep, I was late, and everyone knew it. The bell had already rung, and all my classmates were in their seats. An eerie silence filled the room. Typically, after lunch, Wendy would be in Mr. Razor's seat reading out of the storybook for the hearing pleasure of the entire class. But this time, Mr. Razor was at his desk and in his seat. He dryly glanced at me sternly and sneered, not only because I was late but because of something else. As I gracefully walked past him, I looked over, and out of the corner of my eye, I noticed one of my wanted posters on his desk. Fuck, I was busted!!

The class resumed when I took my seat, but there was no storytime. Instead, Mr. Razor walked us through one subject after another until recess. It was then, when the recess bell rang, that he pulled me aside. He discreetly waited until the classroom was completely empty. Once it was, he didn't waste time getting to the critical issue.

He held up my poster and asked, "What is this all about?"

I just shrugged my shoulders.

"You know, this was not a very good thing to do."

"I know"

"Then why did you do it?"

I remained silent for a minute and tried to think of what he wanted to hear. Then, I finally just told him the truth, "She is a real bitch!"— "She can't be nice to anyone."

"But that doesn't mean you can do something as damaging as this."

Once again, I just shrugged my shoulders.

"Okay, here's what you are going to do. You will write a thousand-word essay on why it was wrong for you to do what you did, and I want it on my desk by tomorrow morning. Do you understand?"

Once again, I just shrugged my shoulders. He knew he wouldn't get any more out of me unless he rammed bamboo shoots under my fingernails. He motioned for me to head outside for recess.

On the playground, many kids came up to me with their posters. They were laughing wildly. Some even said that their teachers had confiscated theirs. Their comments, filled with admiration for my work, made my day.

That night, I began to write the worst essay imaginable. If Mr. Razor wanted some words, I was going to give that fucker some words, some really stupid words. I started off writing really insane sentences until my ramblings became almost intelligible. "Making a wanted poster of a fellow student is really bad. She could have gotten killed when the bounty hunters came for her. And the amount of the reward was way too high. It should have been ten cents instead of $10,000. And the picture I drew of her didn't really look like her. I should have taken art classes before I ever drew up the poster. And black and white posters aren't really that good. It should have been in color. But I wouldn't know what color her dress was. And I don't think she wore pony tales that often, so I guess the poster was wrong. Maybe she should sue me, and I would gladly give her all the nickels I gathered from all the students . . . etc."

In the morning, Mr. Razor read my essay and never said a word to me about it. I think just the fact that he made me write a thousand words was good enough for him. He had claimed a moral victory over me.

When all the excitement died down over the next couple of days, Wendy resumed her after-lunch duties of reading from the storybook for twenty minutes while Mr. Razor sat at the back of the class and corrected papers. Fuck, all my efforts were fruitless. Wendy continued to hold her role as teacher's pet, and if anything, the effects of the poster only bolstered her bitchiness. Her behavior continued to drive me crazy to the point that I had to do something else—I just had to.

One day, after lunch, we all returned to the classroom and took our seats for the usual twenty-minute story time. Mr. Razor turned his chair over to Wendy, then shuffled down the row of desks and took a seat behind me (two desks back and one row over, to be precise). Wendy began her usual reading while half the students laid their heads onto their desks and closed their eyes, and others doodled away. The rest just stared out the window and daydreamed.

I had to think hard of what I could do to derail her. It had been days since the wanted poster incident, and I still wanted to advance my crusade. The answer came to me in a big ball of gas that quickly expanded in my large colon. Oh, I have never felt a surge this large before. A beautiful moment was unfolding right before my very nose. Just before the pressure started to level off and subside, I realized that I couldn't blow this moment—I mean, I had to really BLOW this moment. And so, I leaned forward in my desk, raised my buttocks up ever so slightly, and with all my might squeezed my abdomen and Kegel muscles only to push out the most ferocious, earth-shattering, roaring fart. The deafening ripping sound shredded the seat of my chair and reverberated across all corners of the room. The entire class jumped up in their seats, startled beyond belief. Heads turned every which way to see who had done it. I buried my face into my arms and laughed and laughed as quietly as I could. Mr. Razor sat behind me and just stared and stared at me from behind. He did not know what to say. After a moment, Wendy returned to reading, and Mr. Razor returned to correcting papers. That flatulating kiss was all for Wendy. Love ya, Baby!

The following week, Mr. Razor rearranged the seating in the class. He moved me up near the front, probably to keep a better eye on me after the rectal stunt I pulled the week before. This change didn't faze me at all. My imagination was working in overdrive. The very next project he gave us entailed building a model of some business or factory for our social studies subject. He began unloading a box of supplies on a folding table in front of the classroom. First, all the heavy colored paper came out. Next came the bottles of glue and the boxes of straws and toothpicks. Mr. Razor kept unloading the supplies. Soon, cups, paper plates, and all kinds

Anthony J. Major

of standard household items, which we could cut up and fabricate into any shapes we wanted, all cluttered the table. The first thing I did was to secure the toothpicks, thread, and glue. But instead of putting together a school project, I spent time on something else. It didn't take me long to fabricate a tiny bow and arrow. Without missing a beat, I was shooting tiny arrows all over the room, and without any warning, Mr. Razor ordered me out into the hallway. He had busted me once again. Dammit! I went out first while he followed me, but before joining me outside the classroom, he reached up to a hook near the door frame and secured his large wooden paddle. I knew what was coming. He was going to set my ass on fire.

That day, after he hacked me, I still wasn't totally cured of my ADHD because I merely switched my focus from miniature bows and arrows to paper airplanes. Oh, I loved throwing them all around the room! I couldn't stop. (Unfortunately, there was no Ritalin back then.) Mr. Razor immediately noticed my aberrant behavior immediately but decided to take a different approach this time. Instead of ordering me out into the hallway for another hack, he brought the class to order and made an announcement.

"Everyone, listen up." He began.

The chatter in the room came to a halt.

"We are going to have a paper airplane flying contest. Every student will participate, and you have one week to perfect the best aircraft design you can come up with."

Every day from there, Mr. Razor set aside thirty minutes for us to work on our airplanes, and then we would begin covering our next subject. During the class's airplane construction, I looked around the room and realized that most of the students didn't have a freaking clue as to what they were doing. I laughed at some of their designs. All I knew was that I would make a basic airplane as I had always done in the past because 'there is genius in simplicity'.

The week went by wonderfully because the class fully embraced Mr. Razor's challenge. For the first time since the beginning of the school year, many of them engaged in something enjoyable, something that no other teacher had ever put them up to. I had to hand it to him for putting forth such a project.

14

On the day of the competition, I looked down at my basic but sleek airplane and decided to spruce it up a little bit. I took a pair of scissors and cut a few inches off the back to make it much shorter. Then I got out my colored pencils and started shading it with red, white, and blue. With a pen, I drew stars all over it and wrote the name "Captain America" on both wings. I knew I had a winner.

After the morning recess, Mr. Razor herded the class down to the gymnasium and lined us up at one end of the basketball court. He then produced a roll of masking tape and laid down a four-foot strip on the floor. That would be our launch point. He stood back and probed the entire class, selecting the first student to go. He had Gretta Wilkison go first. She stood up to the line and threw her airplane as if throwing a wet washcloth at her little brother. Her plane did not go but ten feet.

One by one, each of my fellow students took their turn throwing their paper contraptions into the air. None of the flimsy aircraft went very far. Most of them took a nosedive within ten feet and crashed to the ground. One plane flew into the air, reversed course, and went behind us—a minus score for that idiot. Out of all the students, Tim Peterson's faired the best. His airplane made it halfway down the court and landed in the middle of the gym. I was last. Mr. Razor planned this on purpose. I just knew it. The class waited in suspense as I approached the line and held Captain America in my right hand.

Before I made my throw, I looked over at Mr. Razor. Our eyes met. He secretly cheered me on, but in duality, he also wanted to see me fail. Either way, he was determined to make a point. He wanted to see me sink or swim in front of all my fellow students.

I stepped forward to the line with Captain America. I pulled my arm back and took a couple of warm-up lunges forward like a golfer taking a couple of practice swings. I heard an imaginary drum roll, and on my final reach, I flung my arm forward with all my might and let my little plane sail into the air. Captain America shot up like a rocket heading for the stars. He leveled out at altitude and began a long, gentle sloping descent. That little missile kept going and going and going until he made it all the way across the gym, where he disappeared behind the stage. Half the class cheered, and half the class moaned.

Mr. Razor did not look surprised at all. It was time to end the charade. He walked over to a chair and picked up a large, flat rectangular box. He strolled up to me with it and as he tossed it into my arms, said, "Congratulations!"

I was unprepared to catch the box and almost dropped it because it was so heavy. I lowered it to the floor and tore the taped flaps open. When I looked inside, I discovered a large cellophane bag filled with nothing but dirt. The entire class started laughing at me. I looked over at Mr. Razor with total disgust. Once again, I totally believed that he had everything perfectly orchestrated and that he knew deep inside that I would win the contest. Part of his plan was to humiliate me with the dirt, but there was more. I stood up and began to head across the gym to find my airplane. I DID feel humiliated. However, I didn't make it two steps until he said, "Look a little closer inside the box."

When I turned around and took a second look inside the box, I found a smaller bag tucked underneath the dirt, and in that bag were two Baby Ruth candy bars. I smiled and gave one to my best friend, Mike Peterson. Mr. Razor smiled at me and gave me a wink. We had just bonded that much more. After the great competition, Mr. Razor got a break from me, at least for an hour, when I went down to the gymnasium for my afternoon band class. That is where I met up with a real asshole.

For four years, I played the trumpet, and for the life of me, I didn't know why I did. In short, I didn't take it seriously. I never practiced. I couldn't give a shit about playing the trumpet. But it just happened to be an escape from the classroom. Hell, I was in sixth grade now, and everything we played should be as simple as pie (or so I thought). Our class was small. Out of the entire school, only twelve of us played instruments. The band class was nothing but a joke to me. But not to Mr. Watson—this was his life, and I made a gross miscalculation going into this particular session. I underestimated his seriousness. I should have sized him up much more closely before acting up in his class. This attitude of mine, that band class should be simple as pie, lasted only until the second song that day.

Mr. Watson was an interesting character. He stood just slightly over five feet high and was almost as wide. He resembled a human cannonball, not only his body but his head as well. He was completely bald and wore a pair of pair of glasses high on his nose. He had more chins than any

Chinese neighborhood, and his face was always beet red as if he were going to keel over with a heart attack at any moment. His companion was none other than the small wand that he waved around as he conducted us in a song—thinking he was in charge of the Philadelphia Harmonic Orchestra. This dude was passionate, to say the least.

Somewhere during that second song, I looked down at my music sheet and realized I had somehow lost my place. I didn't know where we were in the song. I had no idea how to catch up. But instead of reverently pausing till the end, I decided to have a little fun with it and began bobbing my head back and forth as if I was playing a great ballad in front of a raving crowd. Unfortunately, Mr. Watson looked over and saw that I was goofing off. He would have none of that while he was in charge. He raced over to me, grabbed the front of the shirt, and thrust me over in my chair until my head hit the floor. He yelled, "DON'T YOU SCREW OFF IN MY CLASS!!!"

When the veins in his neck stopped bulging, he let go of me and returned to his position in front of the group. I climbed back into my seat and regained my composure. Everyone in the class peered at me in absolute horror. Yes, I was horrified just the same. Luckily, I didn't have any homicidal tendencies, or that asshole would have been dead meat in no time at all. I now added him to the list of people that I hated. But at that moment, I shrugged it off and took full responsibility. I owned it—but I would take care of that bastard later. After leaving band class that day, Mr. Razor's room looked like pure Heaven. I returned to his classroom with a renewed spirit.

Day in and day out, Mr. Razor's class proved to be an exciting ride through life. After another morning's recess, we were led down again to our familiar gymnasium, but this time, it was for an indoor physical education class. Our trusty P.E. coach, Mr. Curry, lined up half the class on the far end of the gym and the other half on the opposite end. We were going to play a stupid fucking game called Red Rover. My God, I was hoping for something like Naked Twister or something, anything but this pussy-ass shit. Anyway, I realized that to survive and get along, you had to go along. So, I made the best of it, but with one caveat: I had to put my imagination to work. There is nothing more powerful and intriguing than a person's imagination.

As Mister Curry launched the game, I just shook my head, thinking how simplistic it all was. The sole objective of Red Rover was to have individual team members run across the gym and try to break through the clasped hands of the opposing students. If a person broke through, they brought back one of the other team members, strengthening their own team and weakening the other. If a person could not break through, they had to join the opposing team, leaving their own team with one less person, and that much weaker.

After the game began, a couple of my teammates could not break the other students' handgrips (weak ass wimps). When it was my turn, I broke through easily and brought back one of my lost teammates. Then thunder was called down from the heavens, "Red Rover, Red Rover, send Fat Suzie right over." And just as if an earthquake began, Fat Suzie came running, very slowly, with each foot stomping across the wooden gymnasium floor, "Boom! Boom! Boom!" The opposing students began to shake with fear. Their eyes grew wide with horror. Their lower lips began to tremble as Fat Suzie pounded her way closer and closer to their line. It was worse than a herd of cattle; it was a single elephant on the rampage. Fat Suzie easily broke through their line. She thrust her hands into the air and cheered in a sign of victory. Her giant, fat tits bounced and jiggled on her chest—a gruesome sight.

The next person called was Patty Pewtard, a small, anemic girl wearing thick, coke-bottle lens glasses. When the word was given, Patty summoned up all her energy and ran as fast as her little legs could carry her. She indeed built up more speed than anyone had thus far, but when she veered a little to the left and tried to break through where Lonnie Sissons stood holding Kim Crenshaw's hand, at the last second, Lonnie let go of Kim's hand and let Patty crash full speed into the wall. The collision sent Patty flying backward and falling violently to the ground. She barely moved, just laid there and quivered as if experiencing death throes. Mr. Curry ran over as fast as he could and dropped down to help her. With her eyes still shut, she drew in never-ending deep breaths and sobbed. The rest of the class looked down in dread. Lonnie just shrugged his shoulders and slowly inched his way from the scene of the carnage. The game was cut short that day, and we returned to the classroom a few minutes early.

That episode caused me to reflect on the incidents that occurred since school started. I recognized a cloud of strange energy that lingered somewhere in our presence. I watched all the stunts that Lonnie had pulled and those perpetrated by Tim Peterson as well. It caused me to think. At first, I thought it was simply that I was in the sixth grade, but then I realized it was much more profound: I hated conformity. That very afternoon, this sentiment came to a head when the school nurse walked into the class. She looked down at her clipboard and read off a few names of students needing certain vaccinations. I just happened to be one of those names. Since most of the class apparently had all their vaccinations, many erupted in laughter, pointing their fingers at us unfortunate ones. They teased us for having to get our shots. That really pissed me off, seeing most of the class jeer at me. But fuck them, I was going to show all those pricks. The other three students and I followed the nurse down the stairs. I moseyed along behind them, exceptionally slowly. Once they made it to the first floor, turned the corner down the hallway, and headed to the nurse's station, I continued straight out the front door of the building and walked directly home, excusing myself from class for the rest of the day. No one would laugh at me like that and get away with it.

When I finally returned to class the following day, Mr. Razor confronted me about my disappearing act.

"Mr. Major, why didn't you go to the office yesterday and get your required shots, and why didn't you come back to class?"

I thought hard for a moment. "Well, when I left class yesterday and walked down the stairs, I felt really sick. I almost puked right there in the hallway."

He looked at me suspiciously.

"Really. I felt so sick, so I went outside for fresh air."

I continued my story, and he knew it was all bullshit and called me out on it. For my punishment, he sent me across the hall to a small room between the main, third-floor classrooms. This small room just happened to be where the slow students came and went throughout the day to receive special help with their math and reading skills—and if they had seizures, all it took was two sugar cubes under their tongues to revive them. The lady in charge of this class of rejects was an elderly woman, Mrs. Peel, not super old and wrinkly like King Tut's mummified wife, but a gray-haired woman who was a year away from retirement, but still looked really old.

Mrs. Peel knew that my presence there was to be my punishment, and thus, she led me to a desk in the back of the class. She immediately brought me some paper, a sharpened pencil, and a school-issued dictionary. My assignment was to copy the words and definitions out of the dictionary. I was to transcribe them as long as I remained in her class, which I believed would be no more than an hour. The entire exercise made no sense to me. And so, to resist the enemy with all my might, I began to copy the first word from the dictionary. I wrote each letter very, very slowly as if I were a sloth. I dragged out writing those letters, taking up to thirty seconds for each one of them. I moved the pencil as slowly as I could.

Mrs. Peel walked around the small classroom and checked the other students' work. When she looked back at me with some kind of time-lapse footage that was going on in her brain and saw me drawing out each letter as if I was stuck in molasses, she went absolutely crazy. She shrieked with a blood-curdling scream, "You are drawing! You are not writing. You are drawing!!" She held her hands up to her face, turned, and raced out of the classroom. A few minutes later, Mr. Razor came and rescued me from Mrs. Peel, or should I say, he rescued her from me. Mr. Razor would think twice about sending me out to do such senseless bullshit.

After the incident in Mrs. Peel's room, I decided to lay low for a while because I hadn't gotten my ass whipped in some time, and I realized that my father had been gone longer than usual. He was probably due back any day and I didn't want him to get any bad reports about me, or he'd pull that damn belt off for sure.

Time passed by uneventfully for a few weeks until Halloween snuck up on us. And leave it up to Mr. Razor; he tried to be creative once again and gave us a unique assignment. We had to write a Halloween story. How could I screw this one up? We had one week to complete the story before the actual holiday arrived. I had to think fast. Since I wasn't into horror, I decided to write a tale of mischief and all the weirdos that I encountered in the neighborhood. And so, I began to write and write, and what a yarn I began to spin. By Friday, I turned in my story right on schedule and felt so proud of myself. Mr. Razor would look down upon me and see a halo above my head. At the end of that day, I skipped home happy as hell.

I finally embraced a little conformity in my life and would be the star student in the class. The Halloween festivities in our neighborhood were now only a few hours away.

After dark, my brothers and I donned our Halloween costumes and went door-to-door as fast as we could to capture as much candy as possible during the window of time placed by city officials. We ran from door to door and were really hauling in the treats. Near the end of the trick-or-treating time, we decided to push our luck on just a couple more houses. We rang the doorbell of a particular house just a block away from ours. A lovely old lady answered. We blurted out, "Trick or treat, smell my feet, give me something good to eat!"

She suddenly backed up, and with a look of total dismay said, "If you kids are going to be that rude, I won't give you any candy at all!" She was an idiot.

My friend and I stood there dumbfounded. 'It was just a fucking joke, Lady. My God!' After a pregnant moment, she tossed a couple of pieces of candy into each of our bags. After hearing her initial response, I vowed that this bitch was going to get it. I knew whose house I was going to throw eggs at next! Crap, we probably didn't even have another minute to go, but we continued anyway.

Even though we knew the deadline had already passed, we walked down the street and tried one more house. We banged on the door until an elderly man answered. "Trick or treat!" we cried out. But instead of giving us any candy, he informed us that trick-or-treating time was over, and he could not give us any candy. Fuck that! I looked into his living room and saw a huge bowl sitting next to his coat rack, still loaded with snack-sized candy bars. Boy, was I pissed! We reluctantly turned around and walked down his front steps. Now, I had two new houses that I would throw eggs at. An old bitch and an old kodger—just what we need on our street: two more useless neighbors.

Monday arrived, and I sat in my seat like a good little, rule-abiding grade schooler. The first thing Mr. Razor did was pass out everyone's Halloween story assignment. I looked from side to side and watched my fellow students get their papers. I looked closely and noticed the beautiful red markings on the front page displaying each of their grades. I saw A's. I saw B's. I saw C's. When my paper finally arrived, I looked down at the beautiful red marking, but it wasn't an A like I expected, nor was it a B, nor even a C—it was an F! What? A fucking F?

The handwritten note below my grade explained that I was supposed to write a Halloween story based on all the traditional stories about Halloween, like the Charlie Brown Halloween or some shit like that. In my misunderstanding, I wrote an entirely fictitious tale of my personal Halloween fantasy and how I terrorized the neighborhood and held the cops at bay until the town surrendered all the candy within city limits. How could I be so dead wrong with the instructions for such a simple assignment? It reminded me of a similar mistake I had made in the third grade. As enraged as I was, I began to have flashbacks. I started to get dizzy. I began to have visions of the past. No worries, I wasn't going to go aggro or anything like that. It's just that I sat there completely dumbfounded.

Minutes passed by without me hearing a sound or noticing anything that was taking place in the classroom. I mentally found myself back in Mrs. Clary's third-grade classroom. Back then, we studied geography, and it just so happened that we were studying the Sahara Desert. We were given a similar assignment, but this time, we weren't to write a story or an essay; we were supposed to be artistic and draw a nice color drawing of what form of transportation that we would use to cross the hot, inhospitable desert. I grew excited over the project just the same.

I went home that weekend and drew a very detailed picture of a cross-country fitted go-cart. On it, I drew intricate details of the engine with the carburetor and exhaust pipe. I included the steering wheel and roll bar. I even included all the gear I would need: water jugs, spare gasoline, sleeping bags, and even a walkie-talkie to communicate with the outside world. I was so proud of my work. But when I came to class the day of the presentation, it seemed that every student in my grade had understood the assignment—everyone except me. Virtually every one of them had gotten the hint that the most ideal form of transportation across the desert was on a camel, "A camel, ladies, and gentlemen, a fucking camel!" I thought Mrs. Clary meant what type of vehicle we would LIKE to cross the desert with, not what was the most ideal or common, but something of our personal preference. Fuck, I loved go-carts. Okay, I was the dummy this time around. Duh! My mistake humiliated me back then as I stood before the class, showing my desert-going go-cart. I felt like an idiot, and now the exact same scenario played out three years later, here in the sixth grade, with my misunderstanding a Halloween story assignment. I felt humiliated just the same. Fuck, when would I ever learn?

In time, I just gave up worrying about things, even more so because the Christmas season was approaching. Without warning, Mr. Razor announced that there would be a Christmas pageant and that all three sixth-grade classes were responsible for putting on the show. No other classes would participate, only us; this was our gig. He then passed out a sheet of paper to every student in the class. On it, the powers that be had already laid out the entire itinerary. The only thing missing was who was to play what part. The ensuing rehearsals would determine that.

The initial meetings in the gym excited me, not because of the pageant but because of my group of friends who would be joining in this great effort. During the zenith of this great gathering, Bert Hoover made his way across the gym and came up to me with the biggest smile ever. I knew trouble was starting to brew before he even said a word.

"Oh shit," he said, "this will be fun! I am going to pull some shit that we will all remember forever."

Now, this was the Bert that I had been missing since the beginning of the school year.

"Whatcha gonna do?" I asked just to see how much bullshit could spew out of his mouth.

He laughed and looked from side to side to ensure no teachers were listening. "I am going to ruin the entire show!"

"How?"

"Not sure yet, but I will think of something."

Knowing Bert, he would definitely do something. However, it was contingent upon what parts they had Bert and I play. It took several days of meetings in the gym with all three of the sixth-grade classes present for the teachers to formulate a plan of who would play what part in the production. In the end, they decided that I would play a few Christmas songs on my trumpet with the rest of my band members. And Bert . . . I could not believe what I was hearing! Bert Hoover, himself, would play the part of Santa Claus? Santa Claus? "No way!" I thought. Worse than putting him in that position, they assigned me to play the part of the elf that would sit at his feet. No way! I couldn't. I just couldn't do it.

As the complete format became set in stone and what was to be, was to be, Bert and I met out on the playground. "Oh, you just wait and see!" he bragged. "When it comes to my part, I am going to go off the deep end and start farting and flipping boogers at people. You just wait and see! I will give them a pageant that they will never forget!" That is something that I really wanted to see.

The days drifted by, and the rehearsals became more routine and mundane. Our class reached the point just a few days before that pageant where we had a class gift exchange. I hated it. Although there were some exciting gifts, most of them were lame as hell. I opened my package to find a box containing a dozen Life Savers flavored candies. This time, after getting so many lame-ass card games in the past, I figured I would accept it instead of throwing it out the third-floor window.

A few days later, after night fell, it was pageant time. I walked over to the school for the big event. I trudged through the light dusting of snow that had fallen since the sun had set, and in my right hand, hung my old case that held my beat-up trumpet. I really wasn't looking forward to the cheesy little performance I had to participate in, but I knew there was no getting out of it. I climbed the stairs to my classroom only to find my room abuzz with activity.

Earlier that day, I had already brought over the costume I would wear that night. Oddly enough, it was not a typical elf costume. It was a Peter Pan costume left over from a play that my older sister Jeri-anne had starred in. It was hand-me-down, and I felt like a fool for having to put the damn thing on. Despite my inhibitions about the costume and even my trumpet part, I felt warm and sentimental since it was Christmas. In addition to the general sentiment for the Christmas season, I felt a deep sense of appreciation for my very own teacher, Mr. Razor, for nearly the first time during the school year. Maybe I felt this way because I became riddled with guilt about how hard he tried to positively influence us and how hard I tried to disrupt his class. For that, I was genuinely sorry.

A few minutes after my entrance into the classroom, Mr. Razor waltzed into the room, glowing more than I had ever seen him. He wore a pristine white dress shirt with a snappy green and red seasonal tie. He had reason to smile; this was his moment in the sun. He knew all his star students would knock it out of the park with the night's performance. He greeted me with a beautiful smile as I opened my trumpet case and got my costume laid out. On this exciting night, he mysteriously treated me more graciously than he had ever done over the past few months. It was like he was offering me some proverbial olive branch. He wanted us to forge some peace between us. But within minutes of that beautiful feeling coming over me, a dark cloud began to rise, and a deep foreboding feeling sunk deep inside me—Bert Hoover and I had been planning and plotting to ruin the entire Christmas pageant by pulling some inappropriate, off-colored stunt. We vowed to freak out the whole crowd. For the first time since we discussed our little ruse, I began to worry whether we were doing the right thing.

After a short while of hustling and bustling around the classroom, Mr. Razor motioned for all of us band members to shuffle down the stairs and into an anteroom on the first floor. A door leading directly onto the gymnasium stage stood at the room's far end. I clutched my trumpet close to my side and felt butterflies in my stomach. The first opening scenes of the pageant had begun, and we were to be the second act. I had no idea how big the crowd would be; I just felt nervous about being in front of any crowd.

Mr. Razor waited by the door and held his ear close to it. I heard a muffled cheer and a healthy applause from the attending crowd. Suddenly, there was a gentle tapping on the door, and Mr. Razor immediately opened it. One of the teachers from the other class motioned for us to take our place on stage. We all filed out one behind each other. The curtain had not yet been drawn. After taking our places, the curtain was finally drawn. The entire audience cast their eyes upon us. As I stood in my spot, I looked out and was shocked to see that the whole gymnasium was utterly packed. There were even groups of people standing at the back due to the lack of seating. The butterflies in my stomach were really beginning to grow. I hadn't expected this.

Mr. Watson, our beloved asshole of a music teacher, marched out in front of us, held up his little wand, and prepped us for our first song. I held the trumpet up to my mouth and waited for the queue. We played several pieces and then bowed as the crowd cheered. From there, we rushed off stage through the same secret door. I made my way back up to my classroom. Mr. Razor filed in behind me with an even brighter smile than when I first arrived. Without words, he expressed his satisfaction with how well we had done, especially with me. Downstairs, the show continued, and my frustration grew. Bert Hoover was in an entirely different class than I was, and we had no time to coordinate plans on how we would ruin the entire Christmas show or even how to stop it. I needed some goddamn intel!

There was no time to waste with how the itinerary steamed ahead at full speed. One act followed another at what seemed like lightning speed. I rushed into the boy's lavatory with my Peter Pan outfit. I put on the green tights and pulled them up to my waste. I donned the green skirt, put on the green jacket, and buttoned it up. Lastly, I put the hat with the little bell on the end of it on my head. I felt stupid as hell, but there was no backing out now. What I should have done is put a large russet potato in the front of my tights and give the crowd something to really look at.

I came back to my class, and Mr. Razor was absolutely delighted with my costume. He escorted me back down the stairs and into the other classroom where I found Bert Hoover fully dressed in a traditional red Santa Claus outfit. I whispered over to Bert, "Are you ready for this?"

He just smiled and nodded his head.

"What do you have planned?"

Once again, he just nodded and smiled without saying a word. I started to get slightly angry. We had planned to disrupt the pageant most magnificently, and now he couldn't give me one freaking clue as to what wild stunt he would pull in the final moments of our production—or whether we would pull anything off at all. "Gimme a goddamn answer, say something, you asshole!"

Soon enough, we were lined up at the door, and just like before, we heard the cheering and applause of the crowd. Our time was next.

Mr. Razor thrust the door open and ordered us to march out on stage and take our places. As we made our way out in front of the crowd, Bert took his place in the rocking chair in the middle of the stage, for he was the show's anchor. We were going to end the show with Santie Claus and his elf—which was none other than yours truly. Once we found our spots, every student participating in the production fell in behind us and took their place. Every participant would be honored on stage, and that stage was filling up fast!

The noise of the crowd died down while everyone stood still. In fact, with the prolonged silence, the crowd hushed to a point where you could have heard a pin drop. Anticipation ran high. This was it. Off to my right, a good old friend, Mike Peterson, walked out to the front and center of the stage. One of the teacher's assistants, down on the gym floor and in the very front corner, turned on a record player. She lifted the arm and placed the needle on the record. A scratching sound came across the large speakers. Then, the slow melody began to play. At that precise moment, Mike began to sing the words of one of the most beautiful Christmas songs of all time: "Oh, Holy Night." Right then, I felt a chill go down my spine because it was the first time in my life that I embraced a moment in such consciousness where I realized the magnitude and meaning of the memory being made right then. Mike's voice echoed through the gym and cascaded with a growing crescendo. I truly felt the Christmas spirit in the gym that night. The crowd looked up at all of us, totally mesmerized. When he finished and the music stopped, the crowd clapped and cheered more than they had at any previous point in the show.

With only a few moments left in the production, I looked over at Bert, who sat in the rocking chair. I wanted a queue from him, any queue, but got nothing. Oh well, I would merely leave it up to him. The teacher's assistant placed another record on the player. This time, it was the tremendously upbeat song, "Here's Comes Santa Claus". That was Bert's grand part in the play. He started waving at the crowd, rocking in his chair, and tapping his foot to the tune. Right then, I realized he had no plan to disrupt the pageant. He wasn't going to ruin anything. With nothing left but myself, I created a little spectacle of my own doing. That stinking hat I had to wear kept throwing that little bell into my eye each time I rotated my head. When I flung my head to the right, it slapped around and hung an inch away from my left eye. When I flung my head to the left, it slapped around and hung an inch away from my right eye. Each time I did that, I stopped and stared at it with an evil glare. After a few times, I heard audience members begin to chuckle. That only encouraged me to keep it up—which I did. As the laughter in the crowd grew, I looked down to the front row and saw Mr. Razor looking right up at me. He heard the chuckling of the crowd, and with that, he nodded at me in approval. In essence, he encouraged me to continue because, at the very last moments of such a beautiful performance, he knew that it was all in good faith and added to the show's beauty.

27

After the show ended and the crowd dispersed, I returned to my classroom and packed up my costume and trumpet. I happily walked the two blocks home in the snow. At one point, I looked up at the extremely dark, clear sky and admired the millions of brilliant stars. The sound of Mike Peterson singing "Oh Holy Night" echoed on and on in my mind as I walked the rest of the way home. Christmas lay just a few days away. I had no worries because I knew my mother would do all of us well as she had always done despite our father never being around.

For the next week, all nine of us siblings enjoyed the Christmas break. We went sleigh riding on the hill just a block from our house. We tuned into every holiday movie broadcasted over the airwaves, and at times, we snuck out at night and threw snowballs at the passing cars. When the break was all over, we returned to school. I went back and stood before Mr. Razor as a new man, for I was a stately man at eleven years old and all.

This time, with a new start in a year, I embraced Mr. Razor's assignments more enthusiastically than I had ever before. On one such project, I received an "A". A month later, Mr. Razor knew that I was into building model rockets, so he had me prepare a rocket for launch for the entire class to see out on the playground. He and I seemed to be working together. Although things seemed to be working out between Mr. Razor and me, things got gnarly for me and Lonnie Sissons.

On the launch day, the entire class filed out of the classroom, down the stairs, and onto the playground. In front of them all, I proudly set up the launch pad. I placed the rocket on the tiny gantry and hooked the wires to the igniter that I inserted into the little rocket engine. From there, I stretched out twenty feet of tiny wires that I intended to hook up to a battery that would ignite the engine. Unfortunately, I made a disastrous miscalculation. Typically, to launch a rocket, one would need a big, high-amperage battery like a six-volt lantern battery, but I made the mistake of thinking that a tiny nine-volt battery would work because it had a lot more volts. Damn! I was wrong. Although the voltage was much higher, it didn't have all the raw amps required to heat the ignitor. The entire class sighed with disappointment when the rocket refused to launch.

Disappointed, Mr. Razor began guiding everyone back to the classroom. My frustrated classmates went far ahead of me while Mike Peterson and I gathered up the rocket, launch pad, wires, and battery.

We walked side by side just a few feet apart with the wires strung between us. Just then, a latecomer, Lonnie Sissons, came running at full speed between Mike and me. He ripped through the cables and tore the rocket, launch pad, and battery out of our hands. He didn't go far since he became entangled in the wires. I was so mad that I walked up to Lonnie and spun around behind him. I bear-hugged him and arched my back, lifting him into the air. From there, I titled my torso sideways and commenced to body-slam the stupid son-of- a-bitch to the ground. I heard a big thud of meat hitting the dirt and a deep exhalation of air like the sound of a dog whoofing. Lonnie rolled over and held his chest in pain. Mike and I untangled the wires from him and continued to the classroom. Lonnie hadn't learned a fucking thing since Mr. D'Andre picked up in the air and bounced him off the gymnasium floor in fifth grade. Besides, this was payback for what he had done to me in the third grade (that story is a little obscene because it took place in the boys' bathroom).

Once inside the classroom, I took my seat like a good little sixth grader. A minute later, Lonnie stumbled into the room, obviously dazed. The left side of his shirt and pants were caked with mud that clung there after he had picked himself up from the playground. He took his seat and never said a word to Mr. Razor. All the bravado inside me suddenly vaporized, and a feeling of sorrow and compassion came across me. Instantly, I was no longer proud of what I had done to Lonnie; I was ashamed. I looked over at this pathetic kid whose family neglected him, and I hurt inside for hurting him. This type of feeling would follow me for the rest of my life as identical situations arose. I had to get past this moment, so I vowed to cooperate with Mr. Razor for the rest of the year. However, my one great nemesis would still not receive any mercy from me: the angry, wretched Wendy Wieselheimer. She refused to let go of her bitch-hood. It would still be open season for her until the end of the school year.

One spring evening, I had a brilliant idea. With the 1950s television series 'Happy Days' in full bloom, I took it upon myself to come into school the next morning wearing a jean jacket with my collar upturned and my hair slicked back with my father's hair gel. I did my best to act like the character 'The Fonz' from the TV series, and Mr. Razor allowed it and actually found it quite amusing. I relished the newfound dynamic between my prized teacher and myself. Spring rushed by faster than I could have ever imagined. We were only weeks away from finishing the sixth grade and were to move onto the world of Junior High.

One morning, three school buses pulled up outside and waited to take all of the sixth-grade classes on a field trip to the Kellogg Junior High School. We were going to get a taste of what lay ahead for us. The drive over to the Junior High only took a few minutes, but once inside the school, the time began to drag on ever so slowly. We were led into the building and down the empty hallways until we were paraded into several classrooms. The older students looked at us as if we were zoo exhibits. It made me feel highly uncomfortable. Just at the peak of my nervousness, I noticed something so striking, so intriguing, and so mesmerizing: there were a lot of girls with nice perky tits—lots of girls with breasts many times larger than the buds on the girls in my class! Oh my, I grew extremely excited to start my 7th-grade year and find myself knee-deep in young, beautiful mammary glands.

After that field trip, only days remained before school would be dismissed for the summer. I tried a little more to make some peace with Wendy Wieselheimer but to no avail. She treated me with as much contempt as she ever had. Apparently, she had not heeded anything I had said since the beginning of the school year. I had repeatedly warned her that unless she changed her attitude, I would get back at her and make her regret it all. With the school year ending, I increased the severity of my warnings, but she didn't seem to give a shit.

On the eve before our final day of school, I gave her my last threat and told her that the next day, she would be dead meat—I was coming, and hell was coming with me.

In the morning, at our home, everyone in the family, including my mother, departed the house at nearly the same time. I purposely chose to be the last one to leave. I walked down the alley, and before I got to the end of the block, knowing that everyone had left, I turned around and headed back to the house. I decided to ditch the last day of school. It's not only because I was rebellious (which I was) but because I needed private time to think of the best way to end Wendy's school year. It had to be something super traumatic to make her remember me for the rest of her life. To help me think, I decided to hike up the side of the hill and look down at the city in deep thought. And so, I lumbered up the side of the mountain, just two blocks from the school. I reached the top, sat on a clump of grass, and began to think really hard. I began to ponder life. Then it came to me. I was going to slime her with the gooiest, stinkiest slime that I could conjure up.

Eventually, I came down the hill and hung out at the house. With only an hour to go, I found a quart canning jar and began to pour in all my ingredients. First, it was flour and water. I mixed it up into a really thin paste. Then I poured in pickle juice and vinegar. Lastly, I decided to add some yellow mustard. I mixed the goo up really well and took one whiff of it. Whew! I had a prize formula on my hands. I put the lid on it and quickly peered at the clock. I timed it just perfectly. I walked down the alley and over to the school. I ended up out front of the building at the exact time that the school bell had rung. Since I knew what bus she rode home on, I ensured I would cut her off before she could climb aboard.

The kids began to pour out the school's front doors and head to their respective buses. Wendy strutted down the outside steps and looked around, only to find me standing right in front of her. She attempted to get around me to run onto her bus, but I was too quick. She knew that path was not an option. She began running down the sidewalk, desperate to save herself from me.

At first, I thought she would run right back into the school, but she knew I would probably catch up to her as she tried to open the door. Instead, she kept running down the street. She continued across the intersection and kept going for another block with me right on her tail. Too winded to run anymore, she slowed down, but when she turned around, she still tried some evasive maneuvers. I was quicker, though. I ran right up to her and dumped half the floury goo onto her head and into her hair. I flung the quart jar a second time, and it splashed across her face, some of it missing and splattered onto the side of the Pic Wick grocery store wall building. I stopped. I had nothing more to do to her. It was "

'Mission Accomplished'. She received her due.

Wendy began to cry. She tried to wipe the goo from her hair as she defeatedly walked back to the school. She began to sob more painfully. "How could I do this to her?" She thought. Fuck, I warned her the entire school year to stop being such a bitch.

Chapter 2

The Fight

The seventh grade didn't start out much differently than the sixth. I defied authority and resisted conformity as much as ever. I had never seen so many brainless idiots who followed the herd. I almost puked each time I saw so many of my fellow students join the crowd because they could not think for themselves. My seventh-grade year confused me much more than my sixth, but by the time I began my eighth-grade year, I was tempted to make some concessions.

My first test that year came when posters started going up everywhere throughout the school, announcing the year's first dance. I didn't often go to these silly rhythmic rituals, because the few I had gone to the year before terrified me to death. For instance, a beautiful buxom beauty named Amber Cox really put the squash on me since the first day of school the previous year. She had to have been one of the most gorgeous girls I had ever known, fifty-percent Native American—but one-hundred percent tits. From the first time she saw me in the hallway, she chased me down and pinned me against the wall. She started in with her long-standing threat of not letting me go until I kissed her. Oh God! Not a kiss! Our lips touching. Holy shit! But I DID want to kiss her so badly, but when I looked down at her cleavage, all I could mutter was, "Momma, Momma."

This little routine of ours continued for months until it spilled over onto the makeshift dance floor in the school cafeteria. She had tried her hardest to get me to dance with her, but I was too scared. Although it had been nearly a year since I last stood in the darkness with her intimidating the hell out of me, this time around, I still felt I wasn't up to it, but I was going to try.

In the days leading up to the dance, I had tried to prepare myself for that grand moment with her. Unfortunately, all the voodoo rituals and all the questions that I had asked the spirits of the Ougi Board did nothing to spurn my testosterone into action before my biological timeclock was ready—and in the 1970s, there was no such thing as Viagra For Seventh Graders. By Friday, I really thought my mind was made up, that I really wasn't into this dancing bullshit. However, after talking with Joe Mandoli, I had a last-minute change of heart. I was going to give it one last try.

At the designated hour, I took a manly swig of chocolate milk, wiped the mustache off my upper lip, and made my way across town. I could tell by the way I swaggered down the street that I had made much more progress into manhood than I had the year before. I was ready. I arrived at the school, paid my entrance fee, and headed into the cafeteria. To my surprise, cutie pies were everywhere, and I would flirt with as many of them as possible. However, dancing still seemed so stupid to me. I wasn't inclined to twist and wiggle around on the dance floor like an idiot, kick my feet, and shake my ass like some Kansas City moron. I just wanted to get a good whiff of as much estrogen as I could.

I looked around the dimly lit cafeteria and surveyed the crowd. Holy shit, there happened to be more snapper in one place than I had ever seen. Although many well-developed girls from my class huddled together, I happened to catch sight of Amber. She barely looked over at me before she glanced away. It was true. She had indeed given up on me after all her attempts from the year before; three hundred strikes, and I am out. I also reminded myself that she had a couple of hottie friends that terrified me to no end just as well: Toni Murray and Cindy Maxwell. The three of them had all spent time on the cheerleading squad, and I always had a penchant for cheerleaders, whether they had a brain or not. But this year, it was all too late. I knew they wouldn't dare touch me if I was the last male stripper on Earth. Even with a russet potato in the front of my thong, they would still throw rocks at me.

"No worries," I told myself; at least I could still fantasize about them. That didn't cost anything. I still enjoyed full use of my extensive imagination, and I'm not talking about soaping up in the shower or anything like that.

Amber, Toni, and Cindy truly gave me warm thoughts. After watching the TV series, I referred to the three of them as Charlie's Angels. Simply seeing them made me smile. But suddenly, something inside me seemed to have changed from the year before. Something in my reproductive organ must have been coming alive because long before anyone explained what a threesome was, I suddenly found myself way ahead of the curve. I had an overwhelming fantasy about jumping headfirst (little head, that is) straight into a foursome with these three creatures. It was a beautiful thought, but fate would never allow it. I quickly gave up on any of those salacious and erotic thoughts. I was a man who faced reality—it was time to find some new targets.

Shrugging off any of my unrealistic expectations, I scanned the crowd again with new eyes. Several girls from my class looked my way and smiled. I tried to ignore them, thinking it was cute trying to play hard to get, which was really stupid because 'get' wasn't hard to get. The other boys walked right up to these girls, and they were the guys who were going to 'get'. If they played their cards right, they would probably be taking the skin boat to Tuna Town after the dance. Fuck! I just couldn't play the same game as everyone else. At that point, a mail-order Russian bride started to look like a viable option for me—at least I didn't have to speak to them if I didn't know Russian. All that any of those Russian women would have to do is pour the vodka and feed me grapes as they rubbed my back. (I got a lot of the best ideas from my Uncle Bill. Uncle Bill said the ideal wife was a deaf and dumb nymphomaniac who owned a bar. It's funny how great minds think alike!)

Getting control of my senses, I looked out and watched the dancing going on out on the floor. I stood there helpless while all the popular girls were being led out to dance, one by one, by all the popular guys. This shit looked like a no-brainer to me, even I couldn't screw this up. So, I looked around and noticed a thin, not necessarily gorgeous, but at least a fairly pleasant-looking blonde standing alone and gazing out onto the dance floor. She had a distant look in her eyes. I knew her from some of my classes. She was a quiet, well-mannered girl named Chandra Davis, a classmate that I really didn't know much about.

I wasn't sure if she was alone or with the chubby girl standing a few feet away. Ole Chubby could have been her bodyguard because I believe that by merely offering her a sandwich, she could have stomped out half the wrestling team. I remember once, earlier in the year, asking her how often she shaved because the hairs on her chin could have been used to scrub pots and pans. After she let me out of the headlock, I decided to leave her alone, that is, until the day that I would become rich and famous and would either need her to be my bodyguard—or if I was applying for admission to a monastery and needed to keep my mind off sex. One look at her and Mr. Weasel would turn himself inside out.

After shrugging off the thoughts of Ole Chubby, I realized that Chandra had never hung with any of the 'in' crowd. She had never been part of any clique. She just kept to herself and made her way through school as a free spirit, and that is what I really liked about her. Then, with nothing premeditated, I felt compelled to ask her to dance, just one dance. I felt it was my duty because she stood there alone, with no one paying any attention to her. Just then, my deep sentiment got the best of me. I looked intensely at her as I strolled over. It was as if an aura appeared out of nowhere and surrounded her. I suddenly saw her in a different light. Wasn't she just as human as the rest of us? Didn't she also have hopes, dreams, aspirations, and feelings like we all did? Didn't she often daydream about tender moments with some unpretentious guy who could make her smile and fill her life? All these questions were answered instantly, not to say that I was that guy even in the slightest. I just saw her as a person with just as much worth as anyone else in the crowd tonight. When I reached her, I caught her off guard. It was the moment of truth. I would pull the pin on the grenade and see what would happen next. Hellen Keller supposedly once stated that life is either a daring adventure . . . or it is nothing.

The current song stopped playing, and for a moment, there was silence. "Would you like to dance?" I asked.

"Ah, yeah. Sure."

Chandra followed me to the middle of the dance floor, and as soon as I turned toward her, a new song started to play. Oh fuck! It was a mellow song—a slow dance! Shit. Our bodies would be touching. For a split second, I asked myself, "What in the fuck was I thinking? Why in the hell did I ask this girl to dance?"

She wrapped her arms around my neck, and I wrapped my arms around her waist and pulled her closer. I knew the song well. It was a recent hit, a dreamy, sentimental song titled 'Emotion" by Samantha Sang. Her girly voice mixed in well with the backup vocals by the Bee Gees. Although the change in music came as a surprise, I relaxed and suddenly didn't care. I had to follow through with my grand gesture; there was no turning back now. We continued to slowly sway back and forth. Her chest pressed against mine, and I could feel her heart beating through her thin, white cotton shirt. I momentarily forgot everything else in the world and wondered what could possibly be going on in her mind. I knew what was going through mine: I just made a stupid blunder. I hoped she didn't think we'd start dating or anything. I wasn't ready for girls yet. I had pranks to pull, adventures to go on, and mountains to climb. My excuses knew no end. I just had to be a man about it and get through the dance.

When the song ended, she paused briefly, looked into my eyes, and quietly said, "Thank you." With that, we turned and walked away from each other. It could have meant nothing at all to her, or it could have been something very meaningful just the same. I would probably never know. One thing that did come out of that short, fleeting moment was that for the rest of my life I would think of her and that dance every time I heard the song 'Emotion'.

Just as I returned to safety in the dark corner of the cafeteria, I bumped into my greatest nemesis in the school. I could tell by the smirk on his face that he wanted to pick on me a little more, just like he had done for the past couple of months in biology class. In class, he sat in the desk right behind me and loved flicking my ears and dreaming up pet names to call me. He experienced great thrills trying to get a rise out of me. My God, do I have to kick this kid's ass?

This guy was a real asshole. If you were to look up asshole in the dictionary, you would find a photo of this dickhead with a puckered-up, snuff-colored sphincter for a head. Yeah, ole rectum face. This guy was truly a walking prick with ears. In fact, this guy tried to be all things to all people. He was both a prick AND an asshole, a feat which few men are capable of—and now, the nightmare of dealing with him on this very night was all mine.

Well, I guess it was time for the showdown. I looked him squarely in the eyes and said, "I am tired of your shit Jim."

"You are, are ya?

"Yep!"

"Let's go outside then."

"Okay. Let's do it." I agreed, using my best Dirty Harry imitation.

We headed for the doors that led out to the parking lot. My heart raced. Oh fuck, here I go again. We went outside and headed down the breezeway, past the gymnasium, and out to the open parking lot on the south side of the school. We turned toward each other and lifted our fists as we got into our fighting stances.

"You take the first punch," he said. Now, why in the hell, with almost every fight I had gotten into, did the other guy always tell me to take the first punch?

I didn't say anything. I just stood there staring him down. He repeated it once more. I ignored him. Jim looked over at the building and saw a crowd of kids heading our way. With an audience quickly approaching, he decided to act—he had to. He wanted to look like a real big shot. Jim finally realized I was not going to take the first punch, and neither was he—he was going to take the first 'kick'.

For one microsecond, I remember how he bragged that he had earned his yellow belt in karate. Yeah, yellow-stained underwear, maybe. As the crowd grew closer, he sprang into action. He violently kicked at me and yelled, "Kee-eye." He kicked several more times, and with each kick, he yelled, "Kee-eye! Kee-eye!". I finally had enough of his shit and lunged forward. I did a nearly perfect double-leg wrestling takedown on him and he landed flat on his back and started flopping like a fish. He immediately put me in a headlock. We rolled around for a minute on the ground in a stalemate. He frantically held on for dear life.

After a minute of locked horns, he knew the fight wasn't going anywhere. Finally, he eased his grip and let go. We slowly stood up. We looked at each other, huffing and puffing, trying to catch our breath. We simultaneously looked over at the crowd. Someone blurted out, "Whatcha guys doin? You two looked like a couple of gay guys making out on the ground."

Laughter broke out.

There was nothing more to fight over. He knew that I was more than a match for him. We didn't shake hands or give each other a brotherly hug. We just walked back to the school doors and returned to the dance.

Meanwhile, I wondered what the hell was this 'Kee-eye, Kee-eye' shit was that he kept yelling. Later, after some research, I found out that in martial arts, when a fighter strikes out with a punch or a kick, he violently exhales with a shout. That exertion of breath while making a striking move is called a "kiai." You don't SAY "kiai," you idiot, you PERFORM a kiai. Sheesh! What a dumb ass.

As the weeks passed, the fighting for me didn't stop there—another showdown was brewing. A gang of bullies roamed the neighborhood and carelessly picked on my little brother Tim, not knowing that he had five older brothers. This time, the dynamic between us three younger brothers seemed different than it had been between our three older brothers. Never in the past did any of my older brothers step in to fight for me when I was bullied. According to Pete, Kit, and Phil, we had to fight our own battles. Regardless of that smug advice, these thugs committed an act too egregious for me to simply let it go. My brother Tim was so young and so small and still in grade school. Unfortunately for these punks, they never considered the brother question.

When Tim reported to me the harassment that he had received, I became outraged and told him to get me a list of names of who these guys were, and once he did, I would find a way to settle the score. A couple of days later, Tim gave me at least three names of the gang's prominent members, and from that moment on, I was on the lookout.

Tim

Fortuitously, the same weekend I was hunting for these bullies, the carnival arrived in town and set up on the junior high school grounds. The location wasn't far from the parking lot where I had the scrap with Jim

Hemmert a few weeks earlier. Tim, Stephen, and I were delighted with the arrival of the carnival. This festival presented another opportunity for us to cause trouble. Every time the carnival came to town, we loved spitting down on the crowd from rides such as the Zipper and launching handfuls of gravel at unsuspecting guests as we were flung around at high G-forces in the Eggbeater. The haunted house proved to be another exciting ride as we threw eggs at the displays that leaped out at us. My God, we really gave those carnies hell. However, attending the carnival this year had a different meaning for me. I wasn't looking for fun—I was looking for a fight.

Just the fact that someone was picking on my younger brother infuriated me to no end. I took it as a personal insult directed at me. It was as if they were daring me to do something about it. Here I was, fourteen years old, and Tim was only eleven. What in the hell were bullies from junior high doing picking on a grade schooler? I really didn't care why. I just became blind with rage. How stupid could these guys be? Everyone in town knew that there were six Major brothers, and if you picked on one, you were potentially picking on us all, or at least that should have been the rumor, but something must have been lost in translation with these jerks.

In my quest to avenge my younger brother, I went to the carnival that Friday night with Tim and Stephen. My mother had handed each of us five dollars and told us to have a good time, but once I got there, all I could do was scan the crowd, hoping to find one of these bastards hanging around. Steve ventured out somewhere on his own and disappeared while Tim stuck close to my side. I needed his help in identifying any of these guys. As usual, the grounds were packed with people of all ages. The entire town seemed to be there: mothers and fathers with their children, elderly couples holding hands and remembering the days of their youth—and lots of teenage kids embracing life as if there was no tomorrow. I poked through the crowd looking here and there for any one of those inglorious assholes who picked on my little brother.

Just on the other side of the Ferris wheel, I spotted a kid surrounded by a group of his friends. Somehow, I knew he was one of them. I stopped. A sudden rush of fear swept through my body like a poltergeist had snuck up behind me. What? Did I really have the nerve to do this, or would I chicken out now? This feeling wasn't something I expected after all the tough talk I had been doing and all the fights I had already been in. I started to have second thoughts. Maybe I didn't need to do this. Maybe things weren't as bad as I thought. Perhaps it was all being totally blown out of proportion, and I was overreacting.

I looked around at all the people enjoying themselves on the carnival rides, the little kids ecstatic eating their cotton candy, and even the gray-haired couples with their arms around each other and looking into each other's eyes. Right then and then, I decided to give up on the whole idea. It wasn't worth it.

I turned and took a few slothful steps away from the crowd of kids. That's when Tim yelled, "Where ya going? That's him. That's one of the guys!"

Deep inside, I knew I could not betray my little brother's faith in me. I wouldn't quit now and let Tim know I wasn't up to it. I stopped dead in my tracks and rethought the entire scenario. This guy was picking on my little brother. Why? Because he thinks his older brothers are too chicken shit to do anything about it. That's why. That perspective alone boiled my blood once again, just like throwing a cup of gasoline on a fire.

To make Tim think it was all part of my ruse, I spun around and briskly walked up to this asshole still holding court with his cronies. Although this punk was one grade below me, he just happened to be a couple of inches taller and had a much longer reach when it came to a full-blown fistfight. But it didn't matter either way; the fire inside me burned with the images of this jerk pushing Tim around.

At first, this punk didn't see me approaching. He was too busy joking and laughing with his friends. To my surprise, after taking a second look at everyone, he happened to be the biggest guy in the bunch, but it didn't matter—I was past the point of no return. I decided to reverse the roles. I intended to pick on him for a change. To kick things off, I rudely pushed him on his shoulder to get his attention and it knocked him off balance. He immediately stopped smiling and looked over at me.

"Yeh?"

"What's this bullshit? You picking on my little brother?"

He seemed confused momentarily, but when he glanced over and recognized Tim standing behind me, he knew who I was.

"I haven't done a thing," he claimed.

"Bullshit!"

He looked to his left and right as his friends wondered how he would handle this situation. I could see by the look in his eye that his peckerhead was digging deep within his soul to find the intestinal fortitude to deal with me. I was already one up on him with the element of surprise.

"Even if I had, what are you going to do about it?" he said half-heartedly with a smirk but with definite fear in his eyes.

"I'm going to bash your fucking face in," was the best I could come up with on such short notice.

"Oh really?"

Just then, one of his followers yelled out, "Fight! Fight!" And just like a swarm of bees, the crowd closed in on us. This butthead and I stood toe-to-toe, staring each other down. The tension grew by the microsecond.

Finally, with nothing transpiring between us, an older high school kid raised the stakes and threw down the challenge, "Hey," he began, as he held up a string of paper stubs that were used for the rides, "whoever takes the first punch gets these ten tickets!"

"My God," I thought, "How cheesy is this?" But apparently, my opponent took the offer seriously. He raised his fists and changed his stance. With his gesture, the entire crowd backed up a few feet to give us fighting room. At this moment, just like when the ref blew his whistle at the beginning of one of my wrestling matches, all the fear left me. I looked at this punk's face and could see his turmoil. He partly felt he could take me, and the other half doubted he could. I could see his fears wrapping around his nerves like an anaconda choking its prey. It suddenly dawned on me; this guy had never been in a fight before. Of course, this made sense. He came from a decent family; his dad was an upstanding local preacher. Adding two and two together, I knew then and there that I was right—this guy had never fought before in his life.

The match was on, and we began to sway from side to side. He looked for the right opportunity to throw a punch at me; those ten tickets looked like a juicy prize to him. I didn't give a shit about any carnival ride tickets. I raised my fists, knowing full well that my little brother stood directly behind me and counted on me to avenge him.

"Come on!" someone in the crowd yelled. That outcry was just enough to evoke some action from my rival.

He let go, giving all his momma-boy energy, and took a wild swing at me. Luckily, I ducked it perfectly, but instead of swinging back, I instinctively lowered myself into a wrestling take-down position—just like I had done with the fight with Jim. Most of the local kids feared fighting a wrestler because they knew they were dead meat once a wrestler got them on the ground. I knew better than to engage in a full-blown fistfight with Mr. Lanky here, who had the advantage of the longer reach. I would take this bastard to the ground and feed him gravel. I dropped down, lunged forward, and nearly touched my knee in the dirt as I threw myself into him with a powerful thrust, driving my right shoulder into his gut. I pushed him upward and lifted him entirely off the ground. I thought about pulling off a fancy, freestyle wrestling soufflé, but with him resisting, I could only swing him over enough to horrifically body-slam him onto the ground.

I heard the resounding thud and slight crack of his backbone, making contact with the earth. And then, like a wild animal trying to protect himself from the jaws of a predator, he wrapped his arms around my head in a desperate headlock (like scared opponents always do). He lay there and frantically kicked his feet and squirmed below me. With his hold on my head, there was nothing left for me to do but to start violently punching his face harder and harder, landing blows on his nose, cheek, eyes, and mouth. The more I hit him, the weaker he grew until I could finally feel his death throes. He was giving up. He had had enough. In the background, I could hear the cheering of some of the kids—and I hated them for it. This was no laughing matter.

As I slowed down on my punching, the guy let go of his grip, and at that moment, I stopped. I had honor. He surrendered, and I gave him a way out. I knew that I had won, and so did he. I pushed myself off of him and rose to my feet. I looked around at the brilliant lights of the carnival beaming all around us. I could feel the cold, crispy October air on my face. I breathed in and out heavily, fighting to catch my breath. I bent over and brushed the dirt off my pants. At the same time, this kid also slowly got off the ground.

Once on his feet, he wiped the blood off his lip and looked down at his hand. He then immediately looked over at me. Fear no longer filled his eyes; defeat did. He was broken, and just like that, the jerk who offered the ten free tickets for whoever took the first punch walked up and thrust those paper stubs into my opponent's hand. He patted him on the back. "Ten free tickets to paradise, my ass," I thought.

I took one step forward and pointed right into his face. "Don't you ever touch my brother again!"

I turned around and saw Tim standing there, smiling hysterically, with his eyes glowing. I could tell he was excited but slightly distraught by what I had just done. The thrill of my victory elevated him two feet off the ground, but I had nothing to say. I just blew past Tim and walked through the crowd. I headed toward the street.

"Hey! Where ya going?" Tim yelled.

I just kept walking and left that God-forsaken carnival behind me.

A block down the road, under a bright streetlight, I looked down at my right hand and saw the skin peeled back from two of my knuckles. It stung. The adrenaline had begun to subside. The further I walked, the more nauseous I became, so sick to my stomach. Here I was, walking home after kicking the shit out of another kid, and I didn't feel like a hero. I felt horrible. I beat his ass alright, but I also took away his dignity and I didn't feel God gave me the right to do that. But at the same time, this jerk took away my little brother's, and that I could not allow—not on my watch. An eye for an eye mother fucker—to hell with turning the other cheek. I did what I had to do.

When I finally got home, I slipped through the back door as inconspicuously as possible and marched directly toward my room. My mother stood at the sink washing the dishes (my two sisters' job) and instantly noticed me.

"Oh, how was the carnival?" she asked.

"It was okay," I said, trying to fake a happy response.

I stepped inside my room and shut the door behind me. To the left, one set of bunk beds lay empty since Tim and Steve were still at the carnival. To the right lay another set. The top was mine. For a rare moment, I had the pleasure of a little alone time. I knew that if I just climbed under the covers, I could find solace in my sleep, dreams that could take me away, hopefully till morning.

I managed to get into my bed and attempted to be the good little church boy that I was. I said my prayers. "The Lord is my Sheppard; I shall not be in want . . ." In addition to my prayers, I asked: "Dad, what should I have done? Where are you when I need you?"

The time came for me to search the past and try to find out what had gone wrong. Why was I so lost and why did I have to act out and be different than everyone else? Was it all of my dad's bullshit stories that he pumped into my head, the ones that I never knew when to believe or when not to believe? Was he really in the war? Did he really get shot once? Did he really spend time in Africa hunting dangerous animals? I just didn't know. I wanted to believe them, but there was always that lingering smell of hydrogen sulfide every time he spouted off.

With the lights out, new thoughts began to replace the old ones from earlier in the day. I shut my eyes and began to sink into a light sleep. Suddenly, the darkness was replaced by brilliant sunlight. The beautiful green foliage surrounded me, an exotic bird cawed up in the trees, and beads of sweat rolled down my forehead. I held a large caliber rifle in my hands. He lay hidden in the undergrowth, somewhere near me. I could hear his deep breath. He let out a low growl which raised the hair on the back of my neck. I was busy hunting tigers . . . until morning, that is.

Chapter 3

Rose Lake

No one knows when it all began: the noise, the mischief, the mayhem, and the ruckus that the six of us brothers caused during our childhood when we terrorized the entire neighborhood and taunted the local police to no end. Everything that we had done in our adolescence definitely didn't happen under my father's watch because when he was still engaged with our family, he was one m son-of-a-bitch, and the fear of his wrath kept us in line. This hot-headed male figure at the head of our household disciplined us without mercy with his belt for even the slightest transgression—mostly at my mother's behest when she could no longer control us. She sternly warned us a thousand times, "You just wait until your father gets home." While we waited in agony, sometimes for days, my mother continued to compile a copious list of every misdeed we had done in his absence. We lived in constant fear of what lay in store for us when our father returned.

One night, my father came home from a business trip, and shortly after he had walked through the door, my mother handed him the list of our crimes—just as she had promised. While we sat nervously around the dinner table, a violent thunderstorm moved overhead. Several lightning bolts hit the ground, and the power went out. In the darkness, my mother rifled through the drawers until she found the candles. We barely ate in the dim lights, with our appetites all but gone. The candle flames flickered and cast ghostly shadows on all our faces. My father didn't say much as he looked at each of us. He mentally formulated a plan to exact his punishment. As he gorged his mouth with food, we all knew what would happen after dinner.

Once we finally finished our plates, my father took us into our bedrooms, one by one, and tore off his belt. Need I say more? For many years after that incident, my mother, knowing how horrific it was, forbade us to ever talk about that night. It's not that our father was the monster that we believed him to be because he was extremely likable and an utterly fascinating man; it's just that he lost all control when he was forced to discipline us.

It bothers me to denigrate the memory of my father because, in the end, I loved him dearly, but in those days, he was no father at all. He was clueless about how to be there for us, helping us with our homework, cheering us on at sporting events, sitting in church with us, or even attending any school award ceremony. In fact, on the night of my brother Peter's high school graduation, my father sat in his favorite living room chair, sipping on his wine while smoking his cigarettes and watching 'Championship Wrestling' on the TV. However, there were times when we loved him very much for his warm moments—even when he drank because he was a happy drunk. Those were the times when he spewed out all his bullshit. However, even in the happy moments, we still feared him.

My mother and father's meeting seemed too incredulous to believe. On rare occasions, she recalled their romantic moment seventeen years earlier when she met him at a Jewish synagogue in Seattle. Their blind date was set up by mutual friends from Pasco, Washington, an attorney and his wife, an elegant couple known as the Heidelbaughs. We will never know how they knew both my mother, a schoolteacher from Seattle, and my father, a young, wild, adventurous logger from British Columbia. Regardless, their story continued beautifully. After two days of romance in Seattle, my father proposed, and she gladly accepted. Shortly after their engagement, my mother canceled her appointment at the monastery where she was to become a woman of the cloth, a Catholic nun.

Once they crossed the border into Canada and gained the blessing of my Ukrainian grandmother, they were married at a small church in a suburb of Vancouver known as New Westminster. Two of the Orthodox priests conducting the ceremony couldn't even speak English. They mumbled, smiled, nodded, and sent my mother and father along their way. After a short honeymoon touring the countryside of lower BC, all my father's previous bullshit began to unravel. When their week of romance ended, they spent the summer living in a tent at a logging camp on the edge of a remote lake instead of residing in a mansion with a private jet on an airstrip behind their castle, as billionaires should do.

My mother was as beautiful as any woman that one would see modeling in a magazine. Her dark hair and high cheekbones gave her outstanding beauty. She was as pure as they came and ultra-faithful in her religious beliefs.

My mother

After seven years, they bore five children while in Canada, and the day came when my father gave up logging and allowed the entire family to move back to my mother's hometown of Kellogg, Idaho. The stork flew overhead again, and I became the first American-born sibling. Following me came Stephen, Timothy, and Allyson. With so many children to feed, my mother realized she could not count on our father to provide a stable income. In her desperation, she resumed her teaching career. This decision meant that all of us would be in constant care of various babysitters. Life eventually smoothed out, and everything went on uneventfully until the day that everything changed. Something inside my father snapped. His business trips became longer and longer, and days would often turn into weeks.

On a beautiful summer afternoon, my father returned from one of his excursions, smiling like I had never seen him before. Within an hour of being home, he ordered the entire family to pack all our sleeping bags and clothes for a weekend trip. In the morning, we drove off in two different cars and ended up in the small rural town of Republic, Washington. After a short visit with my mother's longtime friend, Cheryl Bair, we headed out again, but this time into the mountains. We arrived at what seemed to be the middle of nowhere. In all his excitement, my father ordered us out of the cars and to follow him up a slight draw. A hundred yards into the thick forest, he proudly showed us a hole in the ground. He claimed this opening into the earth was a gold mine laden with endless wealth. Oh my God, that's what it was; that is why he would rarely come home—he had caught gold fever. That was the moment I knew that he no longer belonged to us.

"We are going to be rich, and I mean really rich!" he boasted.

"Dad, does that mean we'll live in a really big house?" I asked.

"Hell yes, young feller! Our house will be so huge, and we will have our own private jet, and we will have them put an airstrip behind the place, and we will have servants." His tales were too big even to be believed. He was so full of shit, but through all his bullshit, my mother continued to remain faithful.

Time marched on as he came home only to leave again. With each visit, he continued to tell us more and more tall tales, and as he did, we kept uncovering inconsistencies and holes in all his stories. Oddly, we accidentally stumble upon some truths. We learned that he was not who we thought he was. His real name wasn't Jerry Major. He was the son of Ukrainian immigrants who had fled Eastern Europe sometime around 1917 and ended up in Canada on the prairies of Manitoba. My father's real name was Merslau Zablocki—Jerry Major. Instead of being humble about his past, he couldn't help but embellish it badly. The truth wasn't good enough. For example, he claimed he was Prussian and a descendant of the royal family. Apparently, that fact automatically made my brothers and I Prussian princes. (Another one of his bullshit claims.)

One outstanding characteristic about my father was that he was rugged, a man of average height but thin and lean. He exuded energy like that of a nuclear reactor. He wore a thick head of dark hair that he kept cleanly trimmed around the back and sides, almost like a pompadour. Along with his piercing blue eyes, one could quickly notice the thick lines in his cheeks that were a dead giveaway to his Ukrainian roots. He wore a set of upper dentures because all his front teeth had been knocked out in his youth from drunken brawls and violent fistfights. My father's unknown past only added to his mystique, and with his infectious personality, he sucked in many a businessman into his grandiose commercial schemes.

Although these investors had money, they wanted to make even more from my father's billion-dollar fantasies. While so many others fell for his delusions of grandeur, my mother seemed to ignore them when he talked this way. When she found herself living in a tent after their honeymoon, it became instantly apparent that he was all talk.

Seventeen years and nine children later, the writing was undeniably on the wall: my father had zero idea what it meant to be a father. The concept of a devoted father staying home and being involved with his children's lives was worth more than a billion dollars in the bank than with no father at home at all totally evaded him.

With my oldest brother Peter now becoming a teenager and my father drifting further away, my brothers and I embraced a vision of our own. We realized that with him out of our lives, it became time for us to explore the world and figure life out on our own. Overnight, our fortunes were reversed. My mother now faced the biggest challenge of her life: raising the nine of us by herself. My mother summoned superhuman strength and never wavered. Additionally, no matter how challenging life became or what hardship she endured, she never complained.

Up to that point, thanks to her, we had all been well-behaved, church-going boys, but things were about to change.

Stephen, Kim, Jeri-Anne, me, and Tim in
the back of my dad's work truck.

Yes, it did become apparent when it all began. It began that summer when my father ran off into the mountains to chase his dreams. It was that summer that my mother had rented us a tiny cabin on the shore of a small, Lilypad-infested lake known as Rose Lake. It would become the summer of our lives up to that point.

The cabin she leased for us was no mansion at all. It was a one-bedroom shack, and the conditions were extremely crude. The accommodation was so sparse that modern child protective services would have probably intervened for our welfare. The sleeping arrangements were like that of a prisoner of war camp. Each night, the eight of us brothers and sisters slept on the floor in the living room in sleeping bags while my mother, baby sister, and father (when he did come back home) took the bedroom. We weren't so poor that we were forced to live on a steady diet of peanut butter and jelly sandwiches like the Bower brothers did; to the contrary, we ate very well. My mother prepared beautiful home-cooked meals with lots of meat and potatoes and freshly baked bread and cookies. We got along fine. However, shortly after, we arrived at the cabin and began fanning around the lake, knowing my father didn't care about us—that is when all hell broke loose.

After our arrival and with a few days of getting acquainted with our secluded surroundings, my first order of business as a stately man of eight years old was to build a treehouse. If I did, maybe I could hide up there and spare myself the wrath of my father's belt. I couldn't take the thought of any more spankings every time he came home. For some reason, I always caused more trouble than anyone else in the family and got punished a little bit more severely. Another reason to build a tree house: my brother Kit had already built a whopper the first two days we were there. He chose an area in the little patch between the dirt roads, a place I dubbed "Zoxville." However, to begin construction, I had to sneak into my father's tools, which was not a good idea, but I was desperate, I needed a hammer, saw, and nails, and if he caught me, I guess he would tear off his belt and mercilessly whip my ass as he had always done. Against my better judgment, I took a calculated risk and did it anyway.

After rummaging through my father's precious tools for an hour, I found the ones I needed, as well as a rusty can full of nails. In no time, I hammered several short boards up the sides of a pine tree. The boards were my steps. Continuing and following my brother's example, I nailed two longer boards between that tree and another one next to it. I began to construct a platform. While nailing away, I looked down from my perch and saw my older brother Philip running up the road at high speed. His thin white legs were pumping up and down, and his arms were flailing forward. With every frantic step, small dust clouds shot out from underneath his worn sneakers. He huffed and puffed as he desperately sprinted past me and back to the cabin. Without a shirt on his back and wearing only a pair of ragged cut-off jeans, Philip resembled a youthful modern-day Tarzan, just as all of us brothers did.

After veering off the road and continuing down the grassy incline into the yard, Phil bounced up the cabin's front steps, skipping a few along the way. Our brother Kit sat at the picnic table on the open deck, biting off a big chuck of a peanut butter sandwich while staring at the small lake. At fourteen, he had girls on his mind.

"Kit, you should see what I found!"

"What?"

"She's a monster!"

Kit bit off another piece of his sandwich and gasped for air as he chewed and attempted to ignore Phil.

"Kit! Come see this thing. It's huge." Phil pleaded.

"What's huge?"

"A bees nest! It's F'ing huge!" Phil almost screamed 'Fucking' but knew better than to be caught swearing within earshot of Mom out of fear that she would report it to our father.

"Really? Show it to me."

Phil spun around and pranced down the wooden stairs. Kit stayed behind him while still munching on his sandwich. They marched back up the road at high speed and right past me and the treehouse I was building. Something extremely important was happening, and I had to get in on the action. I couldn't help it; I just had to climb down from the tree and run to catch up with them.

Phil stopped a hundred feet up the road and pointed down a slight grassy slope. Kit strained his eyes for a moment, then suddenly noticed the large egg-shaped object hanging from the branch of a pine tree. Phil stood gallantly at Kit's side and puffed out his chest. He beamed with pride as the discoverer of the 'bee's nest from hell.'

"There she is!"

"Holy Shit!"

Kit stood in total awe. Immediately, thoughts of how to deal with this threat began to race through his mind. He had to think fast, not because the nest would be going anywhere, but because he had to destroy it before anybody else could, just as he had done many times before with the giant barn spiders that had built their nests around our house back in Kellogg. Other kids also lived around the lake, and Kit had to beat them to it. Old memories of how he had lit red ant nests on fire, pulled the legs off of grasshoppers, and demolished countless spider webs flashed through his mind. He had to do something drastic with these bees; whatever it was, it had to be something really creative.

"It's too far away," Kit remarked.

"For what?"

Kit turned around and began to walk back to the cabin. Phil stood behind him, almost speechless.

"Kit! Aren't you going to do something?"— "Kit!"

"Come on, I have an idea."

Kit headed back to the cabin and walked faster and faster as the ideas began to form in his mind. He began to trot as if he were in a race against time. Phil chased after him, leaping at his heels, desperate for answers from his older and wiser brother. Phil had already destroyed several nests over the past week by pummeling them with rocks, and he knew as well as Kit that this particular nest was unusual—it was the grandpappy of them all, but it was too high and too far away.

Phil grew frustrated with Kit's silent retreat to the cabin. He pleaded, "Come on, Kit, let's just go knock it down."

Kit abruptly turned to Phil and, just as if he were a military commander squashing a rebellion from within his ranks, pointed at Phil, "We are. But first, I have an idea."

"What's that?"

Kit paused and allowed a sinister smile to spread across his face, "We are going to blow it out of the sky!"

"What?"

"We are going to blow that sucker out of the sky!"

"How are we going to do that?"

"We've got to get those firecrackers out of the cupboard before mom hides them."

"How?"

"You distract Mom, and I'll get 'em."

At that very moment, my mother stood in the kitchen kneading a massive lump of bread dough on the kitchen counter while our baby sister Allyson, stood at the edge of her playpen, shaking a plastic rattle. Kit and Phil cautiously crept through the back door and slithered past our mother as inconspicuously as they could, but she did notice them.

"What are you boys going to do today?" she asked.

Kit paused before answering. He looked at Phil as if to say, "Let me handle this."

"Ah, we're going down the dock and trying to catch some bass."

"Oh, that's nice. Do you know where your younger brothers are at?"

"Yeah, they are out back playing."

Phil winked at Kit. He was going to implement a ruse. He called my mom to the kitchen window to ask what kind of bird it was that had just landed on the porch. When she walked over and looked out, Kit very quietly opened the cupboard door and snatched the two packs of firecrackers that lay next to a bag of potato chips. At the last second, he noticed a roll of masking tape sitting on the shelf just below them and he grabbed that as well.

"Oh, that's a robin," she replied to Phil.

My mother turned around just as Kit walked out the back door and cupped the prized firecrackers and roll of tape against his stomach. She returned to her bread dough while my brother Phil hurried out the back door after Kit. The two of them dashed up the road to the site of the impending battle.

Standing in the same spot as before and giving the scene a more complete survey, Kit bent over and picked a small rock off the ground.

"Hold this," he ordered Phil.

After peeling one firecracker away from the pack, Kit craftily taped it to the small rock. Satisfied with the newly made bomb, he issued another command, "Hey Phil, light this."

Phil fumbled through his pocket and pulled out a pack of matches. (It seemed that all of us brothers carried matches for some reason.) He quickly struck a match, and as it burst into a small flame, he touched it to the firecracker's fuse. The fuse instantly began to sparkle, sending tiny flurries of blue smoke into the air. Kit reached back like an all-star pitcher and heaved the package as hard as he could at the nest. It missed by a long way, and the homemade projectile exploded somewhere down the embankment. Kit tried several more times, taping firecrackers to rocks and throwing them as hard as he could at the huge nest. Unfortunately, the makeshift bombs kept falling short of their target. There just wasn't enough weight or velocity to overcome the air resistance. Understanding the fundamental laws of physics, Kit didn't want to waste any more firecrackers until he figured something out. A sudden thought flashed through his mind. He marched back to the cabin with Phil and I following closely.

Kit stopped at the back of the cabin and looked curiously at the old tool shed. Something suddenly caught his eye. He had an epiphany. "Ah, perfect!" he said. Kit anxiously snatched a deflated ten-speed bicycle inner tube off the shed wall and pulled out his trusty pocketknife. With the skill of a brain surgeon, he carved up the circular rubber tube and, in no time, had it lying on the ground like a skinned-out rattlesnake. It took me a minute of thinking, but then it became apparent that he had just converted the once useless inner tube into a large, makeshift rubber band.

Kit continued to scan the yard. His gaze now caught sight of a rusty hammock frame. The old fabric had been long been rotted and torn away. All that hung from it now were a couple of ancient springs. Within a few minutes, Kit engineered a way to fasten and stretch the freshly cut rubber strips between the two ends of the metal frame. With the sling now in place, he and Phil dragged the contraption up the road.

After skidding it across the backyard and up the dirt road, they set it on the perfect vantage point on the edge of the embankment. If Kit's design was correct, this elastic wonder would be hurtling deadly salvos right into the heart of the bee's happy home. The buzzing insects wouldn't have a clue to what's hitting them—they wouldn't stand a chance.

It took Kit a minute of fussing around on the ground to get adequately seated and to calculate the proper angle and azimuth leading to the heart of the nest. He tested this weapon by stretching the rubber back and letting it go without a round. The long black strip snapped forward and oscillated a few times before hanging still.

"Phil, hand me a rock."

Phil picked up a small rock off the ground and handed it to Kit. Kit pinched it in the rubber sling and pulled back as far as he could. He then released the tension. The rubber snapped violently forward and let the rock fly. It sailed through the air in a perfect arc and flew past the nest. The two of them cheered.

"Alright! Now give me a bomb."

Phil picked up another rock and hastily taped a firecracker to it. He handed it to Kit, and just like before, Kit pinched the makeshift bomb in the rubber sling and pulled back all the way. "Light it! Light it! Hurry! Light it!"

Phil fumbled and finally struck a match. He lit the firecracker fuse, and Kit let the ordinance sail. The rubber slapped forward and released the package into flight. The firecracker sailed through the air but fell a little short of the nest and exploded in the air below it. Dammit! Kit and Phil tried once again. The second round came even closer. With the third round in place, Kit pulled back on the slingshot and adjusted his aim. As soon as Phil lit the fuse, Kit let it go. The projectile flew in an arc that would make any mathematician proud. It sailed and sailed and finally struck the nest, embedding itself in one of the bees' master bedrooms. A split second later, the firecracker exploded and blew away a large chuck of the nest. The paper-like fragments of what used to be the first floor of the nest floated to the ground like pamphlets thrown from an airplane.

At that point, the entire colony was on full red alert. Bees started launching themselves out of the opening and circling the nest in tight formation. Just inside the nest, the guy in charge, a head wasp, stood there with sergeant stripes on his sleeve and a cigar clenched between his teeth. He hollered out orders, "Alright, everybody, off your hocks and grab your socks! It's showtime. Everybody get out there and take care of this menace. Now move! All I want to see is assholes and elbows." Within seconds, hundreds of bees began circling the nest, looking for whoever had created the disturbance. Fortunately, we were so far away that the bees had no idea where the projectile had come from. If they had known, they would have immediately attacked us.

Kit cheered. Phil jumped and shifted his feet around on the ground, almost like he was doing a little dance. Suddenly, we heard something off in the distance. The three of us stopped and listened. The sound of an approaching vehicle grew louder and louder. A car was coming up the road in our direction, but we couldn't see it through all the trees and brush. A sense of dread overcame the three of us. If it was Dad and he caught us right in the middle of this charade, he'd definitely lose his temper, and that belt would come flying off, and he'd set our ass on fire.

"Go see if it's Dad!" Kit barked at Phil.

Without hesitating, Phil ran up the road and disappeared around the bend while Kit jumped up and gripped the metal frame of his weapon. He prepared to drag it into the bushes if need be. The sound of the approaching vehicle kept growing louder. Our fear intensified, even more so when Phil came running back toward us with a look of utter exhaustion from sprinting so hard. He almost tripped and fell when he reached us.

"Is it Dad?" Kit asked.

Phil fought to catch his breath. He shook his head and barely spit out the words, "No. It's just Goodson."

Holy shit! It was only the nearby neighbor, Mr. Goodson. With a sigh of relief, Kit got back onto the ground, seated himself into position, and resumed lobbing the salvos. Some would hit, some would miss, but bit by bit, the nest continued to be destroyed until all that remained was a small stem and a partial paper crown.

With the firecracker supply nearly depleted and the conquest of the bees' nest entirely under their belts, Phil and Kit dragged the large contraption back down the road, skidding it along in the dirt just as before, kicking up rocks in its wake. Instead of stopping behind the cabin, they continued down the yard, tearing up blades of grass as they passed the front deck. They continued pulling it along and made it all the way down to the shore of the lake, this time for a private war against the seagulls.

With sunset not far away, Kit and Phil quickly gathered armloads of dry sticks from the surrounding brush and threw them into the fire pit. With the strike of one match, the dry grass and ferns under the wood took on a life of their own, roaring and crackling as the rest of the sticks ignited. Kit and Phil resumed their mission. Just as they had done up on the road, they carefully positioned the giant slingshot toward the lake's open waters. However, with the firecrackers in such short supply, their assault would be short-lived.

When they were getting ready, my mother walked down from the cabin, "Boys, dinner is ready."

"We will be right there, Ma." However, Kit and Phil were too fixated on the slingshot to head up to the cabin quite yet.

They sent out a few rocks to test the range for an upcoming naval battle. Feeling satisfied, they made another bomb. This time, Kit launched it right at the row of seagulls that were innocently standing on a log that drifted past the dock. The newly made bomb splashed in the water and immediately exploded. The seagulls immediately took flight. Kit and Phil fiendishly laughed as the echo reverberated across the lake and slowly faded away.

Just then, the sound of a motorcycle broke the silence around the lake. The engine of Pete's green Kawasaki Bighorn buzzed like an angry hornet. At sixteen, Peter had saved up enough money from his job at the grocery store to buy the beautiful bike, and he was sure proud of it, so proud that when he reached a straight stretch on the north side of the lake, he raced the engine. He quickly shifted through the gears as if in a desperate race. The high-pitch whining grew louder and louder as Pete closed the distance at a staggering speed. I strained my eyes for a moment to see where he was. Finally, I caught sight of the flume of dust that trailed behind him. Peter, as flamboyant as one could get, sped down the backcountry dirt road like a knight rushing upon his opponent in a joust to the death. That was typical Peter—he couldn't help but make a grand entrance.

After negotiating the final twists and turns in the road, Peter pulled up to the back of the cabin and shut off the bike's engine. He instantly noticed the smoke rising from the beach fire and strutted across the dandelion-covered lawn. He slowly undid the strap to his helmet. When he pulled it off, he spotted Kit lying behind the crudely constructed slingshot-of-war with Phil at his side. Peter stopped next to them with a very puzzled look on his face. Just then, Phil lit the firecracker Kit had held in the stretched sling. Kit let the firecracker fly, and when it sailed out, it fell close to the water. It exploded, shattering the silence of the lake once again.

"You goofy suckers!"— "What in the hell is that?"

"A slingshot," Phil proudly replied.

"For what purpose?"

"Oh crap, you should have seen it, Peter! This giant bee's nest."

"What bees' nest?

"Oh shit! It was huge!"

"No, don't tell me."

"Yep! We got 'em. Wiped 'em all out!"

"Nah, don't tell me. You didn't. Don't tell me that you killed a bunch of bees. Why would you guys mess with a bunch of innocent bees that didn't do anything to you."

Phil just looked blankly at Peter, not knowing what to say.

Meanwhile, Kit pulled back the rubber strap with another firecracker, ready to go. Kit cleared his throat and grunted to get Phil's attention. He intended to demonstrate the awe and terror of their new weapon to Pete. As Phil lit the firecracker fuse, Kit began laughing uncontrollably. He laughed so hard that the firecracker slipped out of the rubber pouch and fell directly onto his chest, immediately exploding. Kit screamed and rolled over, frantically slapping his shirt, but even with the pain, he couldn't help but continue to laugh. Despite the setback and the stinging welts on his chest, Kit resumed his position.

"Phil, hand me another one!" Kit roared.

A bullfrog surfaced between two lily pads just a few feet from shore. Like two soap bubbles, his two round eyes barely pierced the water. A second later, another set appeared. The first bullfrog turned to the other.

"Crazy humans"

"Yeh, no shit!"

"Ribbit."

When the firecracker supply ran out, we doused the fire with several buckets of water and hiked back up to the cabin. Everyone took turns brushing their teeth at the bathroom sink, and we soon crawled into our sleeping bags. My mother turned out the lights and retired to her room with our baby sister Allyson. The day had proven to be just another day in paradise for the six brothers—except for a quick wave of terror that suddenly swept over me. Would my mother report to our father what Kit and Phil had done? Would he come home in the next few days, rip off his belt, and whip our asses? She had already done that on so many other occasions. It was not a very nice tactic because it never deterred us from causing more trouble; it merely caused us to live in constant dread, sometimes for days.

My father eventually came home, and when he did, his demeanor was not as I had expected it. He was happy. He strolled into the cabin with a box of rocks, set them on the table, and pulled out a small eyeglass, a magnifier to examine the rock crystals up close.

"Awe! Look at this, very rich ore. We found the vein." He spoke out loud, hoping that my mother was listening, but she paid no attention.

My curiosity got the best of me. I walked up to the table to have a look for myself. My father smiled at me because he now felt that he had a fellow rock enthusiast. He handed the magnifier to me along with one of the rocks. "Take a look at this. This is Galena. Do you see how shiny it is?

"Yeah," I replied, not knowing what else to say.

After a few minutes of close examination, my father got up and poured himself a glass of wine. He went out onto the deck, lit a cigarette, and sat down, crossing his legs in his own unique style. When he looked down into the yard and saw Kit and Philip throwing a frisbee back and forth to each other, he felt content knowing that his brood was safe and taken care of. Still, visions of wealth and success circulated endlessly in his mind. Thank God my mother didn't ruin his moment by telling him about the firecracker-hurtling slingshot. She let him sip on his cheap wine, boast, and make exaggerated claims about his big pie-in-the-sky operation in Republic. Later that day, over dinner, he began to talk to us. This is when he started to spew out all his shit.

"Dad, can you really speak Chinese?" I asked.

"Yes, I can." Then he began spitting out complete gibberish, "Ping pong wong, ching chang, fong, chin, wu, shu . . . "

"Chinese, my ass!" I thought. "You fucking bull shitter."

Although I knew better than to believe him on that one, there were other times that I wasn't quite sure. He said he served in the war and then said that he had been shot, "It hurt like hell, and it really burned," he claimed with much conviction.

After listening to all his nonsense, one story stuck and intrigued me to no end. He claimed to have hunted tigers in Africa. My father being in Africa was a little hard to believe, but the hunting part was realistic because he had proved himself to be an avid outdoorsman. He had bragged about hunting over the years with my Uncle Bill and my Uncle Bob. In addition to his hunting exploits, he had many high-powered rifles around the house. Those firearms helped bolster this claim, no matter how farfetched it was. I often envisioned my father having a standoff with a tiger in the African jungle and mentally placed myself in his shoes. Would I be frightened?

Could I shoot the beast in time if it charged me? I knew my father would be because he was the toughest man that I had ever known.

For the next several days, while listening to his crazy stories, my brothers and I tried to stay out of mischief. We kept ourselves busy doing wholesome things like jumping off the dock into the cool lake water and swimming through the lily pads. From time to time, we took periodic breaks from the beach and returned to the cabin to fill our hands with hastily made sandwiches only to rush back down to the water's edge—all the while ensuring to stay clear of Dad.

As we sat on the dock wolfing down our lunches, the bumble bees meandered through the thick brush along the beach, and the birds chirped happily away in the trees. Later in the afternoons, after our daily swim, Phil, Steve, and I spent time tossing a Frisbee back and forth on the vast lawn while Jeri-anne and Kim sat contently on the cabin deck. They took turns playing with our baby sister Allyson and listened to the latest pop music on the small AM radio. They also oversaw our youngest brother, Tim, who played in the dirt just below the cabin. Tim made engine sounds as he pushed his Tonka truck and walked his Weebo figures around as if they were real people. For the most part, we were all one happy family. We drank of life, not knowing whether we were rich or poor.

Several peaceful days passed, and after breakfast one morning, my father jumped back into his old, red Chevy pickup and headed off to the mountains of central Washington. He had to return to his precious gold mine, which was more precious than his family. We didn't necessarily cheer his departure, but we knew that once he left, we would once again be free from all his restraints. His departure would re-ignite our youthful ambitions, and in no time at all, the genie would be let back out of the bottle.

Immediately after my father drove away, Phil and Kit walked up to the road behind the cabin and stopped. They listened to the sound of his truck fading away into the horizon. In a matter of minutes, they looked around at their surroundings. In his teenage wisdom, Kit instinctively knew that nature abhors a vacuum. He thirsted for something to do. It didn't take long for his roving eyes to come to an immediate halt. They rested squarely on our dad's old blue and white Rambler station wagon. With a vision now crystallizing in his mind, Kit very slowly and articulately asked Phil the ultimate question, "Hey Phil, do you want to learn how to drive?"

Phil's eyes immediately widened. Knowing he had a captivated audience, Kit motioned with a tip of his head for Phil to look at the old Rambler.

Several months earlier, Kit had been granted his driver's license and now felt eager to empower his younger brother with the same skills that he had learned. With this new thought stuck firmly in his head, Kit snuck through the back door of our little cabin, and just as he had done with the firecrackers, he had Phil distract our mother while he secured the keys to the Rambler. Within minutes, Phil sat behind the wheel of the old station wagon while Kit climbed into the passenger seat.

"The first step is to start the car. Turn the key and turn everything on. Next, push in the clutch. That's the peddle on the very left. The middle one is the brake. The one on the right is the gas." Just then, Kit realized Phil was way too young and too short even to push the peddles all the way to the floor. He brought the class to an abrupt halt. Kit jumped out of the car and strutted to the back door of the cabin. He came back out carrying a rolled-up sleeping bag. Kit walked directly up to the driver's door.

"Get out," Kit ordered.

"What for?"

"You'll see."

Kit moved the seat as far forward as possible, then put the sleeping bag onto the driver's seat.

"Okay, get back in and see if you can reach the peddles now."

Kit went back around the car and climbed through the passenger door. "Okay, turn the key back on and push the clutch all the way in. Then, grab the gear shift and find neutral."

"Find neutral? What does that mean?" Phil asked with a puzzled expression on his youthful face.

"Just push in the clutch peddle, hold it there while you push and pull on the shift lever, wiggle it a little until it clicks and is loose. That is where you find neutral."

Phil thought for a moment, digesting everything that Kit had just said. Since all of us were born with a fair amount of intelligence, thanks to a college-educated mother and an eccentric father with an I.Q. somewhere off the charts, Phil worked the procedure all out in his mind in seconds. He did precisely what Kit told him, and just like magic, the shift lever became free, and the transmission was in neutral. Phil smiled.

The lesson continued. Kit coached Phil on how to start the engine, put the car into gear, and get it off to a rolling start. However, getting the car moving from a standstill was the tricky part. Phil had to find a delicate balance between revving up the engine and slowly letting out the clutch.

Phil let the clutch out too quickly on the first couple of attempts, and the car lurched forward and died. He tried time and time again. Finally, Phil figured it out. He let the engine race a little, then eased back on the accelerator. He let the engine slow down a little, then very slowly let out the clutch while keeping a little pressure on the gas. The car began to move.

"Do it. Do it!" Kit yelled as he aggressively pointed his finger, directing Phil to get the car going. "Go, go, go!"

The car lurched forward and chugged a couple of times.

"Give her some gas! More gas!" Kit ordered.

Phil pushed on the accelerator. They were off, rolling forward as Phil wrestled with the wheel, trying to keep the car on the road. Next, Kit explained how to shift gears. After Phil successfully pushed in the clutch, pulled the gear level, and put the car into second, they went cruising down the dirt road. Phil proved to be a superb student, and in less than thirty minutes of lumbering up and down the path, he had all the procedures down pat. Although he could now reach the foot pedals with the sleeping bag sitting firmly behind him, he still faced the problem of barely being able to see over the dashboard, but somehow, he still managed to drive.

After breakfast the following morning, another lesson began. Phil sat behind the steering wheel, and Kit took his position in the passenger seat.

"Phil, today we are going to go all the way to the bottom of the hill, turn around at the main fork, and come back."

Phil nodded compliantly, and they began to drive down the road. Phil built up speed, going from first gear to second gear, then finally into third. Eventually, they came to the point where the road headed downhill.

"Okay, we are going to downshift now. Push in the clutch and push on the brakes. Now shift back into second gear."— "Nice job!"

Phil smiled, then let the clutch back out. They turned around at the bottom of the hill and headed back up.

"Okay, Phil, give her some gas. Nice."— "Okay, you have to be quick here. Push in the clutch and shift down into first gear as fast as you can. Do it!"

Phil performed beautifully. He let out the clutch, and the engine whined.

"Give her some more gas, and let's get to the top of this hill."

With the car now in first gear and the engine growling away, the tires chewed up the slope and spat out rocks. The road eventually leveled off, not far from the cabin. As they passed the patch of woods where our treehouses lay, figures of several wild teenage boys suddenly appeared out of nowhere. Three Goodson boys came running out into the road in front of the car and waved for Phil to stop. Phil pushed in the clutch, stomped on the brakes, and brought the Rambler skidding to a halt.

"What the hell are you guys doing?" Dick asked. He was the oldest and the leader of the clan. Dick pointed his finger at my diminutive brother behind the steering wheel. He laughed at the sight of a shrimp behind the controls. "What in the fuck are you guys doing?"

"I am teaching Phil how to drive," Kit replied as he leaned over from the passenger side and looked past Phil.

"But he can't even reach the pedals or see over the freaking dashboard," Dick yelled as he and his two brothers began chuckling again. "Okay, well, have fun. We don't want to disrupt your little Sunday drive. Now, let's see you hit it in this hot rod."

Phil started the car back up, revved up the engine, and slowly let the clutch out. The car hiccupped and bounced forward. Once rolling, the Goodson boys ran behind the car and climbed on the bumper. They grabbed onto the luggage rack. Kit turned around and looked at them with disgust. "Get the fuck off our car! How dare they interrupt a driving lesson?" Kit thought to himself. The three Goodson boys rode along the back of the old Rambler like the Secret Service agents on the back of the president's limousine.

As they lumbered up the dusty road, Phil shifted gears at the appropriate time, just as he was taught. The Rambler and all its passengers cruised naively down the bumpy path to the end where Uncle Goodson lived. Phil fumbled with the shifter and turned the car around. The Goodson boys jumped off and waved goodbye. They had had their fun—at least for now.

Kit and Phil returned to the cabin and parked the car. Their deeds had become evident to everyone, including my mother, but she disregarded it all. It might have been due to her many pressing duties of taking care of our large family and feeling overwhelmed, or that she chose to pick her battles, and this wasn't one of them. We weren't really sure what she thought, but at the end of each driving session, when Kit and Phil parked the car behind the cabin and walked through the back door, she said nothing.

Several days passed since the encounter with the Goodsons, but while Phil and Kit were driving up the road one day, those wild boys appeared out of nowhere at the same spot. They jumped out of the bushes and ran behind the car. They climbed up on the bumper and grabbed the luggage rack as if they had preplanned this assault. This time, Kit looked back and shook his head. He glanced at Phil and calmly said, "Just keep driving."

After completing the circuit, with the Goodsons still hanging off the back, Phil returned the car to its resting place behind the cabin and shut the engine off. The boys jumped off and giggled. Kit got out of the car and looked at them as if to ask, "What the fuck do you think you are doing?" But before he said anything, he thought about it for a moment. Kit came up with a brilliant idea, but before Kit could share it, a young girl mounted upon a horse came strolling up to the road. She got close to the Rambler and stopped the animal. It was the Goodson boys' cousin Sandy. She looked so cute with her short, dark, straight hair combed off to the side. She sat upon the back of that horse like Lady Godiva. I was in love. She glanced down at me, then at the others. She had witnessed the carjacking and the ambush game but didn't say much about it. She knew what everyone was up to but merely shrugged her shoulders to let her cousins know that she wouldn't tell on them. She was just out for a leisurely horseback ride, and their secret was safe with her. Sandy commanded the horse to move past us and went merrily on her way.

Kit looked at everyone. "Phil, I think you are ready to drive solo. Take the car up the road, then back, the same route as before. I want to see how you do."

Kit then said to the Goodsons, "Now, here's how we will do it. Phil will come up the road, and we will ambush him, but from a different spot every time."

"Yeah!" Dick replied. "We'll surprise the shit out of him."

"That's right."

After hearing that, Phil girded up his loins and climbed back into the car. He started it up and confidently took off down the road, wrestling with the large steering wheel while Kit and the others ran through the little patch of woods and past the treehouses. At the edge of the road, the four hid behind trees. By this time, Phil had already turned the car around and was now chugging back up the long stretch. After Phil had driven past their hiding spots, they all bolted out and ran up behind the car in an all-out assault. The four climbed onto the bumper, grabbed the luggage rack, and hung on for dear life.

At first, their sudden appearance on the back of the car startled Phil, but Kit yelled down through the window, "Keep driving! Just keep driving!" Phil trusted Kit, and as the four bandits laughed, Phil increased the speed of the hi-jacked vehicle and shifted gears. They reached the turn-around point at Uncle Wayne's and returned to the ambush site.

At the right spot, Kit yelled, "Phil, stop! Stop right here!" Phil followed orders and stopped the car. The four marauders jumped off the back. Kit walked up to the driver's side and looked down at Phil. "Go back up the road, turn around, and then drive by again."

During this entire escapade, I had been sitting on a log near Zoxville, watching everything they were doing. My brother Stephen suddenly wandered up to me. He looked out at the road. He knew something was up but was slightly confused, so I explained it.

"Steve, did you see what they were doing?"

"Kind of."

"Did you see Phil driving the car and those guys chasing it?"

"I saw them on the back of the car."

"Yes. They were."— "Come with me, I'll show you. They were chasing it and climbing up on the back of it."

I got up from the log and headed over to my treehouse. Steve followed me with undying curiosity. I climbed up the steps until I reached the platform. He climbed up the steps right behind me.

"Listen close," I said, then cupped my hand to my ear.

Off in the distance, the sound of the car coming back up the road grew louder. From our vantage point, Steve and I looked at the large stretch traversing the countryside. Suddenly, the silhouette of the old blue and white station wagon chugged up the slight incline, and right where the road leveled off, four juvenile figures jumped off the back of it and scurried off into the bushes. Phil continued to drive down the road and disappeared into the trees. He turned around at some point and headed back. Just as he passed the same stretch, he looked all around and instantly spotted the group of thugs running up behind the car. He reacted aggressively by pushing down on the accelerator to get away from them as fast as he could. The engine raced, and the vehicle lunged forward. The chase was on. Kit and the Goodson boys ran even harder but finally managed to climb up onto the bumper and grab ahold. The four of them barely secured their position on the back of the car, but this time it was close. Steve and I looked down enviously at all the fun they were having. The four half-naked teenagers hanging off the Rambler looked like a scene from a 1960s hippie movie filmed just outside a psychedelic, drug-laden commune. Now, Kit, Phil, and the Goodsons acted like drug-crazed hippies.

After the old Rambler disappeared, Steve and I looked at each other. "Let's do it!" he said, and I agreed.

We quickly climbed down from my treehouse and ran as fast as we could to join up with Kit and the Goodson's. The car returned, and they all jumped off. Steve and I followed them up to their new hiding spot. At first, the others were puzzled when they saw us. Steve and I weren't really going to try to join them, were we? We were too young and too small for this; besides, Dad would kill us. Steve and I hid with them anyway.

Phil had turned around once again and came down from the north. At the right moment, Kit leaped out first and ran behind the car, with all of us following him. This time, Phil didn't wait till anybody got onto the vehicle before he mashed on the accelerator. He took off at high speed. Stephen and I were too late. Kit, Dick, and Stewy made it, but the other Goodson boy didn't . . . well, kind of. Terry climbed onto the back of the car but slipped on the bumper, and his head hit the tailgate. He fell even further, all the way down to the road, but out of desperation, he frantically grabbed the bumper and hung on. He wanted so badly to get on that car.

But as Phil sped away, Terry's body dragged along the ground with dirt and gravel scraping away at his bare legs and belly, filling his shorts with dirt. He screamed in pain but didn't want to let go. Eventually, he had to. Dick looked back at his brother Terry rolling around in a cloud of dust on the road behind them like a discarded rag doll but didn't give it a second thought; his brother could fend for himself. On the other hand, Kit realized things were getting too dangerous and grew worried.

At the turnaround point, Kit climbed off the back of the car and walked up to Phil.

"Okay, here's the new rule: you have to let everyone get on board before you gun the engine." Phil nodded, totally unaware that he had been dragging a body behind the car."

Kit looked over at Dick. "I hope Terry is okay."

"Ah, he'll be all right."

Kit looked stunned at Dick's lack of concern for his own brother.

They took a quick break to re-evaluate everything. Terry eventually walked around the corner and limped slightly as he approached the car. His legs and stomach showed signs of severe cuts and abrasions with streaks of blood running down from them. Stewy remained silent and looked plain scared at the sight of his injured brother. Undeterred by what happened, Stephen and I were more anxious than ever. We were going to make our debut.

Six of us now hid in the bushes, and when the car came lumbering up the road this time, we all ran out and began the chase. We surprised Phil by coming out of a new spot. I managed to climb aboard and find a place on the corner of the car. I grabbed ahold of the edge of the tailgate. Stephen ran with all his might and almost didn't make it. Then, with great compassion for his younger brother, Kit reached down and pulled Steve up onto the back of the car. He lifted Stephen up even higher and let him climb onto the roof. Once over the luggage rack bars, Stephen kneeled and clutched the chrome rails very tightly.

This time, Phil adhered to Kit's rule and did not take off at high speed until everyone was safely onboard—if you could call what we were doing 'safe.' After completing the circuit, everyone got off at the usual spot, everyone except Steve. Phil thought everyone was off the car and had taken off much too quickly. He had no clue that Stephen was still on the roof.

We watched in disbelief as Phil drove down the road, around the corner, and disappeared into the woods with our younger brother's life in peril.

A few minutes later, the old Rambler returned our way with Stephen still on top of the roof, clinging desperately to the chrome bars. The five of us ran out of the bushes and executed the final ambush for the day so that we could get Stephen safely off the roof and back to the good Earth. Luckily, no one died during this little escapade of ours that day. I wondered how Terry would explain to his parents how he got all the cuts and abrasions on his legs and stomach.

Dad came home a few days later, and thank Goodness, my mother didn't tell him anything about our misdeeds. My God, Phil was only eleven years old, driving a car. Kit was a mere fourteen and risking his brothers' lives. Totally unaware of what we had done in his absence, my father sat around as usual, sipping on his cheap wine and talking about his mining projects instead of wondering how his large family had been getting along without him. Dad started to play the actual part of a prospector. He loved being outdoors, living the rugged life, yet he incessantly talked about his visions of striking it rich and living the rest of his days in total opulence. His dreams of glory stirred my imagination because who doesn't want to be wealthy? But there was a moral dilemma going on inside me: would I rather be poor with no spankings at all or be rich and get the belt across my butt all the time.

After a couple of days of listening to more of Dad's cockamamie bullshit and eating picnic lunches with him on the deck, he disappeared this time without giving a single spanking. Something was starting to change. With Dad gone once again, we resumed our fun.

For some reason, my brothers and I didn't interact with our sisters very much. However, over dinner one night, my oldest sister, Jeri-anne, announced that she had a surprise for us. We didn't know this, but Jeri-anne had worked all day long on a special project with our sister Kim. They had produced another one of their homemade movies. No, Jeri-anne didn't have a movie camera or any fancy electronic gear. She had nothing more than a bunch of sheets of paper, a roll of scotch tape, a pack of crayons, two empty paper towel tubes, and a flashlight to spotlight her paper screen. Jeri-anne and Kim had worked tirelessly on this latest production. It told the story of a puppy wanting to find an owner.

Before the show began, my mother made us a large bowl of popcorn and a pitcher of Kool-Aid, and we ate to our heart's content as we suspensefully watched our sisters roll out one hand-drawn scene after another. Jeri-anne narrated the story while I shone the flashlight onto the paper footage. At the end, we clapped and cheered. Our lives were rich beyond measure, and we didn't even know it.

The sun finally went down. Outside the cabin, the six of us brothers (the band of brothers) all stood together and looked up at the sky and saw the evening star beginning to twinkle low on the horizon. That night, we all laid out our sleeping bags on the floor as usual. There was no television set for us to watch, no next-door neighbors, only the nine kids, a mother, and sometimes a father.

Summer ended soon after that, and we returned to our crowded, humble house on Mission Avenue. We came back changed, a little more mature, embracing the fact that without Dad around, we had to figure things out all on our own. At least, back home, we had a television set, a telephone, a couple of rooms with bunk beds for my brothers and me, and the back room for my sisters. Our tiny house was so cute. Our rooms resembled an army barrack, but I loved it.

With all of us finally home after a beautiful summer, we started a new school year and continued to expand our presence in the neighborhood and our adventures on Mission Avenue, but the fun was only beginning. Sadly, my father had no clue what we were doing the entire time we frolicked in the sun at Rose Lake. He didn't care and missed out on so much of our lives.

Chapter 4

The Kellogg Police

Life for my family went on as usual back in Kellogg. We started another school year, and true to form, our father began to spend more time away from us than ever. My mother, on the other hand, deserved sainthood. She taught school full-time and still managed to get us all to the Catholic mass once a week, where we confessed our sins to the priest, only for us to go out and commit them all over again. She cared for us on every front, especially providing us with the most spectacular birthdays and holidays.

While our mother kept us clothed and fed, just like she had done at Rose Lake, she disregarded most of our activities, but we weren't the only ones who noticed that. The fat bastard, who owned the tiny neighborhood grocery store across the street from us did. He noticed how she disregarded our mischief—and he openly stated it. He was correct, to a certain degree, that we ran wild and unabated all over the neighborhood without adequate parental guidance. But where was he when my father returned home to exact his punishment on us? That miserable grocery merchant didn't see any of that shit. Each time Dad came home, my mother, in her usual fashion, handed him her famous shit list of our transgressions. Before my father could even sit down and enjoy a glass of cheap wine, he had the task of ravaging our asses with his belt; only then could relax. He could, but afterward, we couldn't. We had to tend to all the stinging welts on our butts. While life continued this way, we grew older and only began to escalate our feats until we attracted the attention of the local police.

During this time in local history, the town of Kellogg prospered dearly. Cars, boats, motorcycles, and campers crowded the streets each summer as everyone scrambled to enjoy life outside their rigorous work routine. Amid these booming days, the classrooms bulged yearly with students from long-time, deeply rooted families of the valley, as well as many new families that moved into town seeking work opportunities in the mines. To maintain peace and order in such a bustling community, a new police chief had been appointed: One-eyed Charlie. Charlie Galbraith was no newcomer to local law enforcement. He had served for many years on the police force, and at this juncture, it was only fitting for him to be appointed as the chief after all his faithful years of service to the city. It became his turn to take the reins until his retirement.

In addition to the new chief, the department had recruited two new officers to the ranks as well, Meyers and Dugan: a duo of distinctly opposite personalities. Meyers should have never been given a badge. His hot, volatile temper and bad judgment made him a loose cannon. With him, a disaster waited to happen. Completely aware of his tall, lanky figure, he whole-heartedly believed that no one was more perfect for engaging in hot foot pursuits of any fleeing bad guys than he was. The handcuffs, the badge, and the gun dangling from his uniform were synonymous with a swastika, German Luger, and the Iron Cross medal. But, he was too anxious—and was a borderline psychotic.

On the other hand, Officer Dugan was quite the contrast to Meyers. Dugan had recently flunked out of a trial period at the Bunker Hill mine's infamous Zinc Plant. Dugan couldn't handle the torturous work in the hot, acid-bath environment. However, the obligation to support his young wife and new baby at home forced him to seek another form of employment. After much soul-searching and scanning the "Help Wanted" ads, he reluctantly jumped at the chance to get into uniform. Despite his soft physique, he barely met the minimum fitness requirements of a law enforcement job. By the grace of God, he squeaked by and somehow completed primary police officer's training. At first glance, one would wonder how he accomplished such a feat because he thoroughly enjoyed his wife's cooking and the occasional donuts, and around his waistline— it definitely showed. Dugan's round face, black-framed glasses, and impeccably trimmed mustache made him look more like a church usher than a law enforcement officer. He smiled at everyone and everything, fearful as hell of everyone and everything. His demeanor showed that he obviously harbored many deep insecurities, which would impede his duties in the coming days.

Chief Charlie held a department-wide meeting within the first week of the new staff taking their positions. His goal was to orientate his team of officers to the new standards of conduct for the force. Inwardly (and even outwardly), he rehearsed his opening speech to the department, even in front of the mirror that morning. While he did, his wife lay in bed, browsing through an Avon makeup catalog, and wondered who he had been talking to behind the closed bathroom door. Charlie desperately wanted to present and instill his vision of an effective, unified law enforcement agency to his men. In his deep sense of duty, he believed so sincerely that what he had to offer to the city of Kellogg was something that the citizens had longed for: a team of men so well trained, so effective, but yet so supportive of the citizens of Kellogg. Charlie wanted to give a new meaning to the phrase "To Serve and to Protect." With all the years of open criticism from his fellow officers now behind him, Charlie stood proudly in front of the entire department that fateful morning in a neatly starched, dark blue uniform that his wife had prepared for him just an hour earlier. Like an apostle charged with spreading the Word, Charlie knew he had to live up to what he believed was the end-all-be-all of his career. "Where much is given, much is expected."

"Listen up, gentleman." he began, "There are going to be some changes from the old way that we have been doing things in the past. We will get focused and concentrate on some key areas in town that really need our attention."

On the wall behind Charlie, a massive map of the town of Kellogg hung gallantly in a neatly crafted wooden frame. The near horizontal lines clearly indicated the interstate highway that ran through the middle of the city. Every street had been laid out and named in tiny letters. Also distinct was the meandering, blue, snake-like image of the south fork of the Coeur d'Alene River that paralleled the freeway.

Officer Meyers stood among the patrolmen and rolled his eyes with disdain at the chief's frivolous remarks while his new compatriot, Dugan, stood beside him and listened intently to the chief.

"First off, you must pay particular attention to some problem sectors in our community. One is the bar scene here on upper McKinley Avenue." Charlie's index finger touched the map with extreme precision.

"We have had too many reports of underaged minors being allowed in these establishments and served as legal patrons." He paused, looked down, and shook his head in righteous indignation. "What would our local religious leaders think of this?" He mumbled.

Charlie cleared his throat and continued, "Secondly, a certain street in downtown Kellogg has presented a unique set of problems for us. It's a stretch of road on Sunnyside—Mission Avenue, to be exact." He began again, "And on this block in particular." He pounded his finger on the map directly in the middle of the long rectangle. (That particular block just happened to be where my brothers and I lived.)

The mention of Mission Avenue immediately piqued Officer Dugan's curiosity. He held his hand halfway up and asked, "What's going on down on Mission Chief?"

The rest of the force began to chuckle.

Dugan looked around sheepishly and continued, "I don't know, Sir, I'm just curious."

The chief looked sternly down at Dugan, "Let me put it to you this way," He searched for the right words. "Well, those kids down there on Mission cause more ruckus than a polecat in a hen house on any given day of the year. Oh, and that's not to mention the worst day of the year— Halloween. Anytime you drive down this part of Mission after dark, Halloween or not, you take a chance, especially in the alleys."

"What type of ruckus are you talking about, Sir?"

"Dugan!" The chief shouted. "Didn't you ever cause any trouble as a kid?"

Dugan just shrugged his shoulders and allowed the chief to continue.

"I'm telling you, these kids are just plain wild! Screaming up the street on their motorcycles, scaling fences, crawling through neighbor's yards, raiding gardens, bashing cars with everything from eggs to apples to plums—anything they can get their hands on. Hell, they've pulled every prank imaginable. And don't forget the firecrackers. Damn near gave Mrs. Bisaro a heart attack one night."

"Which kids are we talking about, Sir?"

The Chief paused for another moment in disgust. He looked down a second time and shook his head. He couldn't believe he had to explain everything to this wet-nose rookie. Charlie turned around once again and faced the enormous map. He ran his fingers back and forth, traversing our block on Mission Avenue, and continued with a warning, "You drive your squad car down here after dark, and you will be washing it yourself in the morning."

Charlie again tapped his finger on the map directly in the center of the block where our house lay. "There are several families in this area with one or two kids, but then you have this entire clan living in one small house right here—the Majors. The mom's a schoolteacher, a nice, respectable lady, but no one knows where the dad is. To complicate matters, no one knows how many kids are there, maybe eight or nine, or could be as high as eleven, but no one really knows."

Officer Meyer suddenly blurted out from the group of officers, "If my car gets nailed by one of those little bastards, I am going to crack some skulls!"

Chief Charlie immediately snapped back, "That's not what I am talking about!" he yelled. "We've got to round up these kids and get with the parents, with the parents, I tell ya!"

"Don't we have to catch 'em first?" asked Dugan.

Meyers rolled his eyes for the second time.

The chief grew silent momentarily, trying to find the best way to make his point. But before Charlie could continue, another officer joined in on the conversation. "Hey, Chief. Remember last week, the trespassing call I went on Wednesday night?"

"Yeh, what about it?"

"Well, I'm pretty sure I put it in my report, but when I talked to Mrs. Damiano, she said it was the Major boys. She said they would run across the street, jump her fence, and use her yard as a path to the back alley. She said they are pretty damn fast. If that's the case, how will we catch 'em?"

Every officer in the room nodded to each other in agreement, then looked back at the chief for some guidance.

This time, Meyers shared his thoughts, "I ain't worried. I'm going to catch those little sons-of-bitches."

"Meyers! What you're going to do is follow procedures. Is that clear?"

Meyers fought hard to keep from smirking. "Yes, Sir," but the rest of the force knew he felt otherwise.

Charlie finally shifted the conversation and began discussing the general procedures within the department. After thirty minutes of niceties, he finally adjourned the meeting. With their new orders, everyone slowly filed out of the room. Charlie stepped behind his desk and slumped down into his severely worn leather office chair. He spun around and stared back up at the massive map of Kellogg. He gently shook his head, leaned forward, and buried his face into his hands. He wondered what he had gotten himself into.

Unfortunately, a particular episode regarding my father escaped Charlie's memory. My brother Peter was involved in an accident at the intersection by the IGA grocery store a year earlier. He certainly had the right of way, but the other driver ran through the stop sign and caused the accident. The young officer issued a traffic citation to my teenage brother, although it was clearly not his fault. My father went ballistic when he came home and found out what happened. He called the police station, yelling and using swear words I had never heard before. Ultimately, they tore up the ticket they had issued Peter and re-issued it to the other driver. The moral of the story: you don't mess with my dad when he's been drinking.

With the memory of the encounter with my father long forgotten and his first crucial meeting with his officers, Charlie kept a close eye on his men and the daily reports. He had to ensure that his new policies were being followed. But the environment changed soon after the school year ended, and the kids were let out of class. The streets were now teaming with mischievous young men—especially those on one-hundred block of Mission Avenue. After a few reports of underaged adolescents cruising town with open alcohol containers and the pranks being pulled on unsuspecting neighbors, Charlie knew that the resolve of his police force would soon be tested to its limits. The weather had turned hot, and he knew he had to brace himself for the summer's recreational onslaught and the inevitable mayhem.

The first few weeks of June passed with a small but manageable number of encounters between his officers and the local teenagers in hot cars, illegal dirt bikes on the public streets, and senseless neighborhood shenanigans.

However, this peaceful lull was about to change when the fireworks stands opened and sold their wares at numerous locations in Kellogg.

From the very first day of sales, it was as if Pandora's Box had been opened. The rockets raced skyward, the smoke bombs ravaged residents' porches, and the firecrackers exploded indiscriminately from the back alleys. With a pack of firecrackers in one hand and a book of matches in the other, the young men (even down to the early grade schoolers) overran the neighborhood and created a scene found in a bizarre episode of the TV series The Twilight Zone. The typical behavior grew infinitely worse than when these kids were armed with harmless peashooters in the classroom, just as they had been a month earlier. So many of the crazed youth were destined to put somebody's eye out with their fireworks if that was the last thing they would do and leave no doubt about it—my older brothers were right there in the thick of it. All I could do was to listen, observe, and remember, being relegated to nothing more than an innocent bystander.

Day after day, every form of fireworks went off across town: the bottle rockets, the firecrackers, the Roman candles, the buzz bombs, etc. However, one afternoon, I discovered that some kids were modifying some of the pyrotechnics. I walked into our little shop behind our house and stumbled across my brother Kit doing something strange.

"What are you doing?" I asked.

"I am building a bomb," He replied.

I looked over at the bench and saw a firework called the Piccolo Pete. I had seen them before. After you light them, they whistle loudly, shooting sparks out of the top of themselves. Kit held a pair of vice-grips in his right hand.

"Listen, it's an old trick I learned from one of Pete's friends."

"Are you tearing it apart to get the gunpowder out?" I asked.

"No, Dummy. Don't you know anything about explosives?"— "Never mind, let's just go out to the alley."

Just before we headed out the shop door, Kit picked a Piccolo Pete up off the bench and clamped Vice Grips tightly to the bottom of it. I had no idea what the hell he was doing. I followed him out of the shop and out into the alley. He set the Piccolo Pete on the ground and pulled out a book of matches. He lit the fuse. We both stood back and waited cautiously. Sparks began to shoot skyward, and the little cardboard tube whistled like an incoming mortar shell. After about ten seconds, the entire thing violently exploded, leaving nothing but shards of paper, its plastic base, and a happy pair of Vice Grips.

"Yee-haw!" Kit yelled.

"Crap, you did build a bomb!"

"Yep, and I got five more of these babies!"

Within a few days, exploding Piccolo Pete's were going off all over town, and Vice Grips at the local hardware store were in short supply.

There was action all over town, and the police could not keep up with all of it. Each neighborhood seemed to have its own teenage warlord in charge. The regional leader and his gang shattered the peace, independent of the other neighborhood gangs. Just down the street to the west, Mike Margeson and his pack terrorized the 200 block, and on the other side of the 100 block, Mark Walkenshaw held down the eastern front with his gang of misfits just the same. Walkenshaw and his friends had their hands as full as we did with the neighborhood spies and informants who peeked through their blinds only to rush to the phone and call the police. Next door to our house, we had the wilted, emaciated mummy-of-a-woman, Mrs. Williams, reporting everything we did. In contrast, the Walkenshaw gang had Mrs. Stoner spying on them from directly across the street, not to mention the old bag on their corner, Mrs. Migraine. However, my family's greatest nemesis came in the form of the miserable, aging store owner from across the street, Ray Swanson, the same guy who openly commented about how our parents didn't do anything about us running wild. He hated us passionately, and because of his disdain for us, we did everything we could to help him hate us even more. We lit as many fireworks in front of his little establishment as possible. Things might have been different if he had just been a little nicer and not berated my mother and father for leaving us to run wild. Hell, what was done was done, and we gave him what he deserved.

Citing a report from the government statistics office, each time the Halloween and Fourth of July holidays were celebrated in our community, antidepressant sales skyrocketed, and nervous breakdowns among seasoned police officers grew to epic proportions. Patrol cars were continuously sent out on countless calls to quell the unrest, and they were only sometimes successful. Fortunately for us, each time a patrol car came sneaking down our street, someone in our neighborhood alerted us, and that was one of the reasons none of my brothers were ever caught. However, the youngsters from other parts of our community did not know this statistic. So many of them were quickly cornered and apprehended. Most of the other kids were just plain dumb. They needed to learn about the effective ways of all-out neighborhood search and destroy missions and how to avoid direct contact with the enemy. These punks had no formal training on how to evade capture by the police. Idiots. As a result of all the easy apprehensions, a new phenomenon infected the ranks of the Kellogg police force. With all the other simple bastards being hauled into custody so quickly, the Kellogg police officers became lulled into a false sense of superiority. They felt virtually unstoppable after achieving some arbitrary daily quota of squishing enough kids' fun. However, soon enough, the city police would find themselves totally unprepared for what lay in store for them when it came to my brothers—especially Phil and a couple of his close friends.

Of all my brothers, Phil was the most independent in thought and action. He had a mind of his own and no one would ever sway, con, or pressure him. He could size up anyone he met in an instant.

One day, at St. Rita's Catholic school, Phil became friends with a guy named Mike Groves. He had met his match. Like us, Mike came from a family of several boys, and they held a reputation similar to ours. Mike and his brothers had their own standing in the community and were known as the 'wild boys from up the hill' (the 'hill' meaning the upper part of town called Wardner). However, unlike us, Mike and his brothers had a more hands-on mother and father to keep them in line (not to impugn the efforts of my own beloved parents). Although Mike came from a more tightly knit nuclear family, that didn't seem to make any difference in his call to mischief. Phil always claimed that Mike was crazy, but Mike turned around and claimed that Phil was even crazier. However, Mike caused his share of trouble on his own. For instance, one winter day, Mike teamed up with Tony Rinaldi out on the playground. They saw a row of fellow female students all lined up along the brick wall of the gymnasium. The girls wore skirts. Their legs, covered with high stockings, looked so skinny. These innocent cuties became targets of opportunity. Mike and Tony began pummeling these girls' legs with snowballs. After all the shrieks and screams, Sister Patricia finally stopped them and hauled them before the priest. It was rare for Tony to get into trouble, but it was only the beginning for Mike.

Strangely, Phil and Mike were born on the same day, one year apart. Although Mike was one year older than Phil, they shared the same classroom because our Catholic school was so tiny that each classroom housed two grade levels. One of the first tests of their camaraderie came when they had to determine one thing: who could outdo the other. Such a test came during an afternoon classroom session in the sixth grade of the small Catholic school we attended. In that room, they mercilessly terrorized one of the finest teachers at St. Rita's Catholic school. Her name was Charlotte Bushnell. She was among the most revered women in the church and in the community. God had blessed Charlotte with the voice of an angel, beautiful yet powerful enough to shatter windows—a voice she used in every weekly church service. During precise moments in a service, Charlotte so piously and single-handedly led the congregation in every hymn. She was indeed an angel. But despite her high stature, Phil and Mike were determined to test her angelic limits and see how far over the cliff they could push her. They talked about it at recess.

"Phil, I don't think I can handle the religious part of class coming up."

"It can't be that bad."

"It is."

"Should pull the fire alarm or something and create a distraction to get us out of it."

"No, don't do that. Maybe we could talk her into something about science or social studies."

Phil thought momentarily, "Let me think of something when class begins."

"Okay, but do you have any ideas yet?"

"No, but just leave it up to me."

"I can't hardly wait."

On that beautiful fall afternoon in class, Charlotte began to explain the blessedness of the Virgin Mary. Like Mike, Phil wanted no part of it, so he snuck to the back of the class and sat in the far corner. Charlotte didn't even notice. While the rest of their classmates listened in almost perfect silence, Phil began to periodically make frog sounds, complete with croaks and ribbits. Many students took their attention off the subject each time he did and began to look around the room. Meanwhile, Mike sat in the front row and buried his face into his arms. He laid his head, face-first, into the desk and tried to harness his uncontrollable laughter.

After the first few croaks, Mike could not contain himself any longer. As the frog sounds echoed across the room, Mike rose, sat back in his chair, and arched his back. He burst out laughing so hard that he almost fell onto the floor. After another outburst, Charlotte froze. She grew silent and fought to maintain her composure. She breathed in deeply and hoped whatever was happening would soon disappear (wishful thinking on her part, I guess). Mrs. Bushnell, obviously frazzled, continued one last time, but the lonely frog reared its ugly head (more like its ugly voice), and this ribbit, above all, pushed Charlotte to the brink of a nervous breakdown.

She straightened her back up abruptly. She knew that Phil was the culprit and Mike was his accomplice. She threw her hardback instruction book onto the desk with a thunderous clap and yelled, "That's it! One more time, one more time, one more time and you two will be taking a class from Father King for the rest of the year."

This time, the threat did hit home. Phil and Mike knew that Charlotte was serious. She could easily make this happen because she had that much clout, and Father Coleman King was a fearsome and formidable one-on-one teacher. The charade came to an abrupt stop.

Later that school year, during a parent-teacher conference, Mrs. Bushnell shared her concerns with Mrs. Groves and our mother about the questionable relationship between Phil and Mike. After that conference, Mr. and Mrs. Groves wondered if Mike being caught in Phil's whirlwind would be the best thing for their son. They expected the best behavior from Mike and remained determined to keep a closer eye on his involvement from there on out. On the other hand, our mother did heed the warning, but found herself so overwhelmed with her duties as a full-time schoolteacher and a mother to not getting around to doing much about it. And so, the mischief continued, but it didn't get too far out of hand.

The months rolled by until another school season ended, and the local youth were released for their summer vacation. In the same manner as the year before, the local police made their rounds through the neighborhoods, thinking that they were really cracking down on the unruly kids. Phil's great friend Mike decided to venture downtown from Wardner onto our turf, looking for something crazy to do with Phil. In a proverbial sense, the matches were looking for the gasoline. Nothing was out of bounds for either of them; they continuously increased their challenges. Nothing Phil suggested was too much for Mike. If the idea of turning cars upside down in the neighborhood came up, Mike would do it just because Phil dared him to (not to say that they ever did). They went toe-to-toe. For example, who could do the most audacious thing with a firecracker? Mike would unabashedly throw a firecracker anywhere, even onto a neighbor's front porch after beating on the door. They certainly freaked out the local residents.

A time came when Mike was one up on Phil. A week earlier, he had taken Phil out for a drive in the Grove's family car, even though both were too young for a driver's license. Mike took the car out without permission, picked up Phil, and then smoked the tires right through the town's main intersection. Luckily, there were no police around.

Not long after the Fourth of July holiday, Mike came down from Wardner and teamed up with Phil once again. "Phil, I got several packs of firecrackers. How many do you have?"

"Five." Phil replied.

"That ain't shit. I've got ten."

"What are you doing, planning on starting a war?"

"I just figure you've got to go big or go home."

"Okay, let's walk around the block and see what's happening."

Phil and Mike menaced the neighborhood by randomly setting off firecrackers in various places. They annoyed every neighbor in their path. Not long after roaming the other streets and blowing up numerous street corners, they ventured back into the alley behind Mission Avenue— directly behind our house. When the reports started to reach the police station, the dispatcher knew precisely where to send a responding officer (if they had any available).

While the Kellogg dispatcher attempted to mobilize any available officer, Phil and Mike entered our gate and set up a firing position from our backyard. They began shelling the alley with the tiny explosives for over ten more minutes. The two partners in crime kept the alley so dangerous that no one dared walk down it. Reckless enough on their part, of course, but senseless just the same because they had no particular target or objective;

they wanted to keep lobbing the firecrackers just for the hell of it. They didn't mean no trouble; they just enjoyed the sound of the explosions. It was music to their ears. The constant bombardment irritated even more of the neighbors, and the reports kept flooding into police headquarters, eventually overwhelming their phone lines.

With the city's resources waning, the department dispatched the first available officer to the scene, the department's finest: poor Officer Dugan. This donut-eating bastard had no idea what he was up against. Still, in the true spirit of the legendary officer Barney Fife from the Andy Griffith show, Dugan straightened up his necktie and headed out to our neighborhood in his modest police cruiser. He headed downtown and drove directly into the maelstrom—to the location specified on the Kellogg Police Department's large map. He remembered how all those ominous, red pins on the police department's large city map (signifying the recently reported disturbances) somehow all seemed to converge directly on the center of our block.

Mike stood confidently in our backyard, having Phil light the firecrackers one by one while he heaved them over the six-foot fence. Blast after blast rocked the nearby houses, and some of the residents began having nervous breakdowns while others started having flashbacks of the war. Phil and Mike neither knew nor cared if the authorities were coming. Nothing could stop their fun. Besides, what were the cops going to do, take away their dessert?

Dugan finally arrived near the scene and parked his patrol car at the end of the block adjacent to the alley. He exited his vehicle and almost ducked for cover when another firecracker went off. He slammed the patrol car door and cautiously strolled down the alley with one hand on his sidearm. He began to creep along like a well-trained Ninja, hoping not to be detected (which he wasn't). However, Mike prepared another firecracker just as this rookie walked up to the back of our fence in his Kiwi-polished shoes.

Mike said, "Phil, light this one."

As Phil struck the match, Dugan spoke up, and his voice pierced the fence boards, "You're not going to light that!"

Phil DID light the firecracker, and Mike tossed it over the fence at the patrolman. The sizzling firecracker bounced off Dugan's arm before falling to the ground and exploding. BLAM! Phil and Mike ran out of the backyard and into the back door of the house while Officer Dugan bolted down the fence line and ran through our back gate. Not being able to detect where the two culprits had gone, Dugan walked the length of our driveway to the front of the house and entered the gate while Phil and Mike found refuge in one of the bedrooms.

Dugan pounded on the front door. Not only had all the explosions annoyed my brother Peter severely while he tried to watch Star Trek in peace, the fresh pounding on the door nearly pushed him over the edge. After Peter jumped up from the couch and angrily answered the door, Dugan professionally explained, "Sir, I believe that children from this household have been breaking the law and causing a disturbance in the neighborhood."

"What do you mean, breaking the law?"

"Well, Sir, they have been throwing a lot of firecrackers and violating the city ordinance."

"Firecrackers? I haven't heard any firecrackers." (Peter was lying, of course.)

"Sir, they have been going off behind your house for quite some time now."

"I don't know what you are talking about. I haven't heard anything. I have just been here watching TV."

Dugan then realized the futility of it all. His mind raced. He wondered how to bow out of this situation gracefully.

"Sorry to bother you Sir. You have a nice day."

"Same to you, Officer."

The dejected Dugan walked back through our front gate, down the street, and around the corner to his patrol car. While his head hung low, Peter resumed watching TV and felt happy that the constant explosions had finally stopped. Phil eventually peeked out of the bedroom doorway and then came out into the hall. At that moment, he realized the firecracker game was being played too close to home, because now, it had just involved his older brother.

After regrouping for a few minutes in the laundry room and wiping the sweat off their brows after such a close call, Phil and Mike went out to the back porch. They felt so relieved that the danger had finally passed. From our driveway, Phil looked up at the mountainside and fixed his eyes on the small cliff, the jagged rock formation that lay half a block away and two hundred feet above the road. He had hiked on it so many times before and knew every boulder and every crevasse. A lightning bolt suddenly hit him, an epiphany you might call it, a one-in-a-million idea. Without saying much more, he and Mike bade each other farewell for the night, and Mike returned home.

That night, Phil slept on his idea, and in his dreams, he found himself conquering a new level in the game of kid versus cop. As the new day began, he could not get the idea off his mind. He pondered his thoughts all morning and even deep into the afternoon. Finally, when his vision had crystallized that evening, he reached for the phone and called the Groves residence.

"Hello."

"Hi. Can I talk to Mike, please?"

"Who is this?"

"Ah, this is Phil, Phil Major."

She felt reluctant to call Mike after the reports she had heard during the recent school conference. She had good reason to—it was that damn Major boy.

"Well, let me see. I am not sure Mike is here right now."

Mike came out of his bedroom and had just heard what his mom said on the phone. He looked at her sternly, walked up, and reached for the receiver.

She caved in. "Oh, here's Mike now." Once Mike took the phone, she looked at him and waved her finger. There would be no trouble tonight.

When Mike finally responded, Phil spoke, "Mike, get your ass down here as soon as the sun sets. I have an idea!"

"Okay! I will." Mike almost squealed in excitement because he knew Phil was going to deliver something good.

After the sun went down, Mike showed up at our back door. Phil stepped onto the patio with a pack of matches and a bag full of firecrackers. Mike was game for anything and simply followed Phil's lead. In the darkness, they strolled down the street, disappeared around the corner, and climbed up to the top of that little cliff.

Chapter 5

Kit

In the middle of the growing melee in our quaint little neighborhood, my brother Kit (six years older than me) finally reached his high school days and emerged from the family shadows just like a phoenix—and he did it in such a glorious way.

Just a few years earlier, in his junior high days, Kit found himself to be less confident than the rest of his male peers. They had made fun of him for having a slight stutter (something I was unaware of because I had always admired my older brother). This tiny, almost unnoticeable impediment caused him to feel shy around women. At this point, Kit hadn't yet found himself. He looked slightly different from the rest of us in the family line-up. He had the darkest hair among us boys, brown and wavy, contrary to the dusty blond curls that the rest of us had. Additionally, Kit came genetically equipped with relatively broad shoulders compared to the thin, wiry physiques with which the rest of us were born. But he possessed latent talents that the rest of us did not have, which leveled the playing field. As Kit began to blossom, he demonstrated a natural musical ability and wasn't quite sure what to do with it. Out of nowhere, he picked up the accordion and played it like he had practiced it for years. The piano came next. He couldn't read one note of sheet music, yet both his hands and his fingers danced and pounded on the piano keys, sending beautiful music through the rooms of our small and humble home. Not long afterward, making love to the ebony and ivory, Kit tackled the drums and took lessons from a young neighborhood man, the son of a prominent store owner.

Kit's fortunes quickly reversed, and he bloomed like no other in our family. It didn't stop with the music. He looked in the mirror at his developing physique and saw great potential. He fantasized about what he could do at the gym. He soon became enamored with the likes of Arnold Schwarzenegger, and the inspiration that he found in his idol drove him into an obsession with weight training.

It seemed like overnight that all of Kit's cylinders began firing. His reputation spread quickly, and he soon became an overnight musical sensation when he secured a position as a drummer in an adult band at an infamous establishment known as The Rio Club. Although Kit was still underage, the bar management allowed him to play, and this exposure only skyrocketed his fame even more among the very women he failed to impress just a few years earlier. As expected, hordes of young local women began to take notice of the strapping young seventeen-year-old stud who hailed from a small house smack dab in the middle of Mission Avenue—the epicenter of trouble that the local police kept a close eye on.

Between songs at the night club, Kit rested his drumsticks in his lap and had the uncanny habit of brushing the dark brown tuft of hair away from his eyes just like Bobby Kennedy had done during his presidential campaign speech in Los Angeles six years earlier. Kit basked in his newfound stature and developed a style all of his own. The rest of us brothers didn't take that much notice at the time of what Kit was doing because we were all so deeply immersed in the individual pranks we were perpetrating. Our older brother Peter has already catapulted himself into local fame with his rare Kawasaki motorcycle, rogue AMC Javelin hotrod, and a work ethic rivaling that of ten slaves.

One Fall day, after Kit's senior year had just begun, he and his friend Kevin Nolan ventured inside the brand-new A&W restaurant just down from our local high school. The two sat across from each other in a booth and fumbled with the menu.

Kevin read aloud from the new-styled menu, "Papa Burger, Momma Burger, Baby Burger, look at this goofy shit!"

"Yeh, I know," Kit replied, browsing through the various choices.

Kevin wouldn't let up, "All I want is a fur burger, with a side of thighs smothered in underwear." He laughed as idiotically and nerdily as any teenager could have.

"Yeh, me too." Kit agreed with a laugh as he closed the menu.

Suddenly, Kevin's eyes grew wide as he pointed toward the counter. "Kit! Kit! Get a load of her!"

Kit spun around in the booth, twisting his entire body to check out what Kevin was pointing at. His jaw dropped. A cute, young waitress walked out from behind the counter carrying a tray of burgers, fries, and frosty mugs of root beer. This beautiful creature had long, straight, dark brown hair, bright, sparkling eyes, and defined cheekbones that supported the most appealing set of lips God could put on a girl. She had the perfect hourglass-shaped figure. Kit instantly fell in love.

"Damn, who the hell is that?" Kit asked.

"I don't know. I think she might be some college student from NIC."

"Boy, would I like to hook up with her!"

"No shit, who wouldn't"

The sexy waitress dropped off the tray at the far booth to a large, bearded man sitting across from a small, petite woman half his size. Kit stared trance-like as she walked back to the counter. She turned around and surveyed the restaurant floor. Kit quickly dropped his head and looked away, not letting her know he had been checking her out. He wasn't ready to make his move because he had just now laid eyes on her.

Fate intervened. A few minutes later, the manager sent this beautiful waitress to Kit and Kevin's table to take their order. She walked up to their booth as gracefully as a model on the catwalk in a Paris fashion show. Kit's heart began to race with excitement. Even though he had felt shy and possibly insecure a few years earlier, his self-confidence had soared since then—in fact, he had grown cocky. However, at that very moment, his newfound confidence was being tested.

"Hey, what's your name?" Kit asked her directly before she could even take their order.

She scribbled with her pen, trying to get it to write on the small tablet.

"Ah, what?" She wasn't expecting such a blunt question at the moment. She was hoping to take his order as her job description mandated.

"What's your name?" Kit asked again.

"Oh. It's Debbie," she replied, shyly smiling and blinking her eyes.

"Debbie? Gee, that's a pretty name. I'm Chris."

He reached his hand out to shake hers. She shifted the pen and tablet into her left hand and gently shook Kit's. Kevin sat quietly, amazed at Kit's extreme finesse in engaging this princess. She took their order and returned to the kitchen. Kit and Kevin began talking away, awestruck by young Debbie. She eventually returned, laid the food tray on their table, and quickly retreated without saying anything. Debbie was only a shy freshman, and Kit was now playing the part of a bold and brash senior. After their little meeting, Kit could not get her out of his mind.

The next day at school, Kit loaded the weights onto the bench press during the morning PE class. He was going for a record lift: three hundred pounds. Following the advice of Olympic class sports coaches, Kit tested his creative visualization skills. In his mind's eye, he "saw" himself lifting the three hundred pounds, he "saw" himself looking like Arnold Schwarzenegger, and he also "saw" himself with this girl. Deep inside, he felt with certitude that everything in the world during his senior year would go his way.

After a week of daydreaming, Kit decided to marshal up all his courage and see this girl again. He got permission from our mother to take the family car out again for the drive across town. After picking up his wingman, Kevin, he went to no other place than the nearby A&W drive-in restaurant. Kit carefully pulled up to one of the outside car-hop stations. He mentally rehearsed his plan before pressing the microphone button and placing his order. He finally pushed the button as if he were launching a nuclear missile.

A few seconds later, a voice crackled from the speaker, "Hello, may I take your order?"

"Yeh, I want two Papa burgers, two fries, two root beer floats . . . and I want Debbie to bring it out!"

After a slight pause, the voice returned, "That's two Papa burgers, two fries, two root beer floats. That will be six dollars and fifty-nine cents." Unfortunately, there was no mention of Debbie.

"Kit, you crazy fucker!" Kevin blurted.

"Watch, you Doubting Thomas. I bet she comes out."

"Ah, I bet she doesn't."

"Why not?"

"She's too hot for you. That's why."

"Bullshit! I'll bet ya five bucks she does."

Ten minutes later, a young, thin, dark-haired beauty walked out to the car with Kit's order. It was Debbie.

When he rolled down the window for her to hook the food tray on the glass, he just had to ask before she could get away, "Are you busy Friday night?"

With a shocked look over his boldness, she answered, "No, not really."

"Good, because how would you like to go and maybe watch the football game on Friday?"

And just like magic, she responded: "Sure, I'd love to, but it will still be six dollars and fifty-nine cents."

Kit smiled, and Kevin almost choked on the first bite of his hamburger.

"Perfect. Now, I think I might need your phone number."

Debbie ripped a page from her order book, wrote her number down, and handed it to Kit. It was a date.

Kevin gasped for air and held his hamburger very still like a street mime waiting to bite into an imaginary meatball sandwich. He dared not take another bite of anything until the reality of what had just happened had sunk in.

The next night, Kit called Debbie at her home, and when a female voice answered, he almost talked sensuously until he realized that it wasn't Debbie. "Hold on, Chris, I will get Debbie for you," she said with a slight chuckle. When Debbie got on the phone, they chatted briefly and confirmed their Friday night date. During the phone call, he found out where she lived, and they both agreed on a time that he would pick her up. Kit got off the line with a lump in his throat, butterflies in his stomach, and a feeling of disbelief that he had won the hand of this luscious goddess, even if it were for only one night.

Over the next couple of days, Kit's classmates would come up to him after hearing the news that he had a date with Debbie. Many of them commented, "You lucky sucker!" Kit beamed with pride but still felt slightly self-conscious because he had never had things in his life take such a positive turn. And so, he mentally rehearsed the date and saw things exactly how he wanted them to be.

Friday came, and everything went better than the two could have imagined. Kit paid for their entrance into the football game, and they walked around the grandstands holding hands for the entire world to see. After the game ended, Kit took Debbie home and parked the car in front of her house. They talked for a minute, and then, just like a perfect gentleman, Kit walked her to the door. When he wished her goodnight, they stood there in silence, in a timeless moment. That is until Kit leaned over and gave her a quick, discreet kiss on the lips. She went into the house and purposely went up to the living room window. She looked out as Kit walked back to the car. He maintained the best composure that he possibly could. He wanted the night to end perfectly—and it did.

As the weather turned colder, the holiday season soon fell upon the community, and Kit and Debbie became an item. As Kit played the drums for the local band at the Rio Club, every song reminded him of her. His passion came out through his beat, rhythm, and intensity. With every passing weekend, Kit began to earn more money. Right after the Christmas holidays, he felt something was missing in his life. He thought about his bodybuilding. He thought about his music. He thought about his goddess-of-a-girlfriend. What was missing from his senior year in high school?

One night after the Rio closed, Kit retired his drumsticks. He walked out onto McKinnley Avenue just in time to see a hopped-up 1970 Chevy Chevelle idle past him with the most beautiful, beasty sound any car could ever have made. Kit knew right then what was missing: he needed a muscle car.

Over the next week, Kit scanned the newspaper, looking for cars for sale—muscle cars only. There were Chevies in town, Chryslers, and at least one Mustang, but as our older brother Peter had done by setting precedence with his red AMC Javelin, Kit needed to make his mark with something new. Eventually, he came across an ad that listed a 1970 Ford GT Torino. He wasn't even sure what that was. If anything, the oddity of such a different hotrod model prompted him to call the seller.

"Sir, I am calling about the Torino that you are selling. Can you tell me about it?"

"Of course. The car is yellow, has a big block 429 Cobra Jet engine with a manual ten-bolt top loader transmission, a shaker hood scoop, and the typical strobe stripes running down both sides of the car?"

Kit thought, "What in the hell is a Cobra Jet? What in the hell is a ten-bolt top loader? And what in the hell is a shaker hood scoop?" Regardless, these words intrigued Kit to no end. If someone could have only looked at the scenes being painted on the screen of his mind, they would be in the audience with a tub of popcorn, yelling, "Go and get that sucker! Buy the sucker right now!"

When Kit got off the phone, he sat with our mother and presented a plan. He had to buy a car of his own, and he asked what she could do to help him. Although he had never seen such a creature as a Ford GT Torino, he knew then and there that he just had to have one. In a positive gesture and as pragmatic as our mother was, she assured him that she would be inclined to help him secure an auto loan at the bank if that was what he really wanted.

The next day, Kit drove to Spokane to look at the yellow beast on four wheels and realized that it screamed out his name. With a handshake, Kit promised to return the next day with the money.

Back in Kellogg, my mother believed enough in Kit to go up to First Security Bank and take out a $1,500 loan with Kit as the co-signer. When Kit returned to town, there was just enough time to complete the loan application and have the bank manager approve it before five o'clock. After Mom and Kit signed the loan documents, the bank teller counted out the money and sealed it in a bank envelope. She handed it to my mother with a smile and thanked her for her business. The next day, the car would be Kit's, and he could not wait. That night, he called Debbie and asked if she worked the next day. If so, he would be by the following evening with a surprise for her.

The following day, Kit and Mom drove to Spokane and met the seller. After a final test drive, Kit counted out the money on the hood of the Torino. In return, the seller signed off on the title and handed it to Kit along with the keys. After a final handshake, Kit started his chariot and gently drove her to the highway. He pet her mane (the dashboard) as he got onto the highway. Our mother faithfully followed not far behind in the family station wagon.

After arriving back in town, Kit picked up Kevin, and for the rest of the afternoon, they drove around town and showed the car off to all their friends. Even though Kit thoroughly enjoyed how they raved over his car, the grand finale still remained hours away. The minutes seemed like hours, and the hours seemed like days until Debbie started her shift at the local A & W. Although Kit told Debbie that he had a surprise to show her, he also promised to take her home from work that night. Kit kept his cool in the meantime but still paced up and down the driveway, constantly checking out his new car. Did the new air fresheners do their job? Did the interior have a pleasant smell? Were there any smudges on the windows? Were the floorboards vacuumed?

An hour into Debbie's shift, Kit could not wait any longer. He warmed up the Torino and slowly drove down to the very end of Mission Avenue, and pulled into the parking lot of A & W. He expressly pulled up to one of the ordering stations and ordered another Papa Burger, fries, and root beer. And just like he had done the night that he asked her for a date, he specifically requested that Debbie to bring it out. A few minutes later, Debbie strolled out with the food and walked up to the side of the Torino, not knowing that it was Kits.

He rolled down the window. "What do ya think?"

Debbie shrieked and almost spilled the entire tray of food. She calmed down momentarily and set his tray down upon the window. She held one hand to her mouth and almost started to cry. "Is this the surprise?"

"Yes, it is!"

She scanned the car from one end to the next and let the lump in her throat be, and the water in her eyes filled.

"What do you think?"

"Kit Major, what in the hell did you do?"— "I love it! She is beautiful! I wish I could get off work right now. How am I going to go back to work now?"

"Don't worry, I will be back when you get off."

Later, Kit kept his promise. And thus, the love affair continued for quite a few months. One could possibly say that there was a love triangle between Kit, Debbie, and the Torino, but in that era, threesomes weren't talked about much.

At the end of May, Kit graduated high school, and an entirely new world opened for him. He gave up his drumming position with the local band and got a job at the Bunker Hill Mine tending to the concentrator at the mill, but he didn't stop there. A few months earlier, he had enrolled in a diesel mechanic's program at the local college that would begin later in the fall. Thirdly, he had enlisted in the Army Reserve, with basic training starting that summer. His ambitions knew no end. Even with all that was poised to take place, he still devoted all the time that he could to his and Debbie's love affair.

In the interim, as the weather grew nicer, Kit began riding his Kawasaki 500 road bike to work. He had not only had one hotrod (his Torino), but he had two. While his Torino was one of the fastest cars in the valley, the motorcycle he bought, a Kawasaki 500 Mach-Three, broke the record for any production motorcycle with its fastest quarter-mile run.

One afternoon, I went for a hike up to the small cliff where Phil had gone that night with Mike Groves. I reached the top, turned around, and looked out over the town of Kellogg. I thought about life. Down on the streets below, I noticed that Kit had already gotten off work from the mine. He drove down the street, pulled up to our house, and parked his Kawasaki motorcycle on the sidewalk. He went through the back door to drop off his lunch box. A minute later, he came back outside and casually climbed into his Torino, which had laid dormant all day in the driveway. I could not see much from so far away, but I knew his routine well.

He climbed inside his car and inserted the key in the ignition. He tapped the 8-track tape cartridge into the player to ensure it was fully engaged and started to play. He then twisted the key in the ignition. The starter whined as the engine turned over. With a few sputters, the huge V-8 fired and roared to life with a high, loud, window-vibrating idle. The oil pressure rose, and the carburetor jets leveled out the mixture, allowing the engine to regain its composure. Within seconds, the high revs on the engine lowered to a speed just above the engine dying. The humongous machine sucked air through the hood scoop and loped as the high-lift camshaft systematically opened and closed the valves. The hood remained steady, but the shaker air scoop shook back and forth as the engine breathed in its life.

Kit treated his car with as much honor and respect as he would a beautiful woman he serenaded under the moonlight (just like he did with Debbie). Kit pampered the Cobra Jet engine and allowed her to warm up just as he did when he thoroughly stretched before a workout. Once she was purring happily, he pushed the clutch peddle down with his left foot and placed his right hand on the T-handle four-speed Hurst shifter. But before he plunked the car into reverse, he reached up and tilted the rear-view mirror down. Kit looked into his own eyes since the eyes are the window into the soul. He saw his true self. He was good enough. He was worthy enough to become the man he knew he could be. With this new overpowering self-assurance, he slowly released the clutch and methodically backed out of the driveway onto Mission Avenue.

Kit idled down to the stop sign, turned left, and headed for the intersection of Cameron Avenue and Hill Street (where the Chevron service station sat). This particular service station grew to be the meeting place in Kellogg for the street-racing pack of hotrodders. Kit's car was only one of the many big-bore engine showpieces. The rival cars included Tim Shibbler's 1970 Chevy Chevelle SS with a fully punched-out 454 engine and an extremely low-geared 411 posi-track rear end. Next was Randy Smith's Nova 402 Police Interceptor, then Alan Jackson's Chrysler 440 six-pack Super Bird, and lastly, Chet's 426 Hemi Road Runner Challenger. This was the remnant of the late '60s/early '70s big block muscle car era. No one dared show up with a small block Mustang with a measly 289 or a wimpy Camaro with a baby 302 in the middle of this crowd.

Kit pulled into the Chevron station and parked his Torino next to Tim's SS Chevelle. Tim had worked there as an attendant for several years and, after earning the owner's trust, basically had free rein of the place. His Chevelle parked outside became a sign that he was on duty. With the station under Tim's control, all his friends pulled their cars into the bays and lifted them up on the hydraulic racks for servicing. Quite often, after Kit visited Tim at the station, he would get ready to leave, but when the other boys saw this, they jeered him.

"Hey Kit, are you going to burn some rubber?"

"Oh, I don't know."

"Come on, man, do it!" They insisted.

Kit had 'burned some rubber' before, coming out of the Chevron station, and after a few times he learned a couple of things that helped him perfect his maneuver. Since Kit's Torino did not have a complete posi-track rear end, he could not take off from a standstill and have both tires spin. In time, he discovered a particular technique. Since his Torino's differential was 'limited slip', Kit learned that if he mashed down on the throttle and shot out of the station's parking lot in a sharp left turn, the differential would apply power to both tires and allow both to spin on the asphalt and 'burn rubber'. Still, it had to be in a sharp left turn.

While the physics of it all made perfect sense in Kit's mind, his friends learned what emotional buttons they needed to push on him to make him do it. Their taunting always started the same way: "Ah, come on, Kit, do a demonstration for us!" They pleaded. That's what they nicknamed his little display. They called it a 'demonstration', a type of code word. And so, with their taunting, Kit would start up his car, look both ways up and down the street, and if it were clear, he'd let her rip!

One night, Kit drove through the nearby town of Pinehurst. He had been driving a little too fast, and a local cop noticed it. The overzealous officer turned on his flashing lights and attempted to pull Kit over just before the highway on-ramp. Through his rear-view mirror, Kit looked back and decided, "No, officer, I am not going to let you pull me over today."

The moment Kit turned onto the on-ramp, he stomped down on the throttle and let the engine roar until the tachometer reached the redline. He then shifted into second gear and mashed down the throttle again. Once on the highway, Kit went through third gear, and then onto fourth. Within a mile on the straightaway, Kit looked down at his speedometer. The red needle had gone past the 120-mph mark, continued even further, then beyond the last line. Then, the needle disappeared. Kit surpassed 130 mph and was nearing 140 mph. The headlights of the police car grew dimmer and dimmer in the rear-view mirror as Kit skyrocketed down the highway.

Finally, as the town of Kellogg approached, Kit slowed the car down and took the first exit. He drove across the overpass then quickly found his way to the end of Mission Avenue (just across from the A&W restaurant where he had met Debbie). At that point, he turned the car lights off and idled slowly down the five blocks to our house, hoping that he had truly lost the pursuing police car. After pulling the car into the driveway, he ran into the garage to find a tarp. Once he covered his car with the large green cloth, successfully disguising his Torino, he crawled into the lower bunk across the room from me—safe at last. However, this wasn't the first time that he had come in this late. He had been up to more mischief than any of us could imagine.

After the Fourth of July holiday had come and gone, Kit's August induction day into the military approached rapidly. Two days before he was scheduled to leave, he decided to create a lasting memory for himself in his beloved Torino. He idled his car a few blocks across town, past Cameron Avenue intersection, and turned up the westbound interstate highway on-ramp. With the car still in first gear, he pushed down on the throttle, mashing it to the floor. The engine roared, and the G-force threw him back in his seat. The wide racing tires gripped the pavement and the car shot forward.

The tachometer climbed and climbed, and so did the speedometer—30 mph, 40 mph, 50 mph, then 60 mph. The needle on the tach hit the red line at 5000 rpm and kept climbing. 5500 rpm, then 6000 rpm. He hit 70mph when he reached the top of the on-ramp. He eased back and threw the transmission into second gear. Stepping on the accelerator once again, the car sprang forward, 80mph, now 90. He jammed the transmission into third gear and stomped on the accelerator again, 100, 110 mph. He then shifted into fourth—120 mph. Suddenly, the red oil pressure warning light flashed on. Kit knew what that meant and instantly ripped his hand away from the shift lever. He frantically reached up to the steering column and turned off the ignition. The engine sputtered and died. All he could hear after that was the sound of the wind rushing past his partially rolled-down window. The speedometer needle began to drop 110 mph, 100 mph, and 90 mph. Fortunately, he had enough mass and speed to take the Torino the rest of the way down the highway and up to the top of the Smelterville exit.

As he coasted to the end of the off-ramp, he pulled off to the side of the road as far as he could and stopped her. The car wasn't going anywhere until she received some proper care. "What in the world could have gone wrong?" Kit thought. "Why did the oil pressure warning light come on?'

Kit walked across the highway overpass and onto the main street of Smelterville. From a payphone outside the little grocery store known as the Wayside Market, he called anyone he could, trying to get a ride and a tow back into Kellogg. Our cousin Jim came to his rescue, and the two of them towed the Torino back to Jim's place using only a long piece of thick rope (which was not the safest way to tow a car, but it worked). Jim graciously let Kit store the car in his garage because he knew that Kit would leave for his army training any day and wouldn't have time to tear the engine apart to find out what had failed.

The next day, Kit pulled up to Debbie's house in our family station wagon. She looked out her living room window and saw Kit getting out of the family car. Bewildered, she ran out the door and down the front steps.

"Where's your car?"

"Oh, she's dead."

"What? Did you get into a wreck or something?"

"No, just something with the oil pump. Won't know until I tear the engine apart."

"Well, at least you weren't in a wreck or anything like that. But that's still too bad."—"Are we still going to the lake?"

"Of course, we are. We just have to ride in the family mobile, that's all," Kit said as he gestured back at the car with his thumb as if he were hitchhiking. Debbie smiled and let out a giddy little laugh. It was all okay with her. She just wanted to be with her man.

The day was clear, the sky was blue, and the air was hot. On the trip to the lake, Debbie rode in the front seat while the rest of the family rode in the back, with Stephen, and Allyson riding in the far back.

At the lake, everyone swam and snacked on chicken, potato salad, and watermelon. During most of the day, my mother stayed in the shade reading another one of her favorite genres of books while Kit stayed close to his girl. However, an ominous cloud of doom seemed to hang over Kit. He couldn't shake the feeling.

Later that night, Kit dropped all of us off at home and drove Debbie to her house. During those few last precious moments together under the stars, she began to cry. She knew that it would all be over soon when Kit left for basic training. That night, they tried to find a way to prolong the inevitable, but it was all to no avail. When their moment ended, they unwrapped their arms from around each other and said goodbye. Kit turned toward the car but could barely walk. He felt as if he was in quicksand. Every footstep that he took seemed to be like moving a thousand pounds. When he finally drove away into the darkness, neither knew that this night would be the last time they would ever be together, ever.

The following day, Kit sat in seat 19A on the flight from Spokane to Denver. As the plane lifted off the runway, he felt as if he had left part of his soul behind.

Basic training at Fort Leonard Wood, Missouri, progressed perfectly for Kit. He was the most physically fit and the most intelligent soldier in his training company. Midway through the program, he so greatly surpassed the fitness scores of every other trainee that his drill instructor, Sergeant Briggs, began to brag about how Private Chris Major was the top jock out of all the training companies. Soon, all the drill sergeants in the battalion had heard of Kit and grew tired of it.

One night at the NCO club, Sergeant Briggs sat at a table of fellow drill instructors, some who had served in combat in Vietnam at the same time that he had. After having survived combat, Briggs saw training raw recruits as easy duty—a walk in the park. He loved the military. He loved tearing men down and building them up. Sergeant Briggs loved that in his very platoon, he had the biggest stud of all in this current cycle of basic trainees. He had a muscle-headed genius named Major in his unit and would pit him against any man in the battalion. Briggs stirred the pot with his fellow drill instructors on purpose.

"Listen, all you lame assess. I've got a rock star on my hands. This guy is the biggest jock I've had yet come to through any cycle. I got a man who max's everything and can fry any of your guys' asses, hands down."

"Who gives a fuck, Briggs? I had a guy max the PT test last week. You ain't got shit on anyone in my company."

Briggs held a shot glass brimming with Jack Daniels whiskey. Just before he placed it against his lips, he had to say, "I'll pit my man Major against anybody in the battalion. Major can beat 'em all!" With that being said, Briggs downed the shot of whiskey and slammed the thick-bottomed glass down on that tabletop. He had thrown down the gauntlet. The others began to talk among themselves as Briggs looked around the club to see if any female non-commissioned officers had come in while they were talking their bravado.

A few days later, just after a ten-mile forced road march, while all the trainees were checking their M-16 rifles into the arms room, a runner came down from the company commander's office with a message addressed expressly to Sergeant Briggs. The instructions were for him to report to the captain as soon as possible. Briggs immediately turned everything over to his junior drill instructor as he dawned his smokey-the-bear drill sergeant hat and headed down to the commander's office.

When Sergeant Briggs entered the building, the orderly jumped up from his desk and instructed Briggs to go in and see the waiting company commander. Briggs entered and then stepped in front of the CO's desk. He stood snapped to attention and smartly saluted the captain.

"Sergeant Briggs reporting as ordered, Sir!"

The commander returned the salute, "At ease Sergeant."

"Sergeant Briggs, apparently, you have been drawing some attention, bragging about your star trainee. I have just gotten notification from the battalion Sergeant Major that there will be a little competition. The four top fitness jocks from each company will compete and determine, once and for all, who the true fitness freak is."

Briggs could not hold back the grin that spread across his face. It seemed much wider than the Grinch's.

"Here's what you do. You get with this Private Major, and the two of you get your crap together. We've got a shit burger to feed our friends at the other companies."

The following Sunday, after the church-going trainees were let out of the chapel services, the company's first sergeant assembled all five platoons and began marching them off to the parade grounds. Briggs' company commander stood off in the distance with a young lieutenant and watched his entire training company make their way across the post. He couldn't wait to hear the outcome of the competition.

When the company reached the grounds, hundreds of soldiers were already grouped together as spectators. Everyone was set at ease and took a seat in the grass. A head drill sergeant, clad in his boots, fatigue pants, and a plain white tee shirt, called out four names. Kit and three other men responded to the queue and ran up to the sergeant, where they received a quick briefing on how the competition would be conducted. He then ordered them to warm up.

Plopping himself onto the ground, Kit sat in the grass with his other three rivals. The four of them had never met before but were now stretching and warming up in front of each other. A group of drill sergeants stood around them with clipboards and stopwatches on lanyards that draped around their necks.

Kit looked over at his three rivals and wondered who was best. Abernathy was truly muscular. He had a thick neck, broad shoulders, bulging biceps, and frog-like legs. Although Kit had delved seriously into bodybuilding over the past several years, he noticed this guy was much larger and more developed. He was what Kit aspired to be.

The other guy, Kienholz, was much smaller than the four of them, a wiry-built individual with the muscles around his body showing like tight bands of steel. He looked at Kit with a distant look as if he wondered why he was even there. He wasn't out to prove anything to anybody. Then there was Williams, generic looking, like a manikin, no expression, nothing outstanding. The quad, by fate, was a perfect contrast of contenders: an overconfident meathead to his left, a greyhound-built gentleman to his right—a gentleman without an ounce of fat on his frame and not an ounce of confidence in his soul, and lastly, a robotic figure that sat in front of them.

All of Kit's focus was on this event. In that instant, in Kit's mind, Kellogg, Idaho did not exist, his GT Tornio did not exist, and even his girlfriend Debbie did not exist.

One of the drill sergeants blew his whistle, and the four contestants jumped to their feet. The first event was the push-up competition. Whoever could do the most push-ups in a two-minute window would win. Each of them got down into position. The leading drill sergeant counted down until he started the stopwatch, "Three, two, one, go!"

The four of them pumped away on the ground. Each one had an individual drill sergeant counting out their push-ups. After they finished, the sit-up event took place. The drill sergeants counted out once again. Cheers broke out among the massive group of soldiers each time an event ended. As the last event kicked off, the two-mile run, the cheering became uncontrollable. Twelve minutes later, Kit ran across the finish line at full speed, with the other three men far behind him. Sergeant Briggs hooped and hollered as he looked down at his stopwatch. He nearly shoved it into the faces of the other drill instructors. They didn't look so happy having their best men getting their asses handed to them.

Kit staggered up to his company and collapsed on the ground before them. He had won all three events. Briggs had held a massive smile on his face the entire time because he knew Kit would win—he willed Kit to win.

Ultimately, the battalion held an official awards ceremony and bestowed a small plaque upon Kit as the battalion physical fitness champ. To this day, Kit still has the old, faded photograph of him holding that plaque framed and sitting proudly on his fireplace mantle.

Christopher A. Major, High Score B.P.F.T.

Kit

That night, back at the barracks, Kit proudly displayed his plaque upon the footlocker at the foot of his bunk. Just before lights out, he peeled back the coarse, wool, green, army-issued blanket and climbed onto the top bunk. His buddy Spencer did the same by peeling back his blanket and climbing onto the lower bunk.

"Hey, Spencer, tell me more about this Pontiac of yours."

Spencer was lying back in his bed and folding his hands behind his head as he stared up at the bed springs on the underside of Kit's mattress.

"Well, it's just a '69 GTO, four hundred, four-speed."

"Just a 400? Come on, that's hefty."— "Did you do any mods to the engine?"

Spencer had to think for a minute. He wasn't the swiftest guy in the platoon, but at least it was a simple question.

"Ah, yeh, my dad and I put a high lift cam in it and changed the pistons out; eleven to one now." With that statement, the smile on Spencer's face grew wide. He missed his car.

"Damn, what's she sound like?"

Spencer chuckled before answering. "Well, people sure look over at me when I am idling at the stop sign. Boy, does she lope!"

Kit started to wonder about other things regarding Spencer's car.

"Spencer, you pick up a lot of chicks in that thing, don't you?" That question threw Spencer off track for a minute. Kit looked over into the middle of the barracks and noticed a fellow soldier wearing nothing but a pair of socks and olive-drab green underwear as he used a floor buffer on the last patch of tile.

"Come on, Spencer, tell me about the chicks you pick up in that thing. You do pick 'em up, don't you?"

"Ah, not really."

"What do you mean not really?"

Spencer started to feel a little uncomfortable with Kit's probing. "Well, chicks sure look at my car, but I never really talk to them."

"Don't you have a girlfriend back home?" This question was only going to lead to more uncomfortable ones for Spencer.

"Well, kind of. There is this girl that I have taken to the movies a couple of times. But I don't know if she really likes me or not."

Something suddenly dawned on Kit. He smiled with a flash of insight, something he had just realized about Spencer. "Spencer, have you ever been laid?"

Being caught off guard, Spencer began to trip over his own words. "Ah, yeh, sure. I have. Well, just once. Ah, well, almost just once. We came really close."

"Really close!"— "What do you mean by really close?"

Spencer now began to feel really uncomfortable. He then realized that Kit wasn't the only one chiming in on their conversation but continued anyway. "Well, we were at the drive-in, and somehow we just started kissing, and I mean kissing a lot until she finally stopped and gave me this really funny look."

"And then?"

"I wasn't sure what to do, so I asked her if she wanted to do it. And she didn't say anything."

Kit suddenly leaped off the top bunk and landed with both bare feet on the floor, directly in front of Spencer. He had to get to the bottom of this crazy story. "STOP. STOP. STOP! Hold it right there. Now back up for a second."

With his head shaking from side to side and almost speechless, Kit finally continued, "You ASKED her if she wanted to do it?"

"Yeh."

Kit erupted, "You freaking moron! You never, ever, ever ASK a girl if she wants to do it."

"What do you do then?"

The other ears listening to the ensuing conversation could no longer take the idiocracy. Sitting in the next bunk over, Private Darnell Jones cut in on the conversation. "Listen here, Spencer, my man. If you's ever find yourself in that situation again, you's keep doing what you were doing. The ladies like a man with a slow hand. You keep kissin' on her and then reach up and fondle those breasts. If she doesn't stop you . . . then dammit boy, you is gonna get laid!!"

At this point, Spencer was indeed listening intently. He had never heard this kind of stuff before and now had to ask, "What do I do if I get her to that point."

"You crazy fool! Once she starts puffin' like a steam engine, then you's tear her panties off, and you go for it." Darnell laughed fiendishly like some kid who had just pulled a prank on his first-grade teacher.

With over seven trillion brain cells, the best response Spencer could come up with was, "Really??"

Just then, the barracks door burst open, and Sergeant Briggs' assistant drill instructor stepped inside and yelled, "Okay, everyone, lights out. We've got a big day ahead of us tomorrow. Get your rest—and Major . . . good job today. You made us all proud."

With that being said, the light switch flicked off, and 45 tired soldiers lay in the dark on their bunks.

From the beginning of basic training, several times a week, usually in the late afternoon, Sergeant Briggs would hold mail call and hand out all the latest letters that had arrived for the trainees. Debbie routinely wrote Kit several pages at a time with steamy sentiments about how she felt for him while he was so far away. She penned her feelings about how intensely she missed him, how lonely she felt without him, and other things like what she did to keep herself busy in his absence. Usually, as a last thought and as a bonus, she would spray a puff of her best perfume on the letter just before sealing it.

In the last letter Kit received, she mentioned that high school had just started again and that the school was holding its first dance. She explained that to keep herself busy, she was going to it with a guy named Mike, who is just a friend. That seemed a little odd to Kit, all that was from the last letter. Now, this time around at mail call, Sergeant Briggs handed out the letters, and then one came across one for Kit. As usual, just before Seargent Briggs handed it to Kit, he held the envelope up to his nose and sniffed it. The platoon all laughed as always. However, there was no perfume on this letter.

When Kit grasped the envelope between his fingers, he felt something deathly wrong. A cold chill ran down his spine like someone had just walked over his grave. This letter was extremely thin—an ominous sign of doom. Kit froze for at least a minute and then decided not to open it. After eons had passed and glaciers had melted around the globe, he walked over to his footlocker and buried the letter at the very bottom. It stayed there for several days. Eventually, he summoned the courage to open the envelope and unfold the solitary sheet of stationery. His hands began to tremble at the first glimpse of her handwriting.

"Dear Chris, I'm sorry, but I have found someone else. Debbie." That was all she wrote.

Kit folded up the letter and thrust it back into the envelope. He could barely make it through the rest of the day without breaking down. His heart had been ripped out and stomped on by a thing that we call life. Sadly, none of us would ever make it through unscathed. Little did I know that my time would eventually come, just the same.

Chapter 6

The North Country

For several years after our adventurous summer at Rose Lake, my father continued to chase his dreams but only experienced one business failure after another. Since his first mining project in Republic, Washington, he had moved on to the Canyon Silver Mine, up Burke Canyon, in North Idaho. Just when he thought he had breathed life back into that operation, it too fell apart. Ultimately, he stumbled across yet another small mine called Prosperity, just outside of Superior, Montana. Soon after producing their first high-grade ore, they sent several truckloads to the Bunker Hill Mining complex for processing. Unfortunately, something did not add up. My father grew convinced that he was shortchanged and became furious. He vowed that it would never happen again. To assure this, he convinced his investors to sink nearly $450,000 into a hastily constructed mill next to the mine. However, nothing differed with the business outcome. No matter how hard he tried, complications always arose. Time and time again, investors promised so much but only delivered half. Conversely, they expected astronomical results out of my father—totally unrealistic demands. At other times, useless workers had to be fired, leaving the operation short-handed. Other factors were simply out of my father's hands. For instance, at the worst possible time, the price of gold and silver dropped sharply, killing any chance of the operation being profitable. Adding these factors together, Prosperity, just like the others, disintegrated under its own weight.

The never-ending struggle of jumping from one project to another began to take its toll on my brothers. Kit couldn't take it any longer and quit first. However, Peter hung in there longer. He had faithfully stayed close to our father's side from the beginning to the end on each of the disasters. But this time around, when the mill at Prosperity failed, the flame inside Peter flickered and then died. He decided to call it quits as well; enough was enough. After that dismal failure, summer finally ended, and when I stepped into that seventh-grade classroom, my father stepped out of our lives. He disappeared once again, supposedly chasing another dream. However, this time around, there was an intense air of mystery surrounding his absence. We could sense that he was up to something big.

One Saturday morning, not long after my father's departure, Peter sat at the kitchen table, eating a bowl of cereal while he read the newspaper. A car pulled up in front of the house and my brother Kit climbed out. He retrieved a large green army duffle bag from the back seat. Basic training had finally ended, and Kit was now back home. He burst through the back door and smiled when Peter looked up at him.

"Damn, you are finally back. How was the army?" Peter asked.

"Well, it was pretty freaking interesting. Glad it's over though."

"Crap. You look great. Looks like they made a man out of you!" Peter laughed.

"How is everyone doing?"

"Crap. Things have been pretty rough around here lately. Everything caved in at Prosperity. The investors pulled the plug because we weren't producing."

"Where's Dad?"

"I don't know. He just took off a couple of weeks ago. Mom's freaking out."

"What have you been doing?"

Peter grinned. "I got on at the mine, making nearly a hundred and fifty a day, but half that is going to Mom."

"A hundred and fifty a day?"

Peter nodded but then held his index finger up to his lips. He began to whisper. "Shhhhh, don't ever tell anybody this. Mom had to ask Uncle Bill for a thousand bucks to help with the bills."

Kit sat down in the chair, looked up at the ceiling, and slowly shook his head. How could things have gotten this bad? When he looked back at Peter, he had to ask, "How is everyone else doing?"

"Damn, Phil is goofing off and will probably get the worst grade point average in the family. At his rate, he will never make it into college."

"How about everyone else?"

"Shit, Tony is causing more trouble than ever. He is getting hacked by his teachers every week at school, and Stephen is doing the same thing. It's like they are in a competition to see who can be the stupidest."

Kit now looked down at the floor and covered his eyes with his hands. He was exhausted from his flight. He felt so discouraged hearing about the situation with the family.

"What are your plans?" Peter asked.

"I'm going to try to get on at Bunker as soon as I can."

"Good idea. Just get your ass to work, and we will figure it all out."

Tim, Stephen, and I had been watching cartoons in the front room the entire time that Kit and Peter had been talking. We didn't even realize that Kit had come home.

Weeks passed and our family clawed its way forward. Peter continued to work at the mine, and Kit managed to secure a job at the Bunker Hill ore-processing plant (with the help of our Uncle Jim who pulled some strings for him since he had flunked the physical to become a miner). Meanwhile, Tim stayed close to Peter's side, Stephen ventured out on his own as usual, and my three sisters clung ever closer to our mother, fearful of their uncertain future. Me? Well, I did what I did, with everything virtually being done on pure impulse (nothing new for me).

The first month of Junior high school overwhelmed me, and I was correct in my assumption—there were more bouncing tits on the eighth and ninth-grade girls than I could ever imagine. They just looked so nice. I just wanted to reach out and grab them. In addition to the maturing women catching me off guard, so did the bullies. My mouth got me into a lot of trouble. But what's a mouth? I believed wholeheartedly in the right to free speech, and whoever didn't like my opinions could go fuck themselves.

The fall months passed by so quickly, and even with all the noise we made around the house, there was an eerie silence in our home with our father long gone. With Autumn eclipsing, Halloween came quickly, then Thanksgiving, and then, before we all knew it, Christmas fell upon us. We were released from school for Christmas break, but where was Dad?

One evening, Tim sat at the kitchen playing with his Legos, and out of the mouths of babes, he asked our mother, "When is Dad coming home?"

"Your dad is really busy right now with his business, but he will be home soon."

"What's he doing?"

"Well, he has some mining stuff going on and has a lot of partners to deal with."

"Do you think he'll be here for Christmas?"

"I am pretty sure he will be."

Peter stood at the counter, preparing his lunch for the next day of work, but he just had to say something. "Mom, you know how Dad is."

My mother looked over at Peter and gave him a piercing glare. She would not have any dissenting opinions because she still kept the faith in our estranged father. Even without Dad around to help, my mother diligently spent weeks preparing the family for the most beautiful celebration ever. Presents spilled out from under the Christmas tree and ended up halfway across the living room floor.

On Christmas Eve, our house was abuzz with holiday music, treat-making in the kitchen, and festive programs blaring on the TV. After dinner and snacks, only a few hours remained before we would go up to the Catholic church for midnight mass. The events on the eve of the year's most significant holiday were cast in stone for our family. The routine was firmly in place—or so it seemed, until our father burst through the front door. Large snowflakes clung to his hair, and he carried a large, bulging, gunny sack over his shoulder. I had never seen a bigger and brighter smile on his face, ever in my entire life. His grand entrance paralleled the ending of the 1970's Walton's Homecoming movie almost exactly. It was something that I could never have made up, but somehow Dad arrived just like that. Honestly, I think he had planned his timing that way on purpose.

My father dropped the gunny sack next to the couch, strolled into the kitchen, and kissed my mother. After a kiss and a slight hug, my father wasted no time securing a glass from the cupboard and pouring himself a measure of wine. We all got out of his way, let him come into the living room, and settle into his favorite chair. He glowed with happiness and contentment, but this time around, we didn't know why. Something was different about him.

"What's this you're watching?" he asked.

"It's The Grinch," Stephen blurted out.

"The Grinch? Is this a Christmas show?"

"Yeah, he steals their Christmas."

My father sat back, lit a cigarette, and quietly watched the last part of the show. When it ended, he got up from his chair, walked over to the TV, and shut it off.

"I want to tell all of you about my trip up north," he began.

"Up north where?" Tim innocently asked.

"Way up in Canada, in the North County."

Tim looked puzzled.

My father looked over at me and politely asked, "Tony, can you bring me my sack?"

"Sure." I respectfully replied. (One thing most people would never understand about our family is that no matter how much our father let us down, disappointed us, or failed to be there for us, we never, ever, ever, EVER disrespected the man. He was our father.)

I went over to the couch, grabbed his big sack, and dragged it over to him. He began to chuckle as he opened it and reached inside. He fumbled around for a moment and finally pulled something out. It was a red kerosene lantern.

"Tony, this is for you. Next time you go camping, you can have some light."

I reached out and took it into my hands. I loved the gesture, but he wasn't finished yet. He stuck his hand back inside the sack and fumbled around again. He then pulled out a small paperback book.

"This is also for you."

I grabbed the book from him and looked at the front cover. The title read, 'How to Survive in the Wilds'. He knew I loved the outdoors.

After he finished with me, he called each of my brothers and sisters over to his side and pulled out gifts that perfectly suited each of them. Soon, the bag was empty, and our Christmas was full. It became a pleasure to be around my father for the first time in many years, and surprisingly, there were no spankings. Although the presents were nice, they really didn't matter—family did.

For the next several days, my father sat in his favorite chair, sipping on his cheap Italian wine, smoking his toxic cigarettes, and strangely talking about this 'North Country,' a place supposedly so far away but filled with many wonders.

"You guys are going to see this place. We are going to own an entire bay."

"How the hell are we going to own an entire bay," I thought, because I knew how crowded the nearby Coeur d'Alene Lake was. He spoke of this place as if it were the closest thing to paradise. At the end of each of his stories, after emphasizing the mystique, he added, "Yes, Sir, we are all moving up there come summer."

At one point, my mother walked into the living room and heard him say that. She looked at him out of the corner of her eye and scowled at him. She wanted no part of it. That was never going to take place because she remembered the first months of their marriage when he had her living in a tent, and she was not going to allow it to happen again, especially with her large family. Strangely, shortly after New Year's Day, my father walked out the front door and never came home again for the rest of his life.

For the next several months, we wondered if he was serious about moving the entire family up to his place of dreams. All his claims seemed too incredible, and maybe his silence proved that because we hadn't heard a word from him for the longest time. Was it just all talk as usual?

One day, five months later, my mother received a long-distance call from my father. It wasn't a typical call; he was calling on a radio phone from somewhere in the wilderness. During their conversation over the airwaves, he gave her specific instructions to get my brother Phil and me out of school early on Memorial Day weekend.

"Kay, I need you to get Phil and Tony up here as soon as you can."

"What do you mean? Where are you?"

"Remember when I first met you and told you about the place up the coast that I logged during the summers?"

"Yeah, I remember. You promised to bring me there, but you never did."

"Well, that's where I am. All the investors are onboard with the operation, but I need Phil and Tony up here as soon as you can get them out of school."

"Jerry, how am I supposed to get them there?"

"Just get them over to Seattle. I will have a plane ready to fly them here."

After that, he gave my mother all the details. With her being the compliant and faithful wife, she hung up the phone and did exactly what he had asked. She went to work that week and got Phil and me out of school early, that very next Friday. As soon as we got home, we packed up the family car. We said goodbye to the rest of the family. From there, Phil and I, along with my mother and baby sister Allyson, drove off into the sunset onward to Seattle.

Five hours later, we entered the city and found our hotel. Our adventure was just beginning. I couldn't believe this was all happening. It was all surreal. I soon fell fast asleep but woke up in the middle of the night, wondering where I was. I could hear the rushing traffic with the cars racing up and down Highway Ninety-nine and the passenger jets screaming overhead as they came in for the final approach at Sea-Tac Airport.

In the morning, we fought the traffic and met our Uncle Bill for breakfast at a place called The Pancake Chef. When he learned of my father's plans, he yelled in a high-pitched voice, overly exaggerating his excitement, "You guys are going to be million-dollar babies! Your dad will be raking in millions before you know it!"

My mother wasn't as optimistic this time after witnessing so many of my father's business failures, so she changed the subject, "Remember Bill, Allyson and I will be landing back here on Monday afternoon."

"I know, Sis and I will be right there to pick you up. Then you tell me all about it."

I was too excited to even eat. My pancakes and sausage went to waste. I only wanted to get on that plane and see this exotic place that my father touted so greatly. We drove north to Lake Union, met up with the personnel at the air service. From there we loaded everything that we could possibly load onto a tiny float plane—so tiny that we had to leave much of our baggage in the car. But it didn't matter, this small plane would take us to our long-lost father.

We took off from the water with the engine and propeller howling at a deafening roar. As we turned north, the Space Needle became visible out of the lefthand windows. After leveling off, we flew for nearly four hours in rough, cloudy, and rainy weather, barfing our guts out from airsickness

111

most of the way. An eternity seemed to pass until we landed in a place that time forgot: an old, abandoned logging camp, a virtual ghost town in the middle of nowhere, nestled in small cove known as Jennis Bay. As we taxied up to the shore, blue smoke drifted lazily out of the chimney of an old cabin on the point. My father anxiously walked down the muddy trail to the beach to greet us. Even from inside the plane, as I looked out, I could him smiling as intensely as he had when he had walked through our door on Christmas Eve. None of us knew it, but once we stepped off that plane and onto dry land, our family would be changed forever.

After giving my mother a quick kiss, my father began barking out orders, "Phil, you and Tony start taking things up to the cabin."

When Phil and I walked through the back door of the cabin, we felt the heat of the wood stove, and our senses were touched by the scent of the piercing aromatic cedar firewood, the musty smell of the cabin, and the aroma of freshly steamed clams—something that we will never forget.

My father invited the pilot and his girlfriend up to the cabin to share a pot of freshly steamed clams with them. Meanwhile, Phil and I wandered around outside, examining our new surroundings. Everything seemed so green and alive. Behind the cabin, the cedar and fir trees jetted up to the sky, and the alder trees, with their leaves of a lighter shade of green, looked like huge sprouting bean stocks. Thimbleberry bushes with huge fuzzy leaves lined the entire perimeter. A dark black raven flew overhead and cawed, followed by two tiny swallows that seemed to be chasing him. Down on the water, a white speedboat bobbed with its bow and stern lines tied to a log boom that stretched from the shore to a tiny island covered with massive, old-growth cedar trees. The evening westerly wind blew into the bay and brought the sweet smell of the ocean air. Dad was right; we owned the bay.

After the pilot and his girlfriend took off in the plane, my father and mother began to talk.

"I needed Philip and Tony here to help clear out the road to the lake."

"Will they be paid?"

"Of course they will, both of them."

"What exactly is your plan?"

"We have to clear the road to the lake before the equipment arrives. Once we have that done, they'll send the equipment up by barge from Seattle."

"How long will all this take?"

"Oh, probably a few weeks, but once we get that done, you bring the rest of the family up."

My mother's next concern was whether Phil and I would be alright alone in the bush, but she already knew the answer. My father was a rugged outdoorsman, the toughest man I have ever known and could handle anything. Phil and I trusted our father as well. He was hard as nails. That night, after my mother, father, and Allyson retreated to their room, Phil and I got on our bunks, and I began to write a diary by candlelight. Once again, after I fell asleep, I woke up in the middle of the night and wondered where I was.

The next day, my father took us out in the speedboat, and we spent several hours touring the long, narrow inlet. We even went all the way up to the very end where it formed a two-mile-long lagoon. At one point, my father pulled us up to the beach and tied the boat to a huge rock. He wanted to show us something. Just a few feet into the brush, a shiny patch of fluorescent paint highlighted something on a tree. It was my father's name carved deeply into the bark. He had obviously been there in the distant past. Mysteriously, he never talked about the history, especially about Jennis Bay. He never, ever discussed what involvement he had in the operation there at all. The details were something that he would take to his grave.

On the morning of the third day, Phil and I went down to the beach. Since it was low tide, we walked along the barnacle-covered rocks and used an iron garden rake to pull in the large, red, rock crab while we waited for my mother's flight. In time, we heard a plane coming from the south. The sound grew louder and louder until the plane burst over the tree line, circled overhead, and landed. After a quick kiss and a slight hug, my dad said goodbye as my mother and sister, climbed aboard. The plane roared across the water of the bay, took off, and disappeared over the horizon. After a few moments of silence, my father, Phil, and I marched up the muddy trail from the beach and loaded the truck with equipment. We headed up the bumpy road across the upper part of camp, and down the other side to where the huge mechanic's shop lay. We immediately went to work using chainsaws and machetes to clear the overgrown road that led four and a half miles up to a mysterious mountain lake where King Solomon's mine supposedly lay.

Three weeks later and with our food supply running low, just as my father had predicted, we finished our grueling work and saw the beautiful waters of Huaskin Lake. It was as if the heavens opened up and the angels began to sing. Once again, my father smiled like he had during the two monumental times before. It was now time to summon the rest of the family and tell the investors to send the barge. The next day the three of us drove fifteen miles down the inlet in the speedboat. My father used the radiophone at the Sullivan Bay lodge to make his calls and arrange everything that would transpire after that day. Phil and I hung out on the dock, not necessarily lost, but almost like sitting through an intermission during a movie, waiting for the next scene.

After a restful sleep that night in the cabin, Phil and I woke up to the sound of a plane landing in the bay. It was then that my father cracked the news to us that he would be flying down to Seattle to take care of business. The plane would take him away and leave Phil and I in the wilderness with very little food and ZERO contact with the outside world. We had no idea when he would be back, a week or so, maybe. We just had to survive in the meantime. That's it—just survive, until he got back.

A week later, after a meager lunch consisting of pancake and sardine sandwiches, Phil and I boiled up some rock crab that we had caught. We went down to the beach to enjoy our catch. Interesting enough, we sat upon the large rocks, cracking open the crab legs and eating them like natives on a south sea island. Eventually, the silence was broken, and we heard the same sound as when the plane came for my mother and sister. Two minutes later two pontoon planes burst over the tree line and the rest of our family landed in the bay. Just as my father wanted—we were all reunited as a family. I was never happier to see my brothers and sisters.

After their arrival, we lived life to the fullest in that abandoned camp. We had no running water, no electricity, and still had no communication with the outside world. Life was great beyond measure, living so simplistically and having free reign of an old ghost town. Everything we did that summer, from bathing in the nearby stream, to exploring every single old cabin, to fishing for cod for our dinner, was pure Heaven. My father's promises were coming true. (All of these details are disclosed in an entirely separate book.)

Near the end of the summer, the barge arrived with all the equipment for my father's cedar operation, just as he had promised, and with it, the planes began to land. The investors climbed ashore and finally had a chance to see where their money was going. Within days of the equipment arriving and my father setting up the operation, it came time for my brothers and sisters to say goodbye. We had to get back and get ready for a new school year. We climbed aboard separate pontoon planes and flew for hours until we crossed back over the Canadian border and into the United States.

When we arrived back in Idaho, we flooded our brother Peter with stories of this strange, exotic place. The tales intrigued Peter to no end. Although he had had enough of following our father in the past, he now had had enough of the wonderful reports. He wanted in on Dad's big operation. He dropped everything and decided to head north. He was going to join Dad in his last big push. This was the real thing.

Peter approached my mother, "Mom, I will give Dad one last shot. It sounds like he is really going to pull it off this time."

"I am glad that you still believe in him."

"There is one thing. I want Phil to come with me."

"He can't. He must finish his last year of high school."

"I know, but if Dad is pulling off something this big, who cares about a high school diploma if we are raking in the money?"

She tried to resist but then gave in. She trusted her oldest son as much as she trusted his father. Phil didn't seem to care about dropping out of school. He felt that he had all the support he needed with his father and brother at his side. Their cause was noble. It was a crusade. They were going to help Dad's final dream come true. Peter and Philip had now reached manhood, and it was up to them to embrace their own destinies.

Peter and Phil left Kellogg and headed north, leaving our family with two less.

Chapter 7

The Frozen Hell

Within a day of Peter and Philip landing in Jennis Bay, my father enthusiastically took them to work, and they started pulling the precious cedar out of the lake. He taught them how to saw the logs, split the rounds into blocks, cube each block into blanks, and then saw them into beautiful twenty-four-inch processed shakes. Much of it would end up in California to cover the roofs of the rich and famous.

Progress at the lake seemed slow at first. They realized that they weren't achieving nearly the output they wanted. Part of the problem was the small, awkward iron tub of a boat they used out on the water. It wasn't performing well. It bobbed around like a cork without a rudder, nearly uncontrollable and virtually useless in booming the logs. After a few days, my father had had enough.

"It's a fucking abortion, I tell ya! A fucking abortion!" My father yelled. Anything that did not function according to his standards, he furiously labeled an 'abortion'.

As a solution, my father decided to create something better. Like a demon-possessed man, he tore into a nearby yellow cedar log with an Alaskan chainsaw mill. The bright yellow sawdust flew everywhere and covered the ground like a blanket of fluorescent snow. He spent several exhausting hours pushing and fighting with the saw as he transformed the log into a pile of long planks. Peter, Philip, and my dad went on to cannibalize boards and large sheets of plywood from several of the old cabins. While the freshly cut planks would make up the sides of the craft, the boards would become the frame, and near the end of the construction, the plywood would complete the hull and the deck. The newly created, box-shaped vessel became a perfect platform to work on while booming the logs offshore from the mill. Peter dubbed it The Green Barge.

Peter and Philip helping our father construct the Green Barge.

The first few weeks of toiling at the mill seemed like a never-ending honeymoon. Though the working and living conditions slowly worsened and the back-breaking labor intensified, Peter and Philip's faith in their father never wavered. No matter what hardship they endured, the two of them continued to vividly see in their mind's eye the untold riches he had promised. Undeterred, the three of them continued to work like machines for the next several months. Fall neared its end and Winter lay not far away. By then, the weather had grown colder, and the conditions became nearly unbearable. The trio continued to work from dawn until dusk, but in time they grew tired—so tired that tensions began to grow. My father had been living out in the bush for nearly a year, and it is not good for anyone to be so far away from civilization. With my father, it began to show. Their troubles finally reached a climax.

One evening my father received a distressing call on the radiophone, and a bomb was dropped. His entire operation was being nuked all the way from Seattle. The investors had gathered together and decided to pull the plug on the business. Nothing had gone according to plan. There were no profits and there would never be any. In short, they were coming to confiscate all the equipment. They informed my father that a barge and tugboat had already been dispatched to steam up the coast and take possession of virtually everything they had sent up months earlier. My father panicked. They just couldn't do this to him, but they had their reasons. They realized that my father's claims were nothing but delusions of grandeur—just another one of his pipe dreams.

Over the next few days, my father called each of the investors individually and pleaded with them to leave him with something, anything that he could use to continue the operation, no matter how little. Could he keep one of the trucks? Could he keep the band saw? Could he keep the cuber? Reluctantly, they made a few concessions, but not many.

Days later, a tugboat with a massive barge in tow showed up in the bay. The seaplanes began to arrive and land. The head investor came personally to oversee the confiscation of the assets. Miraculously, my father managed to negotiate a small compromise: they would take the John Deere 450 bulldozer, the huge 75-kilowatt generator, the monstrous 6x6 Wittenberg flatbed army truck, and a handful of other miscellaneous pieces of equipment that they could lay their hands on. However, in the end, my father got to keep the two aging trailers, the band saw, the cuber, the old Mercury 350 tool truck, and a couple of older outboard motors. Phil and Peter watched in horror as all the rest of the desperately needed equipment was brought down the road and loaded onto the barge. On the day of its departure, my brothers stood on the beach and watched the barge leave the bay and embark on the long voyage back down the BC coast and onward to Seattle. Sadness fell upon them, but suddenly in a surprise reversal, my father mysteriously became unphased.

"Pete, what are we going to do now?" Phil asked.

"Don't you worry; Dad will come up with something."

"Are you kidding? We don't have anything."

"Relax. Trust me. Watch Dad. He's going to pull something out of his ass. I just know it."

With no hefty generator to power the appliances and heaters, they were forced to move back to the two old cabins where they at least had the wood cooking stove and the other wood heater. Luckily, Dad still had the tiny Sears and Roebuck gas generator, which he wired into the breaker panel of the lower cabin. Fortunately, they had electric lights at night.

The atmosphere over dinner that first night back in the lower cabin was solemn. My father fried the fish that they had caught earlier that day. He smothered it with copious amounts of onions while Pete and Phil thumbed through old issues of Popular Science magazines. Few people in the outside world could have ever comprehend their environment. The three of them had no TV to watch, no video movies on hand to view, and no phone line to call anyone on (except for the radiophone). They had nothing but themselves, a gas lantern for light and the sound of the evening crickets chirping outside.

The next morning as they drank their coffee, they looked out at the wild birds swooping in and landing in the surrounding trees. Just then, a bolt of lightning (a flash of inspiration) hit my father. He came up with a plan—it was purely genius. While the sawmill sat idle up at the lake, it was still wholly intact. However, it no longer had the high-voltage, three-phase generator to power the motor that ran the hydraulics. Also, they were still left with no bulldozer to pull the logs out of the lake. Worse than those two factors, what compounded their problems further was that they did not have the huge 6x6 Wittenburg military truck to haul the processed shakes. In short, they were still screwed—at least at that moment. However, Dad was about to pull off a miracle.

After a big breakfast, Dad ordered Peter and Phil outside.

"You two come with me."

"Where are we going?" Peter asked.

"Just get into the truck."

They climbed into the old blue Dodge pickup and took off down the road as if heading to the lake. As Dad drove, a freshly lit cigarette dangled from his lips. He was deep in thought. Just before they reached the one-mile marker, they came upon a naked patch of hibernating alder trees. All their leaves had already surrendered to the autumn and fallen forlornly to the ground, leaving every last one of them skinny and naked. The alders represented death. Dad pulled the truck over to the side of the road and shut off the engine. He pointed through the bare woods at something.

"Look at that," he said.

Peter and Philip looked over and instantly spotted the carcass of an old 1940s model Studebaker sedan. The body was so dusty and faded that it was hard to tell what color it really was. Cracks and yellow stains filled the windshield.

"What in the hell is that?" Peter asked.

"An engine for the mill," my father replied.

"Engine?"— "What do you mean engine?"

"The engine in that car would power up the mill just nicely."

"Wait. What in the hell are you talking about?" Peter shot back.

After a brief hesitation and no further explanation, they climbed out of the truck and walked up to the old jalopy. My dad raised the rusty hood of the car. The hinges squeaked with pain. He examined the old, flathead, four-cylinder engine that had not run in decades.

"She will do just fine," he said.

Peter and Philip stood next to him, absolutely dumbfounded. They looked at each other and shook their heads in total bewilderment.

Dad walked back to the truck and pulled a heavy rope out of the back. They just stood there and watched as he returned to the Studebaker and tied the heavy line to the car's front bumper. As stupefied observers, Peter and Philip watched helplessly as their father backed the old blue Dodge up to the front of the ancient Studebaker.

"Peter, you get in and steer while I tow. Don't worry about the flat tires. I don't give a shit about them."

They towed the car back to the old shop that lay across from the trailers.

Over the next two days, they worked together and pulled the engine and transmission out of the car. Before sunset, they wrestled the drive train up a long plank and secured it in the back of the Dodge. As they hopped down from the truck bed and sighed, my father smiled bizarrely at them. They didn't have a clear idea of how it would work—but my father did.

In the morning, they headed up to the lake with a sack lunch, two thermoses full of coffee, and their prize powerplant. Once inside the mill, the three of them methodically went to work inside the mill with wrenches and tools flying off in every direction. Dad unbolted the large electric motor from the hydraulic pump. He pushed it aside, and the three of them dragged the ancient Studebaker motor in and put it in its place. It took a fair amount of time to engineer and fabricate motor mounts and to mate the transmission with the drive shaft that turned the hydraulics. With the engine married up to the pump, they hooked a length of exhaust pipe back up to the motor. They vented it outside, away from the internal workings of the mill. Before starting the engine, they mounted a fuel tank, ran a line to the carburetor, and hooked up the radiator and hoses. In his final touches, Dad had rummaged around, found a new set of spark plugs (that were meant for his outboard motor). He installed them in the engine. Reaching that milestone, they stopped and drove back down to Jennis Bay. Later that night, over dinner, they crossed their fingers hoping they would achieve success the following morning.

Once they returned to the mill the next day, Dad drained the thirty-year-old oil out of the crankcase and filled it with brand-new Chevron 30-weight lubricant. As a final measure, he poured a capful of gasoline into each cylinder and re-installed the spark plugs. In final effort, he took a spare battery out of the back of the truck, brought it over, and set it next to the engine. He hooked up to the cables. In his last act of creation, Dad grabbed a short but thick length of wire, bent it into a U-shape, and jumped it across the two terminals on the solenoid. Sparks flew, and the engine flinched. He tried again, this time holding the wire in place. The engine turned over and over and finally fired to life, spewing out a cloud of dark smoke. It roared for a second, then slowed down, sputtered, and died. This time, Dad primed the engine again by dumping a capful of gasoline down the carburetor's throat. He repeated this process several times until the engine roared to life and finally stayed running. It slowed down and calmly purred at a slow speed. With the hydraulics now active, Dad tested the cuber and the bandsaw. The power problem had been solved. My father had pulled off Miracle Number One.

The next day, in front of the old shop, they spent another day removing the camper-like shell from the back of the old, white Mercury 350 pickup. Initially, the vehicle had been used as a plumbing contractor's truck, but they now decided to ditch the shelter and turn it into a flatbed to haul the shakes: Miracle Number Two. However, even with the conversion of the

Mercury and celebrations at hand, one last problem remained: they had to figure out how to drag the heavy water-soaked legs out of the lake without a bulldozer. My father had to think hard once again.

It took another day of fishing and relaxing for Dad to devise a solution. He had another epiphany out on the water while pulling in a giant cod. He had a vision of ancient times. He remembered how engineers of old mathematically calculated the power of torque multiplication using pulleys. When they returned, Dad went into a flurry of activity and raced through the remnants of the old logging camp. He scrounged up a series of pulleys (the bigger ones called blocks) that had been used decades before for routing the steel cables of the skylines that ran up the mountainside. Dad deduced that by routing a steel cable through several pairs of pulleys and hooking it to the back of the old flatbed Mercury pickup, the pulling power of the truck was magically multiplied several times. With the pulley system, the old truck would have the same brute hauling power as the John Deere bulldozer: Miracle Number Three.

Within a few short days, Dad, Peter, and Phil were blazing once again, driving full steam ahead with production. The sawdust started flying, the mill began humming, and they took load after load of the beautiful, aromatic cedar shakes down to the dock at Jennis Bay. Each shipment meant another deposit into the corporate bank account.

Every time they returned to the cabin from work, my father noticed that the heavy Fall rains began forming a large spring that ran down the clay bank and spilled across the road. He had another epiphany and went right to work on it.

Instead of sponge bathing out of buckets of water, baths with hot running water became the next order of business. Dad commandeered a defunct water heater from one of the older cabins in the upper part of the camp and installed it in the lower cabin's bathroom. He then ran a black poly pipe from a little pond he had dug and plumbed it into the house's water system. In a highly ingenious manner, he ran galvanized water pipes from the tank, through holes in the wall, and into the wood cookstove. As long as they had a fire, they had hot water. It worked. After the first night of hot baths and warm dishwater for their dishes, they sat contently around the cabin. Despite all their setbacks, the dream was still alive.

Unfortunately, the December weather hit them hard. The cold environment grew nearly intolerable to operate in. Mother Nature began to freeze everything, including my father and brothers' relations. Work became severely difficult, and the tension between my brothers and their own father became unbearable. By Christmas, Phil and Peter were at their breaking point.

"Dad, can you give us some money and let us fly home for Christmas?" Peter asked.

"There's hardly any money in the account."

"Dad, Phil, and I have to get out of here for a break. Give us something, anything, and charter us a plane. Please."

After much begging and negotiating, they extracted enough money from our father for them to fly out and return to Idaho for the holidays.

Back in Idaho, Peter and Philip sat at the kitchen table and the rest of us listened intently to their horror stories of their life at Jennis Bay. The summer paradise was no longer a paradise. It turned into a frozen hell. The situation sounded bleaker than we could have ever imagined.

"I think Dad is losing his mind." Peter said sadly. Phil simply nodded in agreement.

After a week of holiday rest and renewed spirits, they left again for the North Country. My brothers mutually agreed to slug it out for a few more months until Spring. For now, they convinced themselves that it would be best for them to hang in there and place their last shred of hope in their father's vision, if for no other reason than to clear their own consciences. They justified. They rationalized. Their fortunes just had to turn around. They at least had to keep enough faith that even after a last-ditch effort, they would eventually escape the hell and leave it all behind.

Once they returned to the bay, nothing had really changed at the mill. However, this time, it wasn't Peter and Phil who grew weary of the long days, it was Dad. By January's end, my father drifted off into his own world, losing interest in working. He became obsessed with time-wasting antics and frivolous activities. He found every excuse not to go to the lake. When they did begin to work, Dad grew ever more agitated with the slightest of issues. His mental state deteriorated because of his loss of connection with society. It's called being bushed. My dad had been in the bush for too long and was losing his grip. Peter, much older and more mature than Phil, could finally see the writing on the wall—they had to get the hell out of there.

One cold, frosty day, while working at the mill, my father sent Phil in the truck back to the cabin to pick up some parts. Phil did as he was ordered. After miles of driving on the bumpy road, he loaded the items on the back of the flatbed and returned up the savage path to the lake. Without realizing it, some important items had bounced off and were lying somewhere along the road. When my father looked at the back of the truck and realized Phil's blunder, he went crazy. He swore. He yelled. The veins bulged all over his neck and temples. He foamed at the mouth as he screamed at Phil.

"Relax, Dad."

"Relax? Relax? Don't you dare talk to me that way! You don't even have fucking brain one!" Dad huffed and puffed, nearly having an anxiety attack. "Go back down the goddam road and find those parts before I strap you!" (Strap was Dad's term for whipping us with a belt.)

With his steely eyes, although so burned out over the months of hellish work with no rest, Phil looked directly at his father and refused to blink. He calmly said, "If you touch me, I'll break your arm."

Peter stood nearby, totally horrified over what Phil had just said.

Like a cold wind blowing a door wide open, Phil's comment made my father freeze dead in his tracks. He had no idea how to respond. None of his children had ever spoken to him in such a way. Dad's bottom lip quivered as he and Phil locked eyes on each other like two gunfighters waiting for the other one to draw. Peter stood there motionless and dropped his jaw in total disbelief. My father took a few deep breaths and took Phil's threat seriously. He mumbled to himself about dying in the wilderness. After a moment, he walked away. He nervously lit up a cigarette with his hands shaking, and after a deep puff, began to sharpen the chain on one of the chainsaws. My father was already a dead man because the cancer had been eating away inside him for years without anyone in the family knowing.

Peter walked up to Phil and whispered, "We have got to get the hell out of here!"

"Ya damn right we do. I can't take this shit much longer."

A week after the showdown, Peter hatched an escape plan, one in which he could not let Dad know about. After my father had walked down the trail to the beach to check on the boat, Peter shared his idea with Phil. With Phil more than eager to go along with it, they agreed to set the plan in motion the following morning.

Just after breakfast, as the three of them headed up the hill in the truck and had reached the upper part of the camp, Phil yelled, "Holy shit, Dad. Stop! I forgot all the chainsaw files back at the cabin."

My father immediately slammed on the brakes and stopped the truck. "God dammit!"

As my father tugged on the steering wheel to turn the truck around, Phil opened the door and jumped out. "Hold on, Dad. I'll run back down as fast as I can and will be right back."

"For fuck's sake," my dad said. "Alright but hurry up. We have work to do."

Phil sprinted back down the partially frozen road to the cabin, slipping and sliding the entire way. Just outside the back door, he pulled-started the small generator. When it roared to life, he burst into the cabin. He ran up to the table and flipped the switch on the radio phone to turn it on. The airwaves were silent. Phil grabbed the microphone, pressed the button, and summoned the marine radio operator, just like he had seen Dad do many times before.

"Alert Bay, Alert Bay, this is Five-M-O-Seven-Eight, over."

Silence ensued.

As Philip prepared to call out again, the operator responded, "This is Alert Bay. Go ahead, Five-M-O-Seven-Eight."

"Yes, operator, could you patch me through to Scott Cove, please?

A two-second pause followed before the operator called out, "Scott Cove, Scott Cove, this is Alert Bay Marine Radio calling."

The operator called a couple more times before a response came from Scott Cove.

"Alert Bay, this Scott Cove, over"

"Stand by Scott Cove; I have five-M-O-seven eight calling. Go ahead, Five-M-O-Seven-Eight."

Phil's heart raced.

"This is Phil Major calling from Jennis Bay. I just wanted to know if you guys are hiring. Two of us here are looking for work."

The response was almost immediate. "Ah, yes, of course. We are always hiring. We can put you right to work if you get here soon. We could use a couple of good chokermen."

Phil buried his face in his hand for a moment and thanked God. Salvation was near. However, danger lurked just up the road. My father had heard the generator start and now sat behind the wheel in complete panic mode. "What in the hell is he doing? Why did he start the generator? I'm going to kill 'em!"

My father started the truck. Peter then jumped out just as Phil had done and sprinted down the road as fast as he could in front of Dad. Peter could hear the truck coming up behind him and ran all the faster. He had to alert Phil.

Phil was finishing the conversation when Peter burst through the back door. "It's Dad! It's Dad! He's coming!"

Phil wrapped up the conversation, "Darn! That would be great. I'll try to catch a sked down in the next few days." (Sked: a daily scheduled flight in a pontoon plane between various locations.)

"Sounds good. We are always here."

"Hey, when we get there, who do we ask for?"

"Just come up to the office by the wharf and tell them you are there to see Frank Babbit. He's the foreman."

"Okay! Thanks a lot. I really appreciate it." Phil concluded the call by directing his next message to the marine operator, "Alert Bay, this is Five-M-O-Seven-Eight out."

"Thank you, caller. Alert Bay out."

Just then, my father bolted through the back door and saw Phil sitting at the table with the microphone in his hand.

"What in the hell do you think you are doing?"

Phil just stared directly at his father.

"Tell me! I want to know what the hell you are doing?"

Peter looked at Phil and gave him a nod of support.

"Dad, Pete, and I are getting out of here. We are getting jobs at Scott Cove."

My father's head almost exploded. He screamed, "You cannot get jobs. You two are illegal aliens. The RCMP will come and lock you guys up.

You guys are going nowhere!" (All of this was untrue. Peter and Phil were born in Canada and were Canadian citizens.)

Phil mumbled, "We sure the hell aren't staying here."

My father caught his breath and fought for the words to say. He came up with something, "Shut that generator off, and let's get up to the lake."

The airwaves were once again silent. Philip switched the radio off and followed my father out the back door. He reached down and shut the generator off. The little powerplant sputtered, belched, and then stopped altogether. It had performed magnificently. A minute later, the three of them were in the truck, bouncing up the bumpy road toward the lake. This time, however, Peter and Philip didn't feel any bumps at all; they were too hypnotized by their vision of freedom.

Once they started unloading supplies from the truck, Phil leaned over to Peter and, out of the side of his mouth, whispered, "Scott Cove will hire us as soon as we can get our asses down there."

Dad started barking out orders. "Pete, grab a choker and get on over here! Phil, get the truck going, and let's get that log up on the landing."

Peter whispered back to Phil, "We can jump on a sked any day, but there's one problem . . . I only have enough money to get one of us down there."

"Shit!"

"Don't worry, I will think of something."

Peter and Phil did what their father ordered and worked the rest of the day, sawing, splitting, and loading the truck with the cedar blocks to be taken over to the mill. The entire time, they never stopped thinking about ways and means to flee their father's slave operation.

At the end of the day, before they got into the truck, Peter whispered to Phil, "Here's what we do. I have $200. We get you on a sked and get you down to Scott Cove to start work. I'll stay behind because I can handle Dad."

"Then what?"

"With your first paycheck, you pay for a sked to get me down there."

Phil agreed.

However, they thought it over and tried to give their father one last chance. The weeks passed, and they continued breaking their backs while Dad watched their every move. He was not going to tolerate a mutiny.

Peter and Philip were virtually being held hostage by their own father. Worse than the constant surveillance, was the fact that there was simply no money to be had. There was no way for both of them to get out of there at the same time. Eventually, the situation worsened. Their work schedule began to deteriorate, and for reasons unknown, Dad lost all his drive to keep the operation going. He just didn't want to go to work, other things seemed more important. The wasted time started to drive Peter and Phil crazy, crazy to the point that they even abandoned the idea of working for another logging camp. They simply wanted to leave the country, return to the U.S., and start their lives anew.

As more weeks went by, the weather started to turn warmer. April arrived, and the rain continued. The alder trees began to bud, and the leaves eagerly opened up. Still, Peter and Phil struggled with a father who had basically lost his mind in the wilderness. However, against all odds, with their insistence to go to work, by May, the trio managed to fill the old dock down at the bay with the largest shipment of shakes yet to be sent out—seventeen complete pallets. After calling the buyer in Vancouver, an old wooden cargo ship named the Seymour Princess chugged into the bay and began to lift the precious cedar and secure it in its hold. The vessel took off and headed south. Shortly after receiving the shipment in Vancouver, the buyer wired the money into my father's corporate account. Alas, this was Peter and Phil's chance to weasel some hard-earned cash out of Dad and finally execute their plan.

After receiving the payment for the shakes, my father got on the radio and called to speak with my mother in Idaho. Summer was coming soon, and he had a plan.

"Kay, I want you to get Jeri-anne and Tim out of school early and have them fly up here."

"Again? Get them out of school early like you did with Phil and Tony last year?"

"Yep. Get them ready."

"Okay, but how do I get them up here?"

"Have them fly out of Spokane and into Vancouver. Vicky will take care of them overnight."

"So, don't drive them to Seattle?"

"No. If you get them to Vicky's, they can fly up the coast on a sked. After that, I only have to charter one plane for the rest of you out of Seattle."

"Okay, if that is what you think is best."

The news of Jeri-anne and Tim's impending arrival became a breakthrough for Peter and Phil. They knew that salvation edged itself closer and closer by the day. They could hardly contain themselves, but they had to keep it hush. They didn't want our father to flip out if he discovered that they were leaving for good. My father was already living on the edge of sanity. Thus, it became imperative to execute their plan flawlessly. If my father discovered their ruse too early, there is no telling what he could do. He could extend their tour in the land of eternal torment and make things infinitesimally worse.

Tim and Jeri-anne finally landed in the bay, and after a day of rest, they all made their way up to the lake. They started to work together as a team at the mill. Jeri-anne and Tim learned to bundle the shakes and stack the pallets while my father spent time on the water, booming the logs together. Inside the heart of the mill, Peter and Phil worked feverishly, cubing up the blocks and running the blanks through the band saw. At times, they got so far ahead of Jeri-anne and Tim that they had to shut down and help with the bundling.

Not everything was pure slavery. There were times when they found moments for a bit of leisure. One afternoon, they shut down early and took the boat out partway across the lake to a small island less than a hundred feet wide. There, they held a small picnic with nothing more than sandwiches and potato chips. Peter surprised everyone by climbing into the boat and pulling out a sign he had painted the day before. The sign read, 'Timothy Island', naming the tiny land mass after our little brother. Although Peter enjoyed the moment, deep inside, he seethed. He wanted out of that place so fucking bad. Freedom loomed nearby, but yet seemed so far away.

After completing the first week of work with Tim and Jeri-anne, Peter felt that the stage had finally been set to put the escape plan into motion. In the morning, after breakfast, Peter and Phil went out to the makeshift garden and approached our father, who was busy raking mounds of dirt and planting seeds.

"Dad, Phil, and I would like to take a break from things and head back to Idaho for a bit."

My father stopped raking and looked at Peter with a puzzled look. A break? Go back to Idaho? The request seemed too far out of his comprehension.

"What for? We have too much work to do."

"Dad, all we've been doing since Christmas is work. We haven't seen town in nearly five months."

"You can't go. There isn't enough money to fly you home; we can't afford a week of being down."

Peter had to think fast. "Wait, wait! We can go up to the lake, pull out a ton of logs, and spend two days bucking them up and splitting them. Enough wood to keep you, Tim, and Jeri-anne busy for a week until we get back."

"Oh, I don't know."

"We can do this. Let's set a goal. Let Phil and I get some good rest in Idaho, and when we get back, we can push for sending out twenty pallets this time—beat our old record."

My father leaned on the handle of the rake and thought about it. "Do you really think we can?"

"Hell, yes. Phil and I had started a little competition between us in the mill. We got this."

It seemed like ten minutes of silence went by. The situation forced Peter into becoming the best salesman on the planet, and he instinctively knew that whoever spoke first, lost.

"Okay, I'll call for a plane, and we spend two days loading up the landing at the mill."

"Can you give us some money?"

"Ah shit, we don't have much."

"Come on, Dad."

"I can write you a check, but it won't be much."

Phil stood by the entire time without saying a word. His presence alone contributed to the negotiation. It put Dad under additional pressure. Dad realized that it was two against one.

"Let's get up to the lake and get going," Peter demanded.

"Alright. Make the lunches, brew the coffee, and get Jeri-anne and Tim ready."

Peter and Philip turned around and strutted back to the cabin, trying not to act overly exuberant. Over the next two days, they delivered what they promised their father; they filled the landing site with plenty of fresh wood to be milled.

A day later, a small float plane popped through the clouds and pouring rain. It circled the bay and touched down on the calm, glass-like surface of the water. To Peter and Philip, the plane appeared more beautiful than a winged Pegasus swooping down from the heavens to take them away.

As the plane taxied in, Dad, Peter, and Philip climbed in the rowboat, along with Tim, and made their way out to a rendezvous point where they waited. The tide gently flowed past them, with clumps of seaweed lazily drifting by. Only the droplets of rain pelting the water disturbed what could have been a perfect mirror where the water met the sky. With its propeller slowly slashing round and round, the plane taxied up to the rowboat. Peter and Phil waited anxiously with their packed bags at their side. Their escape lay only minutes away.

The pilot cut the engine, and the propeller sputtered to a stop. The pontoons glided through the water until the plane finally rested a mere hundred feet from the beach, and only a few feet from them. My father rowed the boat closer. He stood up, grabbed the wing strut, and brought the boat alongside the plane. The cheerful-faced pilot climbed out and stepped down onto the pontoon.

"Two passengers bound for Seattle; I was told."

"Yes, Sir," my father spoke up.

"Great, but we gotta get out of here before the storm front moves in."

The pilot edged along the pontoon and opened the back door of the plane. Peter and Philip handed him their bags, and he chucked them inside. Time was of the essence. They had to take off as soon as possible.

Peter and Phil stepped out of the rowboat and climbed aboard the plane. As a last-minute gesture, Peter turned to his father and said, "Okay, Dad, we'll be back next week. We really need this break."

My father looked up, but in a mere second, an intense, sardonic grin spread across his face. At that moment, he knew the truth. He realized right there and then that they were never coming back. My father's heart sank at that moment, and he resigned himself to his fate. He grinned and felt as if Judas had just kissed him, and the bags the pilot had thrown onto the plane contained thirty pieces of silver. Dad had nothing else to say to them. Jeri-anne stood alone on the beach in the rain, remaining an innocent bystander. She knew the score, though. She knew how desperately Peter and Philip needed to flee, but she couldn't do or say anything that could ever help resolve the situation. Now, all my father had left in this world was my youngest brother, Timmy, sitting in the boat with him in the drizzling rain and his oldest daughter standing on the beach.

My father shoved the rowboat away from the plane and gently rowed away. He wrestled with the oars at a safe distance and turned the rowboat broadside to watch the plane take off. Timmy sat in the back with tears welling up in his eyes. Right before him, his greatest mentor, his older brother Peter, was being torn away.

Inside the plane, Peter and Phil buckled up tightly, fighting terribly to keep the smiles of joy off their faces. Peter sat in the co-pilot's seat, and Phil sat behind him. Phil slapped Peter on the shoulder, "Damn, we are finally outta here."

"Shhhh! Wait. Wait! Don't look back now. We can't let Dad see us celebrating."

"Do you think he knows?"

"Damn right, he knows."

Phil sat back and looked out the window with the most somber expression.

The pilot started the engine. It sputtered to life and shook the entire airframe. Peter pulled out his camera as quickly as he could. He pointed it out the window and focused the lens on Tim and Dad sitting motionless in the boat. Peter snapped one last picture, capturing them in one of the saddest moments ever in our family history. The tears were now pouring down Tim's cheeks as he cried, seeing his brother Peter, his guardian, abandoning him in this faraway land.

My father and younger brother Tim in a moment of sadness.

The pilot pushed the throttle to full power, and the propeller bit angrily into the air. The little Cessna desperately fought to pick up momentum. It began to race across the bay. It fought harder and harder to break free from the clutches of the sea. Eventually, the pilot pulled back on the wheel, and she lifted off the surface and embraced the calm air. Droplets of rain splattered on the windshield and were pulled aside by the wind. Peter and Phil's spirits soared along with the plane. The nightmare was over.

Peter turned to the pilot and said, "My God, we are glad to get out of that place."

"Yeah, I can see that." He tried to be polite but wanted to remain professional and get them safely back to Seattle.

Peter strained his neck to look as far back out the window so that he could see Jennis Bay disappearing behind them. Neither Peter nor Philip would ever see their father again.

After several hours of being half-sleep and half-dreaming, my two brothers woke up to find themselves descending from the clouds and circling over the waters of Lake Union in Seattle. The northwest metropolis lay below them with the Space Needle jetting skyward as a welcoming beacon to the two nomads returning from another dimension.

Chapter 8

Phil, Craig, and the Cliff

In one sense, Peter and Philip returned to Kellogg with their tails between their legs, but in another sense, they were extremely empowered and motivated. Peter swallowed his pride, kicked in the superintendent's office door, and secured his old position as a hard rock miner. Phil had done the same and resumed his lowly position as a box boy at the local IGA grocery store. However, that was not all he had to do; he had to re-enroll in high school as a senior one year behind schedule.

With everyone in the family growing older, the setting in the neighborhood seemed to have changed. Ever since Phil and Mike Groves had first ventured up to the small cliff that one fateful evening a few years earlier and terrorized the neighborhood with their firecracker barrages, it became clear that that was where the action would stay. Although that initial move to the rocky bluff and the ensuing show had proved so stellar, Phil and Mike's bond had relaxed, and they drifted slightly apart. As time went on, Phil shifted his attention to a friend in much closer proximity: his good neighborhood friend, Craig Turbak.

It was now Craig who joined Phil on his new spree of cliff shows. Phil introduced him to the fine art of firecracker throwing. After disturbing the peace in the neighborhood a few times in this way, a new routine developed. The police, almost on cue, would show up with their spotlights and loudspeakers—all to Phil's delight. The entire point of the exercise WAS to get the police to show up and attempt to get them off the mountainside. Philip's favorite thrill came when the police tried to scale the hillside on foot in an attempt to apprehend them. The hardest part of their escape was trying not to trip and fall down from laughing so hard as they ran away.

Craig soon became the perfect partner. He had a similar background to Mike Groves. They both came from some of the community's highest quality and extremely upstanding Catholic families. Craig and his younger brother Todd were good boys. It must have come from their genes. No pun was intended because Craig's father's name was Gene. Gene Turbak was a gentle giant and a prince of man. He was the kindest person in the world but also the toughest bastard to have ever come out of the Silver Valley. Before Craig was even a twinkle in his father's eye, Gene spent a vast portion of his time in the military on an army boxing team. Gene got released with a more-than-honorable discharge and a 42-0 winning record—an undefeated contender.

Shortly after his return to civilian life, Gene returned to the valley and married his high school sweetheart. They did what most young married couples did: they started a family. Many years had passed since their matrimony and his children were now growing into teenagers. Gene kept a close eye on his beloved sons. He didn't want them tainted by the other hellions roaming the streets in our neighborhood. Gene tried to shield his prized offspring from any questionable characters. If that was the case, Gene must have been completely oblivious to certain things. He should have never let Craig near the likes of my brother Phil, but we Major brothers had a pass: we were good Catholic church-going boys, and this fact may have let Phil slip under Gene's radar.

Mr. Turbak was no dummy. Although he had let Phil slide on many occasions, he still scrutinized Craig's every encounter with him. Not always, but most of the time, Gene could see right through Phil's ruses to lure Craig away. When he realized Phil's true intentions, he would foil them at every turn. Phil was no dummy, either. He knew right from the beginning that Gene was onto him, and he understood that Gene had good reason to be so protective—he had to preserve his local reputation. Over the years, Mr. Turbak had garnered much respect in the community as a hard-working stalwart and public benefactor. Among his roles were his positions as an upstanding member of the local Elks lodge, a servant in the Catholic Church's Knights of Columbus, and that of an officer in the local workers union. With all these hats to wear in the community, he would not throw away all he had worked for by letting his own children get sucked into a ring of terror and crime. He would protect his small brood of children at all costs, especially from the clutches of the Major boys.

Knowing Mr. Turbak's character, he probably stood on his front porch at night, wearing his red plaid shirt, gripping his favorite brand of cigar in one hand, and looking up at the scintillating lights in the sky that emanated from the Major household just one street over. Gene knew well that the Major boys had something nefarious brewing at any given time. "Damn you, Major boys! Why couldn't you guys just enroll in sports or something? And where the hell is your dad?" He muttered to himself.

On many occasions, Phil verbally sparred with Gene, always trying to gain access to Craig's extracurricular time. However, what made it so difficult for Phil is that his adventures were nothing simple. Phil's ambitions were similar to the great explorers like Magellan, where Magellan would roll out a large marine chart, point his finger at the warning inscribed on the far corner: 'Here Be Dragons'. Similarly, Phil seemed to roll out a more modern chart and point at the warning inscribed on the far corner: 'Here Be Really Big Fish' and would say, "This is where we are going, Craig!" The only obstacle to the proposed trip was Craig's dad.

It didn't take Phil long to learn what language to speak to Gene. In the beginning, Phil tapped danced in the Turbak living room, presenting his latest plan, and would often get no actual response. In the end, with much mental processing, Gene would slowly mull over Phil's request while he looked blankly at the TV. Finally, in a slow, monotone voice, barely annunciating, would say, "Craig, I think you should pass on this one."

Interpretation: "Not no, but FUCK NO! Are you crazy!!"

After a few initial failures to gain Gene's consent, Phil learned that the typical approach would never work. He had to come up with something nasty. Gene was onto his Phil's program like ants on a gumdrop. Phil learned that speaking of such things as 'daring adventures' or 'once-in-a-lifetime experiences', were terms not found in Gene's vocabulary. Maybe in our father's, but not in Gene's.

Phil began to experiment with deception and psychological warfare to counter Gene's strict fatherly oversight. In response to Gene's efforts, Phil launched a new campaign. To demonstrate the wholesomeness of his and Craig's friendship, Phil and Craig jointly agreed to strategically serve as altar boys at the Saturday night Catholic mass. They purposely did it in full view of Mr. Turbak and his family. To advance the campaign even further, Craig secured a job at the local IGA grocery store and worked alongside Phil as a box boy. While they worked there, they looked for every chance to cheerfully help little old ladies out to their cars with their groceries, as well as cheerfully helping themselves to all the snacks they could eat and –and all the beer that Craig could smuggle out the back door of the store. "One case of beer for IGA, one case of beer for me!" and so on. (Until the day Craig got caught and got fired.)

This illusion of reverence and purity that Phil and Craig worked so hard to portray began to take effect on Gene, and just like Novocain, their plan slowly achieved its goals. Gene finally cracked under all the seduction and began to release Craig into Phil's care. One of those times happened to be for an innocent sleepover at our house. However, that was just the cover story. Phil was smart enough to know that whatever tale they came up with, it had to be good. It had to be something noteworthy and commendable, such as mowing neighbors' lawns, playing Monopoly with the Dirt, Grit, and Grime brothers, or playing something like hide-and-seek or kick-the-can. Yeah, that's what it would be next time: kick-the-can! That would get Gene past the kickoff while the real night's purpose was to throw firecrackers off the cliff, taunting the police, then go back to the house and engage in poker games (where Phil would cheat everyone out of their money). This newly panned sleepover was going to be the greatest! The very air screamed out for the duo to wreak havoc in the neighborhood.

Phil, in later years, as the Grand Poo-Bah.

Earlier that week, Peter had come home from work at the mine and inadvertently eavesdropped on Phil's and Craig's conversation where they discussed the frustrations with the cliff operations. Phil and Craig were growing tired of hand-lighting each firecracker (or pack of firecrackers), throwing them down the side of the cliff, and waiting for the police to arrive. Although exciting when the authorities showed up, it became too much work. Peter listened intently for a moment as he cleaned out his lunch box. While Phil and Craig talked, brand-new thoughts began to form in Peter's mind. He listened to their woes and came up with the perfect idea.

The day after Peter heard them talk, Phil and Craig headed off to school, and Peter went to work underground at the mine. Peter knew of something that might be of use to them. He arrived at the mine that day and changed into his work clothes. He then climbed aboard the hoist with a group of other miners and descended over a thousand feet down the mine shaft, deep into the belly of the earth—a dark, dangerous, and mysterious place indeed.

At the end of his eight-hour shift, Peter climbed aboard the hoist to ride it the thousand feet back to the surface. He acted strangely when he climbed inside the cage with the other miners. He clutched his lunch box very closely, keeping it safely at his side. Peter was guarding something.

On the surface, Peter showered as usual in the dry room, changed his clothes, and headed home in his truck. When he walked through the back door and into the kitchen, he found Phil, Craig, Steve, and I sitting around our kitchen table. We were all eating snacks and playing cards—and as usual, my brother Steve and I were there trying to win back all the money that Phil and Craig had won from us by cheating.

At first, we didn't pay any attention to Peter until he walked up to the table and set his lunch box in front of us. "Are you guys really planning to do another cliff show this weekend?"

Phil pulled the popsicle out of his mouth, "Of course we are."

"Well, I have something that might help."— "I was just thinking. Why wait for the police to show up? Why not set everything up for the fireworks show in advance and then leave the cliff? Let the police THINK that you are up there?"

"What the fuck are you talking about?" Craig sarcastically asked.

Like a magician, Peter opened his lunch box and pulled out two spools of what looked like green twine. He laid the two spools on the table before us and said, "Why don't you tie everything together and let the fuse take care of the rest?"

"What in the fuck is that? "Craig blurted out as he pointed to the two spools.

Peter smiled and remained silent for a moment just for the effect of driving Craig crazy. He then answered, "It's spinner cord. It's basically dynamite fuse."

Phil and Craig immediately stopped playing cards, picked up the coils, and held them as if they were the frozen embryos of Adam and Eve. To them, the two plastic rolls of the strange cord contained the meaning of life. Their imaginations went wild. They immediately halted the card game. That night, Phil formulated the plan for the following night—the night of the sleepover.

The next day, as soon as school was dismissed, Phil and Craig ran home and scrounged up all their money. They visited several fireworks stands across town. They bought as many packs of firecrackers, bottle rockets, and Roman candles as they could. Before nightfall, Phil found himself once again in the Turbak living room. He and Craig stood before Gene like two soldiers standing at attention during a military court martial. Phil had to put on his best performance. He just had to get official permission for Craig to spend the night. This time around, Phil had perfected his sales pitch very well.

"Kick-the-can, you say?" Gene asked them.

"Absolutely, Sir. We run the cleanest show in town!" Phil responded.

Gene thought about it momentarily until his wife, Carleen, yelled out from the kitchen. Gene strained his neck and turned away to answer. At that moment, Phil nudged Craig with his elbow, and without any words said, with a mere wink and smiling gesture, "Don't worry about it. We got this one licked!"

Gene turned back around and calmly said, "Okay, you boys have fun tonight,"— "And Craig, remember son, I am always proud of you."

After scoring a victory at the fireworks stands earlier that day and scoring a second victory this evening over the one and only Gene Turbak, Phil and Craig rushed back to our house. They retrieved their huge bag of fireworks and dumped it out on the kitchen table. The two of them began to unspool the spinner cord and intertwine it with the firecracker fuses. They were going to give the town, and especially the local police, a brand-new treat: a fifteen-minute-long display of fireworks, lit by . . . NO ONE!

After nearly an hour of work, the duo wound up the entire assembled fireworks show and carefully stuffed it all into a large paper grocery bag like a Hindu flute player trying to stuff a cobra back into a reed basket.

They waited impatiently for nightfall, and when the sun had completely set and the stars came out, they left the house and disappeared around the corner. They scaled up the side of the cliff, slipping on the loose rocks in the dark until they reached the top. On the summit, they carefully unloaded the bag and spread the entire array of fireworks between the boulders, careful not to overlap the green spinner cord. Once everything was in place, their entire setup looked like some impossible centipede. It was time to light it and run. The slow-burning fuse would take care of the rest.

Phil and Craig caught their breath and glanced down at the small town below them. They looked over at each other. Were they ready for this?

"Craig, go ahead and light it?"

"Bullshit. You light it!"

"Come on, are you afraid?"

"Fuck no! This is your gig. You light it."

Phil capitulated. He reached into his pocket and pulled out the lighter. He brought the flame up the end of the green cord. The moment the cord sparkled, it did not burn slowly as expected. Instead, it raced like lightning from one end to the other like a solar flare. In one microsecond, everything went off simultaneously. All the explosives ignited wildly right in their faces. Bottle rockets started shooting off in all directions. Both Phil and Craig, in sheer panic, scrambled down the side of the mountain in the darkness. Something was wrong with the fuse—terribly wrong. It was supposed to be slow burning like in the Western movies.

As the two panic-stricken fugitives scurried through the darkness, they could hear the mayhem going on behind them. All they knew was that they had to get the fuck off that mountain—and pronto!

They scrambled down the hillside with their feet plowing into the dirt and rocks. They knew the road lay somewhere just below them. Right ahead of Phil, Craig felt the bank's abrupt steepness; meaning the payment was right below. He leaped out, but he jumped too early. The road was much further away than he thought. He sailed through the abyss, waiting for his fall to end. Time seemed to have slowed down. His left foot hit first. He stumbled forward at high speed, and the next thing to hit the ground was his kneecap—and it hit hard. Craig finally stopped his fall with both his hands. Oomph! The pain began to erupt in his knee and spread up his leg.

Phil made it down safely and passed Craig, but then turned around to see why Craig had stopped and was on the ground. "Hurry up, you mother fucker. Let's get out of here."

"My knee, my fucking knee!"

Phil ran over to Craig and lifted him by his arm.

"Ouch! Hold on! Hold on!"

Craig got to his feet and started limping after Phil. He could not bend his left leg. He dragged it behind him and hopped sideways across the road, chasing Phil into the bushes. They tore their way through the brush and trekked across the flats. On the far side, they clawed their way down a small trail until they reached the end of a lone street by the Butler residence. Mr. Butler stood in his yard watering his lawn with a garden hose. He looked puzzled as they made their way around the corner and took the short pathway to Mission Avenue. They stopped under the streetlight. Blood had dripped along the pavement behind them.

"Let's have a look. Pull up your pant leg," Phil ordered.

By this time, Craig winced so severely from the pain that he almost started to cry. "It hurts, it fucking hurts!"

He slowly lifted his pant leg. When he got it so high, they saw a large split in the skin right over the top of Craig's knee that exposed the white kneecap. Blood had dripped down and covered most of Craig's shin, soaking his sock and covering his shoe.

"Oh fuck! Crap, go home, go home right now! "Phil told him.

"What the hell, and I'm going to tell my dad?

"Tell him that you tripped playing kick-the-can."

"I can't tell him that."

"Yes, you can. Your dad will believe you, but he wouldn't believe me."

Craig took Phil's advice and limped across the street and disappeared down the dark alley. When he burst through the door of his house, he alerted his mom and dad, who sat on the sofa watching TV. They shrieked in horror when they saw the blood seeping through Craig's pants. Without hesitation, they raced Craig to the hospital emergency room. Meanwhile, Phil wandered back to our house and gave Peter a full report. However, Peter sat on the couch too engrossed in a Star Trek episode to give Phil much of a reply. Phil asked him what the hell could have happened with the spinner cord. Why did It take off at lightning speed instead of burning slowly? Peter all but ignored him.

Later that night, after returning from the hospital, Gene Turbak went out onto his back porch. He sipped a cup of coffee and puffed away on one of his favorite cigars. He began to digest the events surrounding Craig's accident. Something was fishy about the story. He decided it would be best if Craig stayed away from the Major boys for a while.

Chapter 9

Stephen Attacks

All six of us brothers competed against each other at every step of the way. It's not that we competed at the same type of things; it's that we competed to get the most attention. We did that by doing the most outlandish things that we could think of. The neighbors looked out their windows and saw us running in and out of our driveway on foot, on bicycles, on motorcycles, and in hot cars. They constantly wondered where our father was. They stayed close to their telephones and jumped at any chance to call the police if they felt we were ready to cause harm to their precious neighborhood.

One day, my younger brother Stephen's turn came to try and outdo the rest of us. He had enough of the attention that Kit and Phil received from carrying out their notorious deeds. It had been a while since he had done anything notably crazy, and now, he began to feel left out. Stephen became determined to cast himself into the limelight as well—and in a big way this time.

Out of all my brothers, I loved Stephen the most. It's not that we had a close bond or got along by any means; if anything, Stephen and I were rivals. We were rivals on many levels. Sadly, with me being his older brother, I could easily dominate him in almost every challenging situation, and if I couldn't beat him on the stage, I would beat him up in person. Unfortunately, each time I wailed on him, I walked away feeling sick for what I had done. Years earlier, during a week-long stay at summer camp, I tackled him to the ground and beat on him in front of all our friends. My God, why did I do that? I felt nauseous for a long time afterward. If this was merely sibling rivalry, I wanted no further part of it.

On the outside, Stephen and I were so different, but on the inside, we were so much alike. We both had a spirit that yearned day and night, 'I want to live' and we played that out day by day. Unfortunately, we both lived in the shadows of our older brothers, and we vied for the same attention they had garnered from the rest of the family and our neighborhood friends. We felt like we always played second fiddle to Peter, Kit, and Phil. Another thing we shared was the great insecurities that we harbored. We constantly lived with feelings that we weren't good enough, and because of that, we had to spend twice the energy to get any attention. To make matters worse, if we both failed at things, we failed incredibly. Despite our external differences and living in the shadows of our older brothers, I loved Stephen the most because we had the same demons inside. As the years passed, it began to weigh on me more and more on how mean I was to him over our childhood.

Stephen

The new school year had already begun, and for a short time, Phil kept his distance from the Turbak residence as Craig's busted kneecap healed. Indian Summer (as we called it back then) fell upon us. The morning air grew gradually crisper, and the nights grew noticeably colder, but in all the hours in between, the days continued with the warm, brilliant sunlight and spectacular blue skies. It seemed that true summer would never end. With almost a bang, Autumn besieged the valley as the trees bent to the indomitable will of the season. October arrived with the leaves on the maple trees turning bright yellow. Also, high on the mountain ridges above the town, the needles on the Tamarack trees followed suit with their spectacular bright colors. The mood among the neighbor kids followed suit as well. The thriving, carefree outlook on life that we all shared became slightly more somber. All of us brothers were now entering our teenage years. We were coming of age. We searched for broader horizons in our little, sheltered community. The town grew increasingly smaller for us as our adolescent statures grew larger.

October started to creep by faster than we anticipated. Timmy had joined Bert Hoover and me on many a night as we threw rotten apples and mushy plums at passing cars. Meanwhile, Stephen galivanted around our neighborhood on his own, trying to find his own patch of sky. By the second week of October, Stephen's birthday had arrived like a surprise telegram. We had ten different birthdays each year to remember (and that didn't include our father's (no one really knew when he was born). This time around, only two people remembered Stephen's—Stephen and our always-faithful mother. Our mother never missed a beat in her duties, and as usual, she prepared a round of neatly wrapped gifts for Stephen that came directly from the Sears and Roebuck warehouse. In our home, the Sears catalog, especially the Christmas Wish Book, was the most used paperback; forget the bible, the Catholic priest would tell us what that was all about.

On the evening of Stephen's birthday, most of the available family and a few friends from the neighborhood gathered around our kitchen table. Our mother laid out Stephen's presents on the table, along with the thickly frosted chocolate cake. On this birthday celebration, I looked down upon my little brother and witnessed him savoring a brief moment of personal glory. With a smile on his face, he absorbed the much-needed attention. It was his moment in the sun. A brief wave of emotion, a light melancholy, swept over me. While I openly cheered him on, along with all the others around the table, I still reeled inwardly from all the times I had been so unkind to him. However, we all kept our feelings to ourselves. From birth, all of us children were taught not to display our emotions, so we never did. We never cried at funerals, we never got watery eyes during sad movies, and our parents never directly told us they loved us. We were to take love and sorrow for granted. With this implied protocol among the family, I stood around Stephen and his birthday cake and realized our bond.

As we sang Happy Birthday to him, his eyes twinkled briefly as he became lost in some distant thought. I could see, for an instant, he became mesmerized by some irresistible vision. It could have been the idea of finally becoming a teenager, or knowing him and his modus operandi, he was thinking of something crazy. In his mind's eye, he conjured up magnificent images of conquest, images akin to the great explorers or mighty generals of centuries gone by. After a moment, Stephen snapped out of his short-lived trance and blew out his candles. I could tell by some strange intuition that he made an internal commitment to push the limits of his manhood, somehow, someway.

After his party ended, he played with his gifts. I watched and began thinking more about my wonderful brother. I believe that all the conditioning of the past was finally catching up with him. I had gotten many spankings for all my pranks, but wondered if he got more than I did. I remembered how many times in the past, Mom had caught him in the middle of some heinous act and how she would grab the nearest thing to beat him with. Usually, it was a tennis shoe because the flat-soled, white-tipped J.C. Penny specials cluttered the floors in both of our bedrooms, and they were so readily available. Unfortunately, none of the spankings stopped him from continually seeking more mischief. On this birthday, he secretly vowed to himself that he would no longer live in the shadows of his brothers. Stephen had to make a name for himself, not only in the Major family folklore, but also in town history.

That night, after tearing open all his presents and devouring a huge slice of his chocolate cake, Stephen climbed into bed and planned the most daring stunt he could pull off in broad daylight.

The next day after school, I came home and dumped out a box of old circuit boards onto my top bunk and began looking for parts for a new transmitter I was building. Stephen suspiciously walked through the room and carefully opened the door to Phil's room. I detected something odd about him; it was the way he paused before he slowly turned the door handle and hesitantly stepped into the next room. He looked over his shoulder, and our eyes met for a split second. "What?" I almost yelled out but held my tongue. Stephen disappeared for a minute. He crept across the other room and up to Phil's dresser. He opened the top drawer, reached inside, and snatched a 100-pack of Black Cat firecrackers from his older brother's war chest. He hid the firecrackers behind his back as he exited Phil's room. He made his way through our room and back out into the kitchen, all without me knowing what he had just done.

A few minutes later, I gave up working on the circuit boards. I knew that the transistors I needed weren't there. I would have to buy them at the local Radio Shack. I put the box of circuit boards away and decided to head uptown to see my friend Dizzy Dean. Dean was always up for action, as he always said: "I am looking for some action," or "Let's go find some action." Action was always his operative word. With that in mind, I left the house and started my trip across town to Dean's grandpa's house, where he spent many days. Without my knowledge, Stephen had already begun his march across town as well. I was surprised to find him standing on the street corner by Dean's place.

"What are you doing here?" I asked.

"Nothin'," he replied.

I knew he was up to something because he stood there so nervous, so conspicuous. His eyes scanned the street from one end to the other. Stephen acted really weird.

"Well, I'm going to Dean's," I told him.

Just before I walked away, Stephen finally broke down and said, "Hey, go get Dean, and then watch what I am going to do."

Stephen started to grin. He reached inside his shirt and pulled out a large pack of firecrackers still wrapped in red waxed paper. I didn't want to miss out on whatever Stephen was going to do. He waited while I ran up the steps and knocked on Dean's door.

When Dean answered, I yelled, "Hey, get your ass out here now! Steve's gonna do something crazy."

"All right, give me a second. I've been looking for some action."

Dean shut the door and followed me up to the street corner, where Stephen stood with his explosives.

"Wait here," Steve told us.

Dean looked at me and shrugged his shoulders as if he wanted an explanation from me. Hell, I didn't know what Steve had planned.

Steve looked both ways, then ran across the street. Dean and I waited on the corner as Stephen marched further up the sidewalk, past the library, then disappeared around the corner. When he reached the other side of the big, blue building, He scanned the perimeter. When he felt that the moment was safe, he crouched down like a monkey and slinked along the sidewalk behind the cement parapet. The cement wall protected the walkway up to the front door. Stephen hoped he would not be seen by the personnel sitting behind the desks on the other side of the large windows. At the end of the walkway, he finally got down to his hands and knees and slowly pushed the glass door open with his shoulder. Up above him, a large insignia filled up most of the glass. The letters circling the emblem read, 'Kellogg Police Department'.

With the firecrackers now in his left hand, Stephen fumbled into his pocket with his right one to find a wooden match. Stephen slinked through the first door but still had about six more feet to go. At the end of the small foyer lay another glass door, and to his fortune, this one was propped open by a rubber door stopper. Steve could hear the muffled voices of two people talking, and in the distant background, he could also hear the sudden crackling of a two-way radio. He paused and held his breath, hoping to avoid being discovered this close to his ambush.

As the voices continued, Steve exhaled and ever so gently, unwrapped one end of the firecracker package. He struck a wooden match on the concrete wall and lit the cluster of fuses. Once they sparkled to life, he lobbed the entire pack through the open doorway. The firecrackers landed on a doormat and bounced, sending sparks flying everywhere. Steve got to his feet and ran like hell out the entrance and down the walkway to the street. He sped around the corner and came running at high speed toward Dean and me.

Back at the police station, the firecrackers exploded violently in what seemed like machine gun fire. Inside, near the back wall, a female police dispatcher sitting in front of a large, desk-mounted microphone jumped out of her chair and dove down to the floor. The uniformed officer who manned the front desk flinched back and held his hands up to protect his face from the explosions. Everyone in the building believed they were attacked by some fearless outlaw. The firecrackers continued to explode, sending tiny shreds of confetti into the air in all directions like a New York City ticker tape parade. A thick cloud of blue smoke filled the police headquarters. The last firecracker finally exploded, and then there was silence.

Even from half a block away, Dean and I could hear the muffled popping sounds of the firecrackers. The staccato blasts echoed out the station's front door and reverberated between the buildings of uptown Kellogg. Stephen continued to frantically run towards us with his arms pumping away and feet crashing onto the pavement. When he leaped off the curb and into the street, he nearly tripped and fell but pulled out of it and kept running. He bolted across Division Street and through the traffic, almost getting hit by a car. The driver of one of the vehicles slammed on his brakes and blew the horn. Steve sprinted up to us and came to a screeching halt. He bent over, putting his hands on his knees, huffing and puffing uncontrollably. He finally lifted himself back up and looked right at me and Dean. A huge smile spread across his face. He outdid us all.

"You did it, didn't you?" Dean asked, knowing exactly what Steve had done. "You bombed the police station, didn't you?"

Steve didn't answer. He merely nodded his head in a grim confession, then burst out laughing. He knew that he had just become a legend. He basked in the idea that word would get around the neighborhood, and especially at school. The word would spread like wildfire.

Although Officer Dugan regained his composure after the explosions ended, he ran outside but could find no sign of Stephen. The gods must have been on Stephen's side because even during his slow crawl up the sidewalk on one of the busiest streets in town, and up the walkway to the entrance to the police station, no one had noticed him at all. Even more so, after the explosions had started, still, no one paid any attention to him running madly down the street like a fleeing prison escapee. The incident would go unsolved and sit in the Kellogg Police Department's cold case files forever.

Chapter 10

The Dummy

Phil and Craig had returned to the cliff several times and tried a few makeshift delayed fuses of their own. They tested the old World War II trick of using a book of paper matches and a cigarette as a delayed timer for their fireworks. Unfortunately, their successes were minimal. One day, Peter came home and overheard them talking about it. He decided to help them solve the main problem. He pulled up a chair to the kitchen table and, like a crime scene investigator, began to ask questions. What went wrong with the fuse night that Craig busted his kneecap wide open?

During the exploratory phase of their discussion, Peter had a flash of insight. He anxiously asked, "Wait a minute. What color stripe did the spinner cord have on it?"

"I don't know. All I remember is that it was green, and I think it may have had a red stripe on it."

"A red stripe! Holy shit! That's the problem."

"What's the problem?"

"Crap. I never thought about this. There are three kinds of spinner cords. The one with the red strip is the fast burning. The stuff with the purple stripe doesn't burn as fast, but the one with the blue stripe burns slow like a normal fuse."

"So, you gave us the wrong cord?"

"Ah, suck! Yeah, I did. Dammit! Sorry about that." Peter never used the actual word 'fuck'. He thought that if he used a euphemism, God would be more lenient on him when it came time for him to either enter the Pearly Gates or be sent to the bad place. However, saying 'suck' all the time instead of 'fuck' just sounded stupid.

After discovering the cause of the earlier disaster on the cliff, Phil didn't know whether to be mad at Peter or let it slide as a natural mistake; either way he felt elated and now grew overly enthusiastic about the future possibilities. If they could only get the proper fuse, the cliff shows would instantly be vaulted to a brand-new level.

The next day, Peter returned to work at the mine and came home with the correct spinner cord—the slow-burning kind, the kind with the blue strip. With two rolls of the proper fuse, Phil and Craig immediately made up a massive string of firecrackers and bottle rockets. At the very end of the array, they left an ample fuse that would allow them to safely get off the mountain before the mayhem started.

That night, they laid out their assembly around the summit of the cliff. After they lit the fuse, they ran down the side of the hill, and disappeared into the darkness. The fireworks show went off perfectly. They had made it down the side of the mountain and halfway across the flats before the show started. Once again, Mr. Butler stood in his yard and watered his lawn when Phil and Craig burst through the bushes. He noticed the fireworks going off and he noticed Phil and Craig but was too stupid to put two and two together. Every thirty seconds, another pack of firecrackers went off. It was as if a real person was sitting up there and randomly lighting off the crackers and bottle rocks.

As usual, the police arrived minutes later, and shone their spotlights up on the rocky face. They called with their bullhorn for the perpetrator(s) to give themselves up and come down to the road for imminent detention. Phil, Craig, and the rest of us brothers stood in our front yard and laughed so hard at the deceived officers.

After the first extremely successful show, Phil and Craig returned several times over the next few weeks and continuously improved their fireworks displays. They perfected the timing between barrages and used a wristwatch to see how long it took for them to race down the hillside, and to the safety of front yard, and lastly—for the police to arrive.

Like with any high-adrenaline activity, Phil and Craig eventually grew bored with the same old routine and were just about ready to give it up and move on to bigger and better things. Just out of the blue, Phil came up with the mother of all ideas. Maybe, just maybe, they could seriously deceive the police and make them think that someone WAS sitting up there in plain sight the entire time the firecrackers were going off. Maybe they could freak out the police department by giving them a visual target, a conspicuously noticeable culprit. When Phil mentioned it to Craig, their creative juices started to flow.

"Craig, instead of us running down the mountain after lighting the fuse, why don't you just sit out there on the rocks and let the cops come up and try to get you?"

"Are fucking crazy?"

"No. Come on, it would be fun. Let them climb right up to the cliff, and when they are just twenty feet below you, you run. They would never catch you."

"Fuck that shit! Why don't you do it if you think it would be so much fun?"

Phil paused for a moment. He was leading Craig on. Phil had already figured out the plan well in advance. He was only toying with Craig, who would do almost anything Phil dared him to do.

"How about if we get someone else to sit up there and have them wait for the police to climb up the rocks to get them?"

"Who could we get that could be that stupid?"

Phil smiled and nodded his head over and over. He had Craig hooked on the idea.

"Come on, Phil, who could you get to do that?"

"Think about it, Craig; the cops could shine their lights on this guy, shit their pants, and climb up there to make their long overdue arrest." If the cops were to go after someone, Phil would give them that someone. He had the perfect scapegoat in mind.

That following weekend, Phil and Craig rummaged around our house and found a series of items: an old sweatshirt, a tattered pair of jeans, a pair of worn-out tennis shoes, an old pair of winter gloves, an unwanted baseball cap, and a tattered pillowcase. They didn't have to find a culprit; they were going to build a culprit—a dummy. They were going to do what Dizzy Dean and I had done just a year earlier. We had staged a hanging off the highway overpass on Halloween with a dummy we had assembled, and it went off fabulously. Since Phil had played a part in our hanging by being our wheel man, he remembered it well.

Phil and Craig stuffed the pants and sweatshirt full of balled-up newspapers and used large safety pins to piece him together, just like Frankenstein's monster. They used the pillowcase to make the head. Once they stuffed it and attached to the body, Phil used a black magic marker to draw the eyes, nose, mouth, and ears. Just for effect, Phil drew a cigarette that dangled off of the dummy's lips. You gotta do it right, ya know. The final touches came with the attached shoes, gloves, and the Oakland A's baseball cap.

My mother had no idea what they were up to when she came home from grocery shopping. She simply walked through the back door and into the kitchen. She saw the dummy sitting in a chair at the kitchen table as if he were some distinguished guest. My mother stopped and stared for a moment with a puzzled look. She shook her head and said, "I don't even want to know."

Shortly after unloading the groceries, our mother left again for a teachers' conference. This gave Phil and Craig the perfect time to begin assembling their usual array of firecrackers, bottle rockets, and this time, a couple of Roman candles. They put the entire arrangement together just like an assembly line. At one point, while they performed their handy work, Craig looked over at the dummy and asked, "What are you looking at Fucker?" He then reached up and slapped the dummy along the side of his modified pillow of a head. Craig continued, "I said, what the fuck are you looking at? Mind your own fucking business, Pal!"— "Hey Phil, look at how good this fucker listens. Maybe there's hope for this sad cock sucker after all!" Craig was bad. He used the 'F' word more than anyone on the planet. He seemed to use it in every sentence. Thankfully, he disciplined himself enough not to use it in front of my mom—and rarely at church.

Phil chuckled as he tied another pack of firecrackers onto the fuse. "I don't know Craig. I think he's two bricks shy of a full fucking load. Give that son of a bitch a tipsy." (A tipsy is when one uses their middle finger cocked behind their thumb and flicks someone in the face.)

After finishing the long string of fireworks, they stuffed it all into a large brown paper grocery bag. Craig carried the goodies while Phil grabbed the dummy and threw him over his shoulder. Phil carried the lifeless figure out the back door like a fireman rescuing someone from a burning building. They made their way down to the end of the block, around the corner, and to the base of the cliff. They briskly climbed and soon enough reached the top. When they were done laying out the series of fireworks, they strategically seated the dummy just a few feet over the face of the cliff. The lifeless figure looked down upon the town, totally clueless to the fact that he was being sacrificed. (If only dummies could talk.) Mr. Dummy was placed in the perfect position to be lit up by the police spotlight—and the cops would go crazy at the sight.

Phil lit the fuse, and they hurried down the side of the hill, but this time, instead of running across the expanse of the flats, Phil stopped just on the other side of the road and grabbed Craig by the arm. He halted him and dragged him against his will into a patch of thick brush.

"What the fuck Phil?"

"Shhhh! Listen. When those fuckers come down from the police station and see the dummy, we have to look closely at what they're gonna do."

"Suppose they catch us?"

"They aren't going to catch us. They are going to catch the dummy!"

In the darkness, Craig cracked a huge smile because he trusted Phil and would follow him anywhere into battle. This dynamic would follow the two of them for the rest of their lives.

It wasn't long after the fireworks started for the police to be dispatched to the scene. However, this time, two cars arrived instead of just one. The Kellogg police department must have been desperate to solve these menacing firecracker shows for them to send the additional cruiser. The officers turned their spotlights on and lit up the mountainside. Their beams scanned the base of the cliff, passed over the dummy, then frantically back to it, clearly lighting up Phil and Craig's dear friend. The dummy sat motionless as the firecrackers exploded behind him and the bottle rockets sailed skyward over the top of his head.

Oh fuck, did the police officers ever get excited! They had a live one on their hands! Just think of the promotion they would get if they could only apprehend this bandit. The two of them dropped their donuts where they stood. They salivated. Neither of them had ever caught an actual crook before. They flipped a coin to see who would scale the mountainside and handcuff this dangerous criminal.

Officer Dugan called 'heads' and won the flip. He slowly ascended the side of the mountain with a flashlight in one hand and the other one close to his service revolver. He slipped over and over on the loose rocks below his feet. Eventually, he made it up to the base of the large rock formation. He grabbed at each jetting rock until he had just one more crevasse to climb up. Knowing that the perpetrator was a mere twenty feet above his position, Dugan prepared to jump out and surprise the menace. Just before he made his move, he made the Catholic 'sign of the cross' hoping for God's blessing. The moment of truth came. He stood up and immediately thrust his flashlight forward, illuminating the suspect.

"Freeze, Mister!" Dugan yelled out.

The dummy did as he was ordered.

Dugan almost barked out another order to the dummy but then took a much closer look. Crap! He turned, looked down onto the street, and cupped his hand to his mouth. He yelled down to his partner, "It's a dummy!"

Phil and Craig began to laugh uncontrollably. After regaining his composure, Phil yelled out from the darkness, "Who's the real dummy!" And the cops looked out into the darkness, bewildered.

Dugan didn't bother to use his handcuffs. He merely dragged the dummy down the side of the mountain, threw him in the back of the patrol car, and drove back to the station. He sat behind a desk and began filling out the police report while the dispatcher and the other officers tried to contain their laughter.

Phil and Craig returned home and started another game of Monopoly. It was just another day on Mission Avenue.

Chapter 11

Uncle Bill

Periodically, my Uncle Bill would take a few days off work from his job at United Airlines and fly the short hop from Seattle to Spokane—most of the time landing somewhat inebriated. My older brothers loved to be his chauffeur and took turns driving the hour-long drive to pick him up at the Spokane airport. Every trip we took to pick up our illustrious uncle was exciting as hell because he always showered us with small gifts from United and routinely treated us to a meal at a fast-food restaurant. He urinated in the parking lot several times risking arrest for obscene public exposure. Sometimes, I think he did it just to make us laugh. He loved all of us brothers very much—much more than any of our other cousins and much to our other aunts' and uncles' displeasure. Over the past year, Uncle Bill continually heard the reports of Phil's latest and highly audacious cliff shows. He could only imagine how badly he and Craig must have taunted the local police. There came a breaking point where Uncle Bill could no longer take it. He wanted in on the action, even at the ripe age of forty-two years old.

By the time Bill made it over to Kellogg, the July weather had turned rather hot, and the trees and grass had turned quite dry. Bill spent his first night in town making the rounds in the local bar scene, in a series of stops that he dubbed the 'drunken triangle'. He had only gotten thrown out of one bar that night; typically, it was at least three. When he drank, he would often think about my father. Oh, how he missed my dad, his best drinking buddy. They loved to drink together, but now my father was long gone in Canada. The next best thing to being around my father was to be around his sons—us Major Boys. Although we were too young to drink then, we could go on adventures with him and even cause a little mischief.

The following day, after arriving in town, Bill woke up to a hearty breakfast of biscuits and gravy our grandma graciously made for her boy Billy. (Not hardly a boy. Uncle stood six foot three and weighed nearly three hundred pounds.) He sat at the table, expecting his usual three eggs (not two), and sipped his instant coffee while Gramma's poodle sat at his feet, hoping for a few scraps. After gorging down his breakfast with a few burps in between, Bill bent over, kissed his mother on the cheek, and went outside. He pulled the canvas tarp off his Yamaha 750 road bike. He was ready for a ride and knew his bike was also prepared because my Uncle Bob knew in advance of Bill's arrival. He had already put the freshly charged battery in the Yamaha for him. After that heroic feat, Uncle Bob retired to his room in the attic and fantasized about hunting cats in the neighborhood. He dreamed of crawling through the neighbor's yards on his belly with his old .22 rifle. Uncle Bob's favorite movie must have been the old black and white film, 'To Kill a Mockingbird' because one of the surprise characters in the movie was the spook by the name of Boo Radley—and Uncle Bob resembled that weirdo with his bald head and eyes ten times larger than a raccoon. Rumor had it that Uncle Bob bagged five cats in one night, but his headcount has never been confirmed.

Uncle Bill started his Yamaha and let it warm up for a few minutes while he enjoyed one of his favorite Winston cigarettes. He wore a triple XXX, large-size, white tee-shirt and rolled the pack of cigarettes up in his right sleeve. While he enjoyed every puff of that cigarette, he bathed in his visions of how today's summer ride up the river and over the pass into Wallace would be the greatest, especially with the company of his favorite nephews. Bill savored the 'river runs', as he called them, immensely, whether in a car or on a motorcycle. These excursions brought him back in time to several decades earlier when he and his older brother Bob would hunt on the slopes of Graham Mountain. With these memories freshly unbridled that morning, Bill drove his motorcycle down from our grandmother's house and parked it in the driveway outside our house.

In our living room, my brother Peter held the cereal bowl up to his face and scooped the soggy, milk-soaked cornflakes into his mouth while never taking his eyes off the TV. Nothing would get in the way of him watching his favorite Saturday morning adventure cartoon: 'Johnny Quest'. It took something extra special to divert Peter's attention away from a program he was so engrossed in. The only show that even came close to captivating him in such a way was the weekday reruns of 'Star Trek'.

Just as the Jiffy peanut butter commercial interrupted the morning cartoon, Peter heard the dull rumble of a motorcycle engine just outside the house. Bill purposely revved up the engine to let the sound vibrate the front window before he shut off the engine. Peter jumped up from the couch and pushed the curtains aside from the tall glass window. He smiled as he saw Uncle Bill sitting on his Yamaha 750 road bike. Bill carefully removed his helmet and hung it on one side of the handlebars. He then dropped the kickstand with his left heel. Just as he unrolled his shirt sleeve to retrieve the pack of cigarettes, he looked over and saw Peter standing in the window. A grin spread across Bill's face. He knew that he had gotten Peter's attention.

"Crap!" Peter thought, "Bill's too early. Johnny Quest isn't over yet."

Meanwhile, Phil, combed through the refrigerator and grabbed a popsicle from the freezer. He also heard the rumble of Bill's motorcycle, and just as Phil headed for the front room to investigate, Bill burst through the door and growled, "Okay, Boys, let's hit it!"

"Ah, come on, Bill, give me a few minutes. The show isn't over yet!" Peter pleaded.

"Listen Fucker!" Bill instantly responded, "Forget the God damn show! We made plans."

"I know, but can't you wait for a few minutes?" Peter begged.

"I am not waiting for you to finish some chicken shit cartoon. We are on a mission! Now get your bike ready, and let's get the fuck out of here." Bill ordered.

Phil knew that Peter would never miss an episode of Johnny Quest, so he did his best to cover for Peter. He intervened and distracted Bill. "Hey Bill, I think Turk will be over here any minute. Who else should we get to go with us?"

Bill paused briefly to give a little thought to the invite list. "Anybody you want. Just don't invite that puke, Dizzy Dean. He makes me sick. He gives me double fucking nausea!"

"No problem. Scratch Dean off the list." Phil calmly assured him.

Bill strolled right past Phil and headed out the back door to the serenity of the back porch. He found a chair to sit in, and once seated, he lit a cigarette and enjoyed a nice tar and nicotine-contaminated smoke. Bill could be easygoing when we wanted to be, and this was a choice moment for him to sit back and relax. He was in no hurry. He was just testing Peter. Bill had the next two days off from his baggage handling position at the airlines, but he had to practice being a hard ass on Peter and Phil. It was in his DNA.

By the time Bill finished burning through his cigarette, Peter's favorite Saturday morning television show had ended. Craig pulled into the driveway on his black Honda 400 Hawk with perfect timing. He parked it respectfully right next to Bill's bulky Yamaha cruising machine.

Both Peter and Phil heard Craig pull up in the driveway, and they promptly grabbed their helmets from the washroom bench and shuffled out the back door just like fighter pilots scrambling down the runway to man their planes. Peter and Phil mounted their twin-engine Honda 360s and started them up. As the two engines of their Hondas roared to life, Bill waddled down the driveway and mounted his old, fat,

gold Yamaha 750.

Once all the engines were running and the four bikes sat side-by-side near the street, they all took off across town and headed up the ramp and onto the highway. They cruised west on the interstate for a few miles, then turned up the small river highway. They passed the Bear Creek turnoff that led to Graham Mountain. That is when the flood of memories really flashed through Bill's mind. Peter, Phil, and Craig rode behind Bill, pointing, smiling, and joking, yelling their comments to each other because the oncoming air drowned their communication. At that point in their ride, the four of them found themselves in Heaven.

They continued through the ancient mining towns of Prichard and Murray and eventually came over Moon Pass and down through Wallace. Eleven miles later, they ended up where they started, right back in our driveway. After the pleasant ride, they all retired to the back porch. Bill opened a can of beer with the crisp sound of the pop top coming off. He stayed silent for a while and listened intently as Phil and Craig talked about the latest cliff show, the one with the dummy that had foiled the police. Bill just couldn't take it any longer. He finished a swig of beer and then opened his eyes really wide. "Hey, Phil, can you line me up, Buddy?"

As Phil was talking to Craig, he stopped in mid-sentence. He looked over at Bill and asked, "Line you up? What do you mean line you up?"

"I know all about that sneaky shit that you and Scragg pull all the time on that cliff. You think it's pretty fuddy, don't you? Well, give me some of those fucking crackers, and let me pull some of the same shit."

At first, Phil felt totally baffled. What in the hell was Bill talking about? How could fat-ass Bill climb up to the cliff at night, throw some firecrackers, then run from the cops? He was well over three hundred pounds and had a gut the size of a gray whale. Phil finally responded, "You want me to give you some firecrackers?"

Bill exploded. "NO! You dumb son-of-a-bitch! I want you to set me up with a package with all the same goodies you use on the cliff. Have it all hooked up to that delayed dynamite fuse, just like your shit. I got some freakin' payback to do."

Phil finally understood. "Okay, I can make you up something with crackers and bottle rockets, but where do you plan to light it off?"

Bill grew more agitated and responded in his famous gruff voice, "That's none of your fucking business! Can you line me up, or can't you?"

"Okay, okay!"—" I will line you up this afternoon.

A few hours later, after performing some of their handy work on our kitchen table, Phil and Craig drove their Hondas to up our gramma's house. They drove right up to the front porch and shut off their engines. Phil pranced up the steps, carrying a large paper grocery bag. Surprisingly, he looked up to see Bill sitting at the far end of the porch, wearing a United Airlines baseball cap and a dark pair of aviator sunglasses. Bill grinned at Phil, then took a large swig from a twelve-ounce can of Hamm's beer. When he saw the giant paper bag, he knew Phil had pulled through. Bill relished the thought of what he planned to do. Phil walked right up to Bill and presented the gift to the King.

"Here ya go, Bill. Don't spend it all in the same place."

Bill reached out and took the bag from Phil, "That's just terrif." (Bill created his own vernacular just like mine had.)

Bill opened the bag and took a peek. Inside lay a very neatly coiled array of firecracker packs, bottle rockets, and a couple of whistling Piccolo

Pete's. They were tied together with nearly thirty feet of dynamite cord and ample fuse to give Bill some getaway time, wherever he decided to light it off. Phil's instructions were straightforward. All Bill had to do was light the end of the fuse and get the fuck away. Neither Phil, Craig, nor Uncle Bill knew where he would light off the sacred sack full of pyrotechnics. All Bill knew was that he was going to do it.

With bag in hand and feeling completely content, Bill took charge of the porch like a general. "Why don't you boys grab yourself a beer to settle your nerves. You're making me jumpy."

As the three of them sat there sipping beer, it didn't take long for an idea to galvanize in Bill's brain. He wanted in on the action alright, but he had to outdo his nephews, somehow, someway. His act had to be one so audacious, so flagrant, that it would shine in his memory for years to come. A light bulb suddenly lit up in his head. It was time to act. Bill rose like a sleeping giant, ready to climb down the bean stock. He motioned to Phil and Craig. He pointed at the motorcycles like a crewman guiding a jet airliner to its gate. They had never seen Bill move so swiftly.

The four of them scrambled off the porch and climbed onto their bikes. This time, it was Bill who held the paper bag between his legs. They drove three blocks down to Market Street and made a left turn. One hundred and fifty feet further, Bill turned into the alley and stopped his motorcycle behind the newspaper building. The spot that he chose could not have been more precarious. Behind him, directly across the street from the newspaper office, lay the fire department. Three fire trucks were parked inside the large bays. My God! This is where Bill wanted to light off the package?

He had picked a near-perfect position to lay a barrage on the heart of the Kellogg establishment. That same building also housed the library and the Kellogg police station. Bill would go for the jugular and do it in broad daylight. He was virtually going to do the exact same thing that my younger brother Stephen had done—an all-out frontal attack. How much more abuse could the Kellogg Police and Kellogg Fire Department sustain from the local heathens?

Bill surveyed the area carefully, then set the paper bag on the ground. He waved for Phil and Craig to take off and clear the area. When they hesitated, he frantically pointed his finger up the alley for them to keep going as if he were the head of a Navy Seal team. They both looked back as they idled slowly past him and then up the alley. Bill laid the paper bag on the ground, then puffed off his cigarette. He bent over and touched the glowing cigarette to the end of the fuse. The fuse burst into a sparkling orange glow. Bill immediately put his bike back in gear and drove up the alley after Phil and Craig. The dynamite cord burned and burned for nearly thirty seconds as the three of them got away. Then, all hell broke loose.

Uncle Bill

By the time the three of them made it to the safety of our grandmother's driveway, small, distant explosions could be heard across the community. Along with them came the whistling noises of the bottle rockets shooting out of the burning, tattered paper bag. Some of them shot skyward, and some of them shot down the alley before they exploded in front of the fire department. Meanwhile, Phil and Craig burst into wild laughter in the driveway as Bill sat on his motorcycle, quietly smoking away. Bill glowed brighter than the burning cherry on the end of his cigarette. He had finally gotten in on the action.

Several firefighters scrambled out the fire station door and stood at the edge of the street just feet away from the maelstrom. The staccato popping sound of the firecrackers exploding through what was once a large paper grocery bag continued while the remaining fireworks kept going off. The firefighters dared not to go near the spectacle—not yet. Eventually, the last of the firecrackers went off as several stray bottle rockets launched themselves. One rocket shot along the ground and bounced off a garbage can. Another's trajectory shot it directly into the dry grass of the vacant lot next to the newspaper office. It lay there, no longer airborne. Instead, it simply hissed away as the tiny flame ignited the dry tinder. The parched, yellow grass immediately burst into flames. The firestorm quickly spread from blade to blade and from stock to stock of the tall Timothy hay. At first, no one saw the growing blaze. The now calm firefighters stepped off the curb and walked across the street as if they were approaching the O.K. Corral. All that remained in the alley were thousands of tiny shreds of paper from the firecrackers and the still-burning remnants of the shredded grocery bag. To the firefighters, it looked like the show was over. That is, until they walked a bit further and neared the vacant lot. One of them saw the smoke rising from the grass and the orange flames that began to devour everything in its path.

One of them yelled, "Fire!"

The other one yelled, "Holy shit!"

Two of the three spun around and ran back to the fire station at high speed, while the third sprinted into the knee-high grass and began stomping out anything with flames on it. Within a minute, the other two rushed up the alley in a fire truck, with the lights flashing and the siren blaring. They parked it next to the field and frantically began to pull out the fire hoses. It only took a few minutes for the crew to put the fire out, but it was a good drill for them.

Word quickly made its way into the police station that there was trouble across the street. One of the officers on duty burst into Chief Charlie's office and gave him the news: firecrackers again—and with a grass fire this time. Charlie slumped back into his chair, held his forehead with his hand, and asked himself, "Why me? Why me? Why does this have to happen while I am chief?

After all this had transpired, Uncle Bill made his way up the steps to Gramma's front porch. He sat down, lit another fresh cigarette with a cheap paper match, and held it as the flame burned down the shaft. "Sorry sons of bitches," he said, referring to the scrambling members of the firefighting team. Bill blew out the match before it could burn his fingers. He chuckled with his trademark expression, "Yuk, yuk, yuk!" Believing that the charade was now over, he gave Phil and Craig a glorious thumbs-up. Uncle Bill was now a card-carrying member of Phil and Craig's cliff show team.

Chapter 12

Burn Bean

Over several years since grade school, Craig had become the closest thing to being a brother to Phil and the rest of us. As a bonus to their friendship, Phil's efforts to win over Craig's father, the highly respected Gene Turbak, finally paid off. He received Gene's gold-stamped approval, which allowed young Craig to spend as much time with us Major boys as he wanted. Life moved along at full speed. Phil and Craig continued to work together at the local grocery store, and they also continued to serve as altar boys at our local catholic church, all the while continuing the cliff shows. Not to say that Gene Turbak didn't keep a close eye on Craig—he did, and Phil played it cool with Craig because of that. Our family story was different; we didn't have a father around to guide us, let alone punish us. We had to figure it out on our own, what we could get away with and what we couldn't. Ironically, there came times, after wreaking so much havoc, that we often grew bored, and boredom was one of the cardinal sins to avoid at all costs. During those lulls, each of us branched out and found new things to do, and this mad cycle of high to low adrenaline included Craig, our half-brother, just the same.

Craig and his family sometimes lived in a dull but safe routine. However, one weekly activity became almost unbearable for members of both families. The big problem was the church; my God, church was horrible! The Saturday night Catholic mass bored the living shit out of every one of us—all except my mother. She desperately aspired to achieve sainthood and wholeheartedly believed there was nothing more meaningful in life than being a faithful, rosary-bead-praying, fanatical

Catholic. Ultimately, she would go to her grave with her trusted rosary in her hand. While she felt so edified kneeling in that church pew, the rest of us found ourselves stuck in some kind of indescribable hell for an hour every Saturday night. The sick routine of the Catholic Mass gave us enough of a workout that we didn't need to go to any gym. We had to stand up, sit down, kneel down, stand up again—oh fuck, kneel down yet again! When would the crazy, fucking calisthenics ever end, for God's sake?

I was ready to make a fake cast for my leg and bring a pea shooter to church to shake things up a bit. Fortunately, when I thought I had had enough of the tortuous ceremony, Craig broke down first. He didn't bother going into the confessional to say anything about it. Instead, he openly confessed how horrific the Catholic church services were. He didn't need a Catholic priest to spill his guts to; he needed to see a psychiatrist instead. As each weekly church service ended, Craig began to babble on and on about coming up with something new. His ramblings made it evident that he had descended into a personal madness of his own over the mere thought of attending another boring mass. However, just when he could sink no lower, Craig examined the routine at the church and suddenly discovered a particular facet of the service that he could heap all of his frustrations upon. He found the perfect vent.

Anyone familiar with a Catholic mass knows that there comes a part near the end of the service where everyone in the congregation who had made peace with their soul would come forward and receive communion. The parishioners in each row of pews would file out in an orderly manner, form a line, and walk up to the priest to receive 'the body of Christ', or 'host' as they called it. It was merely a wafer, a type of cracker to swallow. It was during this part of the ceremony that Craig noticed something peculiar: one man bothered him.

There just happened to be a magnificent gentleman with extreme devotion to our congregation who acted as an usher at every service: Mr. Tom Bean. Even outside the church, this wonderful chap served as our priest's right-hand man and performed chores for our parish. Although I knew for a fact that Father P.J. O'Sullivan would suck down all the church wine daily and frequent the local bars, I think that Tom Bean laid off the church wine for some reason. It could have been that Father O'Sullivan wouldn't share any of it with him, but I think Tom stuck straight to pickle juice because his breath was just plain horrible. I don't know about his wife's breath because I never got close enough to her to find out. I especially do not mean to discredit his wife by any means because Mrs. Bean was as wonderful as her husband, Tom. She served faithfully in the meat department at the local Stein's IGA grocery store, always with a smile, and it's true: behind every great man is a great woman.

The pickle breath was my beef with Mr. Bean, but it wasn't Craig's. Something else, some tiny, almost unnoticeable habit of Tom's, drove Craig insane. Why did Craig have to get so bent out of shape over some little habit of Mr. Bean? He was a pillar in the community and could never hurt a flea, but what he did near the end of every church service bothered Craig to no end. Before I get to that, I must confess a grievance of my own.

Several people in the congregation bothered the shit out of me just the same. For example, old Mrs. Migraine sat behind us with her wig and huge dough face that looked like President Nixon high on a mix between steroids and meth. Worse than her looks were her perfume. She must have dumped half a bottle of it on herself before she put on her wig, lipstick, and rubber body suit. No one wanted to sit in the pew anywhere near her. So, I was no more to blame than Craig with my own pet peeves. God knew what was in my heart.

The real kicker for Craig was when communion came, and the members of every pew filed out. They walked up to the priest to receive 'the body of Christ.' It was then, after it was almost over with a mere handful of people left, that Tom Bean would show up and make sure that he was the last person in line, every time—and I mean every time! This bothered Craig immensely, and on occasion, he excused himself from the pew and wandered around to the back of the church to try and find a way to beat Tom Bean as the last person in line. Unfortunately, when he could not see Tom Bean anywhere, Craig moved up and took the last position, but miraculously, Tom Bean crawled out of the woodwork and showed up right behind Craig.

"God dammit!" Craig would mutter to himself as he looked over at Phil sitting in the pew next to my mother.

"Fuck, he did it again!" Phil whispered to himself as he looked over at Craig and shook his head, sharing in the frustration.

As time passed, Craig kept getting more unhinged with his obsession to beat Tom Bean. It has once been written that the difference between a psychotic and a neurotic is that a psychotic thinks that two plus two equals five (that's because they are psycho), but a neurotic knows that two plus two equals four—but it bothers the hell out of them! That was Craig, acting truly neurotic. Tom Bean annoyed the hell out of him, although he had done nothing wrong.

Finally, there came a boiling point where Craig could no longer take it. "I'm going to burn that son of bitch!" Craig claimed one Saturday evening. "I am going to burn his ass! I am going to BURN Bean!" To burn means to beat someone at something, to conquer, i.e. to win.

The following Saturday evening, during communion, Craig did not go forward with the family and get in line to see the priest. Instead, he waited until most of the congregation had received 'the body of Christ.' Craig scanned and scanned the church, looking for Bean, but Bean was nowhere to be found. Thinking he would finally seize the moment, Craig stepped into the aisle and walked up as the last person. He looked back at Phil and smiled from ear to ear. Craig truly believed that he had just won the last place in line for communion, but as soon he took his position, Tom Bean was instantly teleported from another dimension and appeared right behind Craig.

"For fucks sake!" Craig whispered to himself after he looked behind him and noticed Bean.

Phil, Tim, Stephen, and I sat in the pew and chuckled.

After church that night, Craig came over to our house to play a few hands of poker. Regardless of how much fun we were having, he couldn't get Tom Bean off his mind, no matter how hard he tried. "I am going to burn that son-of-a-bitch! I am going to burn him!" Craig kept repeating over and over.

'Yeah, burn Bean Craig. You can do it." Phil jeered.

After that evening, and with no surprise, every day that week when Craig came over, he just had to mention how he was going to "burn Bean." We laughed each time and looked forward anxiously to see what Craig had planned for the next mass. We wanted to know how he was going to "burn Bean."

As usual, we entered the church the following Saturday night and filed into our pews. Craig walked in with his family, and they began to enter the pew right in front of us. He stepped into our pew just as he was ready to walk past us. He bent over and whispered to Phil, "Watch. I am going to burn that son-of-a-bitch for sure tonight." He then joined his family as any good Catholic boy would.

Craig Turbak

Mass went on as usual. We stood up. We knelt down. We sat back in the pew. We stood up again. We knelt down. We sat down again and did it a hundred thousand times until it came time for communion. Just as the first row of pews began to line up in front of the priest, Craig excused himself, telling his mother that he had to go to the bathroom.

Row after row of people filed out and went before the altar. Eventually, there was virtually no one left to get in line, and once again, Tom Bean was nowhere to be seen—and neither was Craig. He still had not come back from the bathroom. It was getting late. Craig had better act fast, or he would miss communion and probably burn in hell. When only six people were left in line, Tom Bean seemed to pop out of a time warp. He appeared out of thin air, just like he always had. Tom slowly approached the end of the line with his hands piously held together as if he were in prayer. Phil and I wondered what happened to Craig.

I looked around the church. Then suddenly, I spotted Craig tiptoeing up behind the far-back pews. He stepped so slowly, as if he were walking on eggshells. When he got to the central aisle, he suddenly bolted forward, raced down, and took up a position right behind Tom Bean. He had done it! He had burned Bean (figuratively speaking, that is).

While the rest of us sat in the pew laughing, Craig solemnly stepped closer and closer to the priest. There were now only four people left to receive communion, then it became three, and just like something out of a comedy movie, Craig reached into his right pocket and fished for something. He pulled his hand back out. Craig looked right over at Phil and me. He motioned with his head for us to look down at Tom Bean's ass. Craig produced a cigarette lighter and ignited a flame. He hovered the burning lighter right below Tom Bean's butt. Having made his point, Craig extinguished the flame and stuck the lighter back into his pocket. Tom Bean, with a pure heart, received his communion. Craig was next. He folded his hands in front of Father P.J. O'Sullivan and said "Amen" as the priest presented him with 'the body of Christ' and laid it on his tongue. Craig was now a brother to the Lord. Surprisingly, with all the heads bowed in deep reflection at this point in the service, no one had noticed Craig holding the cigarette lighter below Tom's butt.

Craig rejoined his family in the pew in front of us and kept looking back at Phil, Steve, Tim, and me. He smiled bigger than he ever had. He had finally burned Bean!

It would take a few years for anyone to top what Craig had just done. He had outdone us all. Looking back at the record: Phil had already taunted the police for several years with his cliff shows, Stephen had blown up the police station, Dizzy Dean and I had hung a dummy off the highway overpass in the middle of town on Halloween, and Uncle Bill had terrorized the fire department. After all this was over, I had a premonition. I think my youngest brother, Tim, might surprise us all in the coming days.

Chapter 13

Joe Mandoli versus the Cops

We spent the summer again with our father in the Canadian wilderness and came back at the very end of August. After a couple of weeks into the new school year, I became highly engrossed in another electronic project—my biggest one yet, a robot. One night, I grew so exhausted after reading the chapter on how to wire in the microprocessor in my robot's brain. After I fell asleep that night, Joe Mandoli and his friend Danny pulled up to the curb in front of Joe's house. They had been cruising up and down the valley for hours that night in Danny's CJ5 Jeep and drinking vast amounts of beer while listening to acid-rock music. As soon as they came to a stop, Danny reached up to the steering column and turned the ignition off. The engine rumbled down and slowly died. He looked over at the passenger seat and saw Joe hanging his head. It bobbed and bobbed—too much alcohol, for sure.

They both straightened up in the newly found silence and leaned back in the black leather bucket seats. Joe raised his beer bottle to his lips and took another swig. He was on the verge of passing out. Tonight's trip was rather lengthy. They had even ventured up to Mullan and returned through Wallace. They had finally made it home to Kellogg, and they had done all of this on a school night. They were both as drunk as two high school sophomores could be.

With nothing more said between them, Joe leaned forward in his drunken stupor. He attempted to come across as very aware as he peered through the windshield, looking down the lifeless street of Mission Avenue.

While Danny clumsily lifted his beer to his lips like his drunk friend, Joe panned his head around and gazed in the opposite direction at the far end of the street behind them. Suddenly, he stopped and stared over at our house, which lay almost directly across the street from his. Right there and then, Joe forgot all about the girls he was chasing. He forgot about the wild music they had listened to and all the beer they had drunk. The sight of our house evoked years of memories. They all flashed through his mind like people who had faced death and had their entire lives pass through their very eyes. Joe thought of all the crazy stuff that we, the Major brothers, had done and continued to do. The mere thought of all our shenanigans began to bother him deeply. He felt a great urge to do something to show us that he had just as much spunk as we brothers did.

"Danny!" he whispered.

With no response, he whispered even louder, "Danny!"

Danny snapped out of his daze. "What?"

"Let's do something nuts."

Danny paused momentarily to allow the idea to register in his head slowly. "What do you mean? What do you mean by nuts?"

Joe began to shake his fist at something out in the darkness. He struggled to find the right words. Finally, he pointed out at some invisible enigma, "I just feel like stirring up some shit."

Danny dropped the beer bottle from his lips and almost spat out everything in his mouth. "What the fuck? Now? Right now? This time of night?"

"I have something in mind."

"Like what?"

Joe suddenly reconsidered, "Ah hell! It doesn't involve you."

Danny sighed, "Good. Because I am getting home before my dad gets pissed and takes the jeep away."

"You do it. I am out of here. I am going to do it!"—" Well, what are you waiting for? Get the fuck home.'"

"I would love to if you would only get the fuck out of my jeep,"— "And whatever you do, don't get caught."

With a seductively evil look in his eye, Joe leaned slightly over toward Danny. A huge smile spread across his face. He boasted, "They ain't never gonna get me. I'm Evil Joe, the craziest bastard this valley has ever seen!"

Embracing his instant flash of inspiration, Joe knew exactly what he would do when he said he wanted to 'stir up some shit'. He didn't need Danny. He was going to handle this one off himself.

After taking the last swallow of beer, Joe threw the empty bottle into the back seat of the jeep and opened the door. "Take it easy, Danny. I gotta go."

Minutes later, with Danny long gone, Joe stood in his upstairs bedroom. He rifled through the top drawer of his dresser. Somewhere under his underwear and socks, he found eight packs of firecrackers and at least ten M-80 bombs that he had saved since summer. Joe started stuffing them into his jacket pockets. "The sleepy town of Kellogg wasn't going to be sleepy much longer," he thought.

Meanwhile, Joe's mother and father were fast asleep downstairs in their bedroom. In their deep slumber, they believed that their innocent Joey was home safe and secure from all the horrible dangers that lurked in the outside world. Their saintly son Joey could never do any wrong nor hurt anyone or anything so much as a flea. They never thought for a moment that an imposter of a teenager lived in their home.

Just before leaving his room and shutting the light off, Joe opened his nightstand and snatched an unopened pint bottle of peach brandy. He stuck it into his back pocket like slapping a six-shooter into a holster. Joe knew better than to be caught without a nip when great ideas needed to be carried out. His catchphrases were 'never run out of toilet paper' and 'never run out of booze'. Luckily, at the last minute, Joe remembered to shut his nightstand to hide the latest edition of the pornographic Hustler magazine he had just stolen from the grocery store. Leaving his bedroom safely, Joe tiptoed down the carpeted stairs. He stealthily stepped out of the house and quietly shut the door behind him, an easy feat he had accomplished many times before.

Joe pranced through his front yard, then walked inconspicuously down the sidewalk. He disappeared around the corner that led the short distance to the base of the cliff. Joe stopped twice to pull the cap off the bottle of brandy and take a gulp. Within a minute, he stood under the last streetlight on North Hill Street. The road continued from there into the darkness, up to the end of the gulch. He stopped there and looked up at the foreboding geological wonder that we all knew as the 'cliff', not quite as impressive as the Swiss Eiger or Africa's Mt. Kilimanjaro, but impressive just the same.

With the small cliff looming in front of him and faintly glowing from the reflected lights from the city, Joe fumbled in one of his coat pockets and pulled out a crumpled pack of cigarettes. He stuck a partly bent Marlboro into his mouth, and with one strike of a match, he was smoking just like any adult. The logo on the pack of matches read: 'U & I Rooms, Wallace, Idaho'; a souvenir from one of the most famous whore houses in Wallace that lay just eleven miles up the valley from Kellogg. It's not that Joe had visited that particular house of sin; he just happened to be in possession of one of their token advertising tools. Good little Joey would never allow himself to go to a place like that.

The great moment had finally come. Joe veered off the road and scrambled up the rocky slope toward the jetting rock formation. In his drunken state, he stumbled and slipped with nearly every step, at times almost falling backward. With each loose footing, he swore at the rocks beneath his feet, "Mother fucker! You dirty mother fuckers! I dare you to try it again fuckers!" he screamed out.

The swearing must have done the trick because he never fell to the ground. Instead, he finally made it to the rocky crevasses that stood between him and the summit. With his fingers and sheer diabolic determination, he found small cracks in the rock which he used to claw at and pulled himself higher and higher. In his mind, his pride soared because he was not only following in the footsteps of my brother Phil and his accomplice Craig Turbak, but he was also going to show the world that he was just as good as they were.

Joe finally reached the top and turned around to look down upon the majesty. Ah! The glow of the hundreds of streetlights! After one last puff on his cigarette, he glanced down at the valley and looked from east to west, trying to spot any patrolling police cars, not to avoid them, but to attract them. That's what he wanted: police cars—and lots of them.

Breathing hard from the climb and needing another drink, Joe again pulled the brandy bottle out from his back pocket. His imagination ran wild. He held the bottle up to his mouth, tilted his head back sharply, and swigged aggressively. He then ripped the bottle away as if he was acting out a climatic scene on a Hollywood set and saying something to the effect of, "My dear Kellogg . . . I don't give a damn!"

Joe had watched too many of Phil's cliff shows and could no longer let his friends from across the street steal all the glory. He would send a wave of terror across that town that not even the Majors could top—Hell or high water!

Relishing the thought of his soon-to-be-achieved glory, he reached into his jacket pocket, pulled out another tattered cigarette, and lit it up. Next, he pulled out the first pack of firecrackers. He pulled back the paper, exposed the fuses, and stuck the glowing end of the cigarette up to it. Once the fuse sparked to life, he threw the entire pack down the hillside.

Seconds later, the popping sounds of the explosions rocked the neighborhood below. What sounded like a machine gun firing, echoed up and down the entire length of Italian Gulch, and throughout the neighborhood. With the last of the firecrackers going off, Joe dropped down and squatted behind a large boulder. He laughed wildly as he peaked over, looking down at the streets below. He spun around, sat on the ground, and leaned back against the boulder. Just then, Devon appeared, sitting across from him; a shady character that Joe knew well. No one in the neighborhood had ever really seen Devon. They just knew of him and didn't like the seedy reputation that preceded him.

"Joe, you crazy fucker!" Devon shrieked.

"Did you just see that?" Joe replied like a little kid who had just pulled on the ponytails of a pretty girl in his kindergarten class.

"Yep. You better do more than just that."

Joe smiled deviously over at Devon and glowed with great pride. Devon and Joe looked as if they could be brothers. They both had longer, dark, rebellious hair and looked like lead guitarists in a hard rock band. However, Devon had a slightly rougher look than Joe. He wore his trademark tattered jean jacket that sported patches promoting anarchy. One patch even read: 'Born To Be Wild', while another displayed a single, green marijuana leaf.

Devon dug into one of the breast pockets of his jacket and pulled out a rolled-up cellophane sandwich bag. He unrolled it and pulled out a single, crudely rolled joint. He placed it between his lips, then pulled out an old, scratched-up zippo lighter to light it with. As he puffed a few times, a large flame engulfed the end of the joint. Devon slapped the Zippo lighter shut and inhaled deeply, closing his mouth to trap the vapors in his lungs. He handed the joint over to Joe. They sat there for a few minutes without saying much, just taking puffs and passing the joint back and forth between them. Joe waited for another minute for a response from the town. He realized that nothing had really happened after one lone pack of firecrackers, no response at all from the inhabitants below or from the police department.

"Where the hell are the cops?" Joe asked out loud.

"What are you waiting for, Joe? Light this town up. They will be here soon enough."

"No shit! I'm going to."

"Give 'em' something to remember you by Joe. Fuck the Major brothers. They ain't shit compared to you!"

Joe jumped up, lit another pack of firecrackers, and threw it down the rocky slope. Blam, blam, blam, blam! Just as before, the battlefield-like explosions reverberated up the gulch and back down. However, this time, the windows of several houses in the neighborhood began to light up. One door opened, and a man wearing a bedtime robe stepped out onto his porch. Joe peaked down at the houses in absolute delight. He was getting a reaction.

"Good job, Dude! That was awesome. Keep going. You can't stop now." Devon goaded him on.

"Don't worry, I will."

"Yeah, come on Joe, don't be a pussy."

Not wanting to expend all his firecrackers so quickly, and also wanting to savor this precious time on the cliff, Joe delicately took apart the next pack of firecrackers. His tactic now was to lob single salvos down onto the citizens below and draw out their agony as long as he could before he ran out of ammunition.

Over the next several minutes, Joe sent ten single firecrackers down the rock formation, followed dramatically by a fourth hundred-pack of crackers that went off like another machine gun. Finally, a Kellogg police car was dispatched to the scene.

The patrol car arrived at the base of the hill with no siren or flashing lights. It just arrived on time as directed by the chief. Officer Dugan inconspicuously pulled to the side of the road and shut the headlights off. He looked through his window and up at the cliff. He was merely summing up the situation. He hesitantly got out of his car and resumed his look up at the vast rocky formation. He had heard stories of what took place up there.

Joe gazed down at the patrol car with intense thrill. The most profound sense of satisfaction came over him. Joseph Gesepi Mandoli was worthy of all the attention of the police that they could give him. He knew the worst insult in Kellogg for any teenage troublemaker was to be ignored by the local authorities. Joe would not settle for anything short of an all-out manhunt being launched for him and seeing his face on a wanted poster.

Joe Mandoli

"Okay, you bastard!" Joe mumbled as he brought out the big guns. He lit the fuse of a single, high-power M-80 bomb. He heaved it down the hill toward the solitary vehicle. The small, red, cylindrical object bounced a few times, then rolled slowly down the rocks with orange sparkles still shooting off its fuse. Without warning, it exploded with the ferocity of a stick of dynamite. KA-BLAM!! Every window in the neighborhood shook violently. Officer Dugan jumped back and shot his arms up in front of his face to protect himself from the blast. Once the echo faded and the cloud of blue smoke dissipated, Dugan scrambled back into his patrol car and slammed the door. He huffed and puffed desperately trying to recover from the shock wave. He fumbled for the two-way radio microphone. He lost grip of it several times and tried to catch it with both hands as it bounced off the seat and onto the floorboard. When he finally secured the microphone, he pressed the talk button. With his pulse rate soaring and his hands shaking, he called for backup.

"KPD headquarters! KPD headquarters. This is car 27!"

"Go ahead, Car 27."

"This is Car 27 requesting immediate backup. I repeat, request immediate backup!" Officer Dugan wasn't sure what he needed immediate backup for. He was just plain scared.

A moment later, the squad car radio crackled, "Car 27, what is your situation? Over."

Officer Dugan twisted back and forth in his seat in a miniature convulsion. He frantically thought to himself, "What? How dare they question me when I request backup? I mean it! I'm in quite a jam here! Now send the goddamn backup!"

Doing his best to regain his calmness, he pressed the talk button once again and did his best to annunciate, "Ah, I, uh, this is Car 27. I need immediate backup . . . I believe the perpetrator is armed and dangerous. Over."

Just a few seconds passed, but it seemed like an eternity to him. "Damn you, Dispatch!" he blurted out as he looked up through his car windshield, panning left and right, trying to pinpoint the location of the troublemaker. Meanwhile, Joe sat down behind the rock in the shadows, laughing and taking a gulp of brandy from his pint bottle. Devon remained seated in the same spot, smoking another joint, and continuing to coach Joe.

"Come on, Joe, nail that fucker! Light some more and show this guy who's boss."

Joe sent down another barrage, lighting the fuse on yet another one-hundred pack and throwing it down the rocky slope. Before they could explode, Joe stepped up to the cliff's edge, exposing himself fully. He wanted to survey the situation and taunt the stooge hiding inside the police car. Joe raised his arms and spread them as if to say, "Here I am. Come and get me sucker!"

Shattering the silence once again, the staccato-popping sounds of the exploding firecrackers reverberated throughout the neighborhood, causing more lights to come on in once-darkened houses.

Officer Dugan sat helplessly in his car, growing increasingly frustrated while he waited for the cavalry to arrive. Suddenly, his extensive training kicked into action. Like a real pro, he turned the squad car's spotlight on and shone it up at the cliff. He traced the beam from the base of the cliff to the top, then immediately spotted Joe standing on the very edge, looking directly back down at him like Lucifer overseeing the river Styx. "Oh shit! There he is!" Dugan muttered to himself. He had to report this to headquarters.

"KPD headquarters, this is car 27. I have the suspect in sight, a white male, early to mid-twenties, setting off explosives," and just before he could finish his transmission, Joe lobbed down another M-80. It exploded with another thunderous boom, KA-BLAM! The windows in all the houses shook once again. "Send backup immediately! I believe the suspect has a high-power rifle, possibly military in nature. Over."

This time, the dispatcher responded much sooner, "Say again. Are you reporting explosions and gunfire? Over."

"That's affirmative. Over"— "Awaiting instructions. Over" Now Dugan had gotten Headquarters' attention. He was no dummy sent out on patrol. They had sent the right man, and he would prove it.

By this time, many doors throughout the neighborhood had opened, and people had come out onto their porches in their robes to investigate the nature of the disturbance. Meanwhile, back at Kellogg police headquarters, the dispatcher had finally made contact with the Shoshone County Sheriff's department. They had a deputy nearby and were sending him to the scene. Dugan would be saved.

"Stand by car 27, County is responding. A deputy will be on-site shortly. Over" This sounded like music to Dugan's ears. But he wasn't going to take any chances and leave the safety of his car until help had arrived.

Back on the cliff, while Devon cheered, Joe continued raining firecrackers one-by-one down on the neighborhood below—all in the full beam of the police spotlight.

After a few minutes of Dugan shuddering from every exploding firecracker, the county vehicle pulled up behind his squad car. The deputy shut off the engine but kept the flashing blue and red lights swirling away on the top of his vehicle. When Officer Dugan saw the deputy get out of his car, he felt safe enough to get out of his as well. They both met between the vehicles.

"Whatcha got?" the deputy asked.

Dugan pointed up at the cliff, and just as he opened his mouth to speak, another M-80 exploded, sending an ear-shattering shockwave down upon the two of them. Both officers instinctively ducked down behind Dugan's squad car.

"Holy shit!" screamed the deputy.

Dugan was nearly speechless. How could he make himself look like he was in charge of such a bizarre situation? This was his town, but he didn't have a clue as to how to handle things. What would his mother think of him now? Dugan looked at the deputy with total helplessness.

"Fuck it. We've got to apprehend him." The deputy advised.

"Apprehend him?" Dugan asked with a trembling voice.

"Hell, yes. We can't leave a maniac like this on the loose. One of us has to go up there and get them." This directive from the deputy made Dugan shutter. The deputy continued, "Well, maybe we will give him a chance to surrender first."

"Yeh! Let's give him a chance to surrender." It sounded like a novel idea to Dugan.

Just as the deputy returned to his vehicle to call the sheriff's department with a detailed situation report, another set of blue and red flashing lights appeared behind both police vehicles. Tires screeched on the pavement, and the door of this new cruiser immediately opened. The Idaho State Patrol had arrived. They had intercepted messages with reports of explosives, guns, and paramilitary hardware. They wouldn't miss out on this, so they sent their nearest patrolman to the scene. The state patrolman left the lights flashing on top of his interceptor just the same as on the deputy's. He put on his Smokey-the-Bear hat and strolled with a near-perfect military strut to Dugan and the deputy.

"Okay, boys, what's cookin?" he asked, following the spotlight beam up to the top of the cliff with his eyes.

The deputy immediately said, "Well, Sir, we've got some crazy maniac up there terrorizing the place with firecrackers, bombs, and who knows what else."

The trooper listened as he studied the cliff. He saw Joe standing up there, looking down. He quickly identified the young Joey as nothing more than a high school kid.

Joe could not believe his eyes. He saw the three police vehicles and immediately squatted down, taking cover behind the rock formation. The entire time, Devon never seemed to move an inch. He seemed to enjoy the show and loved to jeer Joe on. Joe peeked once again over the jagged precipice and felt delighted beyond measure. This was too good to be true! Not just the local police, but the county, AND the state police as well. "There is a God!" Joe whispered to himself. He then thought the only way to top all this was to bring in the Feds—the FBI.

Joe clenched his fists and yelled, "YES!"

Devon spoke up again, "Okay Joe, Mr. Tough Guy. What are ya going to do next? Don't quit on me now."

Joe didn't respond to Devon this time; the adrenaline was too high. Instead, he rolled over and sat with his back against the rock. Joe pulled out the brandy bottle and took an extra-long gulp, then breathed in and out very deeply. It was time for the final showdown. This was an achievement worth celebrating. After a final drink, the bottle was empty. He took out the last pack of firecrackers, lit the fuse, and stood up in the bright spotlight. He threw the pack downward. Suddenly, a vision flashed through Joe's mind: the scene from the beginning of the movie "Warriors." It is a movie about all the individual gangs of New York who decided to unite and take over the city.

Joe stepped up onto the edge of the rock, spread his arms high in the air, and yelled down at the top of his lungs, "CAN. YOU. DIG IT?"—just as Silas had done in the movie.

The state trooper watched momentarily as the firecrackers bounced down the hill and started to explode. From all the challenging and deadly experiences that he had experienced during his career, this incident was nothing but a joke. He shook his head in disgust.

"Hey guys, I'm out of here," the state trooper declared.

"What?"

"Hell, all you got here is some teenage kid who missed the Fourth of July this year. Handle it! I am out of here." The trooper climbed back into his vehicle, shut off the flashing lights, and slowly pulled away from the scene.

For a moment, Officer Dugan and the deputy looked at each other, both feeling slightly abandoned. As another M-80 exploded and again shredded the night's silence, the two men jointly decided on a plan.

"What's your name, son?" the deputy asked.

"Dugan Sir, Officer Dugan."

"Well, Dugan, here's what we're going to do. Get on your bullhorn and order him to surrender. While you do that, I'm going up there to get him."

Officer Dugan responded to this call to duty by forcing a serious look on his face. He straightened his tie, cleared his throat, and returned to his car. He turned on the PA system and grabbed the microphone. "Now hear this. Now, hear this. Cease all your activity and give yourself up now. I repeat, give yourself up now!"

His words filled the nighttime air and could be heard clearly across town.

The deputy stood reassuringly next to Dugan, pressed his lips together, and nodded, approving Dugan's message. "Okay. I'm heading up. Keep repeating that message once a minute until I get up there."

"What? Wait! What are you going to do?"

"Come on, Dugan. What do ya think? I am going up there and handcuffing that punk. I'm going to bring em' in."

"Oh. Ah, yeh. Got it!"

The deputy headed up the steep, rocky hillside with a flashlight in one hand and a nightstick in the other. Just as Joe had done with his recent ascent, this deputy slipped and stumbled over the rocks with every advancing step, but he was determined to get his man. No punk was going to make a fool out of him.

Joe looked once again over the edge. After seeing the silhouette of the deputy fighting his way up the hill, coming after him, he knew that the time had come to wrap up his circus act.

"You did it Dude! You weren't no chicken shit." Devon congratulated Joe. Surprisingly, he had never bothered to look over the edge the entire time that Joe threw the firecrackers down, nor when the police had arrived.

As a final show of defiance, Joe reached into his pocket and pulled out what was left: two lonely M-80s. Without wasting time, he used the last match from the 'U & I Rooms' matchbook and lit each fuse. He threw both bombs down at the deputy. With his mission completed, he stood up and said to Devon, "It's time to go."

With a dazed and stoned look in his eyes, Devon said in an emotionless, monotone voice, "Yes, it's time to go."

Just before Joe started to leave, he looked down at the lights of his beloved town, then over at Devon. Two humungous explosions shook the cliff, and then the image of Devon slowly faded away until he was no more. Joe took off alone, in a drunken sprint up the side of the hill. Within a minute, he disappeared over the ridge and into the darkness. He was well on his way to safety.

After dodging the last two explosions, the deputy clawed his way up the crevasses. He finally reached the summit but found no one there. The peace officer took a moment in the silence to catch his breath. In a defeated manner, he turned and yelled down the cliff to Dugan, "It's over! He's gone. I'm coming back down!"

While the deputy took his sweet time descending the hill and fantasizing about a fresh jelly donut, Joe hastily made his way over the mountain ridge. Soon he was dropping down into Jacob's Gulch just behind the Kellogg high school. Although scratched up and tattered severely by the thick brush, Joe felt that it was all worth it because no one in our town had ever attracted so much attention from local law enforcement ever—not even the Major brothers.

Back at police headquarters, Car 27 pulled up to the front entrance. The dejected Officer Dugan went inside. The dispatcher instructed him to call the chief as soon as he arrived.

The chief rolled over in his bed and answered the phone. "All right, what happened?"— "And then?"— "Who?"— "How did they?"— "What?"— "You're kidding me."— "Who made that call?"— "Oh. Okay."— "Well, you did what you could. Good job, Dugan." The chief hung up the phone.

The chief's wife, awoken by the phone call, heard bits and pieces of the conversation and just had to ask, "What was that all about, Honey?"

"Oh, nothing, it's just the Major boys at it again."

Chapter 14

Peter Takes Charge

Phil had finally graduated high school (a year behind his peers). After securing his diploma, he enrolled at the Montana School of Mines, just as Peter had done a year earlier. The college had sent a recruiter over to Kellogg to speak with Phil and his good friend Jon Serano, hoping to get them into the fall semester. When the recruiter met with the two of them and realized that Phil's GPA was below a 2.00 and Jon's was teetering on a 1.5, he got really pissed off—angry that is. He had driven nearly four hours to meet with the two flunkies. He was so made at the waste of time that he almost swallowed his tongue. Unfortunately, Phil had been rejected on the spot, not to mention Jon. On the other hand, Peter had completed his first year of college at Montana Tech and had made a name for himself. As a brotherly savior, he stepped in and went to bat for his younger brother. This meant facing the same rigid, steely-eyed dean that he pleaded to the previous year for his own acceptance into the prestigious institution.

As Peter sat in the chair before the greatly revered dean, he gave his pitch with every ounce of his heart and soul. "Think about it. The most successful people in life aren't the ones who get the A's in school. They are the ones who get the C's but go on to exceed in ways beyond belief. They are the ones who get the real A's in life. How many times has the person voted most likely to succeed in a high school poll goes on to become a nothing?" Peter explained with great intensity.

The dean sat back in his chair without saying a word. He merely gestured with an almost undetectable nod of agreement. He wanted Peter to continue. He liked what he was hearing.

"Think about the superstars in life. They struggle and fail a million times but never give up. They have something to prove to themselves and prove to the world." Peter became wound up. He stood up from his chair and pointed out the window to some imaginary place off in the horizon. He continued, hoping to tug at the dean's heartstrings. "Both Phil and I had it rough. We had a father once, who was no real father, but then, what father he was, he left us—nine of us. He left us all alone, and we had to make it on our own. Do we have something to fight for? Do we have something to prove to the world? Ya damn right we do!"

Peter had made his argument and spoke no more.

The cold, calculating, methodical dean looked down at his desk in deep thought. After what seemed like several minutes, he looked back up at Peter and said, "Okay, I'll give him a shot, but for only one semester. If he passes the probation period, I will give him another."

Peter slowly sat back in his chair and solemnly hung his head for a moment. He then looked back up at the dean. "Thank you. Thank you very much. I guarantee you that he won't let you down."

Before the dean released Peter, he added, "Okay, let's see what type of superstar your brother really is."

The gracious dean was never to be forgotten by Philip or Peter for what the chance he had given them. They would never forget his name. The dean was none other than the Honorable William Van Matre, Montana Tech's Dean of Science and Engineering.

With Phil now officially admitted to the college for the fall semester, he and Peter went straight to work at a local mine in the Silver Valley. They worked themselves to death for the entire summer and earned enough money to pay for their whole year's tuition, rent, groceries, and other expenses. During that fall semester and with much effort, Phil passed his probation period and earned another precious semester. Time flew by, and the school year had ended. They returned to slaving away in the mines for another summer until the fall semester began. This year, Phil was no longer on probation.

Peter threw himself into his studies as hard as ever, exiling himself to his upstairs bedroom in the old Victorian house that he, Phil, and a few other students had rented. They called their place at 522 Granite Street 'Animal House'. Every day after school, Peter robotically went upstairs, put on headphones, and religiously listened to his most inspiring record: the soundtrack to the classic Clint Eastwood movie The Good, The Bad, and the Ugly. The droning of the music thrust Peter into a state of pure euphoria. In his mind, he painted images, complete in every detail, of how glorious his life was to be, and with every fantasy constructed perfectly according to his carefully prepared mental script. He was the new global hero emerging from an obscure family with an eccentric father who rivaled the likes of Rasputin. Armed with his visions that would be backed by his accomplishments as a freshman and sophomore, he pushed himself relentlessly harder. He had to be the best in class and in any extracurricular activities that he could squeeze himself into. Every waking hour (as well as every dreaming one), Peter fanatically searched for ways to prove himself to the world.

Although Peter and Phil got along great, there still remained a little bit of sibling rivalry. Since the space at Animal House was limited, Phil and Peter had to share their room, which meant they slept in bunk beds, with Peter on the top. Peter couldn't help but snore at night which prompted Phil, on the bottom bunk, to kick the underside of Peter's mattress, waking him up. After a few times, Peter became so angry that he leaned over from the top and swung punches down at Phil in the dark hoping to bash him in the face. Luckily, it never came down to blows like it had many years earlier when they had an argument over the last popsicle. That argument ended up with Peter beating the piss out of Phil. Hell, they were very young teenagers at the time. It was all fun and games.

Peter was by far the most complex out of all of us brothers. Over the years, he devised many wild, farfetched, yet totally ingenious ideas. He so vastly outdid us with his Herculean stunts that we could not keep up with him. He always used his position as the big brother to sucker the rest of us and our friends into joining him. Although Peter was the firstborn and deserved our respect, it became evident that a storm took place inside his mind. Peter found himself in a triad of timeless, bizarre philosophies. His somewhat twisted beliefs were a complex blend of our estranged fathers, those of Alexander the Great, and then the ruthless, murderous, diabolical Joseph Stalin. Peter used these three figures as mentors, pitting each of their dogmas against the others in the recesses of his mind: my father with his lavish dreams, Alexander with his unstoppable drive to destiny, and Stalin with his insatiable appetite to manipulate (and even to murder).

As time marched on, the turmoil taking place in Peter's mind quietly led him to act in mysterious ways. While we all saw it at the time, our mother felt that her prized, first-born son could do no wrong. She noticed nothing unusual, and with her silence as her blessing, Peter believed that he was as great, if not greater than his three mentors. Armed with such unshakeable confidence, Peter began to burn the candle of life at both ends. His mantras oozed out of every pore of his body as he admonished those around him. One line became his favorite, "You can sleep when you are dead!" And because he tackled life this way, he expected everyone in his network to do the same.

In stark contrast to Peter's ways were the ways of my brother Phil. While Peter had rushed up to his bedroom every afternoon to begin studying with great discipline and intense self-flagellation, Phil goofed off downstairs playing pool, eating popsicles and watching the latest movies on HBO. Surprisingly, they both managed to progress, semester after semester, toward their dreams. The two of them wholeheartedly believed that providence would prevail. In the end, their habits served each of them equally, proving that there is more than one way to skin a cat.

January passed, then February, and then March. Each month seemed to leap off the calendar. All of them uneventfully, until one cold, crisp March afternoon, when fate stepped in and made a huge demand upon my oldest brother.

One day, a young female student aid from the administration building tracked Peter down in his last class of the day. Just as it ended, he jumped up from his seat and began tucking his textbooks into his backpack. Before he could finish, this cute, but timid student aid sheepishly handed him a note. With a bewildered look on his face, he thanked her. Before he left the room, he tore the letter open and read the contents. Peter Major was being summoned to the office of the honorable William Van Matre—the man himself requested an immediate audience with my illustrious brother.

Van Matre was no stranger to Peter because now, for the third time, Peter would find himself facing this remarkable figure, a man with a persona as timeless as the mighty Wizard of Oz, a man capable of granting Peter's every wish that he could ever ask of the college.

At this juncture, Peter had just begun his career, while Van Matre found himself nearing the end of his. In his final years, Van Matre, just like Peter, longed for a way to leave his mark on the world. Van Matre concluded that by overseeing some young, deserving underling, he could somehow live vicarious through him. He could share in the glory of what he and his young protégé would accomplish before his academic career would end. With this aspiration, he had kept a close eye on my brother for the past two years, and facing a new challenge himself, he felt that it was a perfect time to meet my older brother once again.

Peter left the classroom, strolled down the hallway, and quickly hustled across the street to the administration building. He strutted confidently through the door of the dean's office and stopped directly in front of the secretary's desk. Before he could even introduce himself, the dean's secretary seized the moment.

"Mr. Major, it is so nice to see you. The dean is anxious to meet with you."

"What's this all about?"

"I'm not sure, but please go right in."

She smiled and pointed at Van Matre's door.

Peter walked past her desk and stepped into the large office. The revered dean sat encased in an oversized, dark-stained wooden desk that gave him a cloak of superiority. Upon hearing Peter entering the room, Van Matre lowered an engineering trade magazine down from his face and leaned back in a tall, diamond-tucked leather chair. The memories of their two previous meetings flashed through both of their minds. Peter reveled in the thought of how he had emerged victoriously twice from the dean's office, once for himself and once for Phil. He now knew, with certainty, that he could handle anything Van Matre could throw at him, for Peter's record at the college by this time was impeccable.

It would not be fair to think of Van Matre's office as a lion's den, but more accurately, a locus of power. The desk, the chairs, and the array of framed certificates and diplomas were nothing more than props. Van Matre was as human as anyone, just flesh and blood, no more significant than the diminutive man exposed from behind the curtain in The Wizard of Oz. While standing before this man, still somewhat in awe, Peter had learned over time how to play everything to his favor. He would listen intently and embrace what fortune had been laid at his doorstep. For a moment, Peter chuckled inside himself as he made an astute observation regarding the looks of Van Matre. In all appearances, Van Matre seemed quite anachronistic. He sported a short, crew-cut hairstyle and wore thick 1960s-style black-framed glasses. With his buttoned-up, white, short-sleeved shirt and black tie, he looked as if he had just walked out of the control room from the early days of NASA. Despite the powerful image that Van Matre fought hard to maintain and his hardnose attitude, Peter knew from their very first meeting that Van Matre had a soft, compassionate side—and how hard he tried hard to hide it.

"Thanks for coming on such short notice"— "Take a seat."

Peter respectfully sat down in one of the chairs that faced Van Matre.

"Mister Major, I have a mission for you."

Peter sighed, realizing that this meeting had nothing to do with any misconduct that he, or our brother, Phil, may have been guilty of, such as disregarding homework assignment deadlines or unruly behavior on campus. Peter's ears perked up. He liked the phraseology Van Matre had just used and suddenly tried to hide the snicker on his face. A mission he said? Ha! To Peter, everything was a mission, and everything was a competition, and just now, Van Matre's words were pure music to his ears. Without displaying any excitement or exuberance, Peter forced himself to maintain his demeanor long enough to discover what this so-called mission was all about.

Without waiting for a response from my brother, Van Matre calmly continued, "I want you to take charge of Tech's mining competition team."

"I didn't know Tech had a team."

Van Matre immediately exploded with his almost year-long, pent-up anger after what happened the year before, "We don't have a team! WHEN YOU FINISH DEAD LAST IN A COMPETITION, THAT ISN'T A TEAM!"

Peter shrunk back in his chair while Van Matre nervously twiddled a mechanical pencil between his fingers as he fought to regain his breath after his uncontrolled outburst.

Ten months earlier, the University of Idaho had hosted the first annual national mining competition. They had invited all the major mining universities across the country to participate in an old-fashioned, hands-on contest consisting of basic mining activities. The events included skills every hard rock miner had to master on the job deep unground. The events included jackleg drilling, hand mucking blasted rock with shovels into ore cars, laying track by nailing it down with railroad spikes, sawing timbers by hand, and drilling into rocks with a sledgehammer and hand steel. (The hand steel was a highly obsolete method of drilling, not used in over a century.)

Van Matre continued, "Maybe you weren't paying attention last year. Obviously, you don't remember the disgrace. We sent six of our students to compete."

"And they finished dead last?"

"Yes. I am not even sure if they placed in any of the events at all."

"Why did they get creamed?"

Van Matre paused for a moment, and the stoic look on his face changed slightly into a controlled smile. "We sent a group of pansies down there who had never been in a real mine in their entire life. Hell, I heard they drank beer most of the way down to Moscow in the school van."

"And you want me to form a team?"

"Precisely. Mr. Major, the word on the campus is that you and your brother are actual miners. You WILL form a team, train them the hardest you can, and you will all fly to Tucson for this year's competition."

"I can do that, Sir."

"I know you can. Unfortunately, I won't be able to fly down there with you. I have an important Board of Trustees meeting that weekend. Oh, and there will be no chaperone. You are in charge, so don't screw this up."

Peter couldn't believe what he was hearing. And so, to advance one of his pawns in his imaginary game of chess with Van Matre, he gave every effort imaginable to feign coyness. (Pete was the best humble bragger the world had ever seen.)

"Now is your chance. You came to this college, and from the day you started here, you acted like you were going to conquer the world. I've watched your cocky little ass strut around here like you own the place, and the entire time I haven't said shit but just kept my eye on you."

"Sir, I don't think I acted quite like that."

"I don't give a rat's ass what you think. I am right on the money with this one. Well, now you will get your great opportunity, you cocky little punk."

Peter shrugged his shoulders and acted like all this was a surprise, but kept his mouth shut and let Van Matre continue.

"Tomorrow night, at 6:00 p.m., you and I are going to the monthly Board of Trustees meeting to convince them to give us everything we need to assemble a winning team. Is that clear?

"Yes, Sir. Clear as vodka."

"Now that this is understood, get the hell out of my office."

"Yes, Sir." Peter got up from his chair and began to walk out of the office with the biggest grin he ever had on his face since starting college. He tried to hide it with his hand as if he were a grade-schooler trying to wipe away a chocolate smear before his mother discovered that he had just gotten into her fudge.

Peter

The next night, Peter and his great benefactor passed muster before the college Board of Trustees. The board unanimously approved the motion to provide all the funding necessary to outfit a new team to represent the college, partially because one of the leading board members was a local businessman. This renowned businessman still relished over the spectacle that Peter had been instrumental in putting together just the year before. Peter and his crew had constructed a float for this trustee's sporting goods business, and its presence in the parade put this trustee's company in a controversial, yet positive light in the community. The float displayed a humungous, cardboard male jock strap It advertised that the business was one of the college's 'athletic supporters'—a definite pun intended. With all the attention his company received from that stunt, the board member never forgot the name Peter Major. Like Van Matre, this trustee became mesmerized by my oldest brother's charisma.

Now that my brother Peter had the blessing of the college's upper crust, the entire team's performance weighed heavily on his shoulders. Being officially charged with the mission, an internal monologue began inside Peter's mind. He heard his own voice spurning him on, or was it that of one or more of his imaginary mentors? It repeated itself over and over, "The heat is on. Sink or swim, Peter Major. The entire world is watching you. Sink or Swim. Now is the time."

Minutes after leaving the Board of Trustees meeting with Van Matre, Peter arrived back at Animal House only to find Phil sitting in front of the TV with an overflowing plate of Banquet fried chicken lying on the coffee table and the movie 'Animal House' blaring away on the TV screen. Phil was now watching it for the twenty-fifth time this school year. To him, it was a fantastic show. The college frat house in the movie became the reason they named their residence 'Animal House'.

"Do you EVER study?" Peter asked.

Phil took another bite off a chicken breast and mumbled with a full mouth as he kept his eyes transfixed on the TV screen, "Ah, yeah."

Peter trudged up the stairs to his room and stayed secluded for most of the weekend, plotting, planning, and perfecting a strategy on which he would pin all his hopes of victory. For two days, he incessantly listened to the soundtrack of The Good, the Bad, and the Ugly. He fantasized about complete and utter victory on the battlefield. Ironically, Peter had never participated in any organized sport in all his adolescence other than Little League Baseball as a young child. He had never tried out for the football or basketball teams and stayed far away from the track team. In fact, Peter probably had fewer credentials than any third-rate jock in the college, and now he had been selected to take charge of such a paramount undertaking. Despite his lack of credentials, Peter vowed to himself and the gods above that he would not let Van Matre down. Although Peter was a devout

Catholic and had summoned every power of the rosary that he could, he was still more than willing to make a deal with the Devil—anything to achieve his means.

After a weekend of hypnotic self-talk, Peter set out early Monday morning to kick things off long before any students dared venture out of their warm dormitory beds. He stepped out onto the frosty sidewalk and tromped up to the college campus. Armed with several rolls of Scotch tape and a generous supply of tacks, he spent two hours plastering the college hallways with the posters he had so carefully crafted over the weekend. In his prose, he challenged all-comers to try out for this year's prestigious mining competition team. He offered them a chance to join an elite group (unselected yet) that would be competing in the Second Annual National Mining Competition in warm and sunny Tucson, Arizona—but only for those who dare to qualify.

Peter's luring invitation emulated the most successful want ad ever published. He virtually plagiarized the 1914 newspaper employment advertisement that Lord Shackleton had run in the London Times looking for volunteers for the upcoming Antarctica mission. Shackleton penned the script to read as such: "Volunteers wanted. Very dangerous mission and with very low pay. The weak need not apply." The response to the 1914 solicitation was the largest turnout ever for a help-wanted ad. In the same vein, Peter copied the spirit of those times and drafted his ad with the same appeal. However, unlike Shackleton's ultimate failure of being lost in the ice for 18 months in a doomed ship ironically named "The Endurance," Peter stayed determined to settle for nothing less than total victory. Where Shackleton failed, Peter vowed to succeed—and he knew exactly what he was doing when he used the famous explorer as an inspiration. Peter wanted to stand on the shoulders of a giant, a historical hero, thereby becoming a giant himself.

These enticing, handcrafted posters hung on the college walls for nearly a week until the day came for all interested parties to meet in the school's gymnasium. At the appointed hour, Peter found himself standing in front of a row of bleachers with my brother Phil at his side. A handful of students sat in the first few rows, joking among themselves, while several more students shuffled in through the doors behind them, curious about the great event. At four o'clock sharp they were all going to find out.

Peter called for the attention of every student in the crowd.

"Listen up. We are putting something together for the first time in college history, and this is nothing to take lightly." He paused for a moment to carefully observe their reaction. Peter quickly looked to his side at our brother Phil for reassurance.

He continued, "Nearly a year ago, this college sent a group of students to Moscow, Idaho, to represent Montana Tech in the first annual mining competition, and our team totally got their asses kicked. They finished dead last!"

Once again, he paused to test their reaction, ". . . a total disgrace for this school. We are here today to wire our heads to our asses off and make a showing this May down in Tucson. For those who qualify, you will get a chance to avenge this college."—"Try-outs begin tomorrow at noon. After four weeks of practice, we will have a mock competition. The top five scoring students will make the team."

He handed a clipboard to the closest student sitting in the first row.

"Everyone put your names and contact information on this list." Peter looked around at the group and made piercing eye contact with each of them before continuing. "Remember, we meet up at the training grounds next to the mining museum tomorrow at noon, gentleman. See you then." He quickly added, "In the meantime, all of you do some sole soul searching. If you don't think you are up to it, don't even bother showing up."

When Peter finished his speech, Phil looked over at him and grabbed him by the shirt sleeve. "Are you fucking crazy? We had no team last year, and you're trying to scare away any chance we have of having one this year."

Peter glanced out across the gym at the dispersing crowd, and with the calmest and somewhat sociopathic look in his eyes, said to Phil, "Trust me. I know what I am doing."

With the unnerving tone of Peters' voice, Phil did not question him further.

As the crowd slowly left the gym, one interested student stayed behind, waiting to approach Peter. He wanted to speak with him one-on-one. At the right moment he walked straight up to Peter and held out his hand, "Hi, I'm Mike Cadem. I want to help with your training program."

Peter clasped Mike's hand firmly and recognized his face, "Damn. I've heard of you. Six years in the Navy Seals, right?"

"That's right. And that's why I think I might be able to help."

For a moment, Peter felt a slight surge of insecurity, standing before a man who had done something he knew he couldn't and would never do in his life. Yet, Peter maintained his steely-eyed composure.

"Alright, Mike, I think it would be an honor to have your help. Let me show you what I had in mind about the tryouts, then you let me know what you think." Peter thumbed through the training notes on his clipboard and began to share them with the seasoned veteran. After a short talk, he and Mike shook hands once again. As Mike turned and walked away, he carried himself in a victory strut, proud that he was on Peter's team. Although Peter and Phil were the last ones to leave, they would be the first ones on the training grounds, as any competent leaders would do.

Later that night, Peter sat at the desk in his room and let his imagination run wild. During one of his visions, he decided to act on his gut instinct. His plans for the competition were not yet complete. He reached into his desk drawer and pulled out a sheet of stationery. He composed a letter to our eccentric Uncle Bill, who resided in an obscure trailer court near the Seattle-Tacoma International Airport.

It read: "Dear Bill, how have you been doing? By now, I am sure you have heard that Phil and I are kicking ass at college just like you wanted us to. I know it may be short notice, but I desperately need your help on a very important mission. I have been put in charge of the college's mining competition team, and we are due to compete in the national competition in Tucson next month. Do you think you can make it? I have a very serious part for you to play if you are up to it, you lazy bastard. Give me a call when you can, and I will let you know what I need you to do" Signed, "Your nephew Peter. P.S. Don't take any shit off those punks at work—and lay off the sauce before you get your ass fired!"

When he finished the letter, Peter licked the envelope, placed a domestic postage stamp on the right corner, and stepped out the front door of Animal House. He walked up the cold, frozen street and dropped the letter into the nearest U.S. Postal Service mailbox. On his way back, he had second thoughts about what he had just done. He wondered if he had done the right thing by inviting our obnoxious uncle to such a prestigious event. Uncle Bill may end up getting drunk and embarrassing the hell out of the team and the college.

196

Minutes later, after the short walk back to Animal House, Peter climbed the steep steps up to his room and got ready for bed. Once under the warm blanket, he reached over and systematically donned his headphones. With the push of a button, he turned his stereo on. He reached over and gently placed the needle of the player onto the record of the soundtrack of 'The Good, the Bad, and the Ugly.' After the initial scratching of the needle came over the headphones, the music from Heaven began to play.

The next day, Peter and Philip showed up at the museum grounds. From the back of Peter's truck, they unloaded shovels, saws, hammers, spikes, and other miscellaneous tools they would be training with. They began setting up railroad ties, rails, and spikes. The two of them anxiously waited for their future teammates to arrive. Peter leaned against the fender of his long-trusted, white and green Ford 4x4, almost hugging the vehicle like a lover. That very truck held such deep sentiment. It was like a close friend that he had gone through combat with, but today was a new day, and he and his good friend would make brand new memories. In the meantime, Peter refused to waver with the image of his team achieving absolute victory over the other colleges. However, starting with nothing but a crew of inexperienced misfits that had just signed up would be tough. Peter became impatient and began to pace. Phil walked around the truck with his hands in his jacket pockets, entrusting a specific part of his future to his brother. In the most dramatic way, just a few years earlier, Peter had pulled him through the frozen hell during the cold, dismal winter at Jennis Bay. He trusted Peter.

Little by little, everyone started to arrive. Most of the guys who said they would be there were there, especially Mike Cadem. Although the sun shone through the scattered clouds and attempted to warm the earth below, the air remained cold and crisp. The ground lay frozen, just as Montana was famous for. Frost covered everything in sight, but it didn't matter to Peter. He clasped his clipboard in one hand and let a stopwatch dangle from his neck.

From the first minute, Peter had every student pick up their trade implements and familiarize themselves with each piece. To demonstrate the most basic skill of a hard rock miner, Peter grabbed a shovel and struck it into the ground to show them the principles behind the art of mucking ore. However, the sharp edge met the frozen rock pile with great resistance.

The ground proved to be too frozen to be of any use. Something had to be done before they could ever think about continuing. "Crap! We have to thaw that out."

"Let's build a fire," someone suggested, and so they did. They stacked a pile of old boards and some unused pallets on the gravel pile and let the heat of the fire do its thing.

Let's get onto the next skill," Peter commanded.

Without missing a beat, Peter walked over to another area where he and Phil had earlier laid out a long row of railroad ties and had placed two parallel lengths of small railroad tracks across them. Phil and Peter measured the distance between them with a miner's rule, then picked up a hammer and several spikes. Phil held the spike next to the track and Peter began hitting it with the sledgehammer, driving it deep into the wood. Peter stopped after the first spike and explained how the spacing between the tracks had to be precisely measured before the initial spikes could be driven in. While Peter explained, Mike Cadem stood before the group and ordered them to move closer and observe. Mike felt as if he were conditioning a group of raw recruits for combat training. With Peter and Mike's instructions, each team member got a chance to drive spikes. As the first hour progressed, a slight sense of awkwardness and confusion hung in the air. They bumbled through all these new activities, and with all their inexperience being exposed, no one in the group knew who would make the team and who wouldn't.

The weeks of after-school training had passed slowly, and sometimes painfully, as one applicant after another dropped off the potential team. The final stretch came, and during the last week, only ten remained out of the original twenty, and only half of them would make the team. All their hopes now hung in the balance. The testing would be totally fair because Peter did not exclude himself from the rigors and requirements of the final testing even though he was the captain. Even Phil had to pass the challenge just like everyone else, or he would not be on the team, even though he was Pete's brother. Peter and Phil threw themselves into the final stages of training with everything they had, which forced everyone else to push even harder to keep up.

Peter held the final test under a setting sun in early May, the week before the qualifying team was slated to fly to Tucson. He staged the events as realistically as he possibly could. He pitted one man against another and each two-man team against the other. Over and over, during event after event, Peter blew the whistle and held up his stopwatch. Each eager student gave it their all, pushing the limits of their endurance, desperately wanting to make the grade. Peter carefully crafted pitting men against each other, just as his idol Joseph Stalin had done in the final stages of World War II where he pitted Marshall Zhukov against Marshall Konev on their drive to Berlin.

Peter recorded the times at the end of every event, copiously writing them on his clipboard in front of all the anxious students. When it became his and Phil's turn, Cadem took command of the whistle and clipboard.

By the time the last session ended, Peter combed through the results on the clipboard with Cadem at his side to double-check the recorded times and the rankings. When he finished, he looked down at the final figures in an eerie silence (staged, of course) to purposely delay the results to make them all sweat. It was one of Peter's mind games he played purely to create as much tension as he could—a sociopathic tendency for sure. Peter had never yielded such for power before and loved his new position as the puppet master.

The contenders waited anxiously, but as they cooled off from the sweaty activity, they began to don their coats. They gathered around Peter and silently demanded the results as all their eyes were upon him.

"Okay, here's the team standing," Peter paused, scanned over the entire group. He looked each of them directly in the eye, just as he had done on the first day in the gym. He then dispensed with the final roster, "Going to Tucson: Phelan . . . Cadem . . . Welch . . . Smith . . . Phil . . . and myself. I want to thank all of you for giving your very best."

Half the group sighed joyfully, and the other half groaned in disappointment. Phil looked over at Peter and captured his gaze. In a silent gesture that Phil made with his astonished eyes, he seemed to ask Peter, "Did I really qualify, or did you fudge the results?"

Sensing what Phil felt, Peter walked over and immediately showed him the squiggly lines on the paper. He pointed out the officially recorded scores. Truth be known, Peter and Phil honestly DID have the highest score on every event, especially with Peter excelling at the jackleg drilling. Their summers slaving away in the mine had paid off handsomely.

The following day, with the team roster in place, the college administration booked the airline tickets for Montana Tech's six up-and-coming competitors. Late that night at Animal House, the phone rang as Peter was getting ready to crawl into bed. He trotted down the stairs and grabbed the receiver long before Phil could put down his ice cream bowl and lower the TV's volume.

"Hello."

"Good evening. This is the AT&T operator with a collect call from William W. Miller. Will you accept the charges?"

"Yes, Mam."

The operator put the call through and got off the line.

A gruff voice with slurred words began to speak, "Good evening. This is Uncle Bill calling, and I would like to talk to my nephew Peter."

"Holy smokers! Bill, this is Peter."

"Hey, Buddy! I can make it. I can make it to Tucson!"

"Well, I would sure hope so. We're counting on you being there because we are going to take the place by storm."

"I know you are, buddy! That's why I'm coming. I only hang out with winners!" On the Seattle end of the phone, Bill stood in a filthy phone booth, holding the receiver up to his ear with one hand and a burning cigarette clenched between his fingers in the other. While he listened to Peter, he periodically took deep puffs, tilting his head backward and exhaling skyward, filling the tiny phone booth with carcinogenic-filled smoke.

Peter stopped talking for a moment and collected his thoughts before he presented Bill with the risky proposal, which was the most critical part of the call, "Bill, I am so glad you're going to make it, but I have this one big idea. I don't know if you are up to it, or if you even have the guts to pull it off."

Bill immediately pulled the cigarette away from his mouth without taking a puff. "What do you mean, mother fucker? You are talking to the king of guts!"

"Hell, I knew that, that is why I am presenting this to you."

"Go ahead, mother fucker, I'm listening; Granny didn't raise no dummies."

Back at the Montana end of the phone line, Peter smiled and nodded, looking at his reflection in the kitchen window masked against the dark Butte skyline. "Bill, do you think you could impersonate a college professor?"

Bill stopped right in the middle of a huge inhale and nearly coughed. He blew out the smoke, and most indignantly, yelled into the mouthpiece, "Ya Goddamn right, I can!"

Peter almost couldn't contain himself and nearly burst out in uncontrollable laughter but maintained his composure. He had to be serious. "Okay, Bill. I was just checking. Because the only way you can attend every event up close—especially the awards banquet, is for you to be associated with the college."

Bill yelled in desperation, "You know it fucker! You know I can do it. As I said, I only hang out with winners, and you are a mother fucking winner!"

"Okay, Bill, get your ass down there. Let me know what time your flight will land, and we will be at the airport to pick you up."

Bill reached over to the small shelf beside the phone and grabbed the glass he carried out of the bar. He tilted his head back and gulped down the last of the watered-down whiskey drink that he had nursed during their short phone call.

"Okay, good buddy, I will call tomorrow with my flight info. See you next Friday night fucker! Over and out for now."

With his signature goodbye, Bill hung up the phone and waddled back across the trailer park to his eight-foot wide by forty-foot long 1952 vintage trailer, which he called the dumpster: a home fitting for a wanna-be college professor.

A week later, a small commuter plane took off from the Butte International Airfield and headed off into the horizon with the six lucky Montana Tech athletes. The aircraft found its altitude and plotted a course south—a collision course with destiny. After a short layover in Denver, they took off again and arrived on schedule in sunny Tucson. The six teammates disembarked the plane and found their way to the car rental agency. From there, they headed off to a cheesy little motel where the college had so graciously rented rooms for them. An hour after they checked into the motel and unpacked their bags, Peter drove back to the airport to pick up Uncle Bill.

Another plane landed on schedule in Tucson. After it pulled up to the gate and opened the door, passengers began to disembark, one of them, a large man of tall stature. He started walking down the concourse, towering over the other passengers. He casually strolled through the airport with his full head of greased hair. He wore a pair of aviator sunglasses, a huge grin, and an oversized, stretched-out, size XXX white tee shirt with a pack of cigarettes rolled up in one sleeve. He continued out through the front door of the arrivals section and found his way over to a cement bench. While sitting down and waiting for his ride, he reached up to his left sleeve and unrolled the fabric just enough to pull out his cigarettes, a soft pack of Winstons. He lit one up, took a big puff, then blew out the match. The man was none other than our infamous Uncle Bill.

Peter pulled up to the airport minutes later and immediately noticed Bill sitting there. He stopped right in front of him and jumped out of the vehicle. Bill stood up and gave Peter a big thumbs-up.

"How was your flight, Bill?"

"It was terrif. They fed me nonstop drinks the whole way. You can't beat that shit with an eggbeater."

Peter laughed. "Let's get going. The team is dying to meet you."

Once they arrived at the hotel and the others heard Bill's thunderous voice, they scrambled out of their rooms and lined up to shake Bill's hand. They all giggled because Uncle Bill's looks and persona fit Peter and Phil's description of him to the tee.

"Damn good to see all of you. You fuckers are going to kick some mother fuckin ass! Like I said, I only hang out with winners!" Bill always used the same canned lines over and over to the point that they almost became annoying.

Peter and Phil chuckled out loud while Cadem, Smith, Welch, and Phelan stood there smiling, awestruck by this eccentric man of great size and never heard of before wit. After Bill checked into the hotel, he and the six teammates walked a few blocks to a local bar that hosted the college teams' initial meeting. Uncle Bill followed not far behind them, wearing his dark sunglasses, sagging blue jeans, and the overly stretched white tee shirt with a pack of cigarettes safely rolled up in the left sleeve.

The seven arrived at the local establishment and were awestruck at the sight that resembled an invasion. Cars, trucks, and even TV news vans with their telescopic antennas raised choked the parking lot. Welch yelled out with his deep nasal voice, "Holy shit! Look at this place. How big is this event?"

Phelan piped in, "I don't want any news cameras filming me."

Smith slapped Phelan on the back. "Come on, man, after this, you are going to be famous."

Phil looked stunned at what he saw. Cadem couldn't care less about the crowd. However, Pete gloated at the sight of all of it. Everything seemed to match up perfectly with what he had dreamed.

As they opened the door and started filing in, Bill flicked his half-smoked cigarette out into the parking lot and followed them in. He grinned fiendishly as if he somehow knew that he might offend someone tonight—someone, if not everyone, in the entire place.

Everyone on the team felt nervous. Butterflies churned in their stomachs. They knew they were coming in as the underdogs, representing the disgraced college from the previous year, but there was no getting out of it now. Their fears quickly evaporated when an aging, wrinkled-faced female bartender came up to them. She used her arthritic fingers to direct them to a scarcely lit anteroom in the back of the bar. The nine other national teams had already crammed into the room. The Boys from Butte were the last to arrive. A simple beer-chugging competition had been staged as the one special event for the night. Although not a noteworthy activity working in a hard rock mine, this kick-off event would serve as the tiebreaker if the top two teams finished the competition with an equal score. While it was meant to be fun, this simple contest had to be taken seriously because it could mean the difference between a trophy or not.

Scores of mugs lined the long table and were filled to the brim with beer. The foam frothed over the sides. Two officials wearing name tags and holding stopwatches stood at the end of the far end of the table. Their sole purpose was to officiate the event by timing it and ensuring no one cheated. You had to drink all your beer just like a good little college boy, not leaving any in the mug after you put it back down on the tabletop.

Phelan looked around the room and sized up his opponents. He loved what he saw. He had just found himself in his element—a barbaric orgy of drinking. With his wild, uncombed hair, which hung well below his collar, and his crudely groomed mustache, he resembled Vlad the Impaler, AKA Dracula. In this event, the Butte team needed Phelan's contribution more than ever.

"Man, look at all those douchebags! I can drink any of these pudds under the table," he boasted.

Welch stood at Phelan's side and mumbled in agreement, slightly puffing his chest out as if he were ready to play king-of-the-hill with the neighbor kids; besides, he was a champion himself, a Wyoming state track gold medalist in the one-hundred-yard dash. Cadem scanned the faces in the room, then looked down at the long row of beer mugs. Memories of his drinking days in the Navy, from Guantanamo Bay to the Philippines, flooded his senses. This was nothing new to him, and he feared not a damn thing. He and Welch, like Phelan, knew that they owned this turf. However, this only encompassed half of the team. Their bravado was not equally shared. Peter, Phil, and the tall, blond, gaunt Smith were caught totally off guard; they hardly ever drank beer.

Being raised in a religious family, none of us brothers delved much into drinking, except on rare occasions when trying to fit in with the other adolescents. We left the wine-drinking to our constantly inebriated priest, Father O'Sullivan. After the drinking competition was set up, my two brothers turned to each other. While still sizing up the event, Peter looked out of the corner of his eye at Phil, and with an inconspicuous tilt of his head, he spoke out of the side of his mouth and growled, "Phil, don't worry about it. We are going to burn these punks."

"Are we?"

"You damn right. We aren't taking our eyes off that freaking trophy. You will drink blood out of a skull if you have to. Just chug that shit as fast as you can—as if your life depends on it!"

'Okay. I'll do whatever I can do." Phil immediately snapped to attention, bolstered by Pete's extreme confidence. His older brother knew what he was doing. At this very moment, he demanded total blind faith from everyone on the team. Phelan, Cadem, Smith, and Welch kept looking over at Peter for reassurance that they were up to the challenge. He nodded at them with an all-knowing grin on his face. That alone inspired them.

As the first few teams glugged their beer and slammed the empty mugs down on the table, the cheering shook the foundation of the tavern. At last, it came Montana Tech's turn. The signal was given. Peter poured his beer down his throat, gulping like a seal swallowing a fish. Phil followed suit, desperately glugging mouthful after mouthful, gasping and gagging, frantically trying not to let the team down.   Cadem, Welch, and Phelan virtually mirrored each other's moves and slammed their mugs down in precise timing—not a millisecond wasted. Smith finally followed suit right behind Pete and Phil.

The judges fumbled with their stopwatches and tablets at the end of a ten-team battle. At first, it was suspected that the judges may have engaged in a bit of partaking of the fermented malt beverages themselves before the event started. Regardless, as the two officials nodded heads at each other, the winning team was announced. Peter and his crew nearly fell to the floor when they heard they had taken first place. While the Montana team pulled off their first win, Uncle Bill had been sitting on a bar stool with his back against the wall. When Pete looked over at him, Bill poked his cigarette into the air as a salute and exhaled the smoke through his tightly pursed lips like a broken steam pipe. He swayed his head from side to side to evenly disperse the toxic fumes. Many members of the other teams sent piercing glances over at Peter and his crew. They were outraged. None of them expected to be upset by a hodgepodge team that consisted of a Neanderthal man, a square-jawed muscle head, a scrawny, unpretentious ex-navy seal, a tall, thin, lanky blond with Coke-bottle lens glasses—and two skinny bothers who looked like that hadn't even got out of their freshman year in high school. In muffled breaths, some members of the disenfranchised teams vowed to get back at those lucky bastards from Butte if it was the last thing they did while in Tucson.

"How the fuck did they pull this off?" one said.

"I don't know. Pure luck, I guess. Just wait till tomorrow. We are going to bury them!" the other one responded.

After the evening of working the crowd and meeting the other teams and officials, the six of them walk out the door as a team with an enhanced sense of camaraderie. They strolled the few blocks back to their motel with pride and with the proud Uncle Bill in tow. Uncle Bill behaved beautifully because he didn't want to blow his cover with the upcoming role he had to play the next day. He wasn't sure how to impersonate a college professor, but he would do his best. For the trip, he had packed a dress shirt, a tie, and a jacket just for the occasion.

Before everyone retired to their rooms, Peter issued an edict to all his teammates. "We haven't won anything yet. Tomorrow is where the rubber meets the road. These guys think we are bums, but we are going to fry their asses."

"Fuck yeah!" the drunken Phelan slurred as he held up his can of beer in a premature toast.

"But we aren't going to win shit if we get cocky. Don't get cocky. I'm telling you now, don't get cocky!" Peter sternly warned them.

Phelan lowered his beer and almost apologetically lowered his head.

In the past (and in a million Hollywood movies that he watched), Peter had seen how cockiness led to defeat, time and time again. On the eve of this great opportunity, he had to keep their bragging to a minimum. Not only did Peter want to win the trophy, but he also wanted to win the adulation that went along with it. He wanted more than anything to impress ole Van Matre, and even Dad, although he was afar. With Peter, everything was ego. It didn't matter if the event was going out to get the mail, he had to do it better and faster than anyone else in the family. He timed everything, probably down to how long it took him to take a shit.

As Peter and Phil entered their room, Bill followed them in, carrying a bottle of Black Velvet whiskey and a paper cup. Just as the door shut, Bill sat at the edge of the bed and opened his big mouth, "You guys are going to kill 'em! And I mean kill 'em!" But he couldn't stop there. He screamed twice as loud, "You guys are going to mother fucking kill em!"

Half the motel probably heard Bill. The screaming was bad enough, but if all they heard was the word 'kill,' there could be trouble.

"Shut up, Bill! You are talking crazy again. You haven't had that much to drink! All it takes is one beer, and you act like you are totally blitzed. Stop your crazy act! Stop it right now! You aren't drunk, so stop acting like it. You know exactly what you are doing, and you know I'm right."

Bill immediately cowered like a little boy, knowing Peter had him pegged. Bill apologized. "Okay, fucker. I know when to behave. Granny didn't raise no dummies." He got up from the bed. "I will see you in the morning, buddy." Bill turned away, went out the door, and silently ambled to his motel room.

In his room, Bill poured himself another shot of whiskey and added some water. He reflected a little on life, but none of us in the family really knew how deeply he did because he shared so little. Something went wrong in his early adulthood because he never dated, married, or fathered any children. He lived alone his whole life but loved being around our father, beyond measure. He equally loved being around his nephews. Now, with our father long gone to Canada, never to return, Bill had a hole inside him, and the only way for him to try and fill it was to live vicariously through us. My brother Peter was the rock of the family. Bill respected him and was now so happy to be caught up in his whirlwind. After thinking of how badly he missed our father, Bill's eyes watered, and a small tear escaped. It rolled down his cheek something no one had probably ever seen before except me. In later years, while in a drunken stupor, Bill would talk sentimentally to me about my father and told me that I was my dad's carbon copy.

Just before lights out, Phil lay on his bunk and turned on the TV. He found a good movie on HBO and turned up the volume. Peter lay on the other bunk and, almost in secrecy, carefully unzipped his travel bag and glanced over at Phil, hoping he did not notice. Peter pulled out a cassette player along with a set of headphones. Still believing Phil hadn't detected a thing, he placed the headphones over his ears and gently pushed the play button. Peter laid his head back on the pillow and closed his eyes to the seductive theme song of the movie, 'The Good, The Bad, and The Ugly'. The soundtrack played with the drums beating in a demonic rhythm and the short, high pitch whistling that tantalized the listener. All this was followed by the famous squawking of a vocal alto section, "Wah, wah, wah"—and then the whistling again. Peter drifted off into his fantasy land where he, against all odds, squared off in a heated battle to the death, but in the end, he emerged the hero.

In the morning, after a hearty breakfast of ham, eggs, and hash browns (and anything else they wanted to eat at the college's expense), the team climbed into their rental van and found their way to the Arizona State University campus. As they rolled out the vehicle and made their way to the awaiting crowd, the defending champions from Tucson instantly recognized the logo on the shirts the Butte team wore. A chuckle erupted from their group.

One of the members from the Arizona team, the biggest and ugliest one, yelled out in a sarcastic tone, "Lookie here! Butte sent their finest!"

The loudmouth asshole from Tucson forgot to look in the mirror that morning, for he was one of the most ridiculous-looking students ever. Standing at over six feet two and probably weighing nearly three hundred pounds (similar in stature to Uncle Bill) he looked formidable in one respect but hilarious in another. He sported an undersized tee-shirt that rose so high it exposed his navel and his huge, dough-like belly. His hair, brown and uncontrollably curly, looked more like a wig that he inadvertently put on backward in haste. Lastly, his chubby cheeks and large, red, overly inflated liver lips severely accentuated his grotesque, misaligned teeth.

In his first glance at the heckler, Phil laughed at the sight. It reminded him of the retarded kid from our neighborhood. And in the most innocuous way, Phil effortlessly ignored this goon's comments and went about his business of finding Butte's staging area.

"Forget them," Peter instructed the team. "We are going to beat their freakin asses into the ground! Trust me, but don't get cocky!" And without further incident, they walked through the mob and found the area assigned to the Montana Tech team.

During the initial briefing for all the teams, they learned that the scoring would be based on nothing more than a simple ranking at the end of each event. First place was given ten points, second place was given nine points, and so on. The first event was the hand steel, a procedure the crew had practiced many times. Butte was poised to be the first team to compete. Cadem and Welch took their positions in front of the growing crowd. The whistle blew, the stopwatch began, and Cadem and Welch went to work in full fury, just like they had done repeatedly in training.

After five minutes of pounding the hammer and twisting the steel, the official blew the whistle. Cadem and Welch stood up and breathed deeply. The officials measured the depth of the hole that they bore into the rock.

In a heavy breath, Welch walked up to Peter and asked, "How do you think we did?"

Peter puckered his lips, then exhaled, "I think you guys did pretty damn good."

Nevada State took the course next and began their attempt. They fumbled with the hardware. Peter looked at the rival college and felt somewhat dumbfounded. They were supposed to be genuine contenders. The Nevada team struggled. They made mistakes. The hammer bearer missed the steel on several occasions. Their five minutes seemed to drag on much longer than theirs did. The whistle blew. The officials measured the depth of their hole and recorded the results on a clipboard. Could it merely be that Nevada was particularly bad, or was Butte just more prepared?

"Look at these guys; they don't know what the hell they are doing," Peter remarked.

"Hell, I thought we sucked," Cadem replied.

Eight more teams ran the gauntlet, and each time, something seemed askew. At the final scoring, Peter and his team waited for the grand announcement. In a suspenseful moment, they discovered they had been miraculously vaulted into first place. Peter shook his head in disbelief. "Awe, Suck!" he said; always using a euphemism. Why couldn't he just say the actual word 'fuck'?

The next event began: the jackleg. Butte somehow had been slated to go last. If any event was to grant Butte the largest lead ever, it was this one. Peter had been a hard rock miner ever since he was a teenager. Although the jackleg weighed almost as much as Peter, he had mastered it over the years and had tamed the wild machine. During their past weeks of training, Peter clearly demonstrated that he severely outclassed anyone on the Butte team by a mile. No one came even close to his time. All the other nine colleges had fought their way into the cement block with the drill, and now there was no one left but Butte. Peter walked up to the large six-foot by six-foot concrete cube and raised the machine off the ground. He pushed the steel tip up to the small square allotted to the Butte team. He nodded to the officials that he was ready.

With the official's violent downward swing of the arm and the word "GO" yelled, Peter opened the valve, and the drill belched to life. The bit hammered away at the cement and rotated in a hellish growl. It began to chew away at the rock. He stopped momentarily, pulled the drill back, and started a second hole. It was a technique called 'collaring'. Peter began to the second hole and pushed with all his might as he became one with the machine. The drill bit bore deeper and deeper until the long shaft had come very close to the end. The team from Butte cheered, as did many from the crowd. Peter, an underdog from Montana, proved to be a very dangerous contender because he handled the drill so impeccably well.

After completing the first hole, Peter eased back on the air valve and pulled the drill back until the bit came out of the recess. He repositioned the tip a couple of inches away to begin to access the second hole, but then had to realign himself. He stepped back with his right foot and then shifted his weight, but when he stepped back, his leg caught the hose, causing him to fall backward. The crowd gasped as he tumbled to the ground. On his way down, he pushed the jackleg away so that he would not be crushed under its weight. He landed on his back, and his head slammed into the dirt. A hush gripped the spectators.

Peter drilling with the jackleg.

With superhuman strength, Peter immediately rolled over and jumped to his feet like a heavyweight boxer racing to recover from a knock-down punch. He picked the jackleg back up and wrestled to get the air hose out of the way of his feet. Once again, he placed the drill bit against the cement cube and began to drill his second hole, but it was too late. He lost such valuable time with his blunder. The whistle blew before he could even get a quarter of the bit into the cube. By the time all teams had finished the event, Butte had taken last place. There were now only two events left in the competition. Peter walked back to his team with his head hung low in disgrace. He had been the ace in the hole for the team, the best of the best, yet he failed his comrades miserably. With only minutes away from the next event, Peter looked skyward and had a personal talk with God, just like General George S. Patton did in World War Two after being left out of the Normandy invasion. Peter cried out inside himself, "Lord, I will not be cheated out of my destiny!"

With the hand-mucking event coming up next, Cadem and Phil headed out to the starting point. But after receiving a sign from the heavens, Peter ran up and stopped Cadem. In a totally unexpected move, Peter blurted out, "Mike, you have to sit this one out."

Cadem looked back at Peter with a mixed look of confusion and disgust. "What do you mean?"

"I mean, you need to sit this one out. I have an angle on this. Trust me."

"What in the fuck are you trying to pull here? I have been training for this for weeks, and now you want to pull me off?"

"Yep."

"Fuck you, Major. Who the fuck do you think you are? Cocky as hell, and then you blow the jackleg. We thought we were going to win this thing, and you blew it."

"Wait a second, Mike! I know what I am doing. I have a big hunch here. You did great on the hand steel but let me have this one. Let me do the mucking. Trust me."

Time seemed to stand still as Phil, Welch, Smith, and Phelan watched the confrontation in total disbelief. They couldn't believe that Peter now wanted to meddle further in the team's affairs after the jackleg catastrophe.

Peter repeated himself to Cadem, "Mike. Trust me on this one. It's going to work out better than we imagined."

As upset as Cadem was, he restrained himself, probably because of his military training. He marched away, absolutely fuming, and returned to where Phelan and Welch stood.

"What's going on?" They asked.

"Peter wants to take my place for some God-forsaken reason."

"Why?"

"Hell, I don't know. But I have a bad feeling about this. He talked all this hype about us stealing the title, and just when we thought we might have a chance, he blew the fucking jackleg event. Fuck! As tired as he is, he now wants to take over the mucking."

"Shit. We are as good as fucked!" Phelan added.

"Yep. We came all the way down here for nothing. We are really going to blow it," Cadem fumed.

Welch and Smith stood together, totally speechless. They were utterly torn between their loyalty to Peter and sympathy for their teammates.

As the team stood together and looked out onto the grounds, the officials came up to the large pile of rock and an empty ore car. Phil stood on one side of the car, then bent over with shovel in hand. Peter took his position opposite Phil as if he were a mirror image. They looked up at each other, and their eyes met. In the most piercing stare he could give, Peter dilated his pupils in a somewhat possessed way and muttered, almost inaudibly to Phil, "Let's do this."

The whistle blew and their shovels simultaneously sunk deep into the rocky soil with a metallic clang. They both lifted their loads together and threw them into the ore car. With each shovelful, Peter began to chant, "Go. Go. Go," and Phil kept up in equal pursuit. Over and over, they repeated the moves: shovel down, shovel up, throw, shovel back down. Although they were the leanest contestants, they worked like two unstoppable machines. The crowd began to cheer louder and louder. Even their four teammates began to see the momentum taking place right before their very eyes.

At one point, Peter and Phil's energy began to wane. They slowed down slightly in heavy breaths but kept the rhythm. After a few moments, Peter noticed that the ore car was nearly full. He burst out and yelled at Phil, "Let's go! Let's win this thing." With newfound energy, their pace increased faster than it had been from the first few minutes. It was now or never.

A minute later, the officials dubbed the car full and gave their signal. Peter and Phil abandoned their shovels and began pushing the heavy car with all their might. Slowly at first, until it began to pick up speed. Faster and faster, the car reeled down the tracks. The crowd started to go wild with cheers. At the end of the track, the car hit the deadhead, and the whistle blew. The official recorded their times. Before they could find out the final ranking, Peter and his crew had to wait for the rest of the teams to complete the same task.

Phil and Peter staggered back to the group, fighting to catch their breath among all the cheering and back-slapping. Phelan, Welch, Smith, and Cadem aggressively shook hands with Peter and Phil, reveling over the way the two of them summoned up the last-minute, new-found energy. The four of them now conspicuously glanced out upon the competition grounds, eager to kick some more ass; each wanting to throw themselves into the fight just as Peter and Phil had done.

Within minutes, the next team took their place at the mucking sight, and the second round began. As Peter and his entourage intently watched, they noticed that the second team wasn't faring well. The disorganized group from Louisiana was somewhat out of sync with each other and fumbled with their shovels. Several of their loads didn't even make it into the car. Peter began to look around at his team and met them eye-to-eye, hinting that they had probably done even better than they had initially thought. To confirm Peter's suspicions, on the final leg of Louisiana's trial, they couldn't even push the loaded ore car down the tracks without stumbling and falling onto the ground.

After Louisiana, another team took to the pile of ore and began. As their shovels hit the ground and dirt and rocks flew through the air, Peter noticed that this team, just like the prior one, wasn't nearly as organized as they should have been. This same sequence played out time and time again as the others took to the pile of ore and awaiting ore car. After eight faltering teams, the final pair took the stage. It was none other than Arizona State, the previous year's defending champions. Silence fell upon Peter and his crew. Arizona fought hard and gallantly, attacking the rock as if they were delivering blows to the Butte team. They were going to defend their title to the end. Meanwhile, Peter had been glancing down at his wristwatch the entire time.

The whistle eventually blew, and the event came to an end. After a few minutes of the officials flipping through pages on a clipboard, they handed the sheet with the results to the commentator. The announcement came over the loudspeaker: "For the hand mucking, in first place, we have The Montana School of Mines." The crowd went wild with more cheers, and the Tech team shook hands with each other once again. A pervasive wave of invincibility suddenly overtook the rest of Peter's compatriots.

The next and last event: the track laying. This time, Butte was slated to be the final team. During the entire showing, Peter closely watched the other teams' performance and concluded that none of them did that well. When Phelan and Smith took up their positions, the official signaled the start, and they rushed out and laid out two parallel steel tracks. One held the spike, and the other swung the hammer. When the first section was securely nailed down to the railroad ties, they quickly measured the distance to the second track and began nailing it down with the spikes. When they reached the end and jumped up, the official stopped the watch and recorded their time. They had worked perfectly together like a well-oiled machine. They appeared to be unstoppable.

One of the officials walked up to the giant scoreboard, and in the box for the Montana team, he wrote a big '10'—first place. After that, he walked over to hand the results to the commentator. No one had to wait for the final announcement of who won the overall competition. It was all in plain sight, right in front of them on the giant scoreboard. Peter and his crew stood as the undisputed champions, having won every event except for the one Peter had botched with the jackleg.

After a few minutes of the officials comparing notes, the outcome became indisputable. The loudspeaker crackled, "Ladies and gentlemen, the winner of the Second Annual Mining Competition: The Montana School of Mines!" The crowd cheered for the victorious underdogs.

TEAM	BEER CHUG	HAND STEEL	HAND MUCK	JACK LEG	TRACK STAND	TOTAL PTS.
ARIZONA	THIRD	5	1	10	7	23*2
COLORADO	SEVENTH	3	3	7	5	18*4
IDAHO	NINTH	0	0	0	1	1**
MISSOURI	FIFTH	7	7	3	3	20*3
MONTANA	FIRST	10	10	1	10	31*
NEVADA	FOUR*	0	0	0	0	0
NEW MEXICO	*TH	1	0	0		1*
DAKOTA	*D	0	5	5		10*
*AH	*T	0	0			0
ISCONS*		0				

Winners of the Second Annual Mining
Competition in Tucson, Arizona.

The boys from Montana Tech were the new national champions. With the announcement having been made, the big, goofy-looking student from the University of Arizona peered over and eyeballed Phil. This time, a look of total bewilderment washed across his face. How could the last-place team from the year before, with the scrawniest members, have pulled off such a great victory? Phil, seeing this goon's gaze, stared right back. Without blinking an eye, Phil reached up as if to scratch his nose. Instead of scratching, he glared right back at his nemesis. Phil conspicuously extended his middle finger and rubbed it up and down the side of his cheek, giving the idiot from Arizona a taste of his true sentiment. The poor bastard just stood there speechless as Phil gave him the 'bird.' The big buffoon defeatedly shook his head and looked down at the ground in a symbolic sign of resignation.

The coaches talked among themselves. They were numb to what had just happened an hour earlier.

"How did they do it? Look at em', ragtag. And how about the two brothers? They look like greyhounds."

"I don't know. Maybe they just trained twice as hard as the rest of us did."

During the entire competition, Uncle Bill remained on the sideline, docile as a teddy bear. He remembered Peter's admonishment from the night before. He had stayed in the foreshadow watching, in total wonder at what his nephews were pulling off. Bill behaved perfectly, but after each event, he hooped and hollered when they announced the winners. With each win, Bill openly toasted with his beer in one hand as he pushed the burning end of his cigarette skyward as if it were an Olympic torch.

When the competition had been finally declared over, the officials summoned the top three winning teams to one corner of the grounds. There, they held a short, impromptu photoshoot with the trophies for each team. However, the official awards ceremony would be held later that night at a formal banquet.

When Pete's team knelt beneath the scoreboard and posed behind the grand trophy, Phil looked out at the crowd and instantly recognized a face that sent a chill down his spine. He gazed out again and saw the highly familiar facial features: the smile, the wavy yet graying tuft of hair, the distinct cheek lines, the creases so representative of a Ukrainian heritage.

215

Phil looked out and recognized his father's face. What in the world was Dad doing here? He had been in Canada for the past five years and now shows up in Arizona. This could not be because our father had never gone out of his way to attend any event supporting any of his children. Could he now be making a last-ditch effort to make an appearance?

In a hushed voice, Phil looked over at Peter and tried to alert him while the photographer snapped photos of the team. "Pete. Pete. PETER!"

Phil looked back at the crowd and saw the same figure, still stationary, looking out upon them with a smile. Phil tried one more time to get Peter's attention.

"What?" Peter responded impatiently out of the corner of his mouth as he kept his smile intact under the camera's view. However, when Phil looked back out at the crowd, he could no longer find our father's face. He scanned the entire mass over and over, almost in a panic. Once the photographers had finished and dismissed the winning team, Phil realized that it had been nothing more than his imagination, or maybe nothing more than a ghost. At that very moment, our father stood alone in the Canadian wilderness, looking out at the waters of the small bay below the tiny cabin that once, several years ago, housed a happy, budding family during the summer months. Our father once believed that the family would be reunited if he could only pull off his one last push, but it was an event that would never be.

By late afternoon, what was left of the crowd finally dispersed from the grounds, leaving the unsung heroes of the Arizona State University facilities department to clean up the aftermath of the competition. Peter proudly carried the trophy up to Uncle Bill.

"I knew it! I knew you fuckers were going to stomp some fucking balls! I am proud of you!" He bragged. No one on the team said much as they climbed into the van. They were beaming so proud, they didn't know what to say, there were no words.

Later that night, one more event required the presence of all the teams and their associated dignitaries. A large crowd of students, faculty, and administrators arrived downtown at the Tucson Hilton. They all filed into the grand ballroom for an exquisite banquet preceding the awards ceremony. The tables on the floor had been neatly set for the occasion, and the three trophies lay on a special table behind the podium.

With Peter's team having won this year's coveted title as national champions, the honor of presenting the awards was bestowed upon the Dean of the Science and Engineering department of the prevailing college, the Montana School of Mines. The person presenting the trophies was none other than Butte's renowned William Van Matre. However, the towering figure behind the suit, tie, and official name tag that read 'William Van Matre' was not William Van Matre at all—it was an imposter. This man held a strikingly similar name as the dean himself. This imposter just happened to be our infamous Uncle Bill, AKA William W. Miller. Instead of an educated, erudite, well-seasoned in academia handing out the trophies, they were about to be fooled by a maverick who hailed from a low-class trailer park on the south Seattle strip. Meanwhile, the authentic college dean sat at a desk in his study nearly a thousand miles away at his home in Butte. He was totally unaware that his team had taken the championship and that he was supposed to be presenting this year's awards. It's true that ignorance is bliss.

As the banquet began and the exquisite dishes were served, the TV crews from the local stations and reporters from the national sports channel ESPN were on site. As the banquet carried on, the crews began setting up their cameras. Although the footage of the competition had already been sent out over a live feed earlier that day via hi-tech satellite links, tonight, ESPN would continue their coverage and broadcast the highlights of the awards ceremony to the world just the same. The banquet progressed while Uncle Bill sat at his table consuming several gin and tonics. While knowing that he was temporarily posing as William Van Matre, Bill wrestled with his conscience. How could he seriously pull this off, presenting himself as a highly educated dean of a prestigious engineering college? How could he do this in front of a massive crowd with television cameras looming in the back of the room, focusing directly on him? He needed a few drinks to build up his courage.

Dinner ended, and the restaurant staff began to collect the plates and silverware. The master of ceremonies approached the podium and gained the audience's attention. The blinding lights of the TV cameras came to life, and the ceremony began.

"Ladies and gentlemen, I want to thank all of you for coming, and I want to thank each and every person from the University of Arizona and the City of Tucson who helped make today's event possible." The MC continued for a few minutes describing the background of the competition, how it started in Moscow, Idaho, then moved to Tucson, and how it would now be moved again, this time to Butte, Montana.

"Now, without further ado, I would like to introduce the person from the prevailing college who has the honor of presenting the awards to each winning team. From Butte, Montana, we have the Dean of Science and Engineering department from the Montana School Mines, the honorable William Van Matre. Now, let's give him a warm welcome!"

The crowd clapped and cheered wildly as the TV cameras panned the room, looking for the grand figure to stand up and make his way to center stage. Peter kicked Bill's shin under the table. "That's you. Get your ass up there!"

Bill took a final swig of his gin and tonic, let out a burp, and plopped the glass down on the table. A bead of sweat began to trickle down his forehead. He stood up and began to meander through the maze of tables until he reached the short steps up to the stage area. When he approached the podium, the MC reached out and shook Bill's hand. After he released his grasp, he handed Bill a list of the three winning colleges and their places. Bill looked down briefly upon the small print that ran across the single sheet of printer paper. He stepped behind the podium, then nervously gazed out at the crowd. Awestruck at the sight, stage fright instantly gripped him. For a moment, he lost his focus, for he had never been thrust into such a situation before (other than at the United Machinists Union board hearing, where he begged to keep his job after he made a racial slur against a coworker).

Bill looked back down at the sheet of paper, and with every bit of intestinal fortitude he had in that fat gut of his, he mustered up enough strength to find the words he needed to say. Since the competition had to do with the mining industry, Bill began to talk about what he knew regarding the rigors of life, especially when it came to hard rock mining. He started off slowly. "You know, I grew up in the depression, and life in the valley was pretty rough. The mines ran non-stop, and no one made very much money . . . and when the mines finally shut down, things became really tough."

Fuck! Bill was getting off-script! He wasn't talking like a prestigious college dean. He sounded more like an uneducated blue-collar worker. Faces in the crowd began to show signs of confusion and bewilderment. Who was this mysterious dean, and why was he talking about mines shutting down? Why couldn't he just get on with the presentation of the awards? Peter and Phil looked over at each other with grimacing faces. They shook their heads and nearly felt like crawling under the table if Bill fumbled much more at such a simple task. Meanwhile, the TV cameras kept rolling, and the reporters stood in the back of the ballroom, taking notes.

Bill continued, "A depression set over the valley and, and . . ." Finally, as if a warm, westerly wind blew through the room, Bill realized that he had drifted away from the original script. He straightened his tie and snapped out his melancholy over the past. In a tremendous act, he grasped the printout he held and looked down at the list. He started over. "It's time to present the awards to the winners of today's competition. Third place goes to Missouri. The crowd clapped and cheered, and as soon as the team captain received the trophy, he exited the stage. Bill resumed his role.

"Second place goes to Arizona." The crowd clapped and cheered once again as the team captain for Arizona rushed up to the stage to receive their trophy. Uncle Bill became more relaxed and almost felt like a true college professor.

"And for the competition's winner, first place goes to Montana Tech." The crowd roared even louder.

Peter strutted up to the stage and received the trophy. As he shook Bill's hand, he whispered but kept his mouth as still as a ventriloquist, "Crap, Bill, you did it!"

Uncle Bill winked back.

After dispensing with the three trophies, Bill glowed up on stage as if he was the one who won the competition. Peter returned to his seat and set the trophy on the table before his team. Both he and Phil sighed. It had been a close call, but Uncle Bill managed to pull off the role of the Dean of Science and Engineering for their college—by a very close margin. As the cheering subsided, the MC walked up to Bill, shook his hand, and thanked him. Bill strolled off the stage and back to his table. The entire way back, he walked two feet above the ground.

That night, Bill immersed himself in heavy drinking with Welch, Cadem, and Phelan at a less than reputable bar just down the street from their hotel. Smith chose not to go with them. Instead, he hung out with Peter and Phil, sipping on a couple of beers at the motel. Just before retiring to his bed, Phil reached over to shut off the TV. Suddenly, they heard a pounding on the door. It was Uncle Bill. In his drunken stupor, he demanded an audience with his ambitious nephews. Peter reluctantly allowed him in. Bill sat in a chair by the door and babbled on for about five minutes before Peter asked him to leave so they could get some sleep.

The next day, Peter and his team attended a minor league baseball game at the local stadium. As they sat in the grandstands eating hot dogs, drinking beer, and watching the game below, time seemed to slip past too quickly. It seemed like a mere instant when they boarded the last flight out of Tucson and headed northward toward the Montana skyline. After their connecting flight in Denver, everyone laid back in their seats, half asleep for the next hour, until they heard the announcement over the plane's intercom. They were descending into Butte. It didn't take long for Welch to peer out of the port window. Looking Northward, he saw the big M on the mountainside above the town of Butte. The lights of the big M flashed on and off like a Christmas tree. It alternately flashed the symbol of a big M, then a giant V, V for victory, a symbol only reserved for a college team returning home after a win.

He pointed it out to the others. "Hey Pete, look at that!"

The other five scrambled out of their seats and went to that side of the plane. The six of them stared out the window and stayed silent as they admired the flashing lights, knowing fully that it was for them. Immense elation overcame each one of them. It was like Noah and his family admiring the first rainbow. Here they were, not a star football team, but a mere grungy, shovel-bearing team of misfits, but champions they were.

After they landed and disembarked the plane, they did not find a reception party fit for a victorious college team. They only found a lone college student waiting outside the terminal with a van. Lackluster indeed, but it didn't matter. They had vindicated the college after last year's total embarrassment, and they thrust themselves into the shoes of national champions.

Monday morning, Phil slipped into his calculus class and sat near the back. He humbly looked out the window, daydreaming of the upcoming softball season. He couldn't wait until his friend Craig came over from Kellogg to play a few games. However, as soon as the class began, the bowtie-wearing professor made a grand announcement. "Good morning, class. I hope you all had a good weekend. But before we get started, I would like to point out that in this very room, we have a member of our mining competition team who took first place in Tucson over the weekend."

A slight hush filled the air while the professor cast his glance upon my brother Phil, sitting inconspicuously in the back row. Everyone in the class turned their heads and looked at Phil, who sheepishly looked out the window, then up at the ceiling, trying his best to avoid the attention. Several class members clapped and cheered while Phil just nodded back at the recognition.

That afternoon, during his last class of the day, Peter shut his textbook and tucked his notes into a folder. Just as he stood up from his desk, a young female student, the same girl from the administration building who had handed him the note just two months earlier, approached him once again. She handed him another note. With a bewildered look on his face, he thanked her. Peter immediately read the message, and just as before, the contents summoned Peter Major to the office of the Dean of Science and Engineering—the office of William Van Matre.

Peter hastily left the classroom and went to the administration building. He walked down the hallway, already sure of how he would present himself to the college dean. He anticipated such a meeting at some point and had already craftily planned something earlier that day. Before Peter had even reached Van Matre's office, he tracked down Marvin, the janitor. "Hey, Marv, if I treat you right, could you do me a favor?"

"Of course, anything for you, Mr. Major"

A few minutes after the exchange with Marvin, Peter walked through the door of the dean's office.

"I got word that Dean Van Matre wanted to see me right away," he told the secretary.

"Oh yes, Peter, go right on in. He is expecting you."

Peter barged through the door and, at the beckoning of the great dean, took a seat in front of the big desk.

Van Matre wasted no time, "Oh yes, Mr. Major, I heard that you did very well in Tucson. You captured the prize!"

Peter smiled but feigned humbleness like he always had. At that precise moment, Marvin walked up to the secretary just outside Van Matre's office.

"Miss Wilson, I have a special delivery for Mr. Van Matre," he said.

"That's fine, Marvin. You can leave it right there, and I will make sure the dean gets it.

"That's fine, mam, but I have special instructions to deliver it directly to the dean as soon as possible."

She hesitated for a moment with a puzzled look on her face.

"Well, if that's the case, let me page the Dean."

She pushed down one of the many buttons on her console. "Mr. Van Matre, you have a special delivery waiting for you out here, but I have been instructed to deliver it immediately."

A muffled voice crackled over her intercom, "Okay, bring it on in."

"Okay, you can go in with it," she told Marvin.

Marvin walked through the door and up to Van Matre's desk. He carried a tall, handcrafted cardboard package. He placed it on the desk directly in front of the dean. After doing so, he promptly excused himself and left the office.

Van Matre continued lecturing Peter, but before he could say much more, Peter stood up and reached toward the tall box that stood intimidatingly on the dean's desk. He pulled the thick band of packaging tape away from the base, then lifted the entire cardboard cover skyward. In a grand unveiling, there stood the first-place trophy the team had won in Tucson.

"Sir, I give you their heads on a platter," Peter said so poetically.

Van Matre's eyes sparkled as he struggled to find the words to reply. He gazed at the scintillating texture of the trophy as if he were looking at the Holy Grail itself. After what seemed to be an eternity, he spoke softly and slowly, "Very well done, Mr. Major. Very well done." Pride soared inside himself as he momentarily lived vicariously through his young protege. A lump developed in his throat, and his eyes began to water—that is, until he snapped out of it and regained his composure.

"Nice job, but this doesn't mean your ass is off the hook."—"Do you know what this victory means?"

Peter hesitated momentarily, caught off guard by Van Matre's capriciousness. Peter abandoned his dreamy thoughts of the recent victory for a moment, "Ah, yes, Sir. I mean, no, Sir."

"This means we are hosting next year's competition here on our campus."

"I understand."

"Do you!" Van Matre yelled. "This means that there is no goddamn way that we are going finish less than absolute first again! Is that clear?"

"Of course, it is. Yes, Sir."

"Good. Now that this is understood, you get your shit together and get us another winning team. You have ten months to prepare."

"Yes, Sir. Definitely."

"Good, Now get the hell out of my office!"

This time, Peter didn't bother to give Van Matre a response; the smile on his face just happened to be too huge to vocalize his true feelings. Peter had been catapulted up another notch of fame across the campus.

As Peter headed for the door, Van Matre added one last snippet to their conversation, "And, by the way, tell your brother I said congratulations." Peter merely looked back briefly and nodded as he passed the secretary's desk. Once outside the office, his walk turned into a strut, and finally into a swagger.

That evening, as night fell upon the renowned Animal House at 522 Granite Street, Peter and Phil retired to their room on seemingly different levels. Phil shut the light out next to his bed and paid no attention to the plate of devoured chicken with nothing left but bones, or to the stack of unopened textbooks with freshly printed assignments sticking out from the pages. They had been on the desk, untouched, since the first hour he got home that day.

Meanwhile, Peter sat at his desk and opened a textbook to finish his daily assignment from his Statics and Dynamics class. He picked up his mechanical pencil and Texas Instruments calculator. Once equipped with those, he donned his headphones. He started the phonograph and laid the needle down on the first track of the album 'The Good, the Bad, And the Ugly'. As the music played, he soared off again into a land of imagination. No longer were Peter and Phil the unfortunate, the disenfranchised, the unruly children of the neighborhood who ran wild without a father figure around to guide them. They would no longer be looked down upon by their relatives, who all lived stable lives with both a mother and father at home. Peter and Philip were now rising stars with so much potential lying before them. Their lives were changed forever by this victory in Tucson.

That night, the sun shone brightly down upon my brothers.

Chapter 15

School Election Upset

News of Peter and Philips's great conquest in Tucson quickly made its way back to the family in Kellogg. When word reached Kit, who was studying at the University of Idaho, he wondered if he should join next year's college team in Idaho and compete against his own brothers on the Montana team. Steve, Tim, and I were elated over their victory and felt so proud to be part of the group of Major brothers.

By this time, Peter, Kit, and Philip had now been slugging away at life, year after year, and achieving one success after another. Me? Well, I was getting into more trouble than ever. I found myself stumbling through my junior year in high school. My grades were suffering badly, so badly that I almost flunked out of geometry. Who gives a shit about geometry. I just didn't feel like doing the homework. Things got really bad when I received a 50% score on a test. Just when I didn't think it could get any worse than that—it did. I received a 0% on the following test. The situation became so precarious that my teacher contacted my mother, and that's when another massive round of guilt trips began.

"Mrs. Major, your son Anthony is a brilliant, intelligent, and capable student, but he just doesn't apply himself. If he flunks this class, he may very well have to repeat his junior year." After hearing this news, my mom shit her pants because she was a teacher herself, and the mere thought of any of her children acting like this was more than she could bear.

That evening, she admonished me like she had always done, year in and year out, over all of my misdeeds. This endless series of lectures all started from the time that I got sent home from kindergarten after being caught red-handed, beating every kid in the class in a pissing contest in the bathroom. (At least I won.)

"You should be ashamed of yourself," she repeated over and over—a comment that I had heard throughout my entire childhood. That statement was almost as bad as when she asked if I needed my head examined.

I would hear her voice echoing in my head for the rest of my life. However, at this juncture, I knew I needed a fire under my ass, but that fire came from the most unexpected place. It wasn't lit by my mother, and it wasn't lit by my teacher. It was lit by this bent nose, snaggle tooth, arrogant bitch who sat next to me in class. She came from a weird, religious, nerdy family. Her entire clan was known throughout the neighborhood for fiercely banding together on everything. I'm not saying they were into incest or anything. They just seemed to have a monopoly on the local newspaper delivery service that served the entire town. Even the emaciated old father and the bony, stretched-skinned, long dress-wearing mother were in on it. Their daughter sat next to me and touted the entire family's persona so well from her neat but scuffed-up wooden school desk.

Every time our weekly tests were handed back to us in class, she held her paper up and showed me her score. One week, it was a 97%, while mine was a 75%. Another week, when I had gotten the 50%, she pompously showed me her 95%. Each time after she lowered her paper and set it gently on the desk, she stuck her nose up into the air. It was her way of telling me she was way too good to have anything to do with a loser like me. When I received the 0% score and was given a strict reprimand by my teacher, I couldn't take her attitude for another minute. It became an all-out classroom war between her and me.

The day I got the embarrassing goose egg (the zero on the test), I took my geometry book home and spent several hours meticulously doing every single problem in the back of the chapter without skipping one.

My mother came through the back door with my little sister Allyson. When they plopped the grocery bags down on the counter, my mother noticed me sitting at the table working on my homework.

"It's nice to see you studying."

"Yeah, this stuff isn't really that hard."

"Well, keep it up, and let's see how things turn out."— "You know, you are a very brilliant young man, probably the most intelligent one in the family. You just have to apply yourself."

Her comment didn't do anything for me. After years of her reviling me for every mistake that I had ever made, her nice comments were equivalent to putting lipstick on a pig.

Just then, the phone rang, and my mother answered it.

"Tony? Yes, just a minute."— "Tony, it's Joe. He wants to talk to you."

I got up from the table and took the receiver from my mother. "Hey," I said.

"Tony, get your Honda warmed up. Let's go up the mountain."

"No. I can't."

"What do you mean you can't?"

"I have to study."

"Studying is for pussies. We are going up there any minute."

"No! I can't. I am doing something really serious."

"Well, shit, man. Don't let me stop you then. I guess I will just go myself."

I hung up and went back to studying. I was going to fry that wench's ass on the next test. That's all I cared about.

I kept this after-school studying routine up for an entire week until our next scheduled test. After the teacher handed out the examination, I sharpened my pencil and went to work. Every question seemed like child's play. The next day in class, our teacher did exactly what he had always done: he handed out our graded papers—and sure as shit, ole Snaggle Tooth did what she had always done. She held up her test and haughtily showed me her score: an impressive 96%. I held up my paper and showed her my impressive 100%. She looked like she had seen a ghost and began to tremble as if she was ordered in front of a firing squad. That night, I went back to the kitchen table and worked out every problem in the next section. I did this every night for the rest of that week. After taking the next test, we waited till the following day to get our papers. This time, she tried again. She held up her paper with a sarcastic smile and showed it to me. Wow, an impressive score of 98%. I then held up my paper and showed her mine, an another impressive 100%. She instantly turned pale and swallowed. I thought she was going to throw up. We did this for another week. Her next score was 97%, mine: 100%. That shut that bitch up for the rest of the semester. She never showed me her test scores ever again.

Now that I had saved my ass in geometry class, I went about my other classes with renewed confidence. As we were reaching the end of the school year, I thought there were no further surprises for me, no more chances to get into trouble. Unfortunately, just when I was minding my own business, a crisis landed right in my lap, with no fault of my own, and I mean by no fault of my own. Certain things in life drove me absolutely berserk: one is stupidity, and the other is conformity. This time, they both came wrapped in the same package and showed up right on my desk, just like a special delivery.

From the very first day of school, the second period class had been deemed our homeroom, which meant that any official school business involving direct participation by the students would be conducted during that hour. With only two weeks of class time remaining before the year officially ended, we were hit with one more collective duty to perform. We had to elect class officers for the following year. This was it. We were preparing for our senior year, which meant whoever won the coveted position of class president would give our commencement speech at our graduation. Additionally, they would lead the entire class across the stage at the ceremony. Just the thought of participating in such a mundane, overrated event made me nauseous. To make things worse than I could possibly imagine, our homeroom teacher was the school's head basketball coach. I don't know which I hated more, the sport itself or this prick. Regardless, I wanted no more trouble this school year and decided to enforce a self-imposed gag order on myself (something I had never been able to pull off before.) I was sure I could do it this time, especially after achieving three perfect scores in geometry. However, it would never happen. I had one huge strike remaining against me, and it had to do with sports. Not only was I a wrestler, and not a basketball player, I had also displayed great disregard for our school's letterman's club.

Since we attended Kellogg Senior High School, the faculty dubbed the letterman's club the 'K' club, K standing for Kellogg—and boy, did I hear enough about it throughout the months. It seemed like every other day during the entire fucking school year, the intercom came to life, and the secretary in the office repeatedly boomed out the message, "K Club meeting in the cafeteria. K Club meeting in the cafeteria!" I heard it so much and had grown so sickened by it that I formed an organization called the 'Anti-K Club'. I even went so far as to print up membership cards, and this homeroom teacher/head basketball coach knew all about it. He had me pegged. I was a marked man. If I just slipped out of line one inch, he would have my ass.

With my gag order supposedly in place and my old reputation all but behind me, this prick began class by making an announcement. "Good morning, class. The school year is drawing to an end, and it's time for us to elect class officers for next year."

At first, I didn't pay any attention because I was looking out the window and daydreaming. This jerk continued his little spiel until he reached the point where he began to solicit nominations for class president, vice president, secretary, and sergeant-at-arms. Still, I really didn't give a shit—that is until some moronic kid with braces raised his hand and made a nomination for class president. I couldn't believe who he nominated. "What the fuck?" I thought to myself, "Is the kid just regurgitating the same popular name that he has heard over the past five years? Didn't he have a fucking brain of his own to be slightly original and think of someone new?"

Our lovely teacher took a piece of chalk and began writing the moron's nomination on the board. One by one, as my fellow brain-dead students made the nominations, I could no longer contain myself. "Oh, my fucking God!" I blurted out.

Mr. Wellington paused and squinted his eyes at me with a total look of hatred and disgust. He knew I was a troublemaker; his blood boiled over my disruption. While he had been so delighted with the nominations because they were virtually the same popular students that had been elected as class officers, year in and year out since the seventh grade, the jocks, the cheerleaders, and the teacher's pets, he instantly grew upset. I was now raining on his parade. First off, the same old names irked me, and secondly, the fact that these retarded students in my class were nothing more than brainwashed sheep who couldn't think for themselves made me puke just the same. The first guy who made the nomination was an idiot and a conformist, one of the lowest life forms in society—a one-celled organism.

"Mr. Major, do you have something to say?"

I looked at Mr. Wellington blankly.

"Mr. Major, do you have a nomination to make?"

For an instant, I was dumbfounded, but then I had to think quickly on my feet. I vowed that I would one-up this pussy of a teacher. I would kick his ass at his own game, somehow, someway! I looked next to me and saw my good friend Gino White. Gino and I had known each other since grade school. We were both nice Catholic boys and had attended Catechism classes together until this year when Father O'Sullivan permanently kicked me out, all because I had no clue how to prove that God exists. Fortunately, Gino remained a good boy and stayed in Father O'Sullivan's good graces. However, he strayed a little bit from the beaten path when he co-founded the Anti-K club with me—a risky move. My uncontrolled spontaneity suddenly kicked in. I just had to do it. I just had to nominate Gino for senior class president.

From the first thought, I knew that nominating Gino for class president was a long shot because he had one major strike against him: he was not an athlete, and I knew he would not get much support from the head basketball coach. Instead of participating in sports, Gino and his friend Todd spent most of their time between classes imitating the famous comedian, Steve Martin. They wore out the phrase, "I'm a wild and crazy guy." But at this pregnant moment, I looked over at Gino and silently prayed, "Thank you, God!" Gino was perfect.

"I nominate Gino for class president."

Gino looked shocked, and Mr. Wellington looked doubtful. So, I boldly repeated my nomination, "Gino for class president!"

Mr. Wellington turned to the chalkboard and very slowly and very reluctantly scrawled out Gino's name. From across the room, I could sense the burning going on inside his brain and see the smoke coming from his ears. Gino becoming class president and beating out this teacher's favorite jock basketball player was his worst nightmare. Getting Gino on the ballet had only been the beginning of the audacious moves that I had up my sleeve. My imagination went into overdrive. Now, I had to actually get him elected.

The following day, I strolled into my second-period class a little earlier than usual. The room was nearly empty except for the several students gathered around Wellington's desk. Not one of them noticed me, not even Wellington. I sat down in my chair and began to doodle in my notebook until I heard my wretched teacher saying to the students around him, "I don't like the idea of this Gino being elected as class president. It would upset everything in your final year in school."

I almost swallowed my tongue. I couldn't believe the gall that this teacher had. Just when all of us students thought we all had a friend in the most gregarious teacher on the staff, I came to find out that he was a snake, a two-faced phony chunk of bologna. My blood boiled. It took me no longer than two seconds to throw down the gauntlet and decide to launch the biggest blitzkrieg of my teenage years. Wellington's ass was toast. I was going to hit that bastard with everything I had. I left my books on my desk and quickly darted out of the room. Near the end of the hallway, I found Gino and Todd laughing and joking with two sophomore girls. Evidently, they were trying to get somewhere with these young cuties, but I don't think Todd nor Gino had the machismo to pull it off.

"Gino! You won't fucking believe what I just heard!"

He withdrew the smile from his face, slightly disappointed in me for interrupting his charm session. "What?"

"Wellington is in there right now talking to the jocks, and he said, I don't like the idea of this Gino White being elected as class president and something else like that."

The look in Gino's eyes grew very distant. He was unsure of what that meant. The actual election wasn't going to be held until Friday. What should Wellington's comment mean to him? Until he could collect his thoughts, all Gino could say was, "Really?"

"You know, I hate that Wellington bastard. Everyone in his classes seems to like him, but he only cares about his little clique of students." Right there in front of Gino, I excoriated our homeroom teacher in the worst way.

"Yeah, I noticed that about him, but what do you plan to do?"

I wasn't sure what I would do but I was outraged enough that I would turn this entire election upside down.

The following morning at school, everything seemed routine except for the campaign posters that started appearing in the cafeteria, gymnasium, and hallways. Nothing had changed in the school elections over the past several years. The typical posters merely said something as bland as: "Kevin Johnson for President"—just as dry and unimaginative as can be. Back in our second-period class, Gino and I took our seats. He turned toward me and whispered, "Did you see all the posters?"

"Yep"

"Well, I haven't made any posters yet. How the hell am I supposed to win?"

"Leave that to me," I reassured him.

I still wasn't exactly sure what I would do, but my plan at this time was to analyze what everyone else was doing and do something that the student population would never expect. Somehow, I had to attack the opposition in a way they had never prepared for. There were still three more days until the election, and I was determined to gather more intelligence. More important than what was happening in plain sight was what was happening behind the scenes. What was going on in the minds of the average student, the voter? Being the instigator I was, I began casually and unbiasedly asking the upcoming senior class students who they were voting for. Most of the time, their choices were for the same old people, the popular ones, the only names they were familiar with. They were too dumb to vote for anyone other than the well-known students. Sadly, nobody in their school experience gave them any reason to vote for someone different.

I went home that night and quickly folded up a piece of typing paper so that when I unfolded it, the entire sheet had creases separating the page into eight different sections. In each section, I wrote the same message repeatedly in each of the squares, "Gino for Class President," along with my traditional smiley face with the pointed ears, my trademark. I ran over to Sunnyside School and had my mother print twenty copies with the school copy machine, just like she had done with my wanted posters of Wendy Wieselheimer back in the sixth grade. (This time, she did it with an upgraded copy machine instead of the old mimeograph.) Once I got home, I used my mother's paper cutter to cut all the sheets up like dollar bills coming off the presses at the U.S. Treasury. I now had 160 calling cards for Gino, Todd, and me to hand out personally to as many students as we could.

After racing to school the following day, I met up with Gino and Todd.

"Hey! Look at what I got."

"Campaign posters. Alright!" Gino said. When he took one look at them, he continued. "But it doesn't say much. It just says Gino for class president."

"I know. I did this for a reason. It's just a beta test."

"A test?"

"Yeah. It doesn't say much because we don't know what's on students' minds."

"Then what's the purpose?"

"The purpose is to hand them out and start getting some feedback. For example, why will they vote for the other guys instead of you."

One thing that I knew about psychology is that Sigmond Freud once claimed that no person can keep a secret; if they do not say it with words, they will give themselves away with the tapping of their fingers or something of that nature. With this in mind, I was going to get the other students to talk, and when they talked enough, I would know what hot button to push on the next poster.

Gino, Todd, and I began handing the newly printed slips out to students between classes and asked for their votes. It didn't take long for me to figure something out. Many students asked why they should vote for Gino. I threw that right back into their faces. "Why would you vote for Kevin Johnson? Hasn't he been a class officer every year for five years? What has he ever done worth a shit for our class?" My response posed a dilemma in many of their minds. At the end of the day, after talking to so many students, I thought of a zinger to throw at the entire student body, but I had to act fast; the elections were just a couple of days away.

The next day at school, I once again opened a dialogue with random students. I still wasn't quite sure what my final message would be. After dinner that night, I sat on my bed and pulled random books off my shelf. Somehow, I had grown to be quite a bibliomaniac. I had collected books from garage sales, flea markets, and sales at the public library. One such book I added to my collection was one of famous quotes. I opened it up and began thumbing through the pages, where I stumbled across a quote: "You will never influence the world by trying to be like it" Anonymous.

It hit me like a bolt of lightning. In every campaign poster at school, the words were all the same. Everyone was trying to influence the voters, but everyone was trying to influence them the same old way with the same old message. Every candidate was trying to be like the others. In an article in a writer's magazine, an agent claimed that during countless auditions in Hollywood, many wanna-be stars imitated the current popular actors and singers. He said, "That's a huge mistake because what the world screams for every day is something new." That was it! Gino had to be totally different, totally new. But the day was nearly over, and there wasn't much I could do at this late hour, but I was going to do something, somehow.

Leaning against my top bunk, I scribbled out some slogans on a tablet. The creative juices started to flow. I was on fire. I drafted up a campaign poster complete with a brand-new appeal. When I finished, I felt proud of my work, but I resigned myself to the fact that it was too little, too late. Gino would just have to let fate determine the outcome of the election. I did all that I could do. There was no way I could get any campaign posters made tonight. The sun had gone down, and the day was nearly over.

I left my bedroom and did what I always did at 8:00 in the evening: I made myself a peanut butter and marshmallow sandwich. As I stood at the kitchen counter laying out even rows of miniature marshmallows onto the thick layer of peanut butter, I reflected on a time six years earlier when I wanted to be a newspaperman and start my own local paper at the ripe age of eleven years old. Then it dawned on me. I had a printing press! It had been boxed up in the basement for several years.

I quickly poured a glass of milk and wolfed down the sandwich. I needed all the energy I could muster to complete my mission. I went into the laundry room, moved the hamper from its traditional spot, and pulled away the rug. There lay the trap door that led down to the basement. Our basement was more like a makeshift wine cellar and reminded me of Dr. Frankenstein's laboratory. I flipped on the light switch, and no matter how creepy the little the basement was, I climbed down the wooden steps. At the far end of the cellar lay an ancient shelving unit that stood leaning at an angle as if it were ready to fall over. On the middle shelf, I spotted a familiar yellow and red box. As I grew closer, I could see down through a clear cellophane window built into the cover. Inside lay my old rotary printing press. It sat unused for years. By a complete stroke of luck, it had not been thrown out over time. Now, it was a Godsend—manna from Heaven.

It took me over an hour, sitting at the kitchen table, to organize all the tiny rubber type and insert them into the metal rails. I spelled out my message as clearly and succinctly as any propaganda minister ever could. Fortunately, years earlier, I had ordered several sizes of type and colors of ink, along with rubber clip art. By 10:00 that night, I had cut up over two hundred sheets of 5"x 8" paper of different colors. I slowly ran the first sheet through the hand-cranked press. Out the other side came my handy work—work that I knew would make its mark on the world. By 11:00 that night, everyone had already gone to bed except my mother. She had been correcting her students' homework the entire time I worked on my propaganda. In a sense, I felt silly being seventeen years old and playing with a children's toy printing press, but desperate times require desperate measures. This toy helped me complete my mission: produce two hundred propaganda fliers for the campaign blitz.

In the morning, I woke up too excited to just lay there and sleep in. I jumped out of bed and looked at the top of my dresser to ensure my precious work was still there and not merely part of a dream. After devouring two slices of toast, I put all my flyers into a brown paper lunch bag. When my mom left the house and headed out the back door toward Sunnyside School, I snuck into her bedroom and rifled through all her drawers until I found the office supplies I was looking for. Bingo, I grabbed several rolls of her Scotch tape and threw them in the bag with the flyers.

When I arrived at the school, I raced through the hallways until I met Gino. I held up the brown paper bag.

"What's that?" he asked, pointing at the bag.

"I just robbed a bank."

"No, really, what's in there?"

"You want to win the election, don't you?"

"Of course, I do, but I don't see how I am going to."

"Well, we are going feed Wellington and our class a real big shit burger!"— "You know how most of our classmates are brain-dead? I am going to give them something for them to all think about." I pulled out one of the flyers and handed it to Gino. He silently read the script, with his lips mouthing the words. At the end, he burst into laughter.

"I love it! Damn, I love it. But where are you going to put them?

"We, WE, are going to plaster them all over the fucking school. But we will need some help, and we will have to dump first period."

He hesitated. "Oh, I don't know if I can."

"Dammit! You want to win the election, don't you?" I almost yelled at him.

"Sure, I do."

"Then we gotta do what we gotta do. We are going to have to get some help, though." As soon as I said that I looked down to the far end of the hallway, near the door leading to the stairs. There I saw two of my brother Steve's friends. I had an idea. I marched down the hallway, almost knocking over a few students along the way.

I walked up to Wilksie and asked, "Hey, do you want to skip first period and stir up some real shit today?"

He almost looked insulted that I would ask such a dumb question. "Why would I want to do anything else?"

Just then, Mr. Wellington walked up the last few steps from the downstairs hallway, turned, and strolled past us. "Shhhhhh!" I said to Wilksie and his friend as I inconspicuously looked in the other direction.

Once Wellington was out of earshot, I pulled out one of the flyers and told them what their mission was: bombard the entire school with these flyers, anywhere and everywhere, and in the craziest places that they could possibly imagine. We had to create the biggest spectacle before the end of the first period. I handed them each a bundle of flyers and a roll of Scotch tape. I could tell by the grins on their faces that they were totally on board. Now, all we had to do was wait until the final bell rang and first-period class had begun. Once the hallways were empty and quiet, we could then disperse in all directions and go to work.

The bell rang, and just like clockwork, all the students obediently disappeared into their respective classrooms. Our time had come—but not quite yet. The sound of footsteps coming up the cement stairs broke the silence. I peeked over the rail and looked down the stairwell. I spotted Mr. Wier, the assistant principal. Oh shit! He was showing up in the wrong place at the wrong time. I motioned for everyone to follow me up the stairs to the next floor. There we waited. I peeked over the railing once again. Thank God, Mr. Wier turned and went down the second-floor hallway.

"Gino, see where Mr. Wier is going."

"Crap, he might see me."

"Do it!"

"Okay, okay."

Gino tip-toed down the stairs and ever so cautiously looked around the corner to see what Wier was up to. He watched our assistant principal stroll halfway down the hallway and make a sharp left into Mr. Adam's history class. Gino looked back up at me with a dumbfounded look. I shrugged my shoulders. He started whispering at me and making hand gestures. I couldn't tell what the hell he was trying to say. Gino looked back down the hallway and suddenly ran back up the stairs. "Forget about Wier," I thought. "We just have to do this no matter what." We agreed to spread out in different directions. Wilksie headed downstairs toward the gymnasium and the shop classes. His friend went to the library, study hall, and office area, while Gino and I took the east wing and the second, third, and fourth floors.

Just as Gino and I were about to go around the corner and head down the hallway, Gino grabbed my arm and pulled me back. In a loud whisper, he said, "It's Wier! He's coming back!!"

"Shit! Let's just wait. He'll be gone in a minute," I said.

We retreated once again to the stairs leading to the third floor. Thankfully, we heard Wier's footsteps on the concrete stairs. This time, they were heading back down and not up. Apparently, Mr. Wier had merely delivered a note to Mr. Adams and was now returning to the office. With the pressure off, Gino and I split up. Our little band splattered the posters everywhere, even above a couple of urinals in the boy's bathroom and in the girl's stalls. Before we ran out of time, we ran out of posters. There was nothing more for us to do except wait for the first period to be over.

We sighed in relief when the bell finally rang. We began to mingle with the students who were gushing out of their classrooms. I watched with much pleasure as they noticed the flyers taped to lockers, the drinking fountains, and even to the bathroom mirrors. One student, very close to us, plucked a flyer off a wall locker and read it to his friend, "Are you tired of seeing the same old jock, egghead, and teacher's pet being elected as class president. Aren't you ready for a change? VOTE GINO—HE'S REAL!" His friend snatched the flyer and looked at it very closely.

"Hey, look at this shit at the bottom: Anti K-Club Publications, Propaganda Department." He laughed. "Who in the hell made this? This is great!"

Gino and I meandered through the crowded hallway and made it to our homeroom class. We sat down next to each other and smiled. The bell finally rang, and although the class was supposed to begin, Wellington was nowhere to be found. After a few minutes of silence, Wellington entered the class and headed straight to his desk. As he sat down, I noticed he was holding one of Gino's campaign posters. He looked down at it and shook his head back and forth in disbelief.

After regaining his thoughts, my favorite asshole of a teacher finally called the class to order. He announced that the voting for the senior class officers would take place in the gymnasium during our lunch break and that we should all attend. Wellington seemed so distressed by our two-hundred poster blitz that he had difficulty focusing on the material he was trying to teach us. He stuttered and paused several times during the instruction. I knew the thought of Gino becoming class president was more than he could bear.

Lunchtime came and went, and the voting took place. At the end of the day, just before our final class ended, the intercom system came to life, and a familiar voice from the office began speaking. "The election results for next year's student body officers are as follows: For All Student Body secretary: Lori Smith, for Sergeant at Arms: Todd Griffith, for All Student Body vice president: Bob Burden, for All Student Body president: John Brower." The long-time school secretary paused and cleared her throat before continuing, "And for senior class president. . . Gino White."

I almost collapsed in my seat and rolled onto the floor. I felt so relieved. I knew it. I just knew that we could pull it off for Gino because my distaste for the status quo was that great. I don't know what class Gino was in at the time, but I could feel his smile. We had done it! We had pulled off the impossible, and school history would be changed.

Just by chance, Gino and I met in the hallway after school.

"Tony, I can't believe we pulled it off."

"Me neither."

"What do you plan to do after graduation? Think you'll go to college?"

"Hell no! I just want to go back to Canada and stay there forever. How about you?"

"Ah, I plan to go to college for sure, probably down in Moscow."

"Well, we still have a year to go. You better make your mark on the school. You are now the new senior class president."

"Yep, and I have plans."

"Gino, as soon as school is out, I won't see you again until the end of summer."

"I know. You have fun up there in Canada. Our senior year is going to be great."

With the election victory out of the way, I still faced a busy schedule preparing for my brother Kit's wedding as well as my sister Kim's. I was to play a major part in both ceremonies (no pun intended). At Kim's Catholic wedding, my brother Steve and I served as altar boys and had to wear the stupid girly robes and stand next to the priest who wore an even fancier girly robe.

At Kit's wedding, Uncle Bill and I were to serve as attendants while Jay Helms would perform the part of the best man. The four of us men were to wear fancy tuxedos, but I didn't want to be seen in a tuxedo any more than I wanted to be seen in a girly robe. I prayed to God and hoped that no girls from any of my high school classes would be there at the wedding to see me all doo-daddied up. Unfortunately, I was bound to get nailed. Little did I know that Kit's ceremony was to come with a unique surprise for me.

It all started a year and a half earlier, during the first few weeks of my sophomore year. I had met one of the cutest girls ever in a chance encounter. She was the next best thing to being a cheerleader; she was on the drill team. My heart melted when I first saw her strut down the hallway in her uniform and cute cowboy-like booties. Somehow, our paths eventually crossed, and we started talking, laughing, and joking around.

After becoming so mesmerized by her, I would go to the gym after school and watch her and the rest of the team practice their moves out on the basketball court. They danced to a top-forty musical hit from the movie Grease, the song: "You're the One That I Want" sung by Olivia Newton-John and John Travolta. This beautiful creature that I suddenly had the hots for was a girl named Ronnie Stuckey. Soon she began to hold onto my arm in the hallways and introduce me to her friends as her boyfriend. I was so petrified. She was too good to be true, but I was too terrified to even know what to do about it.

Then, one day, late in the fall, she walked out of my life. She disappeared from school, and no one knew where she had gone. Throughout the winter and into the spring, I thought of her every time I heard an obscure song by Mellissa Manchester.

The months dragged on until the last week of school. Just before summer vacation, I ran into a friend of hers.

"Did you know that Ronnie is back in town?" She asked me.

"No way!"

"Yep."

"Where is she?"

"She lives in that little house right across from the city park."

Butterflies in my stomach began to swarm. I had to find her. Later that day, I went to the park, sat in the grass, and looked at her house for an hour. I finally got up the nerve to knock on the door. When I did, to my surprise, she answered. What a sight for sore eyes. She was back!

Every day that week, I tripped over myself to go over and see her. Finally, I made a bold move and took her out on a date to a drive-in movie, but I had no idea what the hell I was doing. Everything seemed so uncomfortable. The night ended up being awkward, but it soon ended. In another twist, two days after that date, I left town and spent the summer in Canada with my father, leaving HER behind this time. Would anything ever work out for me?

When I returned that fall, nothing further ever transpired between her and me. We both seemed to have changed. We barely talked to each other that school year. However, in the spring, nearly a year after our one and only date, we would have one last encounter. It happened at Kit's wedding. It was something that would be captured and preserved for a lifetime.

I got caught wearing a tuxedo.

The church was packed, and the ceremony ended beautifully. My brother and his new bride strolled down the aisle with the best man and the maid of honor right behind them. Next came Uncle Bill and the first bride's maid. I was the last to walk down the aisle with the other bridesmaid clinging to my arm. With only a few pews left to pass, Ronnie appeared out of nowhere and staged an ambush. She jumped up from the last pew with a camera in her hand. She snapped a photo, and the flash nearly blinded me. She had caught me on film wearing a tuxedo. Damn her!

A few days later, she ran around the hallway at school, showing off the picture of me wearing the tux. Ironically, sometime during the day, she accidentally dropped the photo on the floor and went her merry way, unknowingly having lost it. In a bizarre event, my wrestling coach (and my future brother-in-law) found the photo on the hallway floor, luckily untrampled. He gave it to me during the last class of the day. The photo was now mine, all mine!

A week later, school was dismissed for the year, and I would not see Ronnie again for many years to come. I would never have her. I would only have her photo, the one that she had taken of me. Fate had it that

Ronnie and I would never date. We would just end up being good friends for the rest of our lives.

Besides savoring the retrieval of the illicit wedding photo, Gino's school election upset had made my year. I realized that an old era had ended and a new one had just begun. Over the next school year, Gino would govern our senior class and give the commencement speech at our graduation. From there, he would go on to college and become the student president at the University of Idaho. Ultimately, Gino became an Idaho State congressman—the youngest in the state's history . . . and it all began with my distaste for conformity.

NORTH-SOUTH NOTES
■ *Betsy Russell*

Gino White adding bite to candidacy

BOISE — HE WAS THE CATALDO boy who became one of the youngest ever to serve in the state Legislature.

So where is Gino White today? The one-time Silver Valley political whiz kid is down in Boise, where after four years as a deputy state controller, he's running for the Legislature again.

Gino's return to politics.

Chapter 16

Tim and the Cliff Inferno

My senior year of high school had finally started. I was now the cock of the walk, just like I was in the sixth grade. The first day of school excited me like no other. I was a senior, the big kid on the block, and the girls were prettier than ever. My head was spinning over the meeting of old friends and new sophomores who had just joined us from the junior high.

At the end of the first week, the Friday night football game attracted much of the town and hordes of students looking for a good time. My God, I hated football almost as bad as I hated basketball, so I rarely went to the games (kind of a self-imposed boycott). Instead of rooting on our high school team, my brother Tim and I again picked up our favorite fall-time sport. We began to hide around the neighborhood at night and throw rotten apples and mushy plumbs at cars. This kept us quite busy.

September flew by pretty fast, and then October began. Tim and I knew damn well what was coming up: Halloween. This year, I planned to do the usual: hunting down the local police cars and pelting them with eggs. That was a given, but I worried about Tim. He was a big freshman now and could fend for himself, but I was curious about his intention. From previous experience, I realized that Tim did have one advantage over me. He must have studied economics because he believed in something called economies of scale. If I bought two cartons of eggs to throw at the police, he bought twenty. If I hooky bobbed one block behind a car on the icy streets, he'd go for five. If I made a homemade rocket from a paper towel tube, he'd make one out of a huge Christmas wrapping paper tube.

I knew Tim was up to something big this Halloween, but I didn't know what. Little did I know, he had been planning for weeks for a surprise prank to be staged up on the cliff. Phil and Craig's antics with the firecracker cliff shows inspired him so. However, this year, Tim didn't stock up on fireworks as Phil and Craig had done, and he couldn't find any of their secret caches hidden in any of the bedrooms. Coming up shorthanded, Tim simply had to improvise. He made the cliff his focus. Every day of the week leading up to Halloween, Tim packed something secret and clandestine up the rocky face of the cliff and stashed it up there. I wasn't sure what it was, but he returned each night from the mountainside with a huge grin of satisfaction.

Halloween night had finally arrived. I got home from school and waited till after dark before I would take off through the neighborhood.

"Hey Tim, are you coming with me in a few minutes?" I asked him.

"I can't."

"What do you mean you can't?"

"I've got a surprise to pull off first."

"What? Are you going to egg someone's house?"

Tim kept tight-lipped. He wouldn't tell me what he was going to do.

"Come on, tell me what you're up to."

"No! You'll see it in a bit. Just go out egging, and I'll catch up later."

Just then, several kids from school came directly to our house and pounded on the back door. When I answered, I was surprised they were some of Tim's freshman classmates. They knew me well from all the hiking and camping we did.

"Hey Tony, let's hit it! We just saw two cop cars down the street."

Every one of them held a carton of eggs in their hands. "Damn, how many eggs do you guys have?" I asked.

"Oh, don't worry, we have more stashed down at the end of the block."

"Okay, let me grab mine."

We went out the back gate and wandered down the dark alley. We began our patrol.

As little kids, dressed in their costumes, banged on doors begging for candy, I went on the hunt for cops, while Tim and his friend, Darrin, snuck up the street. They were armed with a milk jug full of an illicit liquid, a book of matches, and a solitary pack of firecrackers. They started up the mountainside. Halfway up to the summit, they stopped and rested.

"Oh, crap, this is going to be good," Tim told Darrin.

"Do you think we'll get caught?"

"Hell no. We'll be off the cliff before anyone even shows up."

"Well, I hope you're right because my mom and dad would kill me."

"Don't worry about it."

Tim looked back down at the town. Ghoulish visions came alive in his mind—this would be his best stunt yet. After catching their breath, they continued to the top. Once there, they rested before they did anything. They wanted to be entirely prepared for the frantic run down the mountainside.

In the faint light, the two of them admired Tim's handywork. Over the past several weeks, Tim had carried armload after armload of firewood up the mountainside, as well as a few old rubber car tires. The milk jug they carried contained the last ingredient needed to create the most dazzling spectacle of the night. It was a liquid none other than gasoline. Setting it ablaze on top of all the firewood and tires would be like launching the Saturn V rocket during the Apollo moon missions.

Once this monstrosity burst into flames, the neighborhood would know it, the entire town would know it and the police—especially would know it.

Tim laid the jug of gasoline on top of the heap of firewood and placed the pack of firecrackers directly on it, just as if he were placing a cherry on top of a birthday cake. He paused and looked at Darrin. Darrin nodded his head. Tim lit a match and touched the flame to the bundle of fuses. They jumped back, turned, and started to run down the hill. After a mere fifty feet of sprinting into the darkness, the firecrackers all went off, and then there was silence. Tim and Darrin stopped and looked back up. They saw no flames. The firecrackers did not burn through the plastic jug and ignite the gasoline as they had expected. Dammit! Tim didn't have any more firecrackers. He would have to light the gasoline himself.

They walked back up the pile of wood. Tim took the lid off the jug and dumped the entire gallon over the wood and tires. He then dropped the plastic container on top. He stood back and pulled the matches out of his pocket. He struck a match very hesitantly, let it develop into a full flame, and then threw it at the petrol-soaked pile. The moment the match landed, the pile instantly exploded into a giant fireball, almost knocking Tim and Darrin flat on their butts. The searing heat nearly singed their hair and eyebrows.

"Let's get out of here!" Tim yelled. He and Darrin trembled from the horror of what they had just done.

They bounced down the hill into the darkness like young deer fleeing a pursuing hunter. The two partners in crime hastily made their way across the flats and down the same beaten path to the alley behind Butler's place. From there, they sprinted around the corner and down the little pathway from Elder to Mission Avenue.

Once in the safety of our front yard, they looked up at the cliff through the now leafless Maple trees. The entire mountainside had lit up with a devilish orange glow as the flames leaped ten feet into the air. The wood intensely crackled while the tires burned like the fires of hell. The blaze could easily be seen from anywhere in town—especially uptown Kellogg; the location of the Kellogg Police and Fire Department. Like a scene from Dante's Inferno, the townspeople saw the raging fire from a place where there should never be fire since there were no trees around the cliff. They had seen fireworks going off up there before, but not a fiercely burning fire. Phone calls flooded into the police station, backing up the phone lines that were already clogged up with reports of eggings, assaults on kids' candy bags, sightings of Elvis, etc.

A fire truck was sent directly to the scene. The engine and company blew their loud horns as they blasted through every intersection across town. When the emergency crews reached the base of the cliff, a handful of people loitered around the street corners with their eyes fixed upward at the dancing flames, many of their mouths gaping open. Two firefighters in full gear jumped out of the truck and began the ascent up the rocky slope. They both carried large, red, cylindrical fire extinguishers. The sweat started dripping down their cheeks and foreheads within minutes of climbing.

"Hey Joe, what do ya think is burning up there?" One of them asked the other.

"I don't know. There's nothing to burn up there."

"Yeh. I guess we'll find out in a minute."

Down on the street, the crowd waited in deep suspense. Was it an airplane crash? Maybe a KKK cross-burning? Upon reaching the blaze, the two firefighters looked at the black smoke billowing skyward and the flames that angrily spat out molten pieces of burning rubber from the worn-out Goodyear car tires. Within seconds, both red extinguishers unleashed their suffocating cloud of white chemicals and quickly quelled the inferno. The mountainside grew instantly dark.

"Joe, what crazy fool would do this kind of shit?"

"Kids, just kids."

"Well, they definitely need their asses kicked, and maybe their parent's too."

On this very night, Chief Charlie sat in front of his TV, totally mesmerized by the polka dancers performing their act on the Lawrence Welk show. He charged his wife with the duty of answering the door for trick-or-treaters while he enjoyed his one fetish: watching this show. He would not be disturbed.

When the phone rang this time, he didn't even hear it. It rang and rang until his wife finally yelled at him.

"Charlie. Charlie! Answer the phone, dear."

"Ah, ah, yes, honey."

He picked up the receiver and put it up to his ear, "Hello."

"What?"—"Fire?"—"Where?"—"And?"—"Oh, okay."— "Keep up the good work. Just have them put everything in their report, okay? Bye."

He hung up the handset and shook his head in a slight daze. "Why me?" he said to himself. "Why me?"

Once again, he regretted his decision to become the chief of police. The past few years had been a living hell for him. Suddenly, he realized that there was one more thing to do while the night was still active. He picked the phone back up and dialed the police station.

"Maltby, this is the chief. Listen here, even though that fire is put out on that cliff, I want every available car sent over to that neighborhood. Have them patrol the streets and alleys on Mission, Mullan, and Elder Avenue."— "Yes. That's right."— "Yes. Even Meyers. I know he's a sneaky little shit, but I need all hands on that neighborhood. I bet you donuts to dollars that whoever started that fire is still lurking in the immediate vicinity, and I want him found!" The chief slammed the receiver down. He immediately got up to raise the volume on the TV in hopes that he could finish the Lawrence Welk show in peace.

After hearing from the chief, the dispatcher at police headquarters got on the airwaves and ordered all available cars to divert to the Mission Avenue area. The chief wanted some butts. Even if they had to frame somebody, find a scapegoat, pin it on a dupe, anything, he wasn't going to come up empty-handed.

After combing through the neighborhood for a while, my friends and I continued to prance through the dark alleys and lay in wait behind the hedges in random neighbor's yards. For some reason, our neighborhood had suddenly become a target-rich environment. It seemed, more patrol cars were driving around than when we had first started. Just as we ran through one yard to try and get a clean shot at a police car on one street, we turned around only to spot another one coming up the street that we had just left. What the hell was going on? Chief Charlie had inadvertently sent all his available police cars into an unexpected ambush. It was going to be a turkey shoot for us high school kids.

We caught up to one patrol car and splattered the side of it with several eggs. The yellowish yoke splattered all over the driver's side window, and the white eggshells fragmented and went in every direction. The officer instantly brought the car to a screeching halt. He slammed the car in reverse, and with the tires squealing on the pavement, backed up just enough to ram the transmission into drive. He violently turned down the alley with his headlights leading the way. Unfortunately for him, we had already jumped a fence and ran through a yard long before he had even made it off the street. The simple son of bitch didn't have a freaking clue as to where we were.

Before we called off our assault, we wanted to nail one more; one last score for the night. Just as we were discussing it as a group, lo and behold, God answered our prayers and delivered one final Kellogg Police cruiser right into our hands—just a mere block from our house. When he drove by, we let go with everything we had. We each got off about three rounds a piece. Fifteen eggs must have splattered all over that poor car.

The officer driving had to have been a little mentally unstable because he immediately stomped on the gas pedal, and aggressively jerked the steering wheel to one side. He went berserk and made a sharp arcing turn in the middle of the street. Unfortunately, he lost control and ended up plowing up the curb and through a fence into some unsuspecting neighbor's yard. But that wasn't enough for him. Next, as if in a demolition derby, he shifted the car into reverse. The back tires spun like crazy, tearing up the soggy grass and spitting mud and mangled green blades everywhere. This guy was a nut. He began to build up speed in reverse and nearly hit the mailbox before he swerved to miss it. He wanted to catch us in the worst way. But why take out all the structures on the block to find us, you idiot? A flash of insight came over me. This had to be Officer Meyers. He's the only officer on the force that unhinged. Meyers finally got back onto the road and drove down the street in the opposite direction. We never saw his car again that night, thank God.

When the incident ended, I went home happy and proud of our score in the game of Kids vs. the Town Clowns. I entered the house through the back door and found Tim sitting at the kitchen table eating a bowl of ice cream. He smiled and burst out laughing so hard.

"Did ya see it? Did ya see it?"

"Hell yeah, the whole town saw it."

He continued to laugh and almost spit out his next mouthful of ice cream.

Just as usual, my mother didn't have a clue as to what we did that night—and our father was not around to spank us.

Chapter 17

Two-Time Champions

Tim and I decided to lay low after our Halloween activities. We weren't sure if there would be any serious investigation into the events of that night. We also didn't want to have to go to the Catholic church and confess our sins to the drunk priest any more than we wanted to be violated in one of the cells at the Kellogg police station (at least our Catholic priest was always too drunk to get it up).

The first few months of my senior year in school didn't quite go as smoothly as I wanted. My meteoric rise from being the worst wrestler in the district the year before to becoming one of the best wrestlers of the season came to an abrupt halt near the end. When I faced an old rival whom I had not seen since the year before, I choked and lost horribly in front of a home crowd, 19-2, when I should have easily beaten him. I grew paralyzed by fear a mere hour before the match. Then, at the district tournament, I lost again to the same guy when I was beating him in the second round. At that meet, I finished with the bronze medal instead of the gold. In short, when my last wrestling season finally ended, the memories would forever be bittersweet.

With my mind finally off the wrestling scene, I could get on to bigger and better things, like shooting my peashooter in the hallway at school on my eighteenth birthday. Luck had it that I got caught by the same asshole of a teacher who didn't want to see Gino become senior class president; I got my ass kicked out of school for three days. Like always, I fell far short of the accomplishments of my older brothers. Kit stayed steadfast in earning his degree at the U of I in Moscow while Peter and Phil slugged it out in

Butte, preparing for the Third Annual Mining Competition. Peter's senior year of college proved to be more spectacular than my senior year in high school by far. He was destined to go out in a blaze of glory, while I would go out in shame.

When news of my expulsion from school reached Peter, he wrote me a scathing handwritten letter all about it. He started his letter off with, "Dear Idiot"—not really a big motivator, to say the least. Peter could kiss my ass. Hell, I wasn't going to go to college anyway. Instead, I sent a postcard off requesting a free pair of 'ARMY' socks, and when they came, so did the recruiter. I wanted to go out into the world and be an elite soldier, a paratrooper, an Army Ranger, or maybe a Green Beret, and sure as shit, the army recruiter signed me up. I enlisted. I had a guaranteed assignment with the 82nd Airborne Division. After my enlistment, Peter and I didn't discuss college any further.

The contents of the scathing letter were just something he had to get off his chest because he had been Papa Peter, our surrogate father, for the past five years. What else could be expected of him? With the harsh letter out of the way, he focused on the biggest and final push of his college days: hosting (and hopefully winning) the Third Annual Mining Competition right there in Butte. However, this year came with a twist: the beloved Dean Van Matre had been replaced by a hard ass by the name of Finch. It's not that Van Matre didn't play the part of a hard ass; he did, but there were deep, compassionate undertones. He was merely playing a role. Finch, on the other hand, had no compassionate side. He didn't care about touching the lives of his students. He simply wanted to secure power for himself—quite the opposite of Van Matre. However, Dean Van Matre stayed on the college staff and closely watched the Major brothers. He had merely stepped aside and knew that he would put out to pasture in just one more year.

Although Peter studied hard during the fall months and well into winter, he could not keep his mind off the spring mining competition. To occupy himself in the meantime, he looked for a battle, anything to conquer, and he got his wish when they announced the annual men's boxing smoker, "All contenders: Come One, Come All."

Peter was built like a greyhound and was completely aware of his well-toned physique, made up of steel bands of muscle. As far back as I can remember, I can't ever recall Peter ever being in any neighborhood fist fights or bar brawls, but it didn't matter; he was going to throw his hat in the ring, do or die. Donning sixteen-ounce gloves and wearing a protective mouthpiece, he stepped into the ring in front of an overflowing crowd. He had no idea who his opponent was, nor did he care. It was simply a smoker, a show for spectators.

The first round began with Peter throwing a few wild punches—which were easily dodged. After Peter failed to land a single hit, his rival laid into him with a barrage of perfectly timed blows, sending Peter reeling back against the ropes. As one more swing came, Peter ducked down, and it missed. He charged forward and thrust a wild jab into the guy's jaw, stunning him. Peter swung several times, missing twice but landing a solid one on his rival's cheek. Like a cyborg, this stranger seemed totally unphased and continued to pummel Peter repeatedly, driving him into the corner of the ring. Peter did his best to block the punches, but several landed. One hit him so hard that he thought it was over, but he shook it off and charged again—this time with reckless abandon. He totally dropped his guard and went headfirst into a mele of punches, taking a severe bashing. When Peter managed to get one good hit in, his adversary pushed back even harder, landing punch after punch on Peter's face. The crowd began to go crazy; they had a couple of fighters on their hands.

The first round ended, and the second one began. It seemed like a repeat of the first, his contender pummeling him to the verge of a knockout, only to have Peter lunge forward and fight back. By the third round, Peter grew extremely fatigued, not knowing how much longer he could keep it up and take all this abuse.

At one point near the end of the round, Peter got caught in the corner of the ring with his opponent bashing him repeatedly. He then heard a group of Tech students, including Welch and Smith, yelling, "Get off the ropes, you idiot. Protect yourself. Knock the sucker out!"

When it looked like it may end up with Peter getting knocked out, Peter summoned everything he had and began blocking the onslaught with his gloves. In a Herculean effort, he rose and responded to some primal instinct. He broke through his rival's defenses and hit him under the jaw with a surprise uppercut. The pummeling suddenly stopped, and in the lull, Peter stood there dazed but still on his feet. The crowd erupted with a deafening roar, and just then, the bell rang. The fight was over. He dropped his gloves and huffed and puffed, dizzy from the exertion.

After all the matches had ended that evening, trophies were presented to the winners of every weight class. Before they finished, they announced that a final trophy would be awarded to the contender in the best fight of the night. They called Peter into the ring to receive it, and as soon as he did, the crowd began to chant, "Major-Crowley, Major-Crowley, Major-Crowley!"

As the crowd dispersed, people walked up to Peter and asked, "Hey man, when is the re-match?"

The next morning, Peter opened the newspaper to the sports section and was surprised to see the photo of him charging his opponent. From another article he learned that the guy he fought, had a brother on the Montreal Olympic boxing team, thus explained the difficulty of the fight, this guy came from a family of boxers. The events of the previous night satisfied Peter's appetite for adventure—at least for the time being. The mining competition was still this school year's brass ring.

Peter charging his opponent in the most
incredible fight of the night.

Spring had not even begun when Peter sought an audience with the newly appointed Finch to discuss the mining competition. "I am ready to put a team together soon and begin our training."

"Oh yeah, your prized competition," Finch replied. "I know we are required to host it here, but this is a college, not a training ground for professional athletes."

"Sir, we just need permission to use the museum grounds and a certain amount of funding to pull it off right."

"Pull it off, right? What do you mean pull it off right?"

"Well, this is becoming a pretty prestigious event, and I am sure the town will be excited."

"The town excited? Shit what does the town have to do with it? This is just merely a cute, little college stunt."

Peter fell back into the chair. He couldn't believe what he was hearing.

"What are you saying? You don't think we should promote the event?"

"Do whatever promoting you want to, but you will only get so much from the college."

Peter felt horrified at what Finch just said.

"Well, I am going to promote it. I want to at least say thanks for letting us hold it on campus." Peter wasn't serious. It was fake sincerity. He was furious at the lack of support from Finch. This only set Peter on fire. He was more determined than ever.

The tryouts began in late March like they had the year before. The cold weather still gripped the Montana countryside. Old Man Winter held the streets of Butte hostage with its high snowbanks, using them as pawns on a chess board to keep the citizens in check. Van Matre grew as anxious as Peter for the competition to come, but he could only do it from afar since he was no longer the dean in charge. Instead, he peered out the window from the warmth and comfort of his office.

Peter poured everything he had into promoting the event. Still intoxicated by the team's stunning victory the year before, he plotted and planned like never before. A simple trophy wasn't enough. He would suck the entire town into the affair and give them a show like they had never seen. The whole town must be behind this thing, every business, every citizen, and every student—every breathing part of this town must rally. Peter wanted the energy so high, the buzz so intense that it would shake the core of every team that dared to go against them. His team would not only win, but the entire town of Butte would also win. This was Pete's last hoorah, and he would graduate with a bang.

In no time at all, posters went up all around the college, challenging all comers to try out for the award-winning Montana Tech team. After a week of promotion, the tryouts began on the chilled museum grounds. The frozen dirt forced them to build fires on them just like the year before. Often, during their tryouts, the snow began to fall and covered the earth with a thin, white blanket. Not surprisingly, as the weeks of grueling training went on, applicant after applicant began dropping out. The old team members from last year so desperately wanted to make the team for a second time. Being held on home turf, this competition was too big NOT to be a part of the team. There was no way that the last year's victors, who brought this thing home (Welch, Smith, Phil, and Phelan), were going to give up their slots on Butte's dream team to any undeserving punks.

Van Matre knew that Peter was driving the training sessions even harder than last year. This impressed him very much. He slumped back in his chair and threw his glasses onto his desk. He wrung his hands, then pounded both fists onto the armrests of his chair. He yelled out in a jubilant cry, "Yes! We are going to win! We are going to win again!"

However, the weight on Peter's shoulders grew even heavier. In addition to the grueling training, he had to canvass the entire community and find sponsors. It seemed like no one in his inner circle wanted to do anything but train. His delegating wasn't working. And so, Peter, by himself, had to stroll through the door of business after business, promoting the grand occasion. Eventually, the business owners' attitudes began to thaw, and they opened their pocketbooks. Alas, Peter was going to get his support.

When the team trials came in early May, the final roster included the same members as the previous year (all except Cadem). With his original group still intact, Peter went home exhausted, and all those who did not make it went home disappointed. He retired to his upstairs room, feeling that the college, the heavens, and the cosmos were all behind him.

Sitting at his desk, he grabbed a yellow legal notepad and a black pen. He manically wrote in all capital letters, "ONLY THE PARANOID SURVIVE!" Below that, he wrote in smaller letters, "And don't you forget that. You haven't won anything yet!!" Peter now became the paranoid, and he wanted not merely to survive but to thrive. No one knew how close this race would be this year because all the other colleges wanted to exact their revenge on Butte. At the previous year's event in Tucson, every competing college had been caught with their pants down, totally unprepared for the onslaught inflicted on them by rag tag team from Montana Tech. This year, for sure, every team would come back highly prepared.

The next day, after having his team selected, Peter dropped a hastily written letter into the mail addressed to a Mr. William W. Miller, residing at the small trailer court on 42nd Avenue in South Seattle. Peter spelled out the particulars to Uncle Bill about the big event: the dates, the location, and, more importantly, the fact that the college team was looking for sponsors. Sponsorship meant recognition, and Uncle Bill took every advantage to create a spectacle and gain recognition. In the postscript, Peter wrote, "Give me a call at your earliest convenience. This is your chance to be one of the big boys." Peter knew exactly how to push Bill's buttons, and without a doubt, he knew that Bill was going to be a donor, that Bill would love to see his name in the limelight—and hopefully Uncle Bill didn't bump into the real Willam Van Matre while in Butte.

After mailing the letter, Peter called his team together for a meeting. He brought along what he had written down on the tablet. When he had their undivided attention, he introduced this new slogan to his men. team. He loudly proclaimed it as their new mantra.

"Listen here, you guys, only the paranoid survive. If we don't prepare ourselves for the worst, we deserve to get our asses kicked. Now isn't the time to get cocky. We haven't won anything yet!" He reiterated the same message as the year before. His boys knew that they had to push themselves to the limit during their training, and they knew Peter would continue to hound them throughout the competition with the same message.

A week later, the phone at Animal House rang. This time, Phil answered. A polite, professional female voice asked, "Sir, this is the AT&T operator. Will you accept a collect call from a William W. Miller?"

"Of course."

Bill immediately began to rant, "Listen, mother fucker, this your Uncle Bill speaking. I got your letter, and I'm going to be there. Do ya hear me? I am going to be there!"

Phil heard the drunken slur in Bill's speech. It was typical and almost always highly entertaining. "What letter, Bill?"

"The goddamn letter you wrote me about the competition! Who is this?"

"Shit, Bill, this is Phil. Peter must have written you. Let me get him for you."

"Alright, mother fucker. Get Peter on the phone right now."

As Phil yelled up the stairs for Peter to come down and answer the phone, Bill stood in the same filthy phone booth, under the same streetlamp, and took a big puff off his cigarette. Just as he reached down to raise his glass to his mouth and take another drink of whiskey and water (that he had walked out of the bar with), a short, elderly man walked up to the booth. He stood there patiently waiting to use the phone. Bill turned toward the man and yelled, "Buzz off!" Then took another drink. He held out the glass as a salute to the poor guy as if to say, "Get the fuck out of here until I am done." Sadly, the gentleman looked down, shook his head, and slowly walked back into the darkness, totally dejected.

Peter picked up the phone. "Hey Bill, this is Pete."

Hearing Peter's voice, Bill fumbled as began to take another drink. He pulled the glass away too quickly and spilled some of it down the front of his United Airlines coveralls. "I got your letter. I'm coming. I am mother fucking coming!" Bill yelled.

"You better make it over here. It's going to be big."

"I know it is. And you know what? I'm going to be a sponsor."

"I would hope so. Whip out that checkbook. You can't take it with you when it's all over."

"I am writing a check for a G, a fat fucking G. A thousand bucks! Granny didn't raise no dummies."

"Shit, Bill, thanks, man."

"You understand that shit. Thanks for letting me in on it."

"Bill, if it weren't for you, I wouldn't even be where I am today."

"Glad I could do what I could. I am very proud of you and your brothers. You guys are kicking ass and taking names."

The small talk continued for a few minutes until Bill hung up and stumbled back to his trailer. Even in his inebriated state, he still managed to find an envelope, address it, and insert a check scribbled out for an even one thousand dollars. He licked the back of a stamp and pasted it on the upper right-hand corner of the envelope. With his head spinning from the long period of whiskey infusion on an empty stomach, he fell back on his messy, unmade bed and wiggled himself out of his work clothes. Dreamland lay only minutes away (or should I say Whiskeyland).

The week flew by. The college and the City of Butte worked together in a flurry of excitement for the big event. The college students formed a union to assist the local businesses in constructing bulletin boards. They created displays to be strategically positioned on the mining museum grounds. One board, made out of a four-by-eight sheet of plywood, became of particular interest to my brother Peter. He ensured that it contained a very conspicuous entry in its list of sponsors. Of the names included, with their titles, was Bill Miller: Mining Speculator. Peter knew that on the day of the competition, that bulletin board would be hoisted precisely at the entrance to the event site, and that Uncle Bill would stand below it, basking in his own glory.

Two days before the big weekend, Uncle Bill boarded a flight from Seattle to Spokane. My mother tasked me with the duty of picking him up at the airport. As usual, once back home in Kellogg, Uncle Bill stayed uptown at my grandmother's house. He drove her crazy as usual with his loud, obnoxious voice, screaming out every obscenity possible. My grandmother often ran to the kitchen, fetched a wooden spoon, and threatened the three-hundred-pound bore. Bill typically faced two options: shut up and finish watching the TV program with Granny and Uncle Bob (the Spook) or slip out the door and make his rounds between the only three bars that would allow him entry. Most of the time, while out on the Drunken Triangle, Bill grossed out numerous people so offensively that they kicked him out of each establishment. When that happened, he slipped quietly back into the house without disturbing Granny.

The day after Bill arrived, I had to attend all my classes at school. There was no getting out of it. I hated the final months and couldn't wait till they were finally over. This particular day in class had become even more unbearable since we were to embark on the last and final trip to Animal House.

After the final bell rang, I raced home. To my surprise, I discovered that my brothers Tim and Steve had already beaten me there. My mother had already loaded a couple of bags into the car for her and my sister Allyson. Stephen, Tim, and I hastily threw fresh underwear, socks, and a change of clothes into our gym bags. Once we loaded the car, I drove across town and navigated up Division Street. I turned into the driveway of Granny's house. Uncle Bill had been anxiously sitting on the porch waiting for our arrival. My mother systematical got out of the passenger side and moved into the back seat. She allowed Bill to climb in front with me. After he oozed into the car like a starfish entering a crab trap, he gave me a large, goofy grin as I started to back down the driveway. I drove down the hill and neared the highway on-ramp. Just then, Bill spoke up, "Hey buddy, do ya think you can stop at the grocery store before we head out?"

"Sure," I replied.

I knew that when Bill went into the store, he would always come out with a bunch of snacks for everyone. We waited outside for a few minutes, and when he waddled back out to the car, he carried a grocery bag in one hand and a twelve-pack of Budweiser beer in the other. He oozed back inside and set the beer on the floor between his feet. I drove up the highway on-ramp and a minute later we were headed east, bound for Butte. We were on our way.

The car remained completely silent for several miles until Bill reached between his feet and tore open the 12-pack of beer. He opened a can and handed it to me. My mom immediately panicked.

"Bill! He can't drink and drive!"

"He sure the fuck can! Don't worry about it. It's only three-point-two horse piss." (Bill referenced the 3.2% alcohol content in the beer.) "Besides, he handles the wheel like a brain surgeon."

"But Bill, he's only eighteen."

"That doesn't mean shit! I was drinking when I was fourteen."

My mom sat back in her seat, overruled. She nearly had tears in her eyes seeing the horror of her brother Bill sipping a beer and her underage son behind the wheel drinking and driving. Without saying another word, she took a rosary out of her purse and began to pray. "Come on, Ma, you have no reason to worry," I thought, "I was drinking responsibly." I carefully sipped on one can of Budweiser after another as we headed deeper and deeper into Montana. By Missoula, I began to feel the effects of the alcohol. The four-hour trip seemed to transpire a lot quicker this time. It's funny how alcohol alters the space-time continuum. It seemed like we reached Butte in less than two hours.

After arriving in town, I strategically pulled the car up to the front door of 522 Granite Street and shut off the engine. We all got out and went straight up the front steps—everyone but Bill. He was still trying to get his fat ass out of the car.

We burst through the front door and found ourselves in the middle of one of Peter's energetic pep talks. He stood in the living room waving his hands back and forth and poking holes in the sky with his index finger. Welch, Smith, Phelan, and Phil sat around on the couch along with their roommate, ole greasy Pulver. Pulver sat in one of the old chairs, listening intently as he munched on a bag of Lays potato chips. (He was a true sweat hog.) Our presence interrupted Peter's pep talk to his team. On the floor in front of him lay the monstrous jackleg and set of hoses. He took the competition so seriously that he took the damn thing home to inspire himself and the team.

When Peter stopped talking, Uncle Bill lumbered through the door right behind us. Everyone jumped up from the couch to shake the hand of the famous Uncle Bill. Somehow, while Bill had fidgeted to get out of the car, he exchanged his beer for a half-gallon bottle of Black Velvet whiskey that he pulled out of his weekend bag. He waved it around as he shook everyone's hand. "Don't you guys go anywhere until you have a little liquid courage!"

"Bill, we don't have much time before we have to head out to the pub," Peter told him.

"Oh yeah, why so soon?"

"That's where they are holding the beer chugging contest, just like last year."

"Oh, no shit! I do remember."

To add to all the excitement, earlier that day, the Colorado team had landed at the airport and headed straight to the college campus. They asked some Tech students where they could find Peter and his brother Phil. That information was readily available because everyone on campus knew of the famous Animal House on Granite Street—just down from the college. The Colorado team soon beat on the door and yelled, "Where are the Major Brothers? We are here to kick their butts!"

When Peter opened the door, they looked inside and saw Pulver sitting there, gorging his mouth with food, and then they saw the jackleg and hoses on the floor.

"Holy fuck!" One of them shouted, "These lunatics are practicing drilling in their own house. They are fucking nuts, and we are fucking dead!"

At that moment, Peter's confidence rose to the stars after seeing how intimidated the other team became. With the unexpected visit by the Colorado team now behind them, and the family there to support them, Peter and Phil, headed down to the pub that was sponsoring the beer chugging contest.

Since I was eighteen and almost of age, Peter allowed me to ride down with him and Phil. Fortunately, although I was still in high school and looked very baby-faced, the bartenders never questioned my age. Our group found a small table to sit at, and a minute later, Phil returned with a pitcher of beer and several glasses. I poured myself one like a real pro and sat back as confidently as possible. A few cute college girls sat at a table near ours. Oh shit, what was I going to do? (Nothing. I was too chickenshit.)

Just like in Tucson, the teams lined up and chugged their beers, and just like the year before, Peter and his crew won again, possibly because my brother Peter wore a black tee shirt with the U.S. Army's 'Ranger' tab imprinted across the front (an intimidation factor maybe).

The following morning, after Peter and Philip had already headed out to the college, the rest of us drove to the outdoor museum. Rat farts! We couldn't find a parking spot anywhere near the grounds. It seemed like the entire town showed up for the event. We had to park a couple hundred yards away and walk the distance. As the grounds came alive, Van Matre stood in his office, blocks away, and looked out his window. "Well, well, look at that. My boys are to make history again. I just know it," he muttered to himself.

My family and I strolled through the museum gate. I immediately spotted Peter's truck parked just inside the entrance underneath a giant bulletin board. This board listed all the sponsors. A name jumped out from the list: Bill Miller, Mining Speculator.

"Hey Bill, look at that!" I said as I pointed up to the board.

Bill looked up and laughed with his famous 'yuk' 'yuk' 'yuk' chuckle. "Ya know, if ya wanna be big, ya gotta think big!"

"Yeah, just look at your gut," I thought.

Spectators, as well as various teams from across the country crowded the entire area. Each team wore their respective college tee shirts. These young men had flown in from many different states and were extremely anxious to begin slugging it out in hopes of beating the almighty Montana squad. The teams from Idaho and Arizona were the most worried. Idaho had started the competition, only to have Tucson take the trophy away, then to have Butte embarrassingly take it away from them as well. Now, both Idaho and Arizona were out for vengeance. You could see it in their eyes as they looked over at Peter and his crew.

Just as we approached Peter, a familiar figure showed up. It was his roommate, Mark Pulver. Mark presented himself with a large grin and a fancy 35mm camera that hung around his neck.

"What are you doing?" My brother Steve boldly asked him.

"Why, I am doing a story for the school newspaper."

"What? You? Think you're a reporter now or something?"

"Don't worry about it, punk," Pulver replied disrespectfully. He had no respect for us younger brothers. He saw us as smart-ass, rebellious adolescents. Ironically, with all the insults he threw at us, we hurled them back twice as severely. He was fat, sweaty, and severe acne ravaged his face. His hair was greasy, and dandruff filled. Need I say more?

A voice blared across the loudspeakers from every corner of the museum grounds. It called for all the teams to meet at the center of the competition field for a briefing. We stepped back and let Peter and his team go forth. When the meeting ended, all the competitors retreated to their respective staging areas. Peter walked back and joined us with a big smile on his face. "Guess what? The first event is the jackleg, and they are starting it off with me."

For some reason, starting Peter off in the first round of the competition didn't seem to bother him after last year's fiasco. He had developed an extreme level of self-confidence and would now be giving it all in front of the entire college, the town, and his own family. The embarrassment and shame of having botched this event the year before (and coming in dead last) never really haunted him because his powers of visualization were that great. He had listened to the theme song to 'The Good, the Bad, and the Ugly' enough times this year to believe that he was invincible and destined to win. All eyes would be on Peter—and that is what he wanted. He wanted that ego boost. He wanted to be the hero in his own story. That was Peter's way. He had practiced so hard with the jackleg over the past month that he could hardly lift the drill at the end of each day's training.

When the officials signaled that the competition would now begin, another announcement blared over the loudspeakers, "The first event will be the jack leg, and representing Montana Tech will be Peter Major."

Peter walked up to the enormous cement block, covered his eyes with his safety glasses, put on his earmuffs, and donned his gloves. An official started up the large air compressor. Its engine roared to life, and a black puff of smoke belched out of the exhaust pipe. The noise drowned out everything on the grounds. Peter raised the heavy drill and balanced it on its leg, firmly planted in the dirt below. He pushed a lever, and an ear-piercing hiss of air shot out of the port on the drill, signaling that the airflow was fine—all systems go. Peter pushed the tip of the long steel shaft onto the side of the cement block. The official walked up and stood right next to Peter. He held the stopwatch in his left hand and raised his right hand into the air. Peter looked squarely at him and nodded. The crowd stood in suspense. The official dropped his right hand and yelled, "GO!"

Peter then opened the air valve. The steel began to spin as it simultaneously hammered into the block. The machine belched out a deafening growl so loud that people couldn't hear a word the person standing next to them was saying. Peter pushed the drill into the rock with all his might for a few seconds, then pulled the bit out and started a second hole, collaring once again. He continued. The veins in his forearms bulged as all his muscles tensed up in distinctive bands of tissue. The drill snarled deafeningly as the steel bit slowly worked its way into the enormous concrete cube.

Peter had been holding his breath under the initial strain but then fiercely exhaled and grasped for desperately needed air. With the new intake of oxygen hitting his bloodstream, a particular activity began to take place in his brain. He began to relax. The passing of time slowed down in his mind. Amidst the roar of the drill and the muffled cheers of the crowd, Peter felt a peaceful sense of quietness. The locus coeruleus and the dopaminergic pathways deep in his gray matter began to go into overdrive. The drilling now seemed effortless. His breathing returned to normal, his muscles slightly relaxed, and the drilling seemed easy. Peter entered what would become known decades later as the 'flow state'. Science has only begun to discover what happens physiologically or neurologically when a person enters that zone of ultimate human achievement. Peter's incessant training on this particular event burned neural pathways so deeply that everything he did now became instinct.

With the drill shaft all but disappearing into the block, Peter eased up on the throttle. He shot a look behind him to see where the air hose lay so that he would not trip over it as he had in Tucson a year earlier. With his footing secure, he pulled the drill out and repositioned it on the cement surface next to the first hole. He opened the air and began the second drive in. The roar of the drill once again echoed across the museum grounds as Peter pushed with all his might—this time with much more ease. Time had slowed down in his mind, no panic, no stress, just pure vision. He could see nothing around him except the block in front of him. Finding himself encapsulated in a mystical silence, he smiled as he watched the drill sink deeper and deeper into the rock.

The hand of the stopwatch ticked closer and closer to the end. The official walked up to Peter. At a mere two feet away, he raised his arm and yelled, "STOP!" as he dropped his hand down in a cutting motion. Peter immediately shut off the drill and pulled off his earmuffs. The silence seemed deafening to him, but he began to hear talking among the people. There were a few random claps from the crowd, then a huge burst of gallant cheers from Phil, Phelan, Smith, and Welch. Peter pulled the steel shaft out and lowered the jackleg to the ground. He walked back to his crew, his head slightly down to hide his grin. Peter always tried to downplay every one of his exploits, while inside, he wanted all the glory he could get (enough for him to humble-brag later). Everyone on his team patted him on the back while the officials measured the depth of his two holes. How deep could he drill in a mere two minutes?

Next, Arizona took center stage, and then Idaho (Butte's two closest rivals). At the end of every drilling, the officials took the measurements and wrote them down. We all sensed that the other teams were pretty close in the results, but we felt that Peter had outdone them all. Peter and his compatriots held their breath as the last team took the stage: Missouri. They drilled away until finally ordered to stop. The officials took the measurements and then huddled around the judge's table.

Minutes later, one of the officials acted as the scribe and used a large, black ink marker to write down the team's placements, from last to first, on the giant scoreboard. The crowd grew quiet. Box by box, the official wrote in the team ranking: Missouri, Texas, South Dakota, and Nevada, etc. The boxes began to be filled in, but still nothing for Butte. In the end, he wrote a '9' in Arizona's box, then finally a '10' in the Montana box. Once the scribe had finished, a voice over the loudspeaker blared out, "In the jack leg event, in third place is the University of Idaho, Moscow, and in second place is the University of Arizona, Tucson, and in first place, the Montana School of Mines, Butte." The home crowd cheered wildly, and a local TV crew panned their camera from the scoreboard across the crowd, only to rest on my two brothers standing in front of their team. Peter had completely vindicated himself of his last year's debacle. His win put enormous energy into motion among his team, the supporters from the college, and the local townspeople. However, the competition was far from over. Many of the other groups had trained nearly as hard as Butte this time, and they wouldn't give up without a fight.

Uncle Bill raised his plastic cup of beer into the air and saluted Peter as the competition continued. I personally grew bored watching everything. It all seemed silly, a makeshift event attempting to mimic the annual logger's competitions. Whoever thought of a mining competition? Besides all this bullshit, it was all for Peter's glory. I had my share of things to worry about in my personal life. Maybe I was downplaying this. Peter and Philip had come this far with no help from our father. Over the past five years, they had figured it out by themselves.

In my boredom, I asked Uncle Bill to get me a glass of beer the next time he went to concessions. A few minutes later, my mother noticed me standing next to my uncle, sipping a beer. She gave me an extremely disgusted look, but I didn't care. I was thirsty. After finishing that first beer, everything just became a blur to me, partly due to alcohol but also due to my lack of interest in everything. My attitude stemmed from the fact that every one of us brothers was competitive, and I was tired of it.

Each of us wanted our own piece of the action; we wanted to outdo each other, but this act was Peter's. I would eventually find my own patch of sky.

The next couple of hours ticked by as all the teams battled it out in very close races. In the end, Peter and his team took first place once again—as we all expected. They had kept the trophy safe at home in Butte for another year. They were two-time champions.

The Montana Tech Mining team posing with
the first-place trophy after winning the Third
Annual Mining Competition in Butte.

At the end of the competition, Van Matre made his way to the grounds. He stayed off in the distance. He stood there with his black tie neatly tightened around the neck of his pristinely starched, white shirt and his black-rim glasses sitting high on the bridge of his nose. He crossed his arms in deep reflection. He had arrived just in time for the team photos, where the winners held their trophies. A feeling of contentment swept over him. He could now retire knowing he had made his mark on the next generation. He would forever feel the satisfaction of having pushed a handful of promising students to reach their greatest potential in the final chapter of their college experience. William Van Matre walked away while William W. Miller walked into the crowd of celebrating students.

"We're going out and celebrating boys. The drinks are on me!" Uncle Bill said with a snarl.

A week after Peter had made his final mark on the Montana School of Mines, I had a hasty, very last-minute date, taking Denise Hare out to my senior prom. I had called her five minutes before the store that she had returned her prom dress to closed. Surprisingly, no one had asked her out. We didn't go to dinner or anything fancy, and we didn't stay long because I hated conforming and trying to fit into the crowd.

My high school graduation lay just two weeks away and I suddenly had thoughts about another girl, a girl that I had dated earlier in the year. With her now heavy on my mind, I summoned the courage to ask her out again after all these months. I should have taken HER to the prom, but I didn't—stupid me. I only had one chance left to see again before my life would be changed forever. She agreed to go out with me once more, and I took her to the drive-in theater. We only watched half the movie before leaving and finding a place to park on an isolated mountain road. The stars were out and shone so brilliantly, but our time would not last long. We could not fool the tricks of time. I sadly dropped her off on her porch with one last kiss. I knew right then and there that I had made a terrible mistake by joining the military. I was not only leaving her behind but my father as well. He waited in Canada for me to join him as soon as I graduated. I just had a bad feeling about it all.

Once home, I parked the car in the driveway and quietly snuck through the back door. I went directly into the spare bedroom. Too many thoughts stirred in my mind to go right to bed. Although we didn't pay for cable TV, the old black and white counsel in that room could faintly receive the broadcasts from the new HBO station. As I tuned in, I caught the very end of the movie 'Patton'. We had watched it as a family several years earlier in the living room as my younger brothers and I sat on the couch with a large bowl of popcorn. I remembered many of the scenes well.

Although, I was slightly disappointed having missed most of the movie that night, I could at least watch the ending. I listened intently as the actor George C. Scott narrated General Patton's final thoughts as he marched down the cobblestone streets in Bavaria. Patton had just been relieved of his command of the Third Army. He spoke these words:

> *"For over a thousand years, Roman conquerors returning from the wars enjoyed the honor of triumph, a tumultuous parade. In the procession came trumpeters, musicians, and strange animals from conquered territories, together with carts laden with treasure and captured armaments. The conquerors rode in a triumphal chariot, the dazed prisoners walking in chains before him. Sometimes, his children robed in white, stood with him in the chariot, or rode the trace horses. A slave stood behind the conqueror holding a golden crown and whispering in his ear a warning: that all glory is fleeting."*

So powerful were the words that I turned the TV off right then so I could ruminate upon them. I slipped through the side door into my room. My younger brothers were both asleep in their bunk beds. Timmy snored lightly on the top while Stephen lay contorted on the bottom. As I crawled into mine, I attempted to gather my thoughts. I had just got home from a date that I would remember as the most romantic moment of my life, and now I had just turned my back on her and my father. I would graduate high school in just over a week and leave for the army's basic, advanced, and airborne training. Tonight, it was all too much for me to digest. There was nothing I could do but lay my head back on my pillow and close my eyes.

As I began to fall asleep, visions of future adventures grew clearer in my mind. The dreams of the great endeavors that I would undertake knew no bounds. I would jump out of airplanes, fly helicopters, win fights, trek to faraway places, and even rescue a beautiful, exotic princess in some distant land. Ah yes, I found comfort in my dreams, but just before I was out, I seemed to hear a voice, a whisper in my ear, a warning . . . "that all glory is fleeting."

Epilogue

(Two Years Later)

The Air Force crew chief waved at me and pointed up to the cockpit. I took his cue, climbed up the ladder, and entered through the door. I found myself standing behind the pilot and copilot who sat in front of the controls of the enormous aircraft. They were busy keeping their eyes on a hundred gauges and hardly noticed that I was there. It was my first chance ever to see the world from the cockpit of a military aircraft while in flight. As I looked out through the front window, the world suddenly became very bright with the brilliant sunshine and pristine blue sky stretching as far as the eye could see. The two young pilots in green military flight suits finally noticed me. They smiled warmly when I squeezed in between them. The countless gauges, levers, and knobs of the aircraft were absolutely baffling. I could never have been more excited. I was onboard the famed Lockheed C-141 Starlighter jet. I had the privilege to be up there while my fellow soldiers were down in the fuselage with all the equipment, vehicles, and 20mm Vulcan cannons. Accompanying us were the non-airborne troops that we were hauling back from Hawaii. Once a year, we exchanged troops with the Hawaiian division for a few weeks of military maneuvers. Our guys trained there in the tropics while we brought their guys back to train in the woods of North Carolina at Fort Bragg. I could hardly wait to get over Normandy drop zone and see their faces as we jumped out of the plane with our parachutes and full combat gear on.

"How high are we?" I asked the pilot.

The young co-pilot pointed down at the altimeter, then looked back at me, "Right at forty thousand feet."

"No shit!" I replied.

In front of us, I could see the tail end of another Starlifter not far away. The majestic aircraft with its high wing and massive tail looked so large, unlike when we arrived at Hickam Field earlier that day. There, our C-141s had sat on the tarmac next to the enormous C-5 Galaxies and were dwarfed by their mammoth big brothers. Regardless of the comparison, the Starlifters were still so beautiful, long, robust, and elegant in design.

Here I was now, seven hours into a fourteen-hour flight back from Hawaii, still only halfway home. Dammit! I hated how slowly the hours passed while in the air. However, the previous forty-eight hours seemed to slip by very quickly from the moment I jumped out near Schoefield Barracks and parachuted into a Dole pineapple patch. From the instant we hit the ground, it was all fun and games for a handful of us while the rest of the unit had to get down to business unloading equipment and preparing for the training. A few friends and I turned our M-16s in at the armory and changed out of our jungle fatigues. We got on a bus and spent two nights drinking it up on Waikiki Beach. I regret that the only tangible thing I was bringing back from this Polynesian paradise was a ceramic ashtray with a naked woman lying in the sand. The only place to lay your cigarette was in the crack of her ass. The caption read: "Watch your Butt. Hawaii". I bought it for Uncle Bill.

After a few minutes in the cockpit, the pilot motioned for me to leave and head back down to the cargo area. We were very close to the beginning of the in-flight refueling process. The year before, on our return trip, we had landed in San Bernadino to refuel on the ground. However, on this flight, somewhere out in front of us, a KC-135 tanker loomed with its refueling probe extended.

No sooner than I left the cockpit and reached the deck in the fuselage that the engines' whining began to change pitch as we got ready to maneuver in and get the desperately needed fuel. A little turbulence rocked the plane momentarily; then, I felt a bump. The tanker's probe had made contact with our fuel port on the conspicuous hump on the top of the plane. We stayed in a very slow flight during the procedure, and just like a mother robin feeding her young, our tanks were being filled.

Along with us in the belly of the plane were two six-wheel drive Gamma Goat vehicles, two Vulcan anti-aircraft cannons, and a couple of light jeeps with trailers. They were all strapped to the floorboard with heavy canvas ratchet straps. These wicked Vulcans spewed out a hundred rounds in one violent, ear-shattering belch, and in the unlimited mode, they could spit out three thousand rounds per minute. Their firepower was so destructive, impressive, and awesome, and it made me proud to be part of the American military with equipment like this.

While I was serving my country, all my brothers and sisters were doing very well and would continue to go on and excel at everything they did. My oldest brother Peter was making a name for himself as an engineer in the mining fields of South Africa. He would eventually win another prize: an MBA from Cape Town University.

Next, I thought of Kit. He had just finished his engineering degree at the University of Idaho while raising a small family. In addition to achieving his coveted degree, he had reached new heights with his bodybuilding and won a couple of glamorous trophies. Kit finally crushed his critics who said he would never put on enough muscle to exceed the two-hundred-pound threshold. He, too, like Peter, would go on to earn his MBA.

In addition to those two, my brother Philip had also finished his engineering degree at Montana Tech. Before he finished though, he followed in Peter's footsteps and took over as captain of the mining competition team. He led them to two more first-place victories. However, instead of pursuing an engineering career, Phil took a job in Minneapolis and started a sizzling career in sales that would far exceed anything he would have done as an engineer.

While I served as a paratrooper, my younger brother Stephen was also deployed, but with a heavy mortar platoon halfway around the world at a small army base near the North Korean border, a place called Camp Hovey. Stephen referred to this little outpost as the 'armpit of the world' and wanted to get out there as fast as he could, just as I did with Fort Bragg. Stephen's only consolation for serving in such a miserable place was that he could buy extremely cheap cases of Schmidt (Animal) beer and drink it on his off time. During his routine patrols with his infantry squad, he often looked across the expanse of the DMZ and saw the North Korean communist troops conducting their own training operations. Unbeknownst to most of the world, the North Korean soldiers often fired shots across this no man's land at the American troops.

271

Stephen standing in front of a ghastly military
vehicle known as the Gamma Goat.

After hearing Stephen's stories, little did I know that in a few short years, I would in turn, be yards away from communist soldiers on the other side of the globe. I would find myself visiting an East German border town called Hof. There, I would find myself looking up into the face of a communist soldier manning a machine gun in a tower. The tower, that sat upon a wall covered with razor wire, was a mere hundred and fifty feet away from me.

While Steve and I faced the Commies, our little brother Timmy was busy finishing his senior year of high school back in Kellogg. He too, would follow us into the army, but would never be stationed overseas. Tim would be assigned to the Second Armored Division at Fort Hood, Texas as a track vehicle mechanic with a MLRS unit (multiple launch rocket system). The tour afforded him the chance to attend college in South Africa and to secure his bachelor's degree in business management, all at the expense of the U.S. military. Tim indeed, played it smart.

Tim holding an M60 machine gun.

Counting Kit, with his time served with the Army Reserve, the four of us brothers would forever remember the days when we were truly Cold War warriors.

C.A. Major

J.A. Maloney

R.P. Martin

R.S. Martin

J.E. McCombs

Kit's basic training photo.

I finally sat down near the back of the plane on the taunt, red canvas that made up the makeshift seating. Near the tail, lay two pallets of prepacked parachutes, one full of main chutes and one full of reserves. This time, we were jumping with the non-steerable T-10s, not the more dangerous Dash-Ones. The Dash-Ones were slick alright. They had open patches in the back and handles on each side of the risers. The open patches let the air spill out the back and gave you a 9.8-mile-an-hour forward thrust. Unfortunately, the Dash-Ones had recently proved to be too deadly in midair collisions.

Just the year before, eight paratroopers from our division were killed in airborne accidents, several of them directly attributed to the Dash-One's tendency to collapse when colliding with another jumper. I personally knew one of these soldiers. I experienced a near miss myself with the Dash-One during a jump into Fort Bragg when we flew back from El Paso. I came head-on with another jumper, but we both quickly turned. Luckily, our canopies glanced off each other. It scared the shit out of me.

Further up the plane sat Resmini, a dickhead from the New England area. He was the first one in the battery with whom I had an altercation. Instead of me wearing the red-painted helmet on my first jump with the unit, signifying that I was a cherry (a new trooper fresh out of jump school), I told them all to fuck off. As a result of my defiance, a group of soldiers in my platoon continued harassing me for months. I finally had enough of it the day Resmini got in my face. I hit him twice in the chest, the second time, so hard that his beret went flying off (that is if you could call it a beret because he was too inept to form it properly on his head). It looked more like a chef's hat than a paratrooper's headgear. Additionally, when his head was uncovered, the short bristles on his little round noggin made him look more like a concentration camp inmate than a soldier. With his looks, a soiled black and white striped uniform would suit him more than the camouflage jungle fatigues. However, he wasn't the only idiot messing with me. A buddy of his, Rice, became insanely outraged after he saw me push back at Resmini.

Rice hailed from Louisiana. He was a true Cajun, had a southern drawl and all. The most distinctive thing about his looks was his lazy blue eyes with eyelids that always seemed to be at half-mast. He wore a regulation-style, neatly trimmed mustache on his upper lip. It could have easily been waxed and turned into handlebars if he had permitted it to grow out a little more. One night, during a drunken party in my barracks room, Rice slurred as he held a two-foot-long metal bunk adapter. He explained how deadly he was with a piece of metal such as this. I oo'ed and awe'd and feigned intimidation. This set the stage for how he would treat me after the Resmini incident.

For twenty-one days, Rice really poured on the harassment. He kept it up until the day he made fun of my car—a big mistake. First off, don't you ever make fun of my brothers, and secondly, don't you ever make fun of my car. Immediately after his comments, I vowed to kick his ass. I waited for that asshole to show up outside for our noon-time formation. I looked out my third-floor barracks window until I saw him appear. He lit up a cigarette in front of all his buddies. I raced downstairs and approached him under the elm tree. At first, when I tapped him on the shoulder, he turned around and looked at me with his typical, big, sarcastic smile and thought nothing of it.

"What the fuck did you say about my car?"

He smiled, "I said it was a push-start model."

It really hit home when I didn't smile back. I asked him point-blank, "Do you have a problem?" I definitely caught him off guard.

At that moment, he looked like he had just seen a ghost. He slowly took the cigarette out of his mouth. His jaw dropped. He had wanted a fight all along but didn't expect it right there and then. So, without losing the element of surprise, I reached all the way back to Idaho and hit him as hard as I could. At first, I thought I had knocked him out by the way he dropped down to his knees, but then he sprung up, and the fistfight began. It was CRACK! CRACK! CRACK! All my punches connected, but none of his did. He swung and swung and swung. I could feel the wind whistling across my face every time one of his punches flew by and missed. Finally, a sergeant from Third Platoon broke up the melee and made us shake hands. It was over as fast as it started. Rice would never speak to me again. Whenever he walked past me around the barracks or out in the field, he'd drop his head and look down at the ground. He was a broken man. Well, you shouldn't have been so cocky, you fucking idiot.

Next to Resmini and Rice sat Lucier. Lucier stood nearly six feet tall, had six-pack abs, a V-shaped back, and very bright sparkling blue eyes.

He was a smoker and handled a cigarette more debonair than Humphrey Bogart in the movie Casablanca. Quiet he was, different than the rest of his compatriots. Lucier could have easily passed for an iconic 1970s male porn star, except his hair and mustache were light brown instead of the traditional black. Lucier was an alright guy because he kept to himself and never bothered anyone. He just hung around Rice and Resmini so that he wouldn't be the lone wolf of the platoon.

My roommate Arnie sat next to me. Arnie, a Massachusetts boy, came complete with the Bostonian accent. He had a girlfriend back home named Lisa, but with his Boston dialect, he pronounced her name *Lees-ER* instead of Lees-AH. Arnie was probably the toughest guy in the battery with his stocky build, broad shoulders, and Popeye-like arms. Arnie and I had gotten into a few scuffles just for fun. I could out-wrestle him, but he could easily out-muscle me. So, each time, our friendly matches ended up in a draw. When it came to possessions, Arnie owned nothing, and I mean nothing, except for a black leather jacket and a cheap transistor radio. I really liked Arnie. He was the only guy in the unit that I trusted. If we were ever in combat, I would want him next to me.

From the small window just above my seat, I saw small, white cumulus clouds drifting lazily miles below. We had just made it over California but still had so many hours left to trek across the country. With all this time on my hands, I couldn't help but ruminate about the past, and even the future, because the present really sucked. I hated where I was. My father had died while I was away and the love of my life left me for someone else. I let them both down and would regret it for the rest of my life. There was no one to blame but myself. I had betrayed them both.

I slumped down onto my seat and retrieved a tattered letter from my fatigue pocket. On the outside of the pale green envelope were beautifully handwritten 'to' and 'from' addresses, almost like calligraphy. The letter was from her. I pulled out the note and unfolded it. It had been six months since our breakup. I had gotten the same 'Dear John' letter that every soldier seems to get while away from home. It's true, every girl ditches her man when he leaves for the military. Her cutting me loose and moving on hurt so bad inside that I thought I was going to die. Instead of just leaving me for good, which would have been best, she kept writing to me for some unknown reason. It was like twisting the blade in my back.

I unfolded her letter and began to read it. She wrote so beautifully, so eloquently. As I read it, I stopped at the point where she said, *"I'm so sorry about the way things turned out. My feelings for you are so deep. It's like the words of the John Denver song 'Annie': You fill up my senses . . .".* If that was the case, then why did you leave me? I almost wanted to tear up the letter right then and there, but I couldn't.

I should have never joined the military. I had sold my soul to the devil, and it would take many years for the Lord to redeem it for me.

With around seven hours still to go before the jump back into Bragg, I tried to shift my thoughts in a different direction. I forced myself to mentally rehearse the jump procedures over and over. We would be coming in low for the drop, a mere eight hundred feet, so low that it seemed if I sat in the door, my boots would touch the tops of the trees. At least it was a day jump this time, but with full combat gear, naturally.

I rehearsed all the procedures. If my main chute failed, I would have only two micro-seconds to grab the D-ring of my reserve and pull the ripcord. If that chute failed, I would end up splattering on the ground. At that moment, I didn't care—I was in that much pain. Native American legend has it that when you die, you will wake up in the moment in life when you were the most happy. The happiest moment of my life was when my brother Phil and I landed in Jennis Bay as teenagers and taxied up to the beach in the airplane. There, we saw our father with the biggest smile ever, walking down the muddy trail to greet us.

I laid back and covered my eyes with my beret, and my mind wandered again. I realized how much I loved every member of my family, more than words could say, and how they were all so different from one another. All my siblings were extremely precious to me: Peter the Great, Christopher the Ingenious, Philip the Majestic, Stephen the Vociferous, Timothy the Meticulous, Jeri-anne the Beautiful, Kimmerly the Compassionate, and Allyson the Talented. After thinking of my family, I once again thought about her. I still loved her so deeply, no matter how badly she had hurt me. Her name was Jill Young.

In time, all my brothers would go on to accomplish great things with their lives. They would be bastions of strength and accomplishment, and make our family look so good with all they had conquered—but I was different. I was the misfit, the wild card, the black sheep, so desultory in all my ways, flitting from one thing to another, always trying to fill a hole inside myself that could never be filled. Maybe I was too much like my father. Although I had recently earned a slot in the Army's warrant officer training program to fly helicopters, I didn't want to go. I just wanted to return home, go back to Canada, and pick up where my father had left off. He never completed his dream and knowing that he hadn't caused my head to spin. Nothing could get my mind off Jennis Bay. If I went back at the end of my enlistment, I could still save something—anything. I was in a hard place. If I turned down the slot to become an officer and a pilot, it would just end up being another one of my stupid mistakes.

I pulled my beret even further down over my eyes to get some sleep before we came over the drop zone. I wasn't as fatalistic as I made myself out to be because I could always see a distant light in my future. I believed that things would eventually work out for me no matter how many years it would take. To calm my nerves and help me get some sleep, I kept repeating to myself over and over, "Someday, I will find my peace . . . someday."

My roommate Arnie and I on the tarmac at Biggs
Army Airfield in El Paso, Texas, waiting to board the
C-130 Hercules' for our jump back into Fort Bragg.

My father, Merslau Zablocki, aka Jerry Major. Dad, I love
you, and I miss you. When my time comes, I will be seeing
you on the other side. Thank you for giving me life.

Printed in the United States
by Baker & Taylor Publisher Services